Death on the Trans-Siberian Express

An Olga Pushkin Mystery

C J Farrington

CONSTABLE

CONSTABLE

First published in Great Britain in 2021 by Constable

1 3 5 7 9 10 8 6 4 2

Copyright © C J Farrington, 2021

Hedgehog illustration © Anna Morrison, 2021

The moral right of the author has been asserted.

A CIP catalogue record for this book
is available from the British Library.

ISBN: 978-1-47213-313-7 (hardcover)
ISBN: 978-1-47213-312-0 (trade paperback)

Typeset in Caslon Pro by SX Composing DTP, Rayleigh, Essex
Printed and bound in Great Britain by Clays Ltd, Elcograf S.p.A.

Papers used by Constable are from well-managed forests
and other responsible sources.

Constable
An imprint of
Little, Brown Book Group
Carmelite House
50 Victoria Embankment
London EC4Y 0DZ

An Hachette UK Company
www.hachette.co.uk

www.littlebrown.co.uk

Death on the
Trans-Siberian
Express

For Claire and Acacia,
without whom this book could not have been written

1

The Brim of a Poisoned Well

It was eight o'clock on Friday morning, and Olga Pushkin was weeping on the arm of her new sofa. This would surprise you, if you knew her, for she wasn't much given to weeping (or buying new furniture). And even if you didn't, tears looked somehow incongruous on her face, like hipster jeans on an old man, or a Christmas tree in June. Her cheeks were broad, her nose stolid and wind-raw, her eyes deep-set and wary and wise. She had a face like Russia.

The reason for her tears was a crudely written letter that lay on the table under the window. The table, which was brightly painted in red and gold, was one of Olga's most prized possessions. She had salvaged it from a shut-down Chinese restaurant in nearby Tayga the year before, clambering into a skip and plucking off the fast-food wrappers that clung to the table-top like leeches. She'd wiped it down with a discarded shirt, and with the help of her friend Ekaterina Chezhekov had wrestled it into the boot of a borrowed Lada, and brought it home in triumph to the house she shared with her father Mikhail. But now the coveted object held up the letter like a villain's sidekick, taunting her with its venomous, half-literate insults.

You TART, thinking you can waltz in to that poor old mans' dacha and get away with his savings when he Pops his Clogs, and Mr Solotov an Army man with no children of his own . . . Its daylight robbery is what it is, a Railway Worker should know better. (as if youd ever be anything else!) Youll be found out, oh yes in the end Everyone will know what you've DONE.

She had thought the letter idiotic when she first read it that morning. Everyone in the village knew Olga was about as far from a tart as a woman could be. For one thing, she hadn't had a boyfriend since 1996, assuming Piotr Katin could even be placed in the boyfriend category (a story for later). For another thing, she didn't know how to waltz. In fact, she didn't know how to dance at all, unless swaying back and forth to slow 1980s American love songs in the Roslazny church hall (also in 1996) counted as dancing. Since then she'd always found an excuse to inhabit the edges, not the middles, of party rooms. And Vladimir Solotov's tumbledown shack, whose flooring consisted mostly of ancient copies of *Pravda*, could hardly be described as a dacha. Wealthy Russians kept dachas, second houses in the country where they could escape from their busy city lives. Old Solotov was no Roman Abramovich: what did he have to escape from? Even her father Mikhail, who had a nose for roubles that would put a bloodhound to shame, didn't think Vladimir Solotov worth courting for a mention in his will. He made her visit his lecherous old friend not in hope of a legacy but because he thought it made the family look good in the village, and at no cost to himself. (He himself, of course, was too old, and too unwell, to hobble through the winter snow. Friendship had its limits.)

So – a stupid letter. The writer was clearly deranged, she thought, and probably jealous of her in some obscure way. And didn't they come to the same thing, anyway? After all, there wasn't much to envy in Olga's life. It was Olga who envied others, women who had made something of their lives, who had had education and opportunities, who lived in glamorous cities rather than dying railside backwaters – women whose mothers had lived to nurture them, whose fathers had encouraged them, rather than trapped them . . . To be jealous of Olga was to *be* deranged. But on the other hand, Olga was still healthy, still pretty, still on the right side of thirty-five. An old person might well envy those things. Yes – it was probably some old crone, lashing out at a random target as elderly people often do, their inhibitions worn away, like locomotive brake-pads, by the slow passage of years. She knew plenty of old people in Roslazny, where young people rarely stayed longer than they had to. No doubt her correspondent was some housebound invalid whose window she walked past on the way to her job, or to the café, or to Anna Kabalevsky's house. It was someone to ignore – someone to pity, even.

She had shaken her head after her first scan of the letter's contents, as if to empty her mind of troublesome thoughts, and then dropped it on the red-and-gold table from the Chinese restaurant. She'd looked out of the window – heavy snow again – and started to prepare her sandwiches and salted-fish snacks for the day ahead. It looked set to be another cold one, which was saying something in the Kemerovo region of Siberia.

But then she'd paused and picked up the letter again. And this time she couldn't help thinking: was it so idiotic after all? She read one of the lines again: *As if you'd ever be anything else!*

3

Anything else but a railway worker, they meant, of course. The casual phrase, almost tossed away in parenthesis, that she'd barely noticed first time round – *that* was clever, barbed like the fish-hook on which, as a child, she had impaled her finger by the River Tom, except this time the result wasn't torn flesh and a run of blood but a desperate sinking feeling in her heart.

And that phrase had been written with special conviction. The writer's pen had scored through to the other side for those seven words, and those words alone, showing a depth of spite Olga could scarcely imagine. This was no chance insult written by some old relic who barely knew her, but a knowing, well-directed dart, precisely aimed and delivered. The letter hurt not because it accused her of duplicity, of doing good for others in the hope of reward. It hurt because it voiced her own hidden fears. It was as if some cheap ballpoint had scored *her*, had penetrated a paper-thin veneer and punched into her most vulnerable place: the terror, now spelled out in black and white, that she would never be anything else but a track engineer, third class, in a little hut by the tracks near Roslazny village.

Because she *did* so desperately want to be something else. For years, she had fantasised about becoming a writer, of studying literature at Tomsk State University – the Oxford of Western Siberia – and earning her livelihood on an electronic typewriter or computer in a warm, brightly lit coffee-shop instead of a cramped, mouldy railside hut. Her mother would have wanted that for her, Olga was sure of it. Yet she was gone, and with her the magical grace that dissolved difficulties into laughter. And her brother Pasha too, sweet soul, posted to far Crimea with his regiment. She had friends – Ekaterina Chezhekov at Tayga station three miles down the tracks, and

Anna Kabalevsky in the village, and others – but most of them had difficult husbands or small children or both, and were taken up with their own troubles. Most days she was alone, with only the trains weaving across frozen vastnesses to clatter past her hut, and in the evenings her father Mikhail, who scorned her yearnings and drank up her earnings in cheap vodka.

When she was alone she wrote whenever she could, on whatever she could, huddled close to the hut's little iron stove for warmth. New paper was expensive, but old timetables and memos from the railway provided ample white space to fill between track inspections, her scribbled words charting their own route between departure times from Vladivostok and Moscow. She was halfway through her magnum opus, a book she was writing for women like her, who had to struggle through life. After years of equivocation she had recently settled on a title – *Find Your Rail Self: 100 Life Lessons from the Trans-Siberian Railway*. A hundred was a lot, she realised, but surely it was better to have more ideas than fewer. She'd seen some books with just six or seven, like Sasha Ivanov's *Seven Ways to Conquer Your Career* or Nikita Aliyev's *Six Daily Habits of Billionaire Muscovites*. Perhaps that made sense to people who travelled only by car, with room for just a few bags in the boot. But on the railway it wasn't unusual for cargo trains to have fifty, sixty or even seventy wagons, each filled with varied and essential goods. The people waiting for the goods didn't want just six or seven wagons. Some wanted one thing, and some another. You had to have a lot of wagons to be sure of satisfying people in big cities like Novosibirsk or Ekaterinburg or Irkutsk, let alone Moscow or St Petersburg. And Olga was sure it was the same with ideas. The more ideas you had, the more chance you had of pleasing people, because people always liked best the ideas they had already had themselves. And the more people you pleased, the more books you could sell. And the more books you sold, the sooner you could save up the fees for the honours literature course at Tomsk State University.

When there was a big gap between trains, and nothing much to do on the track, Olga would sit in her little hut and get very excited about her book. Her eyes would glow and her pen would fly across the paper as she laid down lesson after lesson that she had learned from her life on the lines, and which she thought would help other women who struggled with similar burdens. But hers was a busy job, and such times were relatively rare. Almost always the telephone would ring, or the alarm would sound for a train, and she would have to stop writing and start working – not that writing wasn't working, but it was a different kind of work. And then she would go home tired and have to start cooking dinner for her father Mikhail, or pick up shopping for her aunt Zia Kuznetsov (Mikhail's widowed sister), or – like the night before – go around to Anna Kabalevsky's house to help with some emergency or other. At times like that, when there were many calls on her time and energy, she had to decide whom to help first: there was nobody else to call on. And then some people would be upset – again like the night before, when she'd had to call Aunt Zia and tell her she couldn't bring her shopping around because she needed to help Anna. Olga would get to bed late, and get up early, trying to please everybody but really pleasing nobody. It was hard, at times like that, to think of herself as a writer, as an artist nurturing an inner and sacred fire.

As if youd ever be anything else . . .

She stared at the phrase until its vicious words burned into her consciousness, eating away at her most cherished ambitions. The ties that bound her to her dreams were thin and fraying, she realised. Perhaps there would be no glittering, bestselling career after all, no triumphant release to follow the long years of struggle. Perhaps there was only more work on the railway, more endurance, more suffering, more trying to please too many people, on and on until the end.

She dropped the letter onto the table and sank onto her new sofa, laying her head on the arm and allowing herself to be engulfed by a tide of despair that washed over her with the exquisite drawn-out misery of decades, as if each sentence in the hateful letter had been drops of poison in a well that had overflowed at last.

When her sobs began to subside, she saw that her mascara had run with her tears, and was staining the fabric of her sofa. She had bought it from the butcher, Nikolai Popov, only a few weeks before, when their old one had finally collapsed under her father's swelling paunch.

'Stop calling it new,' Mikhail had said, when she complained of his cigarette ash one day. 'Popov had it for years. I remember him boasting about it at Odrosov's when he got it – I don't remember when. But it's an old couch. He probably ended up keeping his pig-heads and sausages on top of it.'

'It's new to *me*,' she replied quietly, fetching him an ashtray. But now there was cheap mascara on the sofa as well as cigarette ash, alongside a number of dubious and quite possibly meat-coloured stains on the yellowing brocade fabric.

In a rush of anger she seized the letter and threw it into the fireplace. She drenched it with a dash of the paraffin she used for firelighting and threw a match on top, and soon the evil words were consumed in a fleeting blaze. In some part of her mind she knew she should probably have kept the letter to show to the police, whenever they got around to sending another sergeant to the tiny Roslazny outpost. But with a more primal part of herself she stared fiercely at the fire, as if doing so would speed the flames and their cathartic work.

'*Suka, blyad!*' she cried, then covered her mouth. Her father Mikhail swore constantly, like all the men in the village, but he hated to hear women cursing. Not that she was afraid of him, but the last thing she needed was an irritable, hung-over, ageing man waking up three hours before usual and adding to her troubles with a rant about the proper conduct of the Russian Unmarried Female.

She knew what he would say. 'How will you ever attract a husband and get us out of this dump, talking like that? It's bad enough you look like a man without speaking like one, too.'

And she would reply: 'If I look like a man it's your fault. You made me work for the railway. What am I meant to wear when I'm checking the rails? A ball-gown?'

And he would shrug and make a sound, inarticulate but expressive, as if to say: 'What was I to do? What other jobs were there for you in Roslazny?'

She looked in the cracked bit of mirror that hung over the fireplace, wiping the last teardrops from her eyelashes and pushing a stray blonde hair over her ear. She didn't look so bad, she thought, for having spent the best part of twenty years working outdoors in Siberia. It was many years since her mother had called her the prettiest tsarevna in all Russia, but she still had attractive features and a good figure underneath her outerwear. The old people *should* envy her, she thought. She did perhaps look a little masculine in her fur-lined Russian Railways boiler-suit and high visibility jacket, but so what? She had long since given up any hope of a husband, in Roslazny or anywhere else. Besides, the only men she saw were railwaymen, and she'd heard enough tales from her Tayga friends, and from her father Mikhail, to give them as wide a berth as possible. And so she dressed for comfort and warmth, as any sensible person would who had to stand in snow and ice all day.

And it wasn't as if she didn't wear make-up. Every self-respecting woman wore make-up, she often thought. The tourists on the Trans-Siberian didn't, so they mustn't be very self-respectful, she reasoned. She had often looked at young women from England and Germany and Spain and America as they stood on the platform at Tayga considering which food-stall looked most hygienic – Larisa's, in fact, but Anya was better at attracting their attention – and wondered at their careless hairstyles, scruffy sweatpants and clumpy hiking boots.

'Don't they want to look good?' she would ask her friend Ekaterina Chezhekov, on days when she had to visit the main-tenance depot at Tayga station. Ekaterina sold cigarettes on the platforms from a little box with straps over her shoulders, like an old-time cinema usher.

'They don't think we Russians matter,' Ekaterina would say, lighting one for herself. 'That's why they dress like that, and appear without make-up. If there were more foreigners here, they wouldn't dress like that.'

'But what about the other foreigners on the train – the men?' Olga would say. 'Don't they matter?'

'Nobody could matter who chooses to travel by train,'

Ekaterina would say. 'These girls are clever. They know that a sensible man, a man with brains as well as money, would take an aeroplane instead of a train. They save their make-up for those men.'

'But these girls are travelling by train,' Olga would say, 'so aren't they stupid too?' Then they would laugh, and the tourists, who never spoke any Russian, would smile politely, buy something small, get back on the train and move on.

I look tired today, she thought, as she gazed at herself in the mirror. But that was no surprise, and not just because of her unaccustomed tears. She'd been out until the small hours the night before, after all, helping Anna Kabalevsky with her children in the absence of her husband, Bogdan, who described himself as a local businessman. His real business was to be at home with his wife and three sons, Olga often said, and helping to run the Kabalevsky Hostel, which consisted of two sparsely furnished rooms and a rudimentary toilet in the basement of their house.

'You'd give your right hand away,' Mikhail would say, 'and your left, too, if a friend asked you. You're always out here and there, helping your friends, doing this and doing that. What would they do for you? That's the question to ask yourself.' And he would nod wisely as if universal suspicion were the only truth. 'Be prudent,' he would continue. 'Prudence is the Russian virtue! D'you think I earned all this' – pointing at the walls, or sometimes the ceiling, of the house they shared – 'by giving away my time or money?'

At times like this, Olga had to force herself to hold her tongue, telling herself that a good daughter wouldn't reply with scorn. A good daughter wouldn't reply that her father had never done a day's work since his accident in 1988, or that the house had been bought with his wife's money rather than his, or that her father had since sold off all but one of her mother's precious heirlooms (and that he'd refrained from selling this last treasure only because nobody knew where it was), or that her father had driven her brother into joining the army and herself into working for Russian Railways, or that her father—

Enough, Olga Pushkin would say to herself. A good daughter would say none of those things, but would carry on and help her friends regardless. And Anna Kabalevsky was a good friend despite the fact that she had children. She'd been Olga's friend ever since their mothers had taken them to the Roslazny state nursery together. And it was a proper nursery in those days, since the local *sovkhoz*, the state farm, was still being propped up by the Kremlin, providing jobs and food for many families. Nowadays, more than a decade after the *sovkhoz* had collapsed into the frozen mud, there was no nursery, just as there was no bathhouse or post office or church or doctor's surgery. There was just whatever each mother could do for her children in her own home, with the help of relatives or friends. But Anna was from the east, of the people of Listvyanka on Lake Baikal, and had no relatives within a thousand miles. So she had to call on friends like Olga when she needed help to manage Boris, Gyorgy and Ilya.

Olga had had a tiring time on the railway that Thursday, with repeated breakdowns of the signalling relays, but she hadn't objected when Anna called and asked her to come around. She needed someone to look after Ilya, she said, while she took Boris and Gyorgy to see Dr Zinozev, who held a free evening surgery for children at the community hospital in

Tayga. Ilya was a sweet baby, Olga knew, and rarely difficult to put down. Anyway, as long as Bogdan wasn't there, Olga quite liked being at Anna's. For one thing, it got her away from her father. And Anna had a better television than Olga and Mikhail's 20-inch Sony. So Olga was quite willing, all things considered, to spend some time putting Ilya to bed and watching re-runs of *Ne Rodis Krasivoy*, her all-time favourite soap. It would be considerably more enjoyable than what she had originally planned, which was to help Aunt Zia with her grocery shopping.

That night, however, *Ne Rodis Krasivoy* was bumped from the schedules to allow for yet another televised press conference held by Lieutenant Colonel Grigor Babikov, the head of police in Kemerovo. Every other day, it seemed, his fussy, pedantic voice could be heard exhorting members of the community to offer their assistance in solving some case or other. Olga liked to think of herself as public-spirited, but replacing *Ne Rodis Krasivoy* with hours of gruesome photos and grainy CCTV footage was a step too far – especially as everyone knew Babikov was only doing it to bolster his profile for the upcoming mayoral elections in Kemerovo, the provincial capital.

To make matters worse, Ilya was unsettled that night, and woke several times after being put down. After some investigative work, Olga found a little white stub poking through his gums.

'Aha,' she said, holding Ilya close. 'So now we know the culprit. A tooth! Well done, *detka*, well done! Soon you will be a big boy like your brothers. But first we must get you back to sleep, back to sleep.' She sat down in Anna's rocking chair, wrapped Ilya with faux-fur blankets, and cuddled him gently back and forth.

Anna texted from the hospital: *Long queue, I'll be back as soon as I can. Thanks Olga! You're the best Axx.*

Olga sighed, and carried on rocking the baby. Soon Ilya's eyelids drooped, and Olga's, too, began to close with sleep. But then someone came noisily in at the front door and woke them both up again. It was Bogdan, Anna's husband.

'What are you doing here?' he said, when he saw Olga nursing Ilya in Anna's rocking chair. Bogdan Kabalevsky was short, tubby, and more often inebriated than not, but he tried to offset these disadvantages with heeled boots and shirts with vertical lines, and by walking as straight as possible at all times.

'I'm doing your job,' said Olga, answering his question. 'So's Anna, most of the time. D'you think hostels run themselves?'

'I've got a better job than that,' said Bogdan. 'I've got—'

He belched and tried to refocus his blurry vision on Olga's face. 'I've got bigger irons in the fire,' he said eventually. 'Not that it's any of your business. Go on, get out of here, *grombaba*!' he went on, laughing and falling into an armchair. *Grom-baba*, or 'thunder woman', is usually a compliment; but the way Bogdan said it, with his eyes lingering on Olga's figure, was clearly meant to imply that she was sturdily built – that the ground would tremble as she walked. This was a very insulting thing to say to a woman like Olga, who wasn't really overweight at all.

'Get back to your shack,' he continued. 'Mikhail needs you. Or do you have another family to interfere with on your way home?'

'I'll go when Anna gets back,' said Olga. 'For now, you'd better sleep off that vodka. I can smell it from here. Don't you know Odrosov brews his own? You'll be blind in a year, drinking that much.'

Igor Odrosov was the owner of Café Astana, Roslazny's sole bar, restaurant and general store. The locals called him the Cosmonaut because he was Kazakh and never stopped boasting of his country's achievements in the USSR's space programme. He'd christened his home-made vodka 'Rocket Fuel'. The joke was that it actually tasted like it.

'Better than listening to kids screaming all night,' muttered Bogdan. He closed his eyes and fell asleep in his chair.

Anna returned after midnight with two tired children and a small paper bag of medicine from the hospital pharmacy. Olga handed over the sleeping Ilya in exchange for Anna's whispered thanks and made her way out, stepping over Bogdan's outstretched legs.

How does Anna put up with that *pridurok*? Olga wondered, as she walked home through the falling snow, stupefied with the desire for sleep and navigating the unlit streets from memory. The vodka, the gambling, the stupid business ventures that always failed . . . But at least he didn't beat Anna or the children, as far as she knew. He was a neglectful, but not an abusive, husband and father. There'd been plenty of those in Roslazny over the years. And on the whole he tolerated Olga helping with the family, which was not the case with all fathers in the village, some of whom would rather see their wives die of exhaustion than accept 'charity' from others. Bogdan had called Olga a *grom-baba*, true, but she'd heard much worse. Her own father had never stinted himself when it came to abuse.

'You can't wear a dress like that,' Mikhail had told her one day, in the department store in Tayga. Olga was fourteen, and hoping to persuade him to buy her something pretty for the *sovkhoz*'s annual party.

He pushed her towards the mirror and held up the dress in front of her. 'See? You'll look fat.'

'I'm not fat,' she said. 'I'm just not thin. Mama said I would be a famous beauty when I grow up.'

'You don't need to bother dressing up, anyway,' went on Mikhail. 'You're like a diesel locomotive on the railway. A Luhanskteplovoz. I always tell 'em, you can paint a 2TE116 in all the colours you like, it'll still look like a pig's arse.'

Olga had stared at him in amazement. Had her father compared her to a Luhanskteplovoz 2TE116 diesel engine? And to a pig's *bottom*?

'Just think,' said Mikhail, warming to his theme. 'You're heavy, you go where you're told, but you can't go very fast. Just like a diesel locomotive. Ha! Like I always said, you were born to be a railwayman. If they run short of engines you can pull the carriages for them!'

'Railway*woman*,' Olga had replied. But though she had courage enough for this, she'd never felt able to challenge her father's certainty that the railway would be her career, as it had been his. It wasn't done, in the days when she grew up, for a girl to disobey her father in such an important matter, especially without a mother to back her up. Things were different now, for some women at least; but the changes had come too late for her. In due course her father had forced her to join the Irkutsk Institute of Railway Engineering, which had a satellite college at Tayga; and two years after that, in 2005, Olga had qualified as a track engineer, third class. In theory, this entitled her to apply for important positions at regional depots like Tayga, but in practice the foreman at Tayga, an old Stalinist called Viktor Fandorin, had blocked applications from women since the date of their first admission to the Institute in 1976, and he had no intention of changing any time soon. So Olga had been consigned to her little hut by the tracks near Roslazny, and there she had worked ever since.

I *am* like a railway engine, Olga thought at times. But not a diesel, she said to herself. I'm more like an old steam locomotive – like that old museum piece painted green and red by the platforms at Tayga. Only not dead and quiet and cold, lapped by wandering snowdrifts, but alive with a raging fire inside, forcing the pressure gauge ever higher. A time will come when I *burst*, she thought.

But not today. Today she had to go to work. That was what Russian women did, day in, day out, regardless of drunken fathers or chauvinist foremen or poisoned words from cowardly pens. The tracks lay always before them, the horizon forever receding. Maybe one day they would reach it. Maybe one day.

2

The Fox and the Hedgehog

The snow fell steadily as Olga trudged down the path that led to the railway, a boundless fretted curtain dancing on her eyelashes and resting on her shoulders like frosted icing. The house she shared with her father was on the north-eastern edge of Roslazny, away from the road and towards the tracks, and soon she was beyond the last wooden shacks and outbuildings and into the woods. There, all other noises were silenced. Even the distant drone of traffic from Tayga died away, replaced by the soft hiss of descending snowflakes and the crunch of her shoes compressing them into footprints. The pines on either side of the path formed the only contrast, their black trunks stark against a dazzling alabaster carpet.

We are small and weak, after all, thought Olga, as she looked northwards at the great trees marching off into the distance. We are mere dots of warm blood and skin, and the *taiga*, Siberia's forest empire, is so vast and cold. We should protect each other against the bitter wind, not send vile letters that bring tears instead of joy. She'd hated the short walk through the outskirts of the village, looking at every darkened window and door and wondering if vicious eyes were watching her, formulating new letters to send, new rumours to spread.

And she'd almost thought . . . no, it was nonsense. But Olga was too truthful to say it was nonsense. She *had* seen a face forming in the cold blue shadow of a wooden doorway, a face with hooded eyes and a cruel mouth, the face of a witch. Or was it maybe someone she knew? But then the face had disappeared, resolving into the angles formed by a dilapidated mailbox and its gaping planks.

She shook her head, as she had after reading the letter. She was exhausted, that was the problem – tired and upset and overburdened. She took a deep breath and forced herself to think about something else.

Why did the first people settle here among the frozen woods, she asked herself, when they must have realised that warmer lands lay to the south? Why endure the hostility of endless winter, and forgo the sunshine, lemon groves and olive trees that could be reached in a few months' trekking?

But if such thoughts were distracting, they were also dangerous, for they bred discontent in the hearts of railway engineers. They made her ask why she, Olga Pushkin, did not flee the frozen wastelands for a new life in some European fleshpot . . . Sometimes at night, when she couldn't sleep, she would read trashy novels about women living carefree days on sunny islands in the Mediterranean, or starting brilliant new careers and meeting the man of their dreams in the same week, in decisive turning-points, the hinges of new and blissful lives. And sometimes she would put her novel down and allow herself to imagine that she was one of the protagonists she admired – that she was Lara Bellagio, waitress-turned-actress in Monaco, or Odette de la Tour, millionaire heiress and luxury shoe designer in a far-off country called Mauritius. Surely those kinds of women didn't receive poison-pen letters criticising their achievements or charitable work. But if Olga went off to places like Monaco or Mauritius, who would look after her father and her aunt Zia and her friend Anna Kabalevsky? Who would man the little railside hut, built years ago for a level-crossing that had never materialised? Who would ensure the track was safe and the trains could run on time? Lara Bellagio and Odette de la Tour could hire staff to take care of things like that; Olga could not.

And who would look after Dmitri? she thought, as she turned the last corner in the winding path and came upon the railway tracks glimmering like bright silver threads amid the sombre forest-eaves. Who would feed him worms and snails to protect him from the cold?

Dmitri was a diminutive white-breasted hedgehog that lived near her hut. She had rescued him from a fox's jaws two summers ago, by means of hitting the fox on the head with her handbag, a hard-edged Soviet-era creation in blue leather. She was not convinced that Dmitri was in fact a he, but as there had never been any sign of him bearing a brood of even smaller hedgehogs she'd decided to stick with her original assumption.

'Where are you, little *detka*?' she called as she approached her hut, painted in once-vivid green and sporting a Russian Railways logo that had begun to peel away at the edges. 'Are you there, Dmitri-Dimochka?'

She walked up to the hut, weaving her way through the tree-roots that arched over the frozen path. She picked up the old broom-handle she kept by the signal relay and thumped the base of the roof to remove the snow that lay thickly on the sloping planks. But as she did so she caught sight of Dmitri emerging from the undergrowth, just in time to be buried by a heavy blanket of dislodged snow. Olga gasped and quickly dug him out. Clucking in a reassuring manner and brushing the snow from his spikes, she opened the hut's rickety wooden door and put him by the little iron stove, which she soon got going with a firelighter and some torn-up newspaper.

'There, Dmitri-Dima,' she said, putting a handful of dried worms in front of him and waiting for him to uncurl. 'Now you can recover. That was a nasty shock. It was all Mamochka's fault.'

She carried on talking, thinking that the noise might soothe Dmitri's nerves, and busied herself with her usual preparations for the day ahead. She found the routine a welcome distraction from the morning's events, a defence against hateful letters, frightful visions and malevolent witches. She took the lid off the stove again and put in some more substantial kindling, including several lumps of bog-peat that would burn for hours. She took off her fur hat and shook it, then brushed the snow from her hair and jacket and stamped her feet until her boots were free of mud and ice. She filled her samovar – an urn of water that she kept bubbling on the stove to make tea – and took her clipboard from a nail in the wall. Every Sunday evening she walked to Tayga station to pick up the week's schedule, and every Monday morning she took the previous week's schedule off the clipboard and put the new one on. (The old timetables went into the cardboard box Olga used to store paper for writing.) When she got to the hut every day, she would look at the schedule and work out when she had to signal the passing of a train to the operators at Tayga or Novosibirsk, and when she had to inspect the track or carry out other local maintenance.

Today was a busy day. The first Friday in January was always busy, since the schedulers had to make up lost traffic from the New Year holiday, and for some reason, now lost in the mists of Soviet history, the first Friday was always the chosen day. Olga sighed as she looked over the long list of duties, and tried to remember what she'd been thinking about before the letter arrived that morning. Hadn't she had an idea for the book? Some life lesson or other that she could include in *Find Your Rail Self: 100 Life Lessons from the Trans-Siberian Railway* . . . Was it something to do with Dmitri, now happily uncurled and feasting on his dried worms by the stove – something to do with our need for a helping hand now and then, perhaps? Or the need to protect hedgehogs, who know just one thing, from foxes, who know many things? Olga knew how important it was to give help when it was needed, above all because there had been many times when she herself would have given anything for a friendly face, and few had ever appeared.

But no – this was too general an idea. The life lessons had to come from the railway, or she would have to think of a different title for her book. But the railway always provided plenty of food for thought. There were six thousand miles of track on the Trans-Siberian railway, after all, and more than a hundred main stations across the breadth of Russia, each with their own collection of Ekaterina Chezhekovs selling things on the platforms. There were also thousands of engines and carriages, each with their own crew and their own smell and their own distinctive scrapes and scratches from years of service, each day passing hundreds of different Olgas standing by the tracks, from Moscow to the Far East, or down through Mongolia to Beijing. And each train was like a wedding party, a never-to-be-repeated group of people who might otherwise never have met, eating, talking, drinking and sleeping together, and perhaps forming lifelong relationships in the narrow confines of a *platskartny* third-class berth.

The railway was a form of time travel, too. To rattle and sway over its tracks was to retrace the steps of countless soldiers, convicts and peasants who had laboured to extend its steel embrace through forest, swamp and steppe. It was to journey back through the twentieth century, before Putin and Yeltsin, Gorbachev and Khrushchev, Stalin, Lenin and Trotsky, before Communism and Bolshevism, to the days when the tsar, the Little Father of All Russia, sent out a decree that a railway should exist, and behold! It did.

So her mother had told her once, her eyes glowing as she gazed out over the landscape that flowed past their carriage window, changing and yet unchanging, a thousand variations on an unvaried theme. It is time to name her mother: Tatiana Lichnovsky, who by great misfortune became Tatiana Pushkin, and who yet rejoiced in her misfortune because of her children, who would not otherwise have come to be. One day, when Olga was seven, Tatiana took her to Tayga station three miles away. (Her brother Pasha was at the Roslazny schoolhouse, which had arranged a boys-only sports day, while Mikhail, who was still working in those days, had gone to Tayga in the Lada they owned at the time.) Her mother bought herself and Olga day-tickets to Tomsk. When they boarded the train, she had sought out a table where they could sit opposite each other and watch the *taiga* passing by.

'This was a royal railway first, you know, Olgakin,' she remembered her mother saying. 'Tsars and tsarinas, tsareviches and tsarevnas have passed along these tracks as well as commissars and Party chairmen and all the accomplices of Communism. Princes, boyars and countesses journeyed here long before Stalin used the railway to send succour to the Nazis. The Great Patriotic War, they call it! Only when Hitler changed his mind and attacked us. Only when the peasants and the Jews had already been crushed under his boot . . . '

Her mother stopped talking, realising Olga was too young to understand. 'Ah, Olgakin, let's not think of horrid things today,' she said. 'We're on holiday. Just you and me, and Tomsk.'

Olga could still bring to mind the sight of winter sunlight upon her mother's blonde hair and thin, high-cheekboned face, sunlight that came dappling through the bare-branched trees that flickered past them in endless untidy rows. It was her first trip to Tomsk – her first trip to anywhere farther away than Tayga – and her mother had made it a magical, unforgettable day, a day of sugared confections at the Hotel Magistrat and personal tours of the gardens and the rare book collection of Tomsk State University. (Her mother could charm her way in anywhere.) Magical and unforgettable – until her mother had felt tired, that was. She'd often felt tired in those days, in the months before anyone had known she was sick. Quite suddenly, in the centre of the university's famous botanical gardens, her mother had put her hand on Olga for support, and stood there, gasping for breath, until their guide ran to the nearby café and brought her a chair.

She soon recovered, though, and took Olga to the university bookshop to buy her a row of Russian classics – Gogol, Tolstoy,

Dostoevsky, Chekhov, Bulgakov, and others – which they carried to the railway station in thin plastic bags before tumbling at the last minute, panting and laughing, onto the last train back to Tayga. They half ran, half walked to their house in Roslazny, dashing in and closing the front door behind them moments before Mikhail drove up the muddy road in the family Lada. To this day he remained ignorant of that trip and of several others. Even if he had known, Mikhail had never had any interest in books, and almost alone among Olga's possessions they had escaped his attention. They rested now on her bookshelf in the hut by the tracks, silent reminders of that happy day long ago, set in gold and blue and red, only a little bleached after nearly thirty years' sunlight and frost. Olga read them from time to time, but found them rather difficult to understand. Her mother could have explained them to her but she was gone. One day, though, Olga would go back to Tomsk, and the clever professors there would educate her, until she understood the books as well as her mother had done. Then she would write a great story herself, a new Russian masterpiece – something even better, perhaps, than *Find Your Rail Self: 100 Life Lessons from the Trans-Siberian Railway*.

'Aha,' she cried, banging her gloved hand on the hut's thin wooden wall. She had remembered the life lesson she'd been thinking of before the letter arrived. It was a simple but important insight, she thought, digging into her pocket for a pencil and picking up a sheet of old timetable paper to scribble on.

People are like stations, she wrote. Once a station is built, there it stays – just like people, when they're given their path in life. One must be a doctor, another a railwaywoman, yet another a teacher or a road cleaner. Saying a person's name, for people who know them, is like saying 'Tayga station' or 'Yaroslavsky station' or 'Irkutsk station'. It means something because they all stay in the same place. They are familiar and known. The trouble comes when people try to be something they're not meant to be. It would be crazy to pick up Tayga station and move it ten miles from the railway, just as it would be crazy for a doctor to try to be a railwaywoman. People should be happy to stay where they are, with their position in life. That's what railway stations are telling us.

She frowned as she finished writing the words. Did these sentences not imply that she should stay in her railside hut for ever, and not go to Tomsk State University, the Oxford of West Siberia? But then she shook her head. She was writing these life lessons for other people, not her. She was the author of the book, not one of its readers. It was because she could write a book that she was able to pick up and move, like the imaginary Tayga station newly set down ten miles from the tracks. But not everyone could do that, and if they couldn't it would only raise their hopes to pretend otherwise – it would only bring them sorrow. But she was meant to be a writer, not a railwaywoman. That was just a means to an end.

Her mother Tatiana had been picked up like Tayga station and moved away. Her father Mikhail had done that. It was his hand that had plucked her from her native soil at Astrazov, and like every plucked flower she had died thereafter. Tatiana was the last of the Lichnovskys, and the Lodge at Astrazov had been her birthright. That was her natural habitat, the old hunting lodge that one of the Lichnovsky counts had built in the days of the tsars, buried deep in the woods twenty miles north of Tomsk, and even further from Roslazny. Olga's grandfather had been a man named Ivan Lichnovsky, born on the wrong side of the blanket to Count Evgeny and a chambermaid, and established (for propriety's sake) in an anonymous dacha in Itatka, a few miles from Astrazov. For this reason Ivan had escaped the purges of the Bolsheviks, though he lived to see Count Evgeny's body hanging from the gallows in Tomsk, and his grandmother, the dowager countess, dead on the ground outside the public lavatories in Itatka, worked to death by the local Party leadership.

And when Ivan and his wife Lidiya fell victim to one of Stalin's purges thirty years later, the nurse who had looked after Ivan since his birth (and who was now extremely old) had to gather up all the things she could carry and hobble from the dacha to the school, where Ivan's daughter Tatiana stood waiting in the snow for her father to collect her. There she told her, gasping for breath, that she would never see her parents again – that they could never return home to the dacha where they had lived together. With her last strength, the nurse took Tatiana to the Lodge at Astrazov, and died there, a frozen bundle of rags on the doorstep. Then the housekeeper, Lubov Yuryev, daughter of Adelaida who had been housekeeper in Count Evgeny's time, took Tatiana in and cared for her until Mikhail Pushkin came along and tore her from her natal earth.

Dmitri the hedgehog, having finished his worms, made a chirruping noise that broke in upon her thoughts.

'Dmitri-Dima-*detka*,' she said, smiling at him and giving him some more worms from the bag she had bought from Popov the butcher. 'I know what Mamochka Tatiana, my dear mother, would've thought of you. She would have said I'd no business saving a hedgehog from a fox, and that the fox deserved his dinner if he could hunt for it. She admired hunters. And she was like a fox herself: she knew many things. I'm more of a hedgehog, like you, Dmitri. I do not know many things, but I know that I love you.'

Her mother had been an aristocrat in many ways, not least in her contempt for new-fangled notions of animal rights and vegetarianism – ideas that had begun to make their way into Tomsk, and even Tayga, by the time she died. But even if she had been old-fashioned in that regard, she had suffered a far deeper cruelty as a result. Because if it hadn't been for her love of the old ways, of peasants worshipping secret icons of St Basil and Tsar Nicholas the Second – of hunters living off the land and sleeping in log cabins by the fringe of the forest – she would never have fallen in love with Mikhail in the first place. Olga gazed out of the hut's small rear window, which faced away from the track, towards the trees and their tangled snowy boughs, and remembered a story her mother had told her of a fateful meeting long ago, in the heart of the forest, at the Lodge in Astrazov.

It took place in the winter of 1977, when Tatiana was twenty-five, and at the height of her youthful beauty. One day there came a knock on the door, and when Lubov the housekeeper peered out into the daylight she saw a slender young man of medium height, dressed in the woodsman's uniform of brown trousers, heavy boots and a baggy grey smock. He had three ducks and a hare slung around his shoulders on a piece of twine, and what looked like a rifle on his back. He asked for directions, and a bite of supper. Lubov would have liked to send him on his way, but she had not been to Itatka for some days because of the weather, and their larder was running low.

'Come in, then,' she said to the man, opening the door. 'Come in and give us the hare for the pot, and have your dinner here. Then we'll set you on the path to where you want to go.'

The man grinned. 'A fair price,' he said. 'I'll gladly accept.' He kicked his boots against the doorpost until it shook. Then, unslinging his rifle and his ducks, he handed the hare to Lubov and made his way inside, looking left and right in the Lodge's dim interior like a hound on a scent. His eyes lit up as he saw the cabinet next to the chimney in the sitting room by the stairs, the silver plates and crystal goblets of Tatiana's inheritance glinting in the firelight. Then he saw Tatiana herself standing by the grandfather clock in a plain blue dress, tall and slender like a young birch, her hair flowing over her shoulders like a sunlit brook of golden water. He stooped low and swept off his foraging cap. 'Mikhail Pushkin, at your service!'

'What happened next, Mamochka?' Olga said. Her mother was telling her the story at the café in Tomsk, on that first visit by train so long ago, when they had walked around the state university and the botanical gardens. Her mother's face had lit up as she talked, alive once more with the romance of a tale she had waited her whole life to live. When she looked back in later years, Tatiana felt as if her upbringing and history and all the days of her girlhood had led her to that moment, furnishing (or burdening) her with the precise dispositions required to fall in love with Mikhail Pushkin from the moment he took off his cap in the doorway of the Lodge at Astrazov. Lubov had sown the seeds by insisting on bringing her up as a Lichnovsky countess, with a curriculum gleaned from her sense of what was appropriate for the education of a lady and a Lichnovsky – a *Lichnovsky*. Lubov's mother, Adelaida, had kept a diary in which she recorded the doings of the young Lichnovsky countesses in the tsarist days when family summers were spent at Astrazov. From its faded pages Lubov constructed a demanding schedule of work for Tatiana, spanning the breadth of aristocratic accomplishment from literature to hunting with hounds, and with deportment and dress in between.

In the evenings, or sometimes on Saturday mornings and Sunday afternoons, Tatiana would sit in bed and work her way through the Lodge's immense library of Russian classics that old Count Evgeny, though not a reading man, had purchased by the yard from the bookseller in Tomsk. Like her daughter Olga after her, she would bury herself in the words of each new novel or play she took from the elaborately carved shelves, and try to imagine herself far off and long ago, acting out the dramas and melodramas the writer had portrayed, putting aside her own name and identity until she became this countess or that peasant farmer-woman, this Cossack or that boyar charged with saving the Russian Empire from Englishmen marching on the borders of India.

Above all she devoured Tolstoy. Given her upbringing at Astrazov, with a gun in one hand and a pitchfork in the other, it was inevitable that Konstantin Levin from *Anna Karenina* became Tatiana's most beloved character in all literature – or at least all Russian literature, which in Tatiana's opinion came down to much the same thing. Konstantin Levin was, at once, an aristocratic man who despised pretension, a sophisticated man who revelled in everyday life, and a wealthy man who got his hands dirty on his own land. Tatiana saw parts of herself in each aspect of his character. And Levin's final turn to faith seemed to offer a ray of consolation amid so much sorrow, and a further bridge to the world of the peasants who lived all around her, and who had preserved their own beliefs by burying them in the woods far beyond the cold arm of the Kremlin.

As the years passed in Astrazov, Tatiana began to look towards her own maturity and coming womanhood, and to assess the young men she met in the light of this literary lens, an ideal of Russian manhood that had perhaps never existed, but which for her summed up all that was admirable and worthy of love. And so, when Mikhail Pushkin arrived at the Lodge, he seemed the living embodiment of the Russian paragon she dreamed of, a man of the land, a man *for* the land. But things had worked out rather differently. Mikhail was a Levin, but he was the other brother in Tolstoy's masterpiece – he was Nikolai Levin the drunken gambler, not Konstantin the gentleman-farmer.

'Mamochka, why are your eyes so sad?' said Olga in the café at Tomsk, when her mother didn't reply.

Tatiana Pushkin dabbed her eyes with a paper napkin. 'Oh, Olgakin,' she said, 'I'm sorry. It's just – it's just something Lubov used to say to me, at the Lodge in Astrazov. She would hit me with a ladle, when I danced around telling her about the latest thing I'd read in the library, and my dreams of a dashing woodsman who would come to the Lodge and take me away with him. "You're a romantic, Tatiana Lichnovsky," she said to me once, "for you believe in fairy-tales. But didn't you know? Russian stories always end in sorrow."'

3

Of Bogdan and Baba Yaga

The light had long since faded when Olga set off homewards at the end of that busy first Friday in January, and she tutted as she realised her torch battery was dying. But in truth she barely needed it. After all these years she knew the path so well that she could probably have walked it blindfold and come to no harm. Besides, Roslazny was near. She could see the house-lights and streetlamps twinkling between the tree-trunks, guiding her back through the twilight.

The village looked beautiful in winter, thought Olga, as she tramped past the Petrovs' place on the outskirts, and then her friend Anna Kabalevsky's house. The snow took the ugly concrete outbuildings and corrugated iron roofs and folded them in a uniform whiteness, as if the ramshackle dwellings were decorations on a cake. Then, later, when the temperature fell and the snow froze into a hard crust, the icy crystals would glitter in the night, reflecting the distant starlight like a thousand diadems. Even the people of Roslazny looked different in winter, their bodies bundled into fur and down and scarves until only a nose or a strand of hair or a pair of eyes betrayed their owner.

But there weren't many people left in Roslazny now. The paucity of house-lights and streetlamps betrayed the village like a known pair of eyes, showing how few people were left, how many houses were abandoned and unlit, how many pathways now led nowhere needful. At its height during the days of the *sovkhoz* – the time when Mikhail had brought Tatiana to live there – Roslazny had been home to at least fifty families, most of whom worked on the state farm. Now fewer than twenty households remained, barely enough to support the café that Igor Odrosov ran with his daughter Svetlana. Most nights at Café Astana ended with Odrosov drinking too much of his own vodka and telling whoever was still there that tomorrow he'd shut down, sell up and move to a place where life was easier, like a maximum-security prison in the Arctic Circle. But the following morning, or lunchtime, would find a bleary-eyed Odrosov opening the café shutters and shouting at Svetlana to get up and prepare for another day's work. Still, the Odrosovs were lucky: they had jobs in Roslazny. Most of the villagers had to travel to Tayga for work each day, thumbing a lift or walking the three miles if they didn't own a car.

I have a job in Roslazny too, thought Olga. Or, at least, one near the village, ten minutes' walk through the forest rather than an hour's trek to Tayga on a narrow, sludgy and dangerous single-track road. Could that be why the unknown writer had sent that horrible letter – out of jealousy over her job? Surely not, thought Olga. Who would be jealous of a tiny freezing hut by the side of the railway, with the same mind-numbing duties day after day, and never a word of praise from a superior or a chance of promotion to a job that reflected her real abilities? But, then, any job was better than none, above all in the winter months when food was scarce and expensive. It was something to think about, at any rate.

The café was out of Olga's route home, since it lay towards the far side of Roslazny from the railway, near the narrow road that led to Tayga. But she had promised her father she would pick up his magazines and gherkins, and Odrosov had promised her they would be delivered to the café earlier that day. Mikhail insisted on a jar of the best pickled gherkins each month as well as subscriptions to two magazines, ostensibly because he wanted to keep abreast of current affairs in Kemerovo Province, but really, as Olga well knew, because both magazines featured pretty girls from across the region in various stages of undress. Neither the gherkins nor the magazines were available in Tayga, which in terms of shopping opportunities was only slightly in advance of Roslazny; and so Olga had had to make a special trip to Tomsk several years previously to organise the delivery of these luxuries on a standing-order basis. Their supply was a small but continuous drain on her precarious finances, not least because Odrosov insisted on charging a fifty-rouble administrative fee for each item received, which meant a hundred and fifty roubles per month on top of the thousand roubles she had to pay the Tomsk agency for the magazines and the gherkins. But at least they kept Mikhail quiet for a few days. That was worth every kopek she could spare.

Mikhail was not the only person Olga ran errands for at Café Astana. Every second Tuesday she collected a parcel of groceries for her father's friend, Vladimir Solotov, and took them reluctantly to his foul-smelling house on the south-eastern side of the village. She also picked up her aunt Zia's shopping every Thursday evening and dropped it at her house near the centre of the village, by the little rose garden where she used to play with her mother. By contrast with Solotov's run-down shack, Aunt Zia's house was one of the most attractive in the village, with an elaborate wooden frame on the façade, stoves and samovars in every room, and a small courtyard at the back that in summer was wreathed in fragrance and flowers. The villagers said that her late husband, Ippolit Kuznetsov, had spent all his inheritance on decorating the house for her, when they'd married and moved in together in 1979. They said, too, that even if he had spent a river of roubles it would never have been enough for Zia, who seemed to think herself worth rather more than the humble resources of a *sovkhoz* manager. Now, twenty years after Ippolit's death, the house's décor had faded and cracked, and no new husband had come to repair the leaking roof or repaint the pale green wood of the façade. Zia and Ippolit had had no children, and Zia's few friends had left when the *sovkhoz* closed, or died in the bleak years that followed. Zia had long relied upon her brother Mikhail, and then, when she was old enough, upon his daughter Olga, who had called Zia the day before, on Thursday evening, to say she wouldn't be able to bring the groceries because she was going to help her friend Anna Kabalevsky.

'And what will I have for dinner?' Aunt Zia had said, her voice distorted by the microphone of her ancient rotary-dial telephone. 'I've nothing in the house.'

'What about the mutton in the freezer?' Olga had replied while walking to Anna's house, ducking under a washing-line that Popov the butcher had strung across the pathway the summer before, and which now supported a heavy mass of icicles. 'It'll soon defrost in a pan over the fire. And you've got some potatoes in the cupboard. I put them there myself, last week.'

But Aunt Zia had hung up with a muttered curse. Olga had sighed and carried on to Anna's, making a mental note to remember Zia's shopping the next day. And so that Friday night Olga had not only to pick up Mikhail's magazines and gherkins at the café, but also two heavy bags of groceries for Zia, which meant a further detour before home – and this after a long and tiring schedule on the railway, and with the dark shadow of the poison-pen letter hanging over her all day. And with each house she walked past, each little oasis of lamplight amid the Siberian night, she couldn't help but wonder: is *this* where the letter-writer lives? Is it Alexeyev the mechanic, or Popov the butcher, or Gagarin the office-cleaner? Or could it be Ludmila the waitress, or Nonna the hotel maid?

She remembered the witch's face she'd imagined that morning on the way to her hut and shuddered. She speeded up, her feet crunching noisily on the fallen snow. But the thoughts kept coming. Could it be – the idea made her shake her head as if to deny it – could it be someone she knew and loved? Could it be Ekaterina Chezhekov, her friend who sold cigarettes on the platform at Tayga station? Could it even be *Anna*? Anna Kabalevsky was one of the few people who knew of her ambition to attend Tomsk State University, to write a best-selling book, to escape the humdrum treadmill of her life as a tiny cog in the vast Russian Railways machine.

But it couldn't be Anna, she thought, as she opened the door to Café Astana and saw her sitting at the corner table with Ilya, Boris and Gyorgy. Anna was too good, too kind, too *spiritual* to write such vile things to her best friend. Anna had asked her once if she thought the Christ-Child in his manger could have been more beautiful, more achingly, heartbreakingly beautiful, than her own little Ilya as he slept swaddled in his blankets. Could a person ask such a question *and* write such a letter to her closest friend? Yes, she said in her heart, but only if the person were truly a demon, a prodigy of deceit and cruelty. And nobody could possibly think that this was a description of Anna, with her homely face and plain, traditional dresses. There were such ladies in Kemerovo Province, doubtless, if the newspapers could be trusted – strange, twisted women who lived in hidden corners of the Siberian *taiga*, in places you couldn't see clearly from the road or the railway, women who nursed old injuries like monstrous growths in a sickly greenhouse. Surely, Olga reasoned, ladies like that wouldn't dare to come into the light, into places like Roslazny where the railway and the road and nearby Tayga kept ancient horrors at bay.

But the letter, she thought with a sinking feeling, was from Roslazny …

She had just realised something she had known all day, but only implicitly, a piece of knowledge she'd hidden in a corner of her mind as if to protect herself from the implications that would follow. The envelope she'd torn open that morning had had no postmark stamped on it. So it had been delivered by hand, by a person who lived in Roslazny, by a person who must have walked up to the house she shared with her father Mikhail. She stopped and swore.

'*Chert*,' she said. 'I should've looked at the footsteps.' Olga was no woodswoman and could hardly tell a deer's spoor from a badger's. But even she could have followed a set of footsteps in the snow. The path laid by the letter-writer's feet would have betrayed them, like a known pair of eyes. But now it was too late: the prints would long since have been obliterated by others. And, besides, it had snowed all day, covering previous indentations with a thick new layer. But at least now she would know what to do if another letter arrived at her door.

'Olga?' said Anna. 'Are you coming or going?'

Olga came out of her reverie and found she was standing in a puddle of melting snow in the café doorway, through which blasts of freezing air were flooding in, to the displeasure of all those inside.

'Sorry, sorry, everyone,' she said, blushing bright crimson as she always did when suffering the least embarrassment, and closing the door behind her. She shook the snow from her clothes and made her way to Anna's table, forcing herself to forget her suspicions and to smile at the familiar faces dotted around the café. There was Fyodor Katin at the bar, the man they called Mechtatel, the Dreamer, because he spent his life elaborating wild schemes for the future of Russia, while forgetting to organise his own. He lived with his parents on the northern side of the village, and was drinking his usual – strong coffee with fresh goat's milk.

And there was Igor Odrosov himself, the Cosmonaut, standing behind the bar, surrounded by the largest collection of Kazakh space memorabilia in Siberia. Behind him, pouring drinks and secretly taking a tithe for herself from every second vodka, was his daughter Svetlana, dressed in her standard outfit of short skirt, tight top and sky-high heels. Svetlana used to sit beside Olga in the village school, when there still was a school during the week for the *sovkhoz* families in the single-roomed village hall, but their lives had taken different paths since then. And occupying a different table from Anna was the familiar rounded shape of her husband Bogdan, sitting as usual over a bottle of Odrosov's Rocket Fuel – but he was with someone Olga didn't recognise, a fleshy man with brown hair.

'Who's that with Bogdan?' said Olga, as she sat next to Anna, Gyorgy jumping onto her lap in an attempt to charm from her one of the boiled sweets Olga always kept in her pockets.

'I don't know – Bogdan said he was a business associate,' said Anna, distractedly, while trying to stop Boris waking Ilya, who was sleeping in the pram next to her. 'Listen, Olga, can you lend me some more money? Odrosov won't let me put any more food on the tab.'

Olga looked at Anna, seeing the charcoal pouches under her eyes and the first hint of delicate bone pushing through her cheeks. 'Oh, Anna,' she said, putting her hand on her friend's. 'Of *course*. Only I don't have much to spare, this week. Will six hundred roubles be enough?'

Anna nodded, turning away to hide the tears that threatened to spill from her eyes. 'I don't deserve such good friends, Olga Pushkin,' she said quietly.

'Nonsense,' said Olga. And to herself she added: What you really deserve is a better husband, who looks after his responsibilities at home instead of drinking Odrosov's vodka with gangsters from Tayga.

For Bogdan's companion was clearly a member of the criminal classes, or at least someone in daily conversation with them. He was dressed in a uniform every bit as revealing as Svetlana's: a shiny leather jacket over a bulging pinstripe suit, a large imitation watch in faux-platinum, and round fingers pushed through a surprising number of gold rings.

'He looks like a cheap pimp from Novosibirsk,' said Fyodor Katin to Igor Odrosov.

'And what would you know about pimps or Novosibirsk, Fyodor Ivanovich Katin?' said Odrosov, laughing. 'You live in the freezing cold attic of your parents' house in Roslazny. You've never been further than Tomsk, if you've been as far as that. Not like me. I've been around in my time. And I'm telling you, you never used to get men like that around these parts in the old days. Well, you did, but the Party kept them in line. You knew where you stood with the Party.'

'Here we go,' said Fyodor. 'The glories of the USSR.'

'I'm not saying the old days were perfect,' said Igor. 'I'm just saying things aren't perfect now either. And we got a lot done back then. We kept up with the Americans in the space race, you know.'

Fyodor rolled his eyes. Although a younger man than Odrosov, he somehow managed to look more or less the same age as the barman, with rapidly thinning hair and pallid, unhealthy skin, loosely wrapped in an ill-fitting suit that had once belonged to his uncle Karlov. He spent most of his free time, as he called it, with Odrosov at the café; he hadn't had a job since the ladies' shoe factory in Tayga had shut down in 2006. But really all his time was free. He spent a great deal of it locked in his childhood bedroom, precariously linked to the web on a dial-up connection, and writing an anonymous blog called Dead Square, in which he called for the restoration of the tsars, among other things. He dreamed of Russia before the Communists, of grand balls and soirées and horse-drawn carriages pulling up to magnificent winter palaces. The villagers, for the most part, refrained from pointing out to Fyodor that his family, like all the families in Roslazny, had been serfs until 1861.

'We didn't put up with criminals either, in the old days – not like we do now,' went on Odrosov. 'We had a proper police force, before 'ninety-one. Now it's hard to tell if there are more criminals inside the police or out. Take that Grigor Babikov. You know, the head of municipal police, down in Kemerovo. He was here in Roslazny a few weeks ago, just before Christmas – you remember? Came in to use the toilet, and turned up his nose at the *pirogi*. So did the man he had with him – strange-looking type, all beard and hair. Turned up their noses at my bar snacks – can you credit it? And he's always on TV asking for our help, as if he can't solve the crimes himself! Who wants a man like that for mayor? But this Nazarov seems a good bet,' he continued, seeing Babikov's opponent appear on the café's ancient television set, mounted in a corner above the bar. 'Strong. Passionate. Committed to the president. And not lazy, like most of them are. He built those roads and bridges around Kemerovo, didn't he? And installed those cameras to catch those good-for-nothing vandals? And put up all those campaign posters around town? That's the kind of man we need in these parts.'

Arkady Nazarov was the head of the local state-owned infrastructure corporation. Stung by the buzz generated at Babikov's televised press conferences, he had redoubled his campaign efforts. He put up hundreds of posters in the region, adorning lampposts, railings and trees with close-up pictures of his blunt, rock-like features, and forcing Babikov to respond in kind. Then Nazarov undertook a television campaign of his own, sponsoring lavish mini-documentaries charting his accomplishments in the sphere of municipal infrastructure, and streaming punchy interviews on his dedicated RuTube channel. Locals affected to sneer at the ludicrous soundtracks and melodramatic voiceovers, but it was hard to deny the importance of roads and bridges in a place with ten inches of snow a day in winter, and Nazarov soon pulled ahead in the polls. Unless Lieutenant Colonel Babikov could mount a spectacular comeback, the mayoralty was Nazarov's for the taking.

'Pah! Nazarov?' said Fyodor Katin. 'Arkady Nazarov is a man like every other in Russia: he wants money and power. He's exactly the kind of man we *don't* want around here. Not that Nazarov's ever *been* around here. At least Babikov gets about. You have to give him that. But, then, is Babikov any better in the end? He's probably just after position and influence, like all the rest. How about a woman for a change? Women don't care about things like money and power.'

Svetlana snorted.

'It's not just men who do bad things,' said Odrosov, ignoring his daughter. 'There's women like that, too, you know, Fyodor. Don't you read the papers? There's bad sorts hidden in the forests. Bad like you wouldn't believe. I've heard things that'd freeze your blood. Things that'd make you watch your back and grab your knife, when you see a woman walking towards you at night. And one woman in particular . . .'

Fyodor sat forward. 'You mean the one they call Baba Yaga? The woman who lives in the forests and strikes when your back's turned? But isn't that just a rumour?'

'I wouldn't be too sure,' said Odrosov. 'Someone told me she's killed scores of men – hundreds. And you never see her coming. Don't like the thought of that, myself, when I take the bins out at night.'

Fyodor laughed. 'You don't need to worry, Odrosov. Women run the opposite way when they see you coming, killers or not!'

'You can talk, Fyodor Ivanovich Katin,' said Odrosov. 'You can talk.'

The men carried on their conversation at the bar, their words drifting across the café, echoing from the imitation-wood walls and plastic furniture and finding their way at last into Olga's consciousness. *Baba Yaga . . . Baba Yaga . . .*

As if enchanted by some secret spell, Olga found herself ignoring Anna's tale of the previous night's interrupted sleep. She was borne away across the years to her mother's side, to a bedroom lit by a small candle that cast flickering shadows on the ceiling and walls, with herself and Pasha wrapped up in their sleeping blankets like larvae in a chrysalis. Her mother was telling them the tale of Baba Yaga and Vassilia the Beautiful, the little girl who only escaped the witch Baba Yaga because of the cleverness of her little mouse, who told her to keep all the things she found upon the way, just in case. Her mother Tatiana conjured Baba Yaga as a living reality, a bony old woman with flashing eyes and iron teeth, who moved about by evil magic in a mortar that she beat with a pestle, sweeping behind her with a besom to conceal her movements. Her house was a hut on hen's legs, which moved around in the forest so it never faced the same direction. Sometimes she would line it with railings of tall sticks with skulls upon them, and a deathless fire that would glow through the night until the rising sun outshone the glimmering eye-sockets. And Vassilia the little girl had Baba Yaga's sister for a stepmother, and the stepmother sent Vassilia to Baba Yaga's hut on hen's legs so that Baba Yaga could eat her. But the cleverness of Vassilia's little mouse, and Vassilia's kindness to those she met upon her way, allowed her to escape Baba Yaga's hut and flee to the forest. Baba Yaga pursued her, driving her mortar with great strokes of her pestle, but Vassilia was too quick for her, and Baba Yaga could not drive her mortar through the forest that Vassilia made from the comb she had picked up. And then her father came and drove Baba Yaga's sister away, and Vassilia and the father and the little mouse lived happily ever after.

Bogdan's predicament was more mundane than Vassilia's. He had been playing cards with his new associate, Sergei, the man with the leather jacket, the night before, and the night before that. On the first night, on Wednesday, Bogdan had won a small but significant sum. The next night, on Thursday, he had met Sergei again, not at Café Astana (which was too public for Sergei's purposes) but at a house that belonged to one of his associates in Tayga. This time Bogdan lost a great deal of money, in Roslazny terms – a sum he would struggle to pay back in a year, even if the Kabalevsky hostel was full every night.

But Sergei had come up with a plan. Instead of paying back all the money, Bogdan would pay half the amount a year from now, and in the meantime he would help Sergei with a scheme he was developing – a scheme that needed a place like Roslazny. Bogdan agreed with alacrity: he knew what happened to people like him who failed to pay their debts to people like Sergei, and he was quite attached, all things considered, to his fingertips. And if he went along and helped Sergei, Anna need never know. In fact, it might be quite fun. He winked at Svetlana, who was restocking the liquor bottles behind the bar, and smirked along with Sergei, as if they were best friends instead of creditor and debtor.

Olga knew none of this, of course, any more than Bogdan knew where his scheming would lead him. She merely shook her head to free herself from memories of her mother's storytelling, and made an effort to concentrate on Anna's account of baby Ilya's teeth and their impact on his nightly sleep routine. Soon it was time for her to leave: Aunt Zia was waiting for her groceries, and her father for his luxuries. Olga paid Odrosov for the magazines, the gherkins and Aunt Zia's bags of supplies, said goodbye to Anna and the children, and headed into the snowy night through the village to Zia Kuznetsov's house. She delivered the groceries to her ungrateful aunt in a perfunctory manner, and walked quickly back to the house she shared with her father. He received the desired items with a graceless grunt, barely summoning the energy to remind Olga that the snow was building up again on the branches of the trees that stood close by the house.

'Better clear them now,' he said. 'I don't have money to pay for any more repairs, if a heavy branch falls on the roof.'

'You haven't paid for anything since 1988,' she muttered. 'No, I didn't say anything, Father,' she went on, in a louder voice. 'Don't worry, I'm going out now.'

She stood still when she got outside, looking up at the quiet sky and trying to forget her responsibilities to Russian Railways, to her father Mikhail, to her aunt Zia and her friend Anna Kabalevsky. For a moment, she wasn't required by anyone. For a moment, she could stand there motionless, merely breathing, blessedly alone. She wasn't even Olga Pushkin the aspiring writer, a woman who dreamed of a better life. She was just Olga Pushkin, a good woman who worked too hard.

But it was too cold to stand still for long in the Siberian night, so she took up the snow-shovel that lay by the door and began to clear the boughs that hung low with their fresh burden of thick white flakes. The job didn't take much effort, for the first bough she struck had been weakened by the heavy snow. It snapped and twisted, striking another, which did the same, until ten or more branches had cleared themselves in a small avalanche. She paused, her breath surrounding her like a halo, and looked up at the trees. The snapping branch had saved her a lot of work, and by sheer good fortune hadn't damaged the roof of the house. So why, she asked herself, did it feel like a premonition?

4

A Mouth Stuffed with Gold

A freight train was passing Roslazny when Olga set out for her hut the next morning. She felt it before she saw it, the ground vibrating underfoot as thousands of tons thundered over the track, the wagons pulled to earth by their immense weight but deflected by the thin shining rails that sent them rattling and jingling on to Novosibirsk and beyond. Long after she reached her destination the wagons kept passing, making the hut shudder and sending Dmitri the hedgehog scurrying for cover under Olga's bookshelf. Finally, with a deafening blast of the rearmost horn, the train passed on, bumping and swaying into the distance until the curving track hid the wagons behind the spreading green-white forest.

Olga sighed with relief. 'I've a bad headache this morning, Dmitri-Dima-*detka*,' she crooned, trying to tempt him out of his hiding-place with a dish of mealworms. 'And the trains are too noisy when Mamochka has a headache. Too noisy and too long.'

An idea for her book, *Find Your Rail Self: 100 Life Lessons from the Trans-Siberian Railway*, crossed her mind – something to do with the need for workers with headaches to put up with noisy trains if important consignments were to make the journey from Tomsk to Novosibirsk, just as, in everyday life, people had to put up with all kinds of difficulties to meet their goals – but though she massaged her temples and chewed her pen until ink stained her lips the words wouldn't come. Maybe it wasn't one of her better ideas, she told herself. That was understandable, in the circumstances: she'd slept badly, and still felt exhausted from the day before and its heavy cargo of goods, or rather ills.

Perhaps that's a better idea for the book, she thought. Each day brings its own cargo, and we don't know what's on the manifest till we open the wagon doors. She would write the idea down later, maybe, if her headache improved. But she would add that some goods should be rejected and returned to sender – things like her premonition, the sinking feeling she'd had the night before, standing by the house in the icy air, a sensation that something fearful was about to happen. Olga didn't have time for omens, or signs, or anything like that. That was her friend Anna Kabalevsky's domain, the world of religion and the spirit. Olga had to operate in the world of iron, grease, and diesel locomotives, like the engines to which her father had once compared her when she'd wanted to buy a pretty dress. And by the look of Olga's schedule, today was set to be another busy day, with eleven more freight trains like the one she'd seen that morning, not to mention a Trans-Siberian service, snow-ploughs, and repair units from the Tayga depot, on top of her usual track inspections for nearly a mile in each direction, on foot and in the heavily falling snow, morning and afternoon. Today was a day for stern and unyielding concentration, not airy fancies. Today was a day for getting by on insufficient sleep, fiercely pickled beetroot, and strong tea made on her samovar.

The radio buzzed on the desk by the door in her little hut, interrupting her train of thought and shunting her abruptly from the abstract to the everyday. The call came from her supervisor, Viktor Fandorin at the Tayga depot, who never missed an opportunity to nit-pick Olga's work, and indeed the work of every other woman in the employ of Russian Railways. His insults varied, but usually involved some combination of cooking, sewing, pregnancy and ladies' shoes.

'Sorry to interrupt your knitting,' he said on this occasion. 'There's a problem down at Junction Sixty-two. Jammed switch motor for the points. If it isn't too much trouble, and if you can remember your basic training, get yourself down there and fix it. Watch your stilettos don't get stuck in the tracks! And call it in when you're finished.'

Olga put the radio down, trying to quell the rage she always felt when she came into contact with Viktor Fandorin. But once the jet of anger had passed, she merely felt exhausted, which was even worse. At least when she was angry she didn't feel tired. And it wasn't as if she didn't have enough to do.

She cursed her luck, as she did every time something went wrong down the line. Most of the track in the region was maintained by mobile crews on repair trains, but, for some reason long since lost in history, there was a gap around Roslazny where the work had traditionally been done by hand. And so, on top of her scheduled work, she would now have to shoulder a heavy tool-bag complete with walkie-talkie and technical instruction manual, trudge at least a mile down the track towards Novosibirsk to get to Junction 62, and spend a miserable couple of hours in the open air trying to hammer open the immobile switching system.

Maybe this was why she'd had her premonition of disaster.

'Do you work on the railway? Do you have a feeling of impending doom?' she muttered, as she prepared to set off. 'Don't be afraid! It's nothing spooky, just a prediction of your boss's behaviour tomorrow. Expect chauvinism, stupidity, and a scattering of bullying. Here, Dmitri-Dima,' she added, in a warmer voice. 'Here's some more mealworms for you, while Mamochka's gone. I'll be back as soon as I can. You'll be nice and warm while Mamochka freezes her socks off.'

But as she opened the door, a smile came to her face. She had remembered something – perhaps the only useful thing her father had ever taught her.

'Those Valnejy point switches are bullshit,' he'd said to her, when she had started work on the railway in 2005. Mikhail had insisted on selling the very last piece of Tatiana's silver to pay for a celebratory meal in Tayga, and by now, after the third course and most of a bottle of vodka, he had become rather chatty. 'I told Fandorin, when they installed them. They stick in the cold if they get over-extended, see? When it's a real freeze and even the winter hares run for cover – and when some stupid *pridurok* at the controls throws the switch one time too many. But I know how to fix 'em.'

Olga was only half listening, wishing she was dining with one of the young men in smart business suits in the corner, rather than her ageing, paunchy, greasy-haired, red-nosed father.

'You pour a can of lighter-fluid over the cylinder and set fire to it,' he went on. 'The heat frees it in no time. The blowtorch is too fierce – damages it. But lighter-fluid's just right.'

Olga forced herself to concentrate. 'Doesn't that burn the cables?'

'No, but you've got to catch it quick. Throw a rag over it to put the flames out. Then hit it with a hammer, job done. See, I know things. I was a good railwayman, in my time. Didn't get paid much for it, though. I never got what I deserved.'

His eyes stared, unfocused, past Olga's left shoulder as he tried to collect his wandering thoughts. 'That last treasure from the old Lodge at Astrazov, now . . . If only your *dear mother*' – he spat the words like curses – 'had bothered to tell us *just a little more* about the last of her precious loot from the old 'uns, we wouldn't need to keep scrimping like this.'

Olga looked at the table groaning with expensive dishes and carafes of wine and vodka, and forced herself to bite her tongue.

'Hidden in the wood,' went on Mikhail, looking closely at her. 'The whispering wood. That's what she said, at the end. What does that mean, eh, child?'

Mikhail was talking about her mother's death, about the terrible weeks when Tatiana Pushkin lay dying in the house at Roslazny, gazing out at the cold sky framed by the window and the snowflakes dancing against the glass. One day she spoke to Mikhail of the Lichnovsky treasures he'd taken from the Lodge at Astrazov. First, she reminded him, he'd sold the silver dinner service to pay for the children's clothes and school fees (and a debt incurred to old man Solotov at cards), then some of the enamelled chinaware, and then some of the miniature oils of the Lichnovsky countesses, and so on until the boxes from the Lodge were emptied, one by one. By 1991, when Tatiana fell sick, few remained of the heirlooms she had brought from Astrazov.

'You have taken them all and sold them,' she said to her husband. 'You would have sold the Lodge itself, if it hadn't been swallowed by the family debts. But there is one treasure you will never possess. The greatest of them all.'

'Another treasure?' said Mikhail, his eyes glinting as they had done long ago at Astrazov. 'What is it? Tell me, so I can sell it and use the money for the children.'

She looked up at him defiantly. 'It makes sounds you cannot understand.'

'What is it?' he said again. 'A balalaika? A music-box? What?'

'It is hidden,' she said, 'hidden in the whispering wood.'

Mikhail tutted in irritation. 'You're raving,' he said.

'I'm not,' she said.

Then she saw Olga standing by the door, watching them both. 'Olgakin, come, give me your hand,' she said. 'You comfort me. You comfort your mamochka.'

But the child could not be allowed to stay for ever, and soon Mikhail took her away, and Pasha, too, when he came back from school, and then Tatiana was left alone, her once-blonde hair now lank and grey upon the pillow.

'What does it mean, Olga?' said Mikhail again, rousing Olga from thoughts of her mother and bringing her back to the over-indulgent celebratory dinner at the restaurant in Tayga.

'I don't know, Father,' she said. 'I told you before.'

'Oh, you and your brother are useless. Pasha! Where's Pasha?'

'He's at the barracks in Novosibirsk, Father,' she said patiently. 'You remember – where you sent him to get his training?'

'Don't confuse me,' said Mikhail. 'Now, what was I saying? Oh, yes. The lighter-fluid. No – wait – what was I saying?'

Olga sighed as his eyes glazed over, and she signalled to the waiter to bring the bill.

But now, years later, the memory had resurfaced. It must have been a particularly brutal night to cause the switch to jam – despite what Mikhail had said, the Valnejy hydraulic motors rarely failed, and only in the coldest weather. But at least now she had a chance to fix the problem without getting frostbite in the process. She turned back into the hut, grabbed the can of lighter-fluid that she kept by the stove and tucked it into her pocket. Then, picking up her heavy tool-bag once more, she set off down the narrow path that snaked along the western side of the twin railway tracks.

She wondered how she hadn't noticed the unusually deep cold on her walk to the hut that morning. The railside plants were fragile with frost, and snapped like dried twigs at the slightest touch. Her breath crackled in the air like jet exhaust, and she felt the microscopic build-up of ice at the end of her eyelashes – something she'd experienced only three or four times in her life. Her feet stumbled over the hard-frozen snow, her toes already half numb. At times like this Olga thought that cold was more than just an absence of heat. It felt like a malevolent force of its own, a withering, hostile spirit suspended in the lifeless air like the malice of her poison-pen writer, or unseen witches hiding in forest huts with legs that swivelled in the night.

It was almost with relief that she came to Junction 62. Here at least was something tangible, something *fixable*, unlike the burdens that awaited her back in Roslazny. She dropped the tool-bag and took out the small blowtorch that railside engineers use to thaw frozen locks. Three minutes later, the lock clicked open, allowing her to remove the metal cover that protected the point-switching mechanism. It seemed quiet after the shushing noise of the blowtorch flame. She could hear the metal of the lock clicking as it cooled, and the humming of the rails as they conveyed the distant sounds of the shunters in Tayga station, now more than four miles down the line to the south.

'I've had another idea, Mamochka,' she said, into the silence. She used often to speak to her mother, holding imaginary conversations that were usually more satisfying than those she had with people in Roslazny. She mostly lacked the faith of the old days that made up so much of Anna's life, but when Olga spoke to her lost mother in the quiet spaces of the Russian *taiga*, she felt at times a faint, answering echo, as if someone might perhaps be listening; and it gave her peace.

'It's for the book again, Mamochka,' she went on, getting out the lighter-fluid from the bag. 'You must be tired of hearing about it. But it's a simple idea, this one. It's just to say that engineers are very important, maybe more important than the drivers, although nobody thinks of them when they buy a ticket to go to Tomsk or Novosibirsk or Perm. If the brakes stop working, the train will run out of control. Or if the track breaks, the train will fall over on its side, and many lives could be lost. What's that you say, Mamochka? What does that have to do with everyday people? Well, it's simple. It's just . . .'

She paused, and carefully poured a small amount of fluid over the switch mechanism. Then she took out a match and lit the fluid, sitting back and watching the gentle flames dancing around the jammed cylinder. When she decided that the cylinder was sufficiently warmed, she dropped a heavy rag over the flames to put them out, taking care that the cables that ran around the cylinder were unharmed. Then she took a small sledgehammer and gently banged the motor-arm until it shifted. With a sigh the machinery fell back into its normal position, and a green light winked on in a control panel above the mechanism.

'It's just this, Mamochka,' she went on, smiling in satisfaction. 'We need people in our lives who can fix everyday things, the things we don't notice until they break. We should make sure we're good to those people, for some day we will surely need them.'

She dusted herself down, packed up her tools and took out the bulky radio that track engineers used to communicate with Headquarters.

'Engineer Pushkin for Viktor Fandorin,' she said, pressing the send button. She received a burst of static in return. Perhaps the cold weather was hampering reception.

'Engineer Pushkin for Viktor Fandorin,' she said again. This time she heard a voice coming back over the waves, but broken up with heavy static. 'Report – what – box . . .'

'I've finished the repair, Mr Fandorin, if that's you?'

Again she heard only a few garbled words in response: 'Fix – cylinder – confirm . . .' And then some words that had for her a special and hurtful resonance: 'Hopeless – stupid *suka* – all she's good for . . .' She heard a burst of staccato noise, like devilish laughter, and then the device went silent. She looked down at the radio and shook it, but everything seemed to be in good working order.

Damn Russian technology, she said to herself. Nothing ever works properly. Why couldn't they have Japanese kit?

She finished packing her tools and tucked the radio into her pocket. She locked the motor cover again and shouldered the bag before setting off down the tracks to her hut. But as she went, she realised that tears had come to her eyes – tears not just from the fierce cold that hung in the air like a baleful sprite, but from a memory that Fandorin's abuse had awakened.

Stupid suka . . . *You stupid bitch* . . .

It was what her boyfriend Piotr Katin had said to her the last time she had seen him. Piotr was Fyodor Katin's older brother, who had tried to make Olga sleep with him the night before he went to university in Ekaterinburg, far to the west. They'd been seeing each other for some time, but Mikhail and the Katins kept a close eye on them, and so far everything had been done in a manner that would have pleased an elderly chaperone from the days of the tsars. But that night there had been a family dinner at the Katins', to which Mikhail and Olga were also invited. The vodka had flowed freely, so freely that Mikhail and the Katins stopped paying attention to the whereabouts of their offspring. And when Fyodor went up to his bedroom to play with the American computer his parents had bought him for his eighteenth birthday, Piotr took Olga to his bedroom, closed the curtains, locked the door and tried to make Olga sleep with him.

And Olga had been tempted. Piotr was very handsome, in those days. She'd seen a photo of him since, and had been shocked by the balding, bloated man he had become. But in 1996 Olga wanted nothing more than his lips on hers, to feel his arms holding her, going on without end, their love lighting them from within like a flood-lit train passing through the *taiga* at night. But she hadn't wanted things to happen like that, with their parents drunk downstairs and Fyodor next door, looking at pornography, or conspiracy-theory websites, or whatever he was interested in that night, on his new computer.

Once Piotr had grasped that she was serious, that she really meant her refusal, his words changed in an instant from loving entreaties to violent abuse. And what Fandorin had said on the radio was the phrase Piotr had used most insistently – 'You stupid bitch, you stupid bitch' – as if only stupidity could possibly motivate anyone to reject *him*, Piotr Katin, a university man and Ekaterinburg resident-to-be.

Piotr was the last boy to kiss her. He came back from Ekaterinburg a few years later to marry Irina Malininsky, who (they said in Roslazny) was less protective of her virtue than Olga had been. After that he took Irina back with him to Ekaterinburg, to a luxurious flat overlooking Lake Shartash. Since then other men had come and gone (mostly the latter) in Olga's life, and had attached themselves to her friends and relatives in Roslazny and Tayga and elsewhere, but none had sought her out as Piotr had done. And Pasha, too, her beloved older brother, had left that same month for the Military Academy in Novosibirsk, so she'd been doubly bereft. Only her father Mikhail and her aunt Zia Kuznetsov were left. Them, and Dmitri the hedgehog, and the little hut by the track near Roslazny.

She shook the tears from her eyes. They'd only freeze and cause her more discomfort later.

Halfway back to the hut she heard the rails humming again, but this time more insistently: not a shunter in Tayga, then, but a big train. Probably it was the Trans-Siberian.

Another idea came to mind for the book, and she smiled despite herself. Today was a good day for the book, if nothing else. It was the humming tracks that made her think.

'If you know how to read the sounds you hear, you can tell what's coming, Mamochka,' she said aloud. 'If you can read your life as well as an engineer can read the sounds of the track, then nothing will catch you unawares. People should pay attention to the sounds around them. If a husband sings too happily in the shower, he has a mistress. If a child laughs too cheerfully, they're stealing from the family biscuit-jar.'

She nodded with satisfaction. 'That's idea number seventy, if I remember right. Just thirty more, and my book will be finished. Ha! I'd like to see Piotr Katin, or Viktor Fandorin, write a book like mine.'

All the way back, Olga dreamed of the literary fame that would surely follow the publication of *Find Your Rail Self: 100 Life Lessons from the Trans-Siberian Railway*. Once the book was out, she could go to Tomsk and sit in warm cafés and lecture-halls, instead of trudging miles in the freezing cold. But at least the day was warming up. The air no longer crackled as it passed her chapped lips, though now it was heavy with the hint of snow.

The hut came into sight just as the long-heralded Trans-Siberian service passed her, the bright red engine rumbling by with another deafening horn-blast. She thought she recognised Kiril Leonov, one of the Tayga-based railwaymen, in the driving seat. He waved at her, his hand a flash of white through the grimy locomotive windows. Then the carriages clattered past, first the *spalny vagony* for the rich, then the *kupe vagony* for the comfortably off, and then the *platskartny vagony* for everyone else.

Olga reached her little hut, dropped the tool-bag inside, and stepped out again to watch the train going by, as she always did. A movement in the woods distracted her, and she turned towards the forest. Was that a shape disappearing behind the hut? But then behind her, in the direction of the tracks, she heard an unexpected sound: the solid thud of a carriage door as it swung open against the side of the train.

That can't be right, she thought in an instant. The train's still moving.

She turned back towards the railway, but as she did so a hammer-blow struck her shoulder and sent her flying against the faded walls of her hut, like a rag-doll thrown by a child. She banged her head hard against the planks, the world erupting in a blaze of glittering stars. She fell limp on the frozen ground. But before her vision faded she saw a man – a young man by the look of him – lying on the ground in front of her. He must have fallen from the train and struck her. He had even white teeth, long brown hair, and deep blue eyes. His clothes looked new, and expensive: a tourist, then, most probably.

But he was dead. Yes, he was dead: his head was stretched back at an impossible angle, revealing a long, gaping wound in his throat and a sheet of blood over his neck and chest. His right arm lay folded under him, and he gazed sightlessly at a point above Olga's shoulder. And his mouth was full of – was that *money*? Yes: someone had crammed his mouth with tens, no, *hundreds* of ten-rouble pieces. The coins spilled from his lips as if he were vomiting them, and lay all around like metallic confetti.

With the last of her strength she pulled the radio from her pocket and selected the emergency frequency, hoping it would transmit properly this time. 'This is Olga – Olga Pushkin, track engineer third class, Roslazny. There's a dead man here. The Trans-Siberian's just gone past. I'm at my hut and I need medical – medical . . .'

But Olga's strength failed her, and her eyes closed as the radio slipped from her fingers. She lay still beside the man as it began to snow again, two white statues toppled to earth, motionless by the endless tracks.

5

The Trials of Vassily Marushkin

'Roslazny?' said Vassily Marushkin. 'Let me think . . . Is that the tiny, one-Lada village off the tracks near Tayga?'

'That's the place,' said his superior, the portly, moustachioed Colonel Terekhin. 'And don't pretend you don't know it. It's all here in your personnel file. You lived there for four years when your father was the junior sergeant at the Roslazny station. I met him once, your father – did you know that? Kirill Marushkin was a good man. And now you can follow in his footsteps, and return in triumph as the new sergeant-in-charge! What's wrong with that?'

Terekhin and Marushkin were sitting in the new Novosibirsk police headquarters, a glass-and-steel monstrosity on the city's outskirts. Vassily Marushkin looked at the colonel and smiled incredulously. 'Well, the fact that I'd be based at a tiny rural station, for a start,' he said. 'When my father worked there, the *sovkhoz* was still going, with plenty of hungry mouths to keep the crime rates up. And even then they thought just a junior sergeant was needed. Being a senior sergeant at a station like that? It's practically a demotion. And I've already applied for the new army liaison post. Does this mean I didn't get it?'

Terekhin shifted in his seat. 'As a matter of fact, you *did* get it.'

'What? But—'

Terekhin spoke over Vassily's protests. 'You got it, but I want you to delay taking it up, for your own sake. Listen – it'll only be temporary. There's a job to do there, and once it's done you can move on.'

'A job?' said Vassily. 'What kind of job?'

'There've been a lot of rumours about the Kemerovo area recently, and Tayga in particular,' said Terekhin. 'Maybe Roslazny too, even. Seems there's a good deal of criminal activity going on there or thereabouts. Pornography, maybe, or prostitution. Drugs, too. The usual stuff. Textbook, but the force needs a good man to get on top of it quickly before people start making noise. And Lieutenant Colonel Babikov requested you personally. You must've made quite an impression on him.'

'Can't imagine how,' said Vassily, thinking back to his placement at Kemerovo three years previously. 'We didn't exactly hit it off.' Vassily remembered one briefing in particular, when he had challenged Babikov's fast-and-loose approach to chains of evidence. Vassily himself was hardly a stickler but, as he remarked to another sergeant after the briefing, the police couldn't just do whatever they wanted. Otherwise, weren't they as bad as the criminals?

'Can't say I blame you, Vassily Kirillovich,' said Terekhin, using Vassily's patronym, as he always did when he wanted to appear respectful to subordinates. 'Babikov's an odd sort. Looks like a picky hygiene inspector, doesn't he, with that little moustache? Sounds like one, too. But he's got a ruthless streak a mile wide. I know a lot of criminals – and a few coppers, too – who've ended up behind bars because of Grigor Babikov. He uses a lot of informants and collaborators on the ground. Agents provocateurs, too – that's a fancy term for snitches, Marushkin. Goes against the grain, in my view. Getting small-time crooks on-side in exchange for a plea bargain, and making them act up in front of bigger fish, dangling for confessions and whatnot . . .'

'Not how we do things round here, sir,' said Vassily.

'No, it damn well isn't,' said Terekhin, banging his desk with a heavy hand. 'Still, I can't deny it's effective. Lots of people are talking about Babikov, and in high-up circles, too. Did you know he's running for Mayor of Kemerovo? He might even get it. They need a strong man in charge there, after all that fuss about the money.'

The previous mayor, Ilyich Burtlanov, had left office in November and in handcuffs, following a police investigation led by Lieutenant Colonel Babikov, which found he'd been channelling municipal funds to an account in the Bahamas. Burtlanov was still protesting his innocence from a high-security prison, but by now it didn't matter what he said. Whoever won the election, whether it was Babikov or his opponent Arkady Nazarov, would refuse an appeal, since a retrial might end up reinstalling Burtlanov.

'Anyway, whatever you did at Kemerovo, it worked,' went on Terekhin. 'Like I said, he seems very keen on you – called me personally to tell me so, after sending the request through.' Terekhin leaned forward. 'But there's something else, too, Marushkin, besides the drugs and the girls - something more troubling. We're not sure what yet. Just some whispers from our informants, here and there, plus the usual guesswork online and in the newspapers. But Babikov thinks – and I'm inclined to agree – that there might be an *operator* at work in the area.'

'An operator?' said Vassily, intrigued despite himself. Terekhin was known to reserve that term for serial killers, and no police officer worth his or her salt would turn down the chance to work on a case like that. 'So what's been happening?' he asked. 'What's the evidence?'

'A lot of things have happened,' said Terekhin, turning over some papers in front of him. 'Babikov put a report together with all the details – you can have it later, though most of it's just him boasting about his murder-clearance rate. But here's one case that might interest you. Three couples have gone missing in the Kemerovo region in the past year – and not the usual suspects, not druggies or trafficked teenagers, just normal working people with families. Foster families, in fact, to make it worse. Nobody's safe any more, Marushkin – not even kind-hearted folk who take in stray kids at their own expense. And then, one day in December, the Tayga police found six bodies in the marshes near the railway tracks at Basandayka, north of Roslazny – *but they were bodies of different people.* I'll spare you the details, but even Uspensky couldn't identify them. You remember Uspensky – the forensics man we poached from Chelyabinsk? He said the teeth had been pulled with a pair of rusty pliers, and they couldn't get any prints, because there weren't any fingers left.'

'I thought you said you'd spare me the details,' muttered Vassily.

'I haven't told you what else they did,' said Terekhin. 'Believe me, you don't want to know. And that's just one case. The murder rate in Kemerovo Province is higher than it was when you were there a couple of years back – a lot higher than it should be, between us, Marushkin, despite Babikov's best efforts. As you know, the top brass don't give a damn how many crimes actually take place. They only care about what percentage get solved. And Babikov's clearance rate is fantastic – the best in Siberia. He says so about twenty times in that damn report of his. But in terms of actual murders per capita, Kemerovo's the worst region in Russia, outside the big cities. Worse than Novgorod, even.'

Vassily gave a low whistle. Ivan the Terrible had put Veliky Novgorod on the map with a massacre in 1560 and, from what Vassily had heard, not much had changed since.

'I know,' said Terekhin. 'I'm surprised, in a way – Babikov's so damn clever, whatever else you say about him, and you won't find a more enthusiastic chief of police this side of the River Volga.

'Well, what else can I tell you?' he went on. 'Oh, yes – the rumour of a master criminal in the region. Believe it or not, the snoops swear it's a she. Whether that's true or not, I've no idea – corruption's rife, as you know, so we're taking everything we're told with a pinch of salt. But woman's work or not, it's pretty obvious what's going on with that case I mentioned. Six disappearances and—'

'Six unidentified bodies to match,' cut in Vassily. 'They're taunting us, telling us they can get away with anything – even swapping one dead body for another. Classic serial-killer move.'

'That's right,' said Terekhin, in a satisfied voice, looking at the sergeant opposite him. Vassily Marushkin was a tall, stocky, well-built man with an unruly shock of black hair and a stubborn, unshaven face, like a beet farmer from Nizhnyaya.

But in his case the rustic façade hid a sharp, intelligent mind and a passion for detective work. Most sergeants had to serve at least some time in rural stations as part of their professional development, and Vassily looked like a man who would be at home in the *taiga*, in the depths of the Russian countryside. But in fact Vassily had for many years worked exclusively on inner-city crime. And his recent application for secondment to the army's 24th Special Purpose Brigade in Novosibirsk would allow him to stay on in the city for at least three more years.

Terekhin knew why Vassily was reluctant to leave. It was in a secret part of his file, marked 'Family', which only men (and a very few women) of the rank of colonel and above could access. Vassily had followed his father's example, becoming a rural *ryadovoy politsii*, a rank-and-file police private, and taking up a post in the small village of Berezkino, outside Tomsk. He was there for several years, and married a local girl, Rozalina. They had a child – a boy called Kliment. But then his wife had become involved with another man, Pavel Prokofy, a former soldier who had reinvented himself as a local businessman – a common type, after the end of the USSR. While Vassily threw himself into policework, Prokofy had followed the usual protocol in such cases: jewellery for the lady, expensive trips to restaurants and hotels in Tomsk, costly presents for the boy . . . And then one day Rozalina and Kliment had disappeared, swallowed, no doubt, into the networks of people-trafficking and prostitution that had spread across Russia like a virulent cancer. And of Prokofy there was no trace.

After their disappearance, Vassily Marushkin had thrown himself into searching for Rozalina and Kliment, scouring the countryside around Berezkino for months before extending his search into Tomsk and other regional centres, on the basis that most trafficked women and children end up in cities. But no trace was ever found of his wife and son, and eventually Regional Headquarters had had to force him to close the case and resume his routine duties. But he didn't give up: he merely applied repeatedly for postings to large cities until finally his superiors gave in out of sheer irritation, and posted him to Terekhin's organised-crime unit in Novosibirsk, with regional secondments to Kemerovo and Ekaterinburg. After those postings, too, led nowhere, Vassily started applying for army liaison jobs, having become convinced that someone somewhere in the vast Russian military must know something of Pavel Prokofy, the soldier-turned-businessman who had stolen his family. And now, when he was close to the longed-for position, here was Colonel Terekhin telling him he had to go back to Roslazny! Serial killer or no serial killer, nothing was more important than finding his family. A wave of anger and frustration rose inside him.

'Look, sir,' he began, but Terekhin waved him into silence.

'I know about your family, Vassily Kirillovich. Your wife and your boy. But you've got to do this, for your own sake.'

Terekhin lit a cigarette. Smoking was officially forbidden in the new headquarters, but the colonel had got the janitor to disable the alarm in his office. 'Want one?' he said to Vassily, who helped himself from the crumpled packet, hoping the familiar tang would lower his blood pressure.

'People are asking questions about you,' Terekhin continued, as the room began to fill with smoke. 'Questions like how you've managed to get all your preferred postings in one city or another. Senior sergeants still have to serve their time in the sticks, you understand? Do this for six months and you can come back and take up the army post, carry on looking for your family. And you might do some good in the meantime. There hasn't been a policeman in Roslazny for ten years, let alone a man of your experience. You'll soon get on top of whatever small-town stuff you find there. And if there is an operator on the go, we need a man like you to put an end to him – an end to *her*, if it really is a woman. Those bodies – and the three couples who vanished – are the tip of the iceberg, I'm sure. The people at Kemerovo will tell you all about it. And besides,' he went on, leaning forward, 'if there is people-trafficking going on in the region, Roslazny isn't all that far from Berezkino, where your family disappeared.'

Vassily looked at the colonel and shook his head. He was a wily old bird. But men don't become colonels in the Russian police for nothing. Terekhin had guessed he'd be willing to delay the army post to follow up another possible lead, however tenuous it might be. And maybe Terekhin had some angle of his own, besides the rumours and the serial killer. Possibly there was something he wanted cleared up on the army side before Vassily got to the barracks. Few people's hands were entirely clean in the new Russia. But that didn't make what Terekhin had said about his career – and about Berezkino and his lost family – any less true.

'Fine,' said Vassily, after a moment's silence. 'I'll do it. But as soon as the six months are up I'll be back in Novosibirsk. I'd better write to the army liaison officer to postpone my application.'

'Don't worry,' said Terekhin. 'I've already told them. Now listen,' he went on loudly, before Vassily could protest at this unwarranted and probably illegal course of action, 'here's Babikov's report, with what we've got so far. Past homicides, rumours, allegations, leads and so on. You can get more info from Police Headquarters at Kemerovo, if you need it. You'll have a local *ryadovoy politsii* assigned to you, too. Private Anatoly Glazkov. An old-timer – based in Tayga. Not much good, really, says Babikov, but he's been around Tayga for ever, so he knows the ground. He'll give you a hand setting things up in the old station at Roslazny. He can look after your mongoose, too –'

'It's a ferret, actually,' said Vassily, stubbing out his cigarette.

'– or mole-rat, or badger, or whatever the hell it is,' went on Terekhin, 'when you're out catching that operator.'

Vassily was famous in Novosibirsk for the ferret he kept in his office at Police Headquarters. He'd found it one day during a fraud investigation, abandoned in a one-bedroom flat, and had taken it away with him. It was a golden ferret, a name that implies a lustrous, aureate fur. Vassily's specimen, however, was of a more disreputable hue, best described as dingy ochre. On account of his ragged appearance and occasionally unpredictable behaviour, Vassily had christened him Rasputin.

'When do I start?' said Vassily, picking up the folder.

'Next Saturday,' said Terekhin. 'You'd better pack up your desk today. Make sure you close up your cases and hand them over properly. And take that damn polecat with you.'

The conversation between Colonel Terekhin and Vassily Marushkin took place the week before Olga received the letter from her unknown detractor. On the day she got the letter, the first Friday in January, Vassily was driving his ageing Volvo 240 up the P-255 highway from Novosibirsk to Tomsk, chain-smoking Belamorkanal cigarettes to dull an incipient toothache, and half listening to local radio stations whose reception faded after a few miles. While Olga was walking to Café Astana for Mikhail and Zia, Vassily was bumping along the one-track road that leads from Tayga to Roslazny, in search of the tiny police station. And as Olga left Café Astana for her aunt Zia's, Vassily pulled to a halt outside a low, single-storey building on the south-eastern side of the village, surrounded by abandoned houses with collapsed roofs and gaping, empty windows. He switched off his headlights and sat for a moment in silence, as people do after a long drive, listening to the exhaust-pipe ticking as it cooled and the swishing noise in his ears that spoke of utter quiet. Even Rasputin's chitterings had temporarily ceased: he'd been lulled to silence by the car's motion and the stuffy air pushed out by the car's antiquated heater.

After a few minutes he got out, inhaling sharply as the freezing air washed over him, like a cold shower. He closed the car door again to keep Rasputin warm and looked over the top of the Volvo at his new home. Or, rather, his old home: he'd lived there from 1990 to 1994, when his father was sergeant-in-charge of the station. Then it had been a family home as well as a police station, a place full of life and noise and light. He was an only child, but his parents had surrounded him with so many animals that he'd hardly missed not having a sibling: dogs and cats in the house, hamsters in his bedroom, two or three pigs outside, depending on the market and the weather, and a goat for milk. But now his parents were dead, his mother twenty years since and his father nearly ten years after that. The animals were long gone, too. Even the building looked as if it had died, sinking under the weight of endless snow and rotting from disuse. The brightly painted walls that Vassily remembered from his youth were discoloured from years of frost and wind, and the police sign that hung over the door was damaged and lopsided.

Nevertheless, there were definite signs of life inside. Dim lamplight streamed out through the barred windows, vanishing briefly as a shadow crossed the brightness; then the door creaked as someone tried to open it from within. Vassily walked up to the door, lending his weight to shoulder it open. It juddered aside, and a man stood in the low doorway, his figure looming blackly against the soft light within.

'Sergeant Marushkin?' said the man. 'I'm Glazkov. Anatoly Glazkov – police private at Tayga. I was told to expect you.'

'Private Glazkov,' said Vassily, nodding at him and shaking his hand. He ducked his head to enter the station, but as he did so he heard the crunch of tyres on frozen snow and turned to see a gleaming Mercedes in police livery pulling up, headlights blazing, behind his battered Volvo estate.

'I think it's the chief,' said Glazkov.

'*Babikov?*' said Vassily. It was highly unusual for a sergeant to be welcomed to a new posting by the local head of police, especially when arriving at night in the middle of a half-deserted village.

'I didn't know he was coming,' Glazkov said defensively. 'He never tells me anything.'

The driver of the Mercedes switched off the engine, and a man got out of the car on the passenger side. 'Sergeant Marushkin,' said a precisely enunciated voice. 'Welcome to Roslazny. Or, rather, welcome back to Roslazny, and Kemerovo Province.'

'Thank you, sir,' said Vassily, squinting against the glare of the headlamps. Lieutenant Colonel Babikov rapped on the Mercedes bonnet until the driver killed the lights. Then he stepped forward, and Vassily saw him clearly: a man of medium height, just into his middle years, but with a marked streak of white running through his dark brown hair, on the left-hand side of his head. He had a leather bag slung around his shoulder.

'It's good to be back, sir,' said Vassily, doing his best to sound convincing amid the snow-covered tumbledown ruins.

'I very much doubt that, Marushkin,' said Babikov, 'but we're delighted you're coming on board – eh, Glazkov? Quite a feather in our cap to land an experienced senior sergeant from Novosibirsk for our little outpost here in Roslazny. Shall we go inside?'

'Er – yes, of course,' said Vassily. 'After you. But what about your driver?' He gestured at the man sitting behind the wheel of the Mercedes, staring at Vassily, his face lit by the red glow of the dashboard. An odd face, thought Vassily, framed by a pointed beard, like a forest sprite.

'Don't worry about him,' said Babikov. 'That's Wolansky. Since your time, Marushkin. He heads up our media unit in Kemerovo, helps me with public relations and suchlike. He's a technology expert – used to work in a digital start-up. And he hired a whole desk of IT nerds who can do things you wouldn't believe. Anyway, he's a man of the city. Rural police stations aren't his métier. He's happier where he is.'

Vassily shrugged his shoulders and followed Glazkov and Babikov inside the station. It was odd enough that a lieutenant colonel of police should come in person to greet a new sergeant, especially when the sergeant in question had been a thorn in his side some years previously – but it was stranger still that a lieutenant colonel should be driven around after hours by his head of PR. Vassily knew that media relations were more important than ever, in this age of social media and smartphones; and he knew, too, that Babikov was running for the Kemerovo mayoralty – but what was there to spin about the appointment of an obscure sergeant to an even more obscure station? Unless, of course, they had somehow stumbled across— But no, Vassily told himself. There was no way they could have found out about any of that. Vassily had been careful. Nobody knew about those things except himself. As long as he carried on being careful, and kept his nose clean, they'd never find out.

As they walked along the narrow entrance corridor to the reception desk, Vassily's puzzlement turned to dismay at the condition of the station.

'This place has gone to the dogs, hasn't it?' he said to the others.

Babikov and Glazkov looked around them at the damp walls and faded, curling government posters. One showed a youthful President Putin following his first election victory in 2000. 'It could be better,' Glazkov admitted, 'but we've kept the heating on, two hours a day, since it was closed down. That's more than you can say for the houses nearby.'

Vassily looked at his new *ryadovoy politsii*, a short, round policeman with white hair and a face like a favourite uncle's. He was moving constantly from foot to foot, and fiddling with small change in his trouser pockets. In Vassily's experience, men like Glazkov usually simpered and smiled and did whatever they could to impress new superiors, instead of acting like a nervous teenager working up the courage to ask someone to the prom. Glazkov must have something to hide, too, thought Vassily – some local scheme or other, like taking a slice of drug money in Tayga, or looking the other way during rail-freight inspections in exchange for a roll of notes. Probably he had cursed his luck when he heard about Vassily's appointment to Roslazny. Maybe that was why Babikov had come, to make sure Glazkov got the message: the good times are over. Well, we all have something to hide, thought Vassily. But he resolved to keep a close eye on his new subordinate nonetheless.

'All right, Glazkov,' he said. 'We'll get someone in to renovate it, once I've settled in. Assuming there are funds for that, sir,' he added, addressing Babikov.

'Oh, I wouldn't worry too much about that, Marushkin,' said Babikov, smiling again at Vassily. And then, after a pause: 'Yes, of course – I'm sure we can find some money for repairs. But these things take time, and budgets always need a bit of massaging. You'll have to make the best of it for now.'

'Understood, sir,' said Vassily. 'The cells are still through here, I suppose.'

'That's right,' said Glazkov, following him down the corridor, with Babikov close on his heels.

'I'll make my quarters here for now,' said Vassily. 'It's the warmest room in the place. I remember my dad telling us the prisoners had better accommodation than we did.'

'Very good, Sarge,' said Glazkov. 'Well, I'll be off, if that's all right with you, Lieutenant Colonel?'

'Aren't you going to tell Marushkin about the radio?' said Babikov. He turned to Vassily. 'Mobile reception can be patchy here, so you need to keep your radio on you at all times. Reception's a bit ropey for that, too, if you're far from Tayga, but you should be fine hear Roslazny.' He turned to Glazkov, who was hovering by the corridor as if he couldn't wait to get away. 'All right, Glazkov, you can go, but don't forget to take your camera with you for the – for the potholes tomorrow. He likes a drink in the evening, does Glazkov,' he added, after the private had left them. 'If you're ever looking for him, try Café Astana, in the centre of the village. Though, of course, you probably won't need to.'

Vassily glanced at his superior. 'I won't need to, sir?' he said.

'Well, because – because Glazkov has a radio, too. If he remembers to charge it, of course! Anyway, here's yours,' said the lieutenant colonel, reaching inside his bag and producing a small plastic device in camouflage colours. 'It's set to the local frequencies. Line one for standard comms, line two for emergencies – not that you'll have many of those. The fire service and train crew are on that frequency, too. Oh, and if you need ammunition for your pistol, you'll have to come to Tayga and sign it out from the armourer. But again, you probably won't need too much of that. I mean – well, you'll find it a quiet station here, after Novosibirsk.'

'Not too quiet, I hope, sir,' said Vassily. 'And, anyway, sometimes it's the quiet places where the darkest things are hidden.'

'Sometimes it is, Marushkin,' agreed Lieutenant Colonel Babikov. 'Well, I'll leave you now. Got to get back to Kemerovo – Wolansky and I have work to do.' Babikov set off back down the corridor to the entrance, saying over his shoulder, 'Glazkov forgot to mention there's food in the kitchen – you'll know where that is – and wood and paraffin for the stove. Call in to Tayga every day or two on the radio, so we know what you're doing. We don't want another Glazkov, sitting on his arse all day and pickling himself in vodka. I'll close the door myself. Goodbye, and good luck!'

Babikov walked back to the Mercedes and got inside with relief. Wolansky had kept the engine running – everyone who could afford it kept their engines running in winter – and the interior was pleasantly warm.

'All well?' said Wolansky, putting away his phone. He kept it in a chequered wallet, by Burberry, that he'd bought on a recent trip to St Petersburg.

'All well,' said Babikov. 'He's got the radio.' He patted his leather satchel. 'The clothes are in here, and the hair, too. And the bank stuff from the lock-up. Everything's arranged at Tayga?'

'Loyal serfs summoned, podium ordered, press release prepared.'

Babikov nodded.

'And the woman,' said Wolansky. 'She's left Yaroslavsky?'

'She'll be near Novosibirsk by now.'

'You're sure she's reliable?' said Wolanksy.

Babikov laughed. 'The second time she came in, she gave me a babushka doll. As a gift! Who does that? My only concern is that she's *too* simple. It's like dealing with a ten-year-old child.'

'You should keep the doll as a souvenir.'

'I will,' said Babikov. 'I'll put it on my bookshelf, and every time I look at it I'll remember the biggest coup we ever pulled off. The biggest coup *anyone* ever pulled off in Kemerovo region. One week of media frenzy, one fifteen per cent bump in the polls, and we'll be home and dry, and that idiot Nazarov will be back in his workshops where he belongs.'

'I hope you won't forget me when you're in that big office in Kemerovo, Grigor. And then an even bigger one in Moscow.'

'Don't worry, Wolansky,' said Babikov, patting the other man's arm. 'We'll go there together. Then you can have all the clothes and cars and jewels you could possibly desire. You'll have earned them. Maybe you'll even get your hands dirty at last, eh? Do some of the rough work yourself, have a bit of fun? That's what a real Russian would do – that's what Putin did! Probably still does, for all we know.'

Wolansky laughed briefly. 'You can bet he does. But, no, Grigor, that's not my field. I prefer to work behind the scenes, like all the best directors. Anyway, it's bad luck to count chickens. A lot of things have to happen before you get that big office, and all of them in the right order.'

'You're right, Wolansky,' said Babikov. 'You know, you're always right. It's almost uncanny.' He glanced across at his head of PR, thinking again what an odd man he was. He was short, and always wore heeled boots, like Bogdan Kabalevsky – but they didn't seem ridiculous, somehow, on Wolansky. His pointed beard, hot, restless eyes and shaggy hair made him look more like a member of some radical collective than the head of PR at a provincial police force. His appearance had prompted unfavourable remarks at the Kemerovo headquarters two years previously, when Wolansky had turned up for interview fresh from a thriving tech company in St Petersburg. He had ruffled some feathers, too, by disregarding rank and addressing everyone by their first name, including the lieutenant colonel (or Grigor). But Babikov had warmed to the PR man's frank acknowledgement that policework was a kind of theatre, after one reached a certain level, complete with actors, producers and audiences, and had insisted on hiring him on the spot.

Wolansky flashed a smile at Babikov. 'It's just the way I am, Grigor. Anyway, we'd better get moving. Marushkin will be wondering what we're up to, sitting out here. Yes – there he is now. He looks like a prisoner already, behind that barred window! I'll wave – and now we can go.' He put the car into reverse and backed the Mercedes into the alley that ran to the south of the Roslazny police station, then swung in a wide turn and set off along the narrow road that led to Tayga and beyond. 'We'll need to move fast, to get to Yurga in time. But don't worry, Grigor. This car's got three hundred horses at my command. German engineering and Russian driving – it's the fastest combination on the planet.'

'I'm not worried, Wolansky,' said Babikov, as the Mercedes picked up speed, bumping and rocking along the frozen track. 'With you at the helm, I'm not worried at all.'

The next morning, at around the time when Olga was making her way to her little hut and watching the freight train go by, Vassily began to get himself organised in the Roslazny police station. He had passed an unsettled night in the cells, during which several unidentified animals had made their presence known in the darkness, before finally giving up on sleep as the grey dawn began to creep through the low windows. Seen in this clear, wan light, the station looked even less attractive than it had the night before, with long tongues of mould reaching up the walls and running down from the ceiling, and with a warped floorboard sticking up through the frayed carpet like a badly hidden pistol. Tired and cold and sleepless, Vassily felt profoundly depressed. To have gone through so much, and laboured so long to get the postings he needed to find his family, and then to end up in a rotting old station in the back of beyond . . . He had tried to keep up his enthusiasm by telling Babikov that country policing had its surprises, but he'd barely believed it even then, last night in the lamplight when everything seemed sinister and threatening. Now, in the cold light of day, and the unbroken silence from the abandoned buildings surrounding the station, things appeared more hopeless than ever.

After making a half-hearted start on cleaning the rest of the station's rooms, Vassily lit a cigarette and made himself breakfast from the meagre provisions Glazkov had left for him. He boiled water in a saucepan on the portable gas cooker and made some instant coffee in a chipped china mug that he found at the back of a cupboard, wincing as the hot liquid twinged a nerve in his troublesome tooth. He dipped the remains of his bread in some brandy and fed it to Rasputin, who seemed happy enough in his cage under Vassily's bed in the cells. Then he lit another cigarette, sat at the desk, and took out the report Terekhin had given him when he left Novosibirsk, cursing the colonel again for forcing him to take the posting at Roslazny.

After twenty minutes or so Vassily had finished the first part of Babikov's report, dealing with recent homicides in Kemerovo Province. Before starting the second, which presented a series of (doubtless favourable) comparisons between Kemerovo and other regions in Siberia, he sat back and glugged tepid coffee from his mug. Babikov might be a bit of a maverick when it came to procedure, thought Vassily, but he knew how to put a report together. Every murder in the past twenty-four months was listed, with photographs of the victim or victims, suspects and known accomplices, and a detailed breakdown of the outcome of each case. Babikov's clearance rate was impressive, as Terekhin had said, but then again, so was the sheer murderousness of the Province's inhabitants. Was it too cynical, he asked himself, to suspect that the more murders there were, the better Babikov would be pleased? No, he decided, it was not – especially with regard to a Babikov running for high office. It was odd, in a way, to think of Babikov as an elected politician. Didn't politicians have to stand up for the rule of law, protect the people, and all that kind of thing? Babikov had hardly come across as someone who respected the rule of law, when Vassily had known him before.

Something else bothered him, though. He couldn't put his finger on what it was, or even what kind of thing it was. Perhaps I'm just over-tired, he thought. It had been a long drive from Novosibirsk the day before, and a long, sleepless night after that.

He had just decided to go back to bed for a nap when a sudden noise made him jump. His police radio had burst into life, speaking a name that reminded him of something buried deep in the past.

This is Olga – Olga Pushkin, track engineer third class, Roslazny. There's a dead man here. The Trans-Siberian's just gone past. I'm at my hut and I need medical – medical . . .

The radio displayed a small '2' on its LCD display, indicating that this Olga Pushkin, whoever she was, was using the emergency frequency. Babikov had said the train crew used that frequency when necessary. And the woman had said the Trans-Siberian had just gone past . . . She must be somewhere by the tracks, thought Vassily. He threw the report onto the table, grabbed his thickly lined jacket and fur Ushanka hat, thrust the radio into a pocket and wrestled open the front door to get to his Volvo. Within seconds he was driving down the rutted track, cursing as the wheels skidded on the ice and crashed into the deep potholes that dotted the surface. He swung the car's nose north, towards the railway, and speeded through the village as fast as the narrow roads allowed. He came to a halt near the edge of the forest, his front wheels burying themselves in last night's snow. Cursing, he jumped out and ran in the direction of the tracks. To his surprise he hadn't needed to radio Tayga for directions to Pushkin's location: a memory from his teenage years, of lazy summer-afternoon strolls by the track, and the little railside hut where the engineers worked had come to mind without conscious effort.

There's a dead man here . . .

He unclipped his holster and drew his pistol, taking off the safety catch and raising the weapon into an aiming position as he made his way through the forest towards the railway. If someone was dead, that could mean a shooter, or a knifeman, or even a drunken farmer with a pitchfork. Whatever had happened to Olga Pushkin, Vassily wasn't taking any chances.

He pulled out his radio again and called Tayga, telling them that he was approaching the tracks, pistol in hand – that he could see a body on the ground covered with blood, and another body, too, with a man kneeling by it.

'Hands up! Move away from there,' he shouted. But then he stopped in astonishment as the man stood up.

'Glazkov,' he said. 'What the hell are you doing here?'

6

Enter Ivanka

Olga came slowly to her senses, realising to her surprise that she was surrounded by the familiar pinewood walls of her bedroom in the house she shared with her father Mikhail. He was there, too, in his usual indoors outfit of an ancient knitted jumper paired with shiny sweatpants and plastic sandals. He was hovering by the end of her bed and leaning on the crutch he needed to walk – or that he seemed to need when other people were around anyway. Then Olga saw there were indeed others in her room – notably her friend Anna Kabalevsky, who was standing next to Mikhail with a worried expression; but also someone she didn't know, a tired-looking man in glasses with a plastic badge on a blue lanyard, who stepped forward to her bed as soon as he saw her eyes flickering open.

'What's your name?' he said sharply. When Olga replied, he demanded, in the same brusque tone, that she tell him the day's date, the full names of her father and mother, and lastly the name of the president. The tired-looking man, she realised, was a doctor. Anna must have called him in from Tayga community hospital.

'Vladimir Putin,' she replied to his last question. 'But what does that tell you? He's been president for about a hundred years.'

The tired-looking man smiled briefly. 'True enough. And tell me, do you remember what happened to you?'

'I remember falling,' said Olga, trying to clear her mind. 'I was standing next to the track. I hurt my head. And then – then I was lying on the ground next to a man. A tourist, I think – a foreigner, anyway. He hit me when he fell. From the Trans-Siberian. The man – is he all right?' She sat up, her voice rising in panicked urgency. But then she remembered the vacant gaze of his eyes as they stared, sightless, at the falling snow. 'No. No, he was already dead. I remember now. There was money – coins – in his mouth. And his throat – someone sliced his throat from side to side . . .'

'It's all taken care of,' said the doctor, laying a reassuring hand on Olga's shoulder. 'There are some people here from the police to talk to you, when you feel up to it. But don't worry about that for the moment. How are you feeling physically? Any pain – any nausea?'

'A bit of both,' she said, putting her fingers to the right-hand side of her head, where she felt a small bandage covering a bump under her hair. 'But nothing too serious. I've had worse after Karaoke Night at Café Astana.'

The doctor smiled again. 'Well, you don't seem too bad to me – just a mild concussion. Take plenty of fluid and get some rest. No agitation, and no work. I spoke to a Mr Viktor Fandorin on your behalf. He's a pleasant man, isn't he? He said he'll organise someone to cover your shift.'

'Thank you . . .' Olga read his badge '. . . Dr Zinovev. What do I owe you for coming?'

All Russians were entitled to free state healthcare. In practice, though, those who could afford it took out private insurance, and those who couldn't, like Olga, relied on paying doctors whatever they could afford.

'Don't worry about that,' said Zinovev, with a tired smile. 'Anna's an old customer of mine. I was happy to come.'

'He's a good man,' said Anna, as the doctor left.

'A good man?' said Mikhail, with a snort. 'He's a doctor, isn't he? He gave you a free pass today so he can charge you even more next time round. The amount of cash they filched out of me when I had my injury . . .'

'How is your leg, Mr Pushkin?' said Anna. 'It's a long time since we saw you at the café.'

'Oh, it's pretty bad, pretty bad,' said Mikhail, rubbing his nose and slapping his right leg – the one he claimed was injured. 'Well, if Olga's all right, I'll be getting back to my stories.' Soap operas were Mikhail's main occupation during the winter months, apart from reading the magazines Olga picked up for him at the café. In the summer he made Vladimir Solotov and a couple of other elderly friends come to the house to play poker for money. The Kremlin had banned gambling in Russia in 2009, but Mikhail had sworn that wouldn't stop him taking money from his friends. It was one of the few promises he'd ever kept.

He hobbled to the door and disappeared.

'I'm sorry, Anna,' said Olga. 'You see why I come to yours instead of inviting you here.'

'Don't be silly,' said Anna. 'He's old. The old have their own ways. Anyway, are you really feeling all right, Olga? I had such a shock when I saw you.' She told Olga how she'd looked out of her window to see Vassily and Glazkov carrying her, her head lolling in their arms and a trickle of blood running down her face. The men were trying to get her into an old Volvo, but Anna quickly ran out into the cold and told them to take Olga to her own house instead. 'Then I rang the doctor, and he came straight away,' Anna went on. 'He bandaged your head while the men went back to the track. They said something about fetching a man – they must've meant the dead man, God rest him. They didn't say anything about him being a tourist, though.'

'I don't know that for sure,' said Olga, 'but he didn't look local. His teeth were too perfect. The only people I see with teeth like that are foreigners at Tayga station, buying food and cigarettes from the platform vendors. And his clothes looked expensive, too.'

'So he fell from the train? And hit you on the way down?'

'He didn't fall,' said Olga. 'Someone cut his throat, stuffed ten-rouble coins into his mouth and pushed him out the door like a sack of turnips.'

Anna crossed herself. 'All we can do now is pray for his soul,' she said, 'that the good Khristos might give to him the well of water that springs up into eternal life.'

But Olga didn't want to think about souls and prayers and eternal life just then: the gory realities of death were too near. The dead man's face haunted her, his staring eyes, gaping throat and money-filled mouth circling through her mind, like an undesired earworm of a melody.

Olga jumped as the thin wooden door resounded with a heavy blow, then another. The door opened and Private Anatoly Glazkov poked his head awkwardly through the gap.

'Thought I heard voices,' he said. 'Are you all right to talk to Sergeant Marushkin now, Miss Pushkin?'

'Oh, I think she should rest—' began Anna.

'No, Anna,' said Olga. 'I want to talk to the sergeant – I want to help. And I don't feel that bad. You can send him in,' she said to Glazkov, who retreated in search of Vassily.

'He's quite handsome, you know – Vassily Marushkin, I mean,' said Anna, smiling. 'Dark hair and brooding eyes – quite trim, too, in a well-built kind of way. Just your type, I'd say. And he's an animal-lover, like you. Glazkov told me he's known for it.'

'An animal-lover?' said Olga, surprised. Many local police-men were keen hunters, and were more often seen blasting wildlife to pieces than caring for it.

'Yes – Glazkov says he keeps a pet ferret.'

Olga recoiled in horror. 'A ferret? Anna, don't you know that *ferrets eat hedgehogs*? Hedgehogs like my little Dmitri?'

'Well, I suppose that's true,' said Anna, thoughtfully. 'But it's probably a very tame ferret. It's just a pet, after all.'

'Anna, stop trying to defend this man's ferret!' said Olga, laughing despite herself. 'And stop trying to set me up with him. I've got better things to do than dream of a love affair with some ferret-owning policeman.'

Anna opened her mouth to reply, but the door swung open again and Glazkov entered, followed by a tall, solid-looking man with black hair that bristled untidily beneath his police cap.

'Miss Pushkin, this is Sergeant Marushkin,' said Glazkov. 'He's just been posted here from Novosibirsk. He'd like to—'

'Thanks, Glazkov,' said Vassily Marushkin. 'I'll handle it from here.' He took out a notepad and pen, and glanced up at

Olga. 'I just want to ask a few questions. I'll start with . . .' He paused, looking at her curiously. 'I know you from somewhere. Your name's familiar.'

'Of course it is, Vassily Marushkin,' said Olga, smiling at him. 'Don't you remember me? From the village school? Anna and I sat three rows behind you, for a couple of years. I remember your father Kirill, too. He ran the police station here, for a while.'

Olga hadn't remembered Vassily's name at first, but his dark, wayward hair had instantly brought her back to a day many years ago, when an awkward, gangly teenager walked into the class behind the teacher, Elvira Volkov, and reluctantly took a seat beside Piotr Katin. By then, Olga had already become infatuated with Piotr so paid little attention to the newcomer. Besides, he was a quiet boy who kept himself to himself, talking mostly to the rather nerdy group that gathered around Aleksei Popov, the butcher's son. They had wealthier parents than the rest, and were mostly destined for university or community college – Olga seemed to remember Popov's son studying computing, or something like that. Probably Vassily had gone to some kind of college too – he certainly spoke like an educated man.

Vassily nodded. 'I do remember,' he said. 'You were always talking to Piotr. I think you'd won him over by the time my family left Roslazny. Did you marry him in the end?'

Olga looked down at her hands, which rested on a patchwork quilt her mother Tatiana had brought from the Lodge at Astrazov. 'I thought policemen were meant to be observant, Vassily Marushkin,' she said. 'Didn't you hear Private Glazkov call me Miss Pushkin? And can you see a ring on my hand?'

Vassily looked at her bare fingers, then glanced down at his own hand. He still wore the gold ring that his wife Rozalina had placed there sixteen years ago, eyes filled with love in the chapel of St Grigor at Berezkino.

'No,' he said, 'I can't see a ring, Miss Pushkin.' She had striking green eyes, he noticed, and her hair had an attractive way of curling around the contours of her cheeks. Yes, she was prettier than he remembered. But then, Vassily hadn't been interested in girls when he attended the school in Roslazny. Not like Piotr: he was the ladies' man of the class.

He shook his head, forcing himself to focus on the investigation at hand. He didn't have time to be thinking about whether ladies were attractive or not. And, besides, he was still a married man. It didn't matter that he hadn't seen Rozalina for fourteen years. And it didn't matter that she'd betrayed him with Pavel Prokofy. Vassily blamed himself for that. If it hadn't been for his obsession with his career, and the constant absences that had resulted, she'd never have felt so alone, so *desperate*, as to escape with a man like Prokofy. Whatever she'd done, he would gladly forgive her for it: she was still his wife, his first and only love, and the mother of his child, his little Kliment.

'Well, *Miss* Pushkin,' he said, in a sterner tone, 'you're now a key witness in a murder inquiry. It looks as if the man was dead before he reached the tracks. His throat was cut – pretty expertly, too, if I'm any judge. And I don't know if you remember, but someone put money in his mouth and down his throat. Ten-rouble coins, to be precise.'

Anatoly Glazkov broke in: 'So we need to know if you saw anything suspicious – *anything at all.*'

Olga knew Glazkov a little. He was based at Tayga, and she'd seen him there from time to time, usually on one of the platforms at the station, talking to her friend Ekaterina Chezhekov or one of the other sellers. She knew him well enough, anyway, to see that he was not quite himself. His usual air of rotund bonhomie was absent, replaced by a restless nervousness that sat uncomfortably with his friendly uncle's face and generous paunch. But perhaps he was nervous about the arrival of the new sergeant. Glazkov was hardly a man to do things by the book, and he might be worried about Vassily picking up on some of the corner-cutting that went on at Tayga. In any case, it wasn't her concern.

'I can't remember much,' she said to them both. 'I remember coming back along the tracks from the junction. Fandorin – that's the foreman at Tayga – had sent me to fix a jammed point switch. I heard the train coming. The Trans-Siberian, of course. Then I thought I saw something – well, someone – in the woods beyond my hut. But I couldn't really see anything. Then I heard a door open on the train – it banged against the side of the carriage. I turned to look, but the dead man hit me from behind and I slammed into the wall of the hut. I remember seeing him lying on the ground, with his throat wide open and money spilling out of his mouth. I passed out. Or – well, I passed out after calling for help on the radio.'

'Thank God you did,' put in Anna. 'And thank God you got there quickly,' she added, nodding at Vassily and Glazkov. 'It doesn't take long to freeze to death out there.'

'And the dead man – was he someone you knew, someone you'd seen before?' said Vassily.

'No,' said Olga. 'I was just saying to Anna that he looked like a foreigner – like a tourist from the Trans-Siberian, the type you see on the platform at Tayga.'

'But the *someone* you saw in the woods,' said Glazkov, a faint sheen of perspiration on his balding head, 'can you remember who it was?'

Olga thought back. All she'd seen was a shadow disappearing behind the hut. It had almost seemed to her that she recognised the figure, but when she tried to clarify the recollection it slipped away from her. 'No,' she said. 'I don't think so.'

'You're sure?' said Glazkov, leaning forward.

'I think we've covered that, Glazkov,' said Vassily, staring at him. Terekhin had warned him to expect a lazy old-timer, but so far Glazkov had surprised him with the energy he'd brought to the investigation. He had even got to the scene of the crime before Vassily – by chance Glazkov had been in Roslazny early that morning, having been ordered to photograph potholes for the local authorities, and had raced to the tracks on foot after hearing Olga's message. Straight away he'd seen that the man on the ground was dead, and had crouched over Olga to see if she, too, had been killed. It was then, said Glazkov, that Vassily had come along.

Glazkov had wasted no time in getting on his radio, either, walking up and down the track while Vassily attended to Olga, and trying to get in touch with Babikov (though he had only managed to track down Wolansky). And now he seemed to be taking a particular interest in questioning Olga. Too much of an interest, in Vassily's opinion. Vassily was the sergeant-in-charge at Roslazny, after all, and he couldn't have a mere *ryadovoy politsii* undermining his authority.

'Well, that'll be all for now, Miss Pushkin,' he said, closing his notebook. 'We'll get in touch if we need anything more.' He turned to leave, indicating to Glazkov to follow him.

'Wait,' said Olga. 'What are you going to do now?'

'The train's been stopped at Tayga so we can question every-one on board,' said Vassily, turning in the doorway. 'But you don't need to concern yourself with that. Get some rest, and drink plenty of fluids.' Again he turned to leave, and again Olga spoke.

'Wait,' she said. 'I'm coming with you.' She flung aside the quilt and jumped out of bed.

Anna gasped and stepped forward to restrain her. 'Olga, you can't go to Tayga now!' she said. 'Remember what the doctor said – and the good sergeant here. Rest, and plenty of fluids.'

'I do remember what the doctor said,' replied Olga. 'He said it's only a mild concussion. Look, Anna, I can't stop thinking of that poor boy's eyes staring past me into the sky, and those coins around his head, like a saint's halo in an icon. He really was a boy, you know – he couldn't have been more than twenty. I can't just lie here and do nothing. And, Sergeant,' she said to Vassily, 'I can be more useful than you think. I know all the vendors on that platform, and they hear more rumours than the police ever do. If something's going on, you need to speak to Ekaterina Chezhekov and the others. I can help you with that.'

Vassily looked at Olga, trying to weigh her potential contribution against the risks of involving a civilian – and not just any civilian, moreover, but a recently injured witness – in an ongoing investigation. She was right, though, that he needed someone who could liaise with local informants – and he suspected that Olga Pushkin would be rather better at that than Private Anatoly Glazkov. 'Fine,' he said. 'Thanks, I mean. But you'll have to sign a waiver. I don't want to be responsible for you hurting yourself on my account.'

'I'll sign whatever you want,' said Olga, wriggling into her fur jacket for the second time that day. 'Now let's get going.'

As Vassily's battered old Volvo bumped along the road that led out of Roslazny and towards Tayga, Olga, who was sitting in the seat behind him, looked out at the familiar houses and wondered why she was really going along. She hadn't lied to Anna when she'd said she couldn't stop thinking about the dead man's unseeing eyes: she was desperately sad at the thought of such a young person's death, of his mother's grief – perhaps a young wife, too, and maybe even a child, although she knew from television that foreigners got married later than people did in Russia. And she hadn't lied to Vassily – she really could help him with the platform vendors. But there was something else, too, something more personal that had risen unprompted within her and forced her out of bed to go to Tayga with Vassily Marushkin and Anatoly Glazkov. It was, she acknowledged, a simple desire to prove the letter-writer wrong.

As if you'd ever be anything else . . .

The person who had written those words thought of her as an unimaginative worker drone, deluding herself with dreams of literary grandeur while confined for ever to a third-class engineer's railside hut. Olga would prove them wrong in time, of course, with the publication of *Find Your Rail Self: 100 Life Lessons from the Trans-Siberian Railway*. But here was a more immediate opportunity to show everyone in Roslazny – and Tayga – that Olga Pushkin was made of sterner stuff than people imagined. Here was an opportunity to face up to danger and triumph over evil, over the web of violence that stretched across Russia and in which she had by chance become entangled. People wouldn't expect Olga to respond by getting *more* involved, by going further in instead of taking to her heels. People would react like her friend Anna Kabalevsky, who, for all that she loved Olga, had expected her to stay safely wrapped up in bed while the investigation proceeded without her. People would be amazed at Olga – Olga *Pushkin*, you know, old Mikhail's daughter, the stay-at-home who works on the railways – assisting with a murder investigation! And perhaps this would help to ease them into a new way of thinking about her, even before she published her book and went off to Tomsk State University to study literature and write Great Russian Novels.

Besides, it wouldn't hurt to have more material for her book. She hadn't thought of including any life lessons about policework, but now that it occurred to her, she realised there were always policemen around the railway. Most Trans-Siberian services had a policeman or two on board, and she had often seen them standing at the station by the trains, checking luggage, using sniffer-dogs to look for drugs, explosives and guns, keeping an eye on the small-time criminals who haunted the tracks, dealing drugs and rifling through tourists' luggage while they left their compartments to buy cigarettes and *pirogi* on the platforms. Olga still had almost thirty life lessons to write in order to finish the book, and it might be a good thing, she thought, to supply some of these from her experiences with the investigation – if Vassily Marushkin would let her. Perhaps, with his help, she could learn to think like a policeman, or a detective, even; she could learn to see things from a different perspective. Wasn't that how you got new ideas – not by seeing new things, so much as seeing the same things differently?

She looked at the back of Vassily's head, his black hair tousled and disarrayed beneath his cap, his head swaying from side to side as the Volvo passed over the bridge of uneven concrete that separated Roslazny from Tayga's jurisdiction. He seemed such a stern man, so unlike Glazkov – so unlike any policeman she had known. He was different from his father, too, whom she remembered as a lazy, work-shy kind of man, when he ran the station at Roslazny. But, then, Olga wasn't like her father, either. If Olga ever received a slight injury to her leg, as Mikhail had done in 1988, she would be back at work as soon as she could, instead of pretending the injury made work impossible for ever.

If she ever had children, would they be like her? she wondered. Sometimes characteristics and personalities leapfrog generations. If she had a son, would he be like her father? She hoped not. But then she tutted to herself, just as Vassily had when distracted by Olga's curling blonde hair. How could she ever have children? She was alone, and nearing thirty-five. No, she would not have children. But she would not always be a railway worker, either. Nobody could make her that if she didn't want to be.

Before long they were on smoother roads, winding through patchy forests punctuated by farm buildings and the small industrial estates that straggled around Tayga's outskirts. They crossed the new railway bridge and merged onto Lokomotivnaya Ulitsa, and then Oktyabr'skaya Ulitsa and Ulitsa Prospekt Kirova in turn, roads that led past the football stadium and the park into the heart of Tayga. At the business centre they turned right and headed south to the station, passing through stark rows of trees whose leafless branches were domes of frozen white tracery. The station came into view ahead: a long building running west to east, painted like Aunt Zia's house in cream and a cool pale green, like lichen under ice, and reached by several footbridges that spanned the three tracks between the station and the square. Normally these were full of people carrying heavy Chinese canvas bags packed with belongings and food for long journeys, but now the bridges were empty apart from a few lingering snow flurries. The usual bustle in front of the station buildings was also absent. Even the vendors had left their normal places, and were now standing in groups, some by the station's main entrance and some over to the right, towards the old steam locomotive that had come to rest at Tayga one day and never left. Beyond the station building, Olga saw the halted Trans-Siberian service, with passengers milling about on the platform while a sniffer-dog team made its way onto each carriage in turn.

Journalists, too, were present in surprising numbers, marked out by their cameras, laptop shoulder-bags and digital recorders. Olga imagined their editors rubbing their hands in glee at the TV, radio and online features to come, and the lurid headlines the newspapers would run for tomorrow's editions. She hoped they wouldn't find out about the money the murderer had stuffed into the young man's mouth. It was a horrible thing to do, she thought, to make money the thing the tourist would be remembered for, as if the whole of his short life, and the lost, uncountable years he would have lived afterwards, could only be defined by notes and cheques and cold hard discs of impressed metal with St Basil's Cathedral on the back.

There was an access way across the tracks for authorised vehicles, and Vassily drove towards this, holding his identity badge out of the window for the benefit of the armed policemen who stood guarding the station entrances.

'The on-board police saw nothing,' one of them said to Vassily. 'But we've got the crew waiting for you. Inside, by the café.' He tried to say something else, but Vassily had already driven on, the Volvo's tyres bouncing over the tracks until they reached the smooth concrete of the first platform. He stopped the car, switched off the engine, and turned in his seat to talk to Olga, his all-weather jacket rustling as he moved. 'You'd better stay here for now,' he said. 'I'll come and get you when I need the vendors. Come on, Glazkov,' he said, and together they got out and walked to the station building, leaving Olga alone.

She peered out of the car windows, trying to work out what was going on. But Vassily had parked in a most inconvenient place for this purpose, with only an oblique view of the first-class *spalny* carriages, and none at all of the vendors or the train crew. Much of the station, moreover, was obscured by the snow, which, after a brief hiatus, was falling heavily again. The car's windows were rapidly misting with Olga's breath and without the engine running the temperature inside had begun to fall. All things considered, she would certainly be justified, she thought, in going into the station building to buy a cup of coffee to warm herself.

She got out of the Volvo and walked quickly towards the station, keeping her head down and digging in her pocket for some change. The station coffee was notoriously expensive, and she didn't normally allow herself to spend money on unnecessary items, because she was saving every rouble she could for Tomsk

State University. After a decade of scrimping, she now had more than six hundred thousand of the nine hundred thousand roubles she needed for the three-year course. On the other hand, though, this coffee was an investment in her future. It was a down-payment on ideas for her book. And if she could write a best-selling book, she would earn more money, so it would take less time to save for the course. It all made sense.

She pushed through one of the station doors and went to the café counter, hoping her Russian Railways jacket would fend off awkward questions from the police. She ordered the cheapest coffee on the menu, and looked around the station interior. She saw Vassily Marushkin and Anatoly Glazkov standing by a large group of men and women, also in Russian Railways uniforms – the crew of the Trans-Siberian. But a movement outside drew her eyes beyond them, through the windows on the platform side, to a woman in a suit and a fur-lined jacket holding a clipboard and talking to what looked like passengers. Tourists, judging by their clothes and hairstyles. Two, a woman and a man, seemed to be crying, and a third had his face in his hands. Then the woman in the suit put her arm around the man with his face in his hands, an act of sudden kindness that brought tears pricking at Olga's eyes. These tourists must have been friends of the dead man, she thought, and the woman in the suit an official sent by the railway to console them. Perhaps his friends had just learned the terrible details of the murder, ten-rouble coins and all, and couldn't bring themselves to believe it.

Olga could hardly believe it herself. She shook her head, wincing as the motion sent a hot dart of pain through her forehead. She breathed out slowly, massaging her temples and remembering Dr Zinovev's prescription of zero agitation. You're here to work, she told herself, to gather ideas for the book, and show people in Roslazny that Olga Pushkin is made of stern stuff. Getting all emotional isn't going to help anybody, least of all the dead traveller.

She forced her gaze past the grieving tourists to the metal staircase on the platform, where two uniformed police were setting up tables and chairs and putting clipboards and pens on the tables, thinly protected from the snow flurries by a small canvas shelter. Beyond them, Olga could see other policemen chivvying the passengers into long, straggling lines that snaked into the distance, the farthest-off people hidden from view by the snow. They must be planning to interview every traveller one by one, Olga thought. She whistled softly. There were often three hundred passengers on the *Rossiya* services that catered for tourists.

'A cold day for working out of doors, Olga Pushkin,' said a man standing next to her at the café counter, with lank hair and a faded leather jacket.

'Sasha Tsaritsyn!' she said, turning to him. 'I didn't see you there.'

'Nobody sees a good journalist coming, Olga,' said Tsaritsyn, giving her a toothy grin. 'That's how we get exclusives.'

'Are you still with the *Kemerovo Herald*?'

'That's right. But we city types slum it sometimes in the sticks, if there's a decent story. And I hear it's more than decent. It's positively *in*decent. They say there were— Hang on, Olga, there's the man himself. See you soon!' Tsaritsyn grabbed his notepad and headed to the station doors on the platform side, where several other journalists had already gathered around a short, bearded man making his way back into the station building. Olga watched Tsaritsyn as he hurried towards his colleagues. She knew him, as she knew Vassily, from shared days and years spent on hard benches in the Roslazny school. Without the school, she sometimes thought, she'd hardly know anyone her own age. But, then, she didn't really *know* Sasha: he was one of the few who'd escaped the gravitational pull of Tayga and made his way to the bright lights of Kemerovo, and she hadn't seen him for years.

Kemerovo . . . Olga frowned as she tried to work out how long it would take someone to get to Tayga from there. Well over an hour and a half, she thought, and then only by taking risks on the icy roads. What time had the body struck her? She didn't know, exactly. And of course she'd been knocked unconscious, which made the immediate past seem rather blurry. But she was sure it wasn't all that long ago: perhaps two hours, or a little more. Wasn't it odd, then, that all these journalists had managed to get to Tayga station so soon after the incident at Roslazny? And what did Sasha mean, talking about an indecent story? Could he already know about the dead body, about the tourist's gaping jaws filled with money?

The small man surrounded by journalists bustled into the station and thrust them aside, saying brusquely that he had no more information as yet, and that they'd have to wait their turn like everyone else. Olga could hear his voice rising shrilly above the hubbub. What was it Sasha Tsaritsyn had said to her, before rushing off – 'Here's the man himself'? What had he meant by that? Was he hoping for another exclusive?

If so, he was disappointed and surprised – puzzled, even. Olga saw Sasha turn and whisper in another journalist's ear as the small man pushed past them with a face like thunder, glanced down at his smartphone and strode towards the main doors on the town side of the station. He wore an expensive grey suit and brown leather boots, which contrasted strangely with his wild-man-of-the-woods hair and pointed, red-tinged beard. Where had Olga seen him before? He didn't look like the sort of person you saw in Roslazny. Then she remembered: she'd seen him on TV, hovering in the background on some political advert or public broadcast, fiddling with a tablet and issuing instructions to an aide. His bohemian appearance, so different from all the smooth politicos in identical suits, had stuck in her mind.

She took another sip of her coffee and tried to recall which politician the man worked for. But just then, as if by magic, the politician himself walked through the main doors and refreshed her memory. Grigor Babikov! Of course. Not a politician yet, then, but a policeman who wanted desperately to be one, judging by the amount of time he spent on TV these days.

Everyone in Kemerovo region knew the lieutenant colonel's appearance by now. He looked like a dull but competent middle manager – perfect for local politics, since people were always ready to persuade themselves they had voted for a safe pair of hands. Like the small man, he wore a smart business suit, and was in the act of pulling on a city overcoat, rather than the shiny fur jackets most men wore in Tayga. His opponent in the Kemerovo mayoral race, Arkady Nazarov, made much of being a worker and a man of the people, and often appeared in overalls bearing the logo of the infrastructure corporation he directed. It didn't take a genius to see that Babikov was trying to mark himself out as a higher kind of individual. Olga remembered a recent interview on local television in which the chief of police had first outlined his poverty-stricken upbringing in the outskirts of Kemerovo, then emphasised how he had transcended his humble origins by rising to the heights of local policing. He portrayed himself as the ultimate self-made man, an affluent member of the new middle class that towered above mere labourers with tranquil ease.

Babikov didn't look very tranquil at the moment, however. His brows were knitted and his jaw tightly clenched as he looked around the busy hall. He nodded curtly as he saw the small man walking towards him, then hurried him up by waving an impatient arm. Olga was a Nazarov supporter, when she thought about it. He was ridiculous, she freely admitted, but on the other hand she admired his energetic stunts, given his age, and there was no denying the sheer quantity of things he'd already accomplished in the region. But now she almost felt sorry for his opponent, Babikov, as he stood conferring urgently with his well-dressed assistant. Any murder could make a chief of police look bad, but a murder on the Trans-Siberian, and the murder of a tourist into the bargain, with the whole world watching . . . That alone could put paid to Babikov's chances of becoming Mayor of Kemerovo. Such bad luck, with a fortnight to go before the polls.

Or was it? she wondered. Having the eyes of the world on you could be a good thing. Perhaps this could be an opportunity for Babikov, if he solved the crime quickly. And whatever one said about the lieutenant colonel – however much one might criticise his love of the limelight – he seemed to be pretty good at tracking down murderers. Or so he kept saying in his press conferences, anyway.

She edged nearer to see if she could snatch any fragments of their conversation. 'Don't worry, Grigor,' she heard the small man say. 'It looks bad, I know, but we've still got the leading lady. That's the key, after all. She won't see it coming – she's loyal as a dog. And it could just be a random job. She—' but the rest was lost in another deafening tannoy announcement. After that she thought she heard Babikov saying something about keeping the show on the road. The small man nodded and said, 'You'd better not get your hands dirty, though. Anyway, it's a chance for him to redeem himself.' Were they talking about Babikov's mayoral campaign, wondered Olga – about some unsatisfactory employee, perhaps, a man who was to be stealthily replaced by a more competent woman? It seemed an odd time to be focusing on the campaign, with a murder at hand . . . But then the men saw some of the journalists milling towards them, and spoke in lowered voices that Olga couldn't hear.

After a few minutes the small man nodded to Babikov, tapped again on his smartphone screen, and stalked out of the station's main doors. Babikov stood for a minute, then breathed in sharply as if to strengthen himself against a coming ordeal. Olga watched him as he strode towards Vassily and Glazkov, who straightened their backs the way people do when they see their superior approaching. Then the three of them began to talk, looking at times towards the train crew, and at times outside towards the passengers shivering in the snow. The crew, meanwhile, were speaking loudly among themselves, and Olga saw an opportunity. She walked towards the group and took up a position between the crew and the policemen, sipping her coffee and trying to appear inoffensive. Several journalists, she noticed, had done the same.

She could just hear Babikov talking to Vassily and Glazkov. 'I hope you realise the seriousness of the situation,' he was saying in his fussy, high-pitched voice. 'This railway is the longest in the world, covering seven time zones and a twelfth of the world's land surface. This is only Tayga, but the eyes of the world are on us. The dead boy was a foreigner, after all.'

I knew it, said Olga to herself. Not many Russians had teeth like that.

'And as everyone knows, relations with the outside world are worse now than they have been for years,' continued Babikov, glancing over his shoulder at Sasha Tsaritsyn and his colleagues, who were edging steadily nearer the group of policemen. 'I came straight down from Kemerovo as soon as I heard – that shows you the kind of importance we're placing on a quick resolution.'

'Of course, sir,' said Vassily. 'I can only assure you we're doing everything possible to expedite the investigation.'

Babikov nodded. 'Good. We have to be seen to be doing our best. We've got uniforms talking to the passengers outside, but I want you two interviewing the crew in here. The coroner said the victim was probably killed thirty minutes or so before the body hit the ground, so you can focus on that timetable. The restaurant's got tables and chairs we can set up in the corner – here they are now,' he added, glancing at two men in railway uniforms staggering towards them with a heavy oak table, and three women in aprons carrying chairs. Beyond them, inside the restaurant, Olga could see two other men dusting something down – it looked like the kind of stand maître d's hovered over in the more expensive cafés and wine-bars in Tomsk.

'You and Glazkov will talk to them,' Babikov went on, 'in detail, one by one, until you find something useful. The last thirty minutes before the body was thrown out, remember. What do you want?'

Olga realised with horror that Babikov had addressed the last words to her, and that she'd edged so close to the policemen she was almost standing in their circle. She smiled at Babikov in what she hoped was an ingratiating manner and glanced at Vassily, hoping he would put in a good word and allow her to stay.

She was in luck: Vassily seemed too distracted to notice that Olga had come into the building against his orders. 'Oh, yes,' he said. 'This is Miss Pushkin. Miss Pushkin, this is Lieutenant Colonel Babikov. Miss Pushkin's helping us with our enquiries, sir – she's the one who found the body.'

Olga frowned. She hadn't just found the body: she'd almost been killed by it. But she wasn't going to contradict Vassily now. She'd already begun to formulate a new idea for her book, Life Lesson No. 71: *One person can stop even the biggest train.* She didn't want to frame the lesson in terms of murder, though. Of course a murder could stop a train service! She wanted to convey the message that one person can make a difference in the world. But ideally, in the book, she would make it clear that the person she was talking about would make a difference without becoming a murderer.

'So she's the one,' said Babikov, in a tight-lipped voice, staring hard at Olga. He'd turned pale, she saw, and again she felt sorry for him. Olga had thought the Trans-Siberian murder could be an opportunity for Babikov, if he could solve the case. But she was beginning to understand how complex a task that might be.

At that moment the small bearded man in the expensive suit came running back into the station building, phone in hand, saying something about the American ambassador in Moscow. Babikov sighed and took the phone, waving Vassily and Glazkov towards the crew of the Trans-Siberian, and walking with the small man towards the far side of the station.

'Come on, then, Glazkov,' said Vassily. 'Let's see if this lot know anything.'

Olga followed at a discreet distance as they made their way to the chairs and table that Babikov had organised, then took up a position where she could hear everything without looking too obtrusive. This was her introduction to routine police work, and at first she found the experience exhilarating. Twenty minutes later, though, she had to admit that it was less exciting than she'd hoped. The crew was very large, with four guards, a transport policeman, six cooks, two engineers, three drivers, and more than thirty *provodnitsi*, or carriage attendants, all of whom had to be individually identified and interviewed about what had happened on board. It soon transpired, however, that none of them knew anything at all. Olga heard the transport policeman, a surly-looking man called Meganovsky, telling Vassily and Glazkov that the only people who might know something were the *provodnitsi* of the carriage from which the body had been thrown. (Each carriage had two attendants, so that a twenty-four-hour service could be maintained.) But since nobody knew which carriage that was, this was not very helpful information.

After a while she stopped listening to Glazkov and Vassily's questions, and began studying the faces of the crew instead. She found this much more interesting than the policework. Some were surly and ungracious, like the *provodnitsa* with a ring of dirt around her unwashed neck, and ugly, misshapen teeth. Olga shuddered, imagining her as the murderous Baba Yaga of whom Fyodor Katin had spoken, and picturing her leering from the windows of a shack on hen's legs on the fringes of the forest. Another *provodnitsa*, by the name of Alyona Vasiliev, gave answers so terse as to flirt with rudeness, which seemed ill-advised when interacting with policemen undertaking a murder investigation. But Olga could see dark bags under Alyona Vasiliev's eyes that spoke of extreme fatigue. Who knew what else might be going on in her life?

(Life Lesson No. 72: *People who seem rude might just be tired*. Being a *provodnitsa* was hard work even if a person was on tiptop form. If a person was struggling with heavy burdens, and was then questioned by policemen as if she might be suspected of murder, it wasn't unreasonable for that person to be a little short with her answers.)

There were others – rather fewer in number – who were friendly and solicitous. She had noticed one *provodnitsa* making her way to the head of the queue, chatting to the others and making jokes. Olga didn't care for her three golden teeth, two on the top jaw and one below, thinking them vulgar, but she admired her smiling, energetic good humour, and was proud to think that tourists and travellers from far-off lands would come across her during their journeys. They would see this woman trying to be helpful on board, just as she was trying to help the police now, and would think better of all Russians as a result. The other crew members could learn a thing or two from her, she thought.

Olga turned back to the policemen and saw that Glazkov had gone pale, and was running a finger around the inside of his collar. He wiped a faint sheen of sweat from his forehead, and Olga detected a tinge of green on his pallid skin. She tutted disapprovingly. She'd noticed him sweating earlier, too, when he and Vassily had interviewed her in her bedroom. Obviously Glazkov had overdone it the night before and was now paying the price.

He grimaced, clearly trying to pull himself together.

'Name and contact details?' he said to the woman in front of him, the cheery, smiling *provodnitsa* Olga had noticed in the queue behind the desk.

'Ivanka Kozar,' she said.

7

All That Glitters

The *provodnitsa* called Ivanka Kozar smiled at Vassily and Glazkov as she sat on the chair in front of the desk. 'Good morning, Anatoly,' she said.

'Do I know you?' said Glazkov.

'Of course! Don't you remember the time we met in Kemerovo – and then again in Tayga? On Platform Two?' she said. 'Well, never mind. A policeman meets many people, and he can't be expected to remember them all. Isn't that right, Sergeant – now, what was your name?'

'It's Marushkin,' said Vassily, rather sharply. 'Vassily Marushkin. But never mind that. Let me see your phone.'

'My *phone?*'

'Yes,' said Vassily, firmly. 'I want to see your phone.'

'But why?'

'I'm asking the questions, Miss Kozar,' he said. 'We're doing spot checks to see if people have been sending suspicious messages – coordinating movements, and things like that. It's standard practice in Novosibirsk. Is that good enough for you? Now, your phone, please.'

The woman shrugged, smiled obligingly, and reached into

her jacket pocket. 'Here you go,' she said, passing him an ancient Nokia mobile held together with elastic bands. 'See what you can find!'

Olga felt a little sorry for the woman with golden teeth, even if she did look rather strange. Vassily was doing his job, but it seemed churlish to demand that she hand over her elastic-banded phone, just like that. Phones were private objects, with personal messages, family photographs, and all kinds of things that others shouldn't see. And, anyway, if Ivanka Kozar, the friendliest *provodnitsa* in the queue, was involved in nefarious activity, she would hardly have left incriminating material on her phone. And even if she had, she could easily pretend to have forgotten her phone, or lost it, or recently changed her number. You see? said Olga to herself. It *was* worth coming. You're already thinking like a policeman – like a detective!

'All right, then,' said Vassily, after a few moments, handing the phone back to the *provodnitsa*. 'Seems OK.'

Ivanka smiled and took it, and was about to speak when Glazkov spoke brusquely across her. 'What were you doing in the thirty minutes before the train stopped in Tayga?'

Vassily frowned at Glazkov, who was once again at risk of overstepping his authority. But Ivanka Kozar seemed happy to answer him. 'Well, you'll have to ask Mr Zonov,' she said, still smiling. 'Andrian Zonov, I mean. There he is – in the queue. Andrian! Come here a minute.'

Vassily made as if to protest, but before he could speak a large, overall-clad man in his fifties stepped forward and took off the woollen hat that rested crookedly on his thick grey hair. 'The name's Andrian Zonov, Russian Railways locomotive engineer, second class, sir,' he said to Vassily, with an air of respect. (Zonov had recently driven away from a minor road crash without stopping, and had attempted to propitiate the crime-fighting gods ever since.)

'Yes – well, er, thank you, Mr Zonov,' said Vassily, rubbing his forehead and feeling that the situation was getting away from him.

'Please tell the good sergeant here – and Anatoly – what we were doing before the train stopped in Tayga,' said Ivanka.

'Oh, well, that's easy,' said Zonov, with relief. 'We were fixing the samovar.'

'The samovar?' said Vassily.

'Yes – you know, the samovar in my carriage,' said Ivanka, tilting her head and looking at Vassily as if he were not quite all there. Everyone knew – at least, everyone who lived near the railway knew – that each carriage on the Trans-Siberian had its own vat of hot water used for tea and washing and toothbrush-rinsing and making instant noodles in packets bought from platform vendors huddled deep in their fur jackets for warmth. Among many other responsibilities, the *provodnitsi* had to ensure the samovars were kept in full working order at all times.

'What happened to it?' said Vassily, looking from Ivanka to Zonov.

'Blocked *dushniki*,' said Zonov. 'Happens now and then, when there's dirt in the system.'

'So I called in Andrian,' said Ivanka. 'About five o'clock this morning, just after I got up for my morning rounds. Yelena was asleep the whole time.'

'Yelena?' said Vassily.

'Yelena Koriakin,' said Ivanka, as if Vassily should have known her name. 'The other *provodnitsa* in my carriage. She does nights, I do days. Going east, that is. Then we switch for the way back.'

'I'll be speaking to her later,' said Vassily, making a note of the name. 'So, Mr Zonov,' he said to the engineer, 'it took you four hours to clear the steam-holes?'

'You try doing it with a . . . ' Zonov had been about to say 'with a crashing hangover after drinking moonshine with the driver until well past midnight', but with his recent hit-and-run in mind he said '. . . with a full load of tourists walking past you all the time, tripping over your tool-bag, most of them still drunk from the night before.'

'And you were with him the entire time?' said Glazkov to Ivanka. 'You didn't take a single break?'

'Of course I was with him, Anatoly,' said Ivanka Kozar. 'Someone had to pass Andrian his spanners and pliers! Besides, there isn't much for me to do on the morning run into Tayga – not with my routine. I do most of the cleaning before I turn in.' Olga nodded approvingly: she, too, liked to do all her housework before going to bed. A new day was bad enough, without all the dirty dishes from last night's dinner to deal with.

'And you didn't see anything suspicious?' said Vassily.

'Not a thing, Sarge,' said Zonov. 'Like I said, we were fixing the samovar. We didn't see anything, apart from rusty old pipes and steam valves that should've been replaced a decade ago and more.' Ivanka nodded in agreement.

'Well,' said Vassily, after a pause, 'I can't think of anything else for the moment. Can you, Glazkov?' But the older man shook his head, with a haunted look in his eyes that surprised Olga. Did policemen always take their cases so seriously, so *personally*, she wondered?

'All right, then,' said Vassily. 'That'll be all for now, Miss Kozar. And I suppose you can go, too, Mr Zonov.'

Andrian Zonov flashed a grin, squashed his woollen hat over his hair once more, and walked quickly towards the exit before Vassily could change his mind. Ivanka Kozar, by contrast, took her time.

'Sorry I'm of no use, Sergeant Marushkin,' she said as she got up to go, smiling at Vassily. 'Nothing makes me happier than helping our brave policemen in their work. If you only knew *how* important it was to me . . . But if anything comes back to me, I'll get in touch. It probably won't – my mind's full of holes. It's like a piece of Swiss cheese! Oh, I'm no good, no good at all.'

Vassily nodded. 'Make sure you do get in touch if you remember anything, Miss Kozar,' he said. 'Perhaps you could ask the next person to come up.'

Ivanka's teeth flashed a final golden grin, and she walked away, beckoning to the next person to come forward – a cook from the restaurant car, judging by his food-stained sweatshirt. What a shame, thought Olga, that the rest of the crew didn't share Ivanka Kozar's work ethic. She would think twice before ordering food from restaurant cars in future, if that was the level of hygiene they maintained.

Vassily waved the man towards the chair, and nudged Glazkov to remind him to take his name. But then Vassily turned in the direction that Ivanka had left. He half stood up, and raised his hand as if to call her back – but then, seeing she'd already walked out of the main door, he sank back into his seat. Olga saw him tap his upper lip three times and gaze into the distance, deep in thought.

What was he thinking? she wondered. Why tap his lip three times? Could that be one tap for each golden tooth? Ivanka's golden teeth were her most distinctive feature, after all. Maybe he thought there was a link between the *provodnitsa* and the dead man, the tourist who'd hit Olga on his way to the ground . . . He, too, had had gold in his mouth, even if it was only the gimcrack gold of a ten-rouble piece.

No, surely not, thought Olga. Ivanka Kozar was a helpful, friendly worker, not an evil murderer capable of cold-bloodedly killing a man and stuffing his mouth with money! And even if she were, Ivanka would hardly have given the police such an obvious, golden-mouthed clue to her identity, or engineered such a convenient alibi with the broken-down samovar. An alibi like that, arranged with a man like Zonov, would be more suspicious than no alibi at all. Vassily must have something else on his mind. Perhaps Olga could find out what it was later on, if he was amenable.

The cook coughed to signal his irritation at being kept waiting, and Vassily nodded wearily, looking down at his list of questions as if to remind himself of what he was doing. Olga realised how tired he looked. No wonder, then, that he'd been brusque with Ivanka Kozar a few minutes ago. She smiled: she'd neglected to remember her own Life Lesson No. 72: *People who seem rude might just be tired.*

Lieutenant Colonel Babikov came back into the station then, and stalked over to the table where Vassily and Glazkov were interviewing the cook. He waved the policemen to the side, away from the line of crew members.

'Nothing from the passengers so far,' said Babikov, Olga straining to hear his words. 'A couple of people saw something falling from the train, and an old man says he heard a door opening, then slamming shut again, but that's it. What about the crew – any leads?'

Vassily opened his mouth to respond, but Glazkov spoke first. 'Nothing so far, sir, though we've kept right at it,' he said, looking nervous.

Babikov stared at him. 'Nothing? Have you talked to all the *provodnitsi*?'

'All the ones that mattered, yes, sir,' said Glazkov. 'Like the last one – an Ivanka Kozar. She had some alibi with a samovar, and—'

But Vassily cut across him. 'Thank you, Private,' he said in a pointed tone, before turning to Babikov. 'Yes, sir, Glazkov's right. The last *provodnitsa* we spoke to had an iron-clad alibi, going back hours before the time when the man was killed. And the others are the same. No leads so far.'

Babikov seemed at a loss for words. He must have pinned his hopes on finding the killer among the train crew, Olga thought. Perhaps he had received a tip off to that effect. Vassily seemed to be thinking on similar lines.

'But there are still a few people to talk to, Chief,' he said, waving a hand behind him at the untidy queue of crew members waiting to be interviewed. 'Hopefully something will come up.'

'Yes, yes, Marushkin,' Babikov said distractedly. 'I'm sure you're right.'

He caught sight of Olga, who was perching on a luggage-stand near the side of the table and trying to look unobtrusive.

'Look, Marushkin,' he said, in a low voice, 'we can't have civilians listening in. Get rid of her.'

'But, sir,' said Vassily, 'we haven't used her for the vendors yet.'

'You've got her contact details?' said Babikov. 'Then call her later, if you have any problems with them. She can speak to them for you. Better still, you can arrest them if they won't cooperate – threaten them with a night in the cells. Problem solved. Wolansky can handle any fall-out.'

Vassily opened his mouth to protest, but Babikov cut across him. 'Take her back to Roslazny, will you, Glazkov?' he said. 'I think you've done enough for today. Marushkin can carry on here alone.' And then, to Olga: 'Thanks, Miss Pushkin, but we don't need you after all. We'll be in touch if we require any more details from you.'

Olga shrugged. It looked like it was time to go.

Glazkov drove Olga back to Roslazny in the Volvo. Olga would have preferred Vassily behind the wheel, not least because she knew Glazkov had been drinking. But that wasn't unusual on a Saturday in Kemerovo Province. The joke was that you could spot drunk drivers because they drove in a straight line; the sober ones wove from side to side to avoid the potholes.

They made it to Roslazny in one piece, and Glazkov left her outside her house. She was greeted by Mikhail, who had been brought to the front door by the sound of the Volvo's engine.

'So, you're back, then,' he said. 'Good. I haven't had my lunch yet.'

'Coming, Father,' said Olga. She was hungry too, and tired. She could feel a headache coming on, and perhaps it was time, after all, to obey Dr Zinovev's prescriptions. It had been exciting to be involved with the investigation, to feel she was doing her duty by the dead tourist with the haunting eyes and beautiful white teeth. She would be able to tell people about it, at Café Astana and elsewhere, if anyone ever suggested she was only a railway engineer. It had been a useful source of ideas, too, for her book, and she'd learned how to think like a policeman, a little. But she was glad to be home, all the same. Vassily, like the fox, had to know many things: how to conduct an investigation, how to squirrel the truth out of people, how to track down and capture liars, cheats and murderers. But for now Olga was happy to be a hedgehog like her little Dmitri-Dima-*detka*, and to know just one thing.

Well, maybe two things. Yes, she was a clever hedgehog, she said to herself – a hedgehog who knew about writing as well as railways. And that, she thought, was enough for anyone to be getting on with.

The news that a man had fallen dead from a train outside Roslazny, striking down their very own Olga Pushkin in the process, had caused great excitement in the village. The new sergeant-in-charge at the hitherto abandoned Roslazny police station had also occasioned considerable comment, not least because he had arrived just hours before the dead body.

'It's an instance of Divine Providence,' said Anna at Café Astana later that day, crossing herself. 'It was ordained from above, so that Sergeant Marushkin could help us in our need, and prevent Olga freezing to death.'

'It was actually me who found her first,' said Private Anatoly Glazkov, sipping his beer. (Technically he was still on duty, but his view was that alcohol didn't count if it was consumed slowly.)

'If I was still in the military police, I'd almost say it's suspicious you were on the scene so soon,' said Odrosov, the

Cosmonaut, from behind the bar. Then he laughed. 'I'm only joking, Anatoly, for God's sake. Don't look so serious!'

'I think Anna's right,' muttered Fyodor Katin, who was drinking Odrosov's excuse for coffee while hammering furiously at an ancient typewriter. 'There's a divine renewal happening in Russia, these days.'

'Oh, is that what it is?' said Odrosov. 'I haven't noticed much difference.'

Fyodor stopped typing and looked at him. 'Listen, my friend, there have been three great periods in Russian history. First, the time of the tsars. Then Communism. And now capitalism. An age of corruption and inequality, of godlessness and materialism. Why else do the people leave the villages where their fathers lived – villages like Roslazny?'

'Because they closed the *sovkhoz*,' said Glazkov, into his beer.

'Well, yes, they did,' admitted Fyodor. 'But that's not quite what I mean. The people would've left anyway and gone off to the big cities in search of consumerist lifestyles. Places like Tomsk, Ekaterinburg, Tayga—'

Odrosov snorted. 'You think Tayga's a big city? You need to get out more. You'll be saying Roslazny's a thriving metropolis next, just because we've got a new sergeant.'

'No, but my point is that now, because of all this materialism, all this consumerism and hedonism, a counter-effect has begun to take hold, constituted by essentially spiritual forces that go back *beyond* the Stalinist days. That's what I'm writing – yes, here, today, among you all, the everyday folk. It's a Manifesto for a New Russia. If we can channel these new forces at work across the country and use their power to reinstate the tsars and tsarinas – within a constitutional framework, of course, limited by the rule of law, and with the blessing and guidance of the Church – then Russia can rediscover her divine mission, to exert a benign, but guiding, influence over both Europe and Asia.'

Odrosov laughed again, Anatoly Glazkov joining him a minute later. 'I see now why they call you the Dreamer,' said Odrosov. 'Look, Fyodor, we don't want all that religious mumbo-jumbo, and we certainly don't want a tsar. Russians don't need some hoity-toity ponce in a crown, telling them what to do.'

'But that's exactly what Russians *do* need,' said Fyodor. 'Look, Odrosov, the problem with presidents is simple: they're chosen by election. That gives them legitimacy, *da*? Even if the elections themselves are not quite what might be desired. Presidents can do anything they like, because it's the will of the people. But a *tsar*,' he went on, eyes glowing behind his greasy spectacles, 'a tsar, or a tsarina, has to remember Red Sunday in 1905, when the Imperial Guard mowed down thousands of poor peasants, who'd done nothing but come in peace to petition the Father of All the Russians. A tsar has to remember the May Laws and the pogroms that followed against the Jews. A tsar has to— Well, I'll spare you many other examples. But, above all, a tsar has to remember what happened at the House of Special Purpose in Ekaterinburg, when the Romanovs perished from the Earth. A tsar, in short, has to tread carefully. Can you say the same of our glorious President Putin?'

Odrosov stared at Fyodor. 'Are you saying you want a *weaker* leader?' he said incredulously. 'Listen, Fyodor, Putin got Crimea back for us, didn't he? He put a lid on those Chechen separatists, didn't he? And he's always hanging round those churchy types, too. Patriarch Something-or-other. What more do you want?'

Fyodor sighed and turned back to his typewriter. It was true that Putin had been partially responsible for the resurgence of religion at the heart of Russia's national life. But if Odrosov couldn't see the difference between the present regime and what he, Fyodor, was proposing, he wasn't worth talking to on the subject.

Fyodor knew he was in a minority in the village, where Putin's popularity remained stratospheric despite the burdens of everyday life. It often seemed that the harsher the struggle and the more ineffective the government's response, the more Putin was fêted by the people of Roslazny. 'Just see what poor President Putin's up against,' people would say. 'Look at the mess the oligarchs made of the country in the nineties, when that drunkard Yeltsin was in charge. But Putin will bring order to Russia again. Say what you like about the Soviet days, but there was order then. People knew their place and stayed in it – they stayed in the villages that now are empty. These days, people do whatever they like. It's the Wild West out here. But Putin will save us.' The means by which he would save them was, however, rarely specified.

People in Roslazny often mentioned America when they were talking about their own country, Fyodor had noticed, and always in a critical way. They didn't see that some of their criticisms were inconsistent: on one day a person might criticise America for being a lawless country of reckless cowboys, and on the next for being a masterly conspirator rigging the world economy at Russia's expense. But this didn't seem to matter: America was always the most reviled country. Vladimir Solotov, for example, had a much-admired doormat with the American flag on it, ensuring that the Stars and Stripes was always covered with a thick coat of mud. (He also had a Photoshopped poster he'd bought in Tayga years ago during President Putin's first term, showing the bare-chested head of state riding a bear with a machine-gun in one hand and a grenade-launcher in the other.) Other countries were also disliked, for varied reasons: France, because of Napoleon, and Germany, because of the war, and the Dutch – well, just because Russian people didn't like the Dutch very much. The English, too, were mildly disliked, because England was a poodle of the Americans. But in terms of public enemies, America was always at the top of the list.

This caused a divide among the villagers of Roslazny when Popov the butcher arrived at Café Astana that evening with exciting news to share.

'I just heard something about the railway murder at Tayga police station,' he said to Odrosov and his daughter Svetlana. 'I was – er – assisting the police with another matter. Nothing to do with food hygiene inspections. Nothing at all.'

Popov took out a handkerchief and mopped his large, bald forehead – Odrosov kept the stoves running hot in Café Astana so that people would get thirsty and buy more drinks. 'I happened to walk by one of the meeting rooms in the police station,' he went on, 'the room that Lieutenant Colonel Babikov was working in. Babikov's the man in charge of the investigation, you know. You'll remember him from his TV ads. And didn't you say he was here in Roslazny a few weeks ago, Odrosov? Anyway, I heard him talking about the dead tourist. A trainee lawyer or something. Turns out he's got a name, of a sort: Nathan *Brrryce*.' Popov pronounced Bryce with a long roll on the *r*. 'Bit of a tongue-twister, that. But he's American, so what would you expect?'

'So he was American,' said Svetlana, who was polishing a beer glass on the hem of her miniskirt. 'Big deal. Everyone's from somewhere.'

'No, but you don't understand,' said Popov. 'That's not all I heard. You know his throat was cut – blood everywhere. Well, that's nothing new. You remember that tramp they found in the sewage works at Tayga on Christmas Eve? Windpipe laid open with a wood-saw, messy as anything. But this *Brrryce* was different. They say his throat was slit as neat as you ever saw – a cut as fine as a butcher's. A cut I'd be proud of myself. And that's not all. Listen to this: his mouth was stuffed with gold!'

When Olga came into the café in search of dinner supplies an hour or so later, she encountered a surprising number of people. Word had spread about Popov's news, and the café regulars – Fyodor Katin and Anna Kabalevsky among them – had been joined by a host of villagers who rarely came to Odrosov's premises. Even Olga's aunt Zia was there, summoned by a telephone call from Popov's wife Nadya. Zia was sitting next to Nadya Popov, drinking a tiny glass of vodka and pretending not to be interested in how a young American had managed to get himself murdered in such a fascinating manner – and right next to Roslazny, too!

'Ah, here's our lady detective!' said Odrosov above the din. 'Maybe she can tell us more about the gold.' Silence fell over the café as everyone turned to look at Olga, who stood in the open doorway as she had on the day her poison-pen letter had arrived.

'I'm not a detective,' said Olga, 'though I did help Sergeant Marushkin with his enquiries, earlier on. And – wait, what gold?'

'Shut the door, woman, for God's sake,' said Odrosov, 'and come and have a drink. Why didn't you tell anyone about the gold?'

'What gold?' said Olga again, closing the door.

'*Well*,' began Odrosov, but Popov was revelling in his new-found role as village raconteur, and was not about to give it up for anyone – least of all Odrosov, who had twice bought horse-meat from Tayga instead of from him.

'I was there, Olga,' Popov broke in. 'At the police station in Tayga, I mean. I was there for another reason. Nothing to do with safety regulations. And I *happened* to hear the police talking among themselves, saying that the dead man was called Nathan *Brrryce* – and that his mouth was stuffed with golden coins, worth millions of roubles!'

'No,' said Olga wearily, kissing her aunt Zia, and perching next to her on the last available seat in the café. 'No, it was only ten-rouble coins. I told Anna this morning.'

Odrosov looked reproachfully at Anna Kabalevsky. 'Why didn't you say anything?' he asked.

'Because I'm not the village gossip,' Anna replied, 'any more than Private Glazkov is. You knew, too, didn't you, Anatoly?' Glazkov grunted his assent, took another swig of beer and shrugged at Odrosov as if to say *More than my job's worth*. 'Anyway,' Anna continued, 'I think it's horrible to go on about how he died, even if there *were* roubles stuffed into his mouth. Just think of his poor parents! He was such a young man. And he was going to be a lawyer, they say. He was going to spend a lifetime fighting injustice, protecting the weak and vulnerable, making criminals pay for their wrongdoing . . .'

Olga thought Anna might be promoting a slightly rosy-eyed view of lawyers – they tended to feature as duplicitous villains in the soaps she watched in the evenings, when Mikhail finally went to bed – but she, too, felt a wrench at her heart when thinking of his young life cut short. She knew he had been loved. She had seen that from the way his friends had wept at Tayga station.

'At least he wasn't married, and had no children,' went on Anna. 'That's something. But now his parents have to send for his remains. They should be getting postcards and souvenirs, not a body to bury.'

'Ah, so what?' said Mikhail to Olga, when she got home that night and told him the news from Café Astana. 'One American, two Americans . . . There could be twenty, for all I care. Good riddance.'

'Father!' said Olga. 'Think of how you'd feel if I was killed on the railway. It nearly happened today, you know!'

'I'd claim that life insurance your mother made us take out, for a start,' muttered Mikhail beneath his breath, but aloud he said, 'I'd be devastated, of course, Olgakin,' and smiled unconvincingly.

Olga hated it when he called her that. He only did it when he was trying to appease her or get something out of her – usually money, when he'd drunk his (very generous) weekly allowance of vodka early, or when he'd lost money to his friends in the poker games he made Olga organise. But it wasn't the transparent falseness of the endearment that upset her. It was the recollection of her mother Tatiana, who had always called her that. Sometimes Mikhail called her Olgakin when he wanted her help in tracking down her mother's hidden treasure, the last and greatest of the heirlooms, hidden somewhere in the whispering wood, and that was when it hurt most of all. For in the absence of treasure, all she had was memory.

8

An Unexpected Jail Guest

The villagers' interest in the murdered American faded as days passed without any further revelations. No murder weapon had been uncovered, let alone a murderer; and no explanation had been found for the ten-rouble coins, which had proved to be innocent of fingerprints. The Kemerovo police PR department released a public-information announcement on TV, which set out what the police did and didn't know about the incident. They were sure, for instance, that a man, Nathan Bryce, had been murdered, but they weren't at all sure why. Who would wish to murder a trainee American lawyer, the presenter wondered, a man still too young to have made any enemies? The Kemerovo police had established, furthermore, that the murderer had killed Bryce by cutting his throat, and they had therefore deduced that the murder weapon was a knife of some description – but they were perplexed as to its location and as to who had wielded it, and when. They were clear, too, about how the man's body had been found, by a certain unnamed employee of Russian Railways – but they were all at sea as to why the murderer had thrown the body out of a train, and why he'd chosen tiny Roslazny as his favoured spot to do so.

Up to now the broadcast had been conventional, by local standards. But then the programme took a strange slant, indulging in ever more outlandish speculation regarding the murderer's motivation for stuffing Bryce's mouth with ten-rouble coins. One theory was that the murderer was rich and wanted everyone, or perhaps someone in particular, to know it. But if someone wanted to show off their wealth, thought Olga, why wouldn't they just walk down Ulitsa Prospekt Kirova in Tayga and cast their roubles to the wind?

Another line of conjecture, even more unlikely to Olga's ears, was that the coins in the dead American's mouth amounted to a political critique of the USA – an oblique allusion, the narrator speculated against the backdrop of old Spanish engravings, to the death of the conquistador Pedro de Valdivia in Chile in 1553, when the Mapuche people poured molten gold down Valdivia's throat in token of the Spaniards' endless thirst for gold. By analogy, the Kemerovo police suggested, perhaps the murderer wanted to draw Russians' attention to the exploitative character of American capitalism. But Olga found this, too, unconvincing: American capitalism seemed more like a pretext for protest marches than the brutal murder of a (presumably blameless) tourist on the Trans-Siberian.

Then the broadcast elaborated another and even stranger theory, and Olga lost her train of thought, badgered by the endless flow of hypothesising into a general sense of hopeless bewilderment. How could any particular theory be proved right or wrong, she wondered, when so many different explanations could be found for the same events?

At length, and following a stern rebuke of the American president's recent condemnation of Russian lawlessness, the broadcast concluded on a pessimistic note. Barring the sudden emergence of new and certain evidence, the case seemed destined to remain an enigma. But the people of Kemerovo could be confident, stated the presenter, that Lieutenant Colonel Babikov and his men would continue to investigate until the wrongdoer was brought to justice.

While the lack of progress was most disappointing, in one sense Olga felt relieved. She disliked being the centre of attention, as she inevitably was whenever the murder was discussed in Roslazny, and she hoped that the police's announcement, conspicuously lacking in novel discoveries, would lead to a decline in public interest. Being known as a capable and competent person who could be something more than just a railway worker was one thing, but being questioned all day about an investigation she now had nothing more to do with was quite another. She was also aware that any one of the friendly faces who smiled at her in Café Astana or asked her for news in the streets of Roslazny might be her poison-pen letter-writer – a thought that limited her willingness to discuss events with all and sundry.

There were people from outside the village who pestered her, too – journalists for the most part, who'd discovered from the locals that the unnamed employee of Russian Railways was in fact Olga Pushkin, and who wanted to keep the Bryce story going with an exclusive interview. At first they badgered her to provide lurid details of the incident, with one writer going so far as to bring a sketch artist along so he could recreate Olga's memory of how Bryce's body had looked, lying by the track surrounded by hundreds of coins. But after a day or two a different narrative appeared, prompted by developments in the

Kemerovo mayoral race, and drawing the journalists' interest elsewhere.

Much to everyone's surprise, Babikov had hardly appeared in public since Bryce's death – he hadn't even appeared on the Kemerovo police's TV feature. This created a vacuum into which his rival in the mayoral race, Arkady Nazarov, stepped with relish, taking to radio, TV and social media to raise questions about Babikov's handling of the case. In one memorable mini-documentary streamed on RuTube, Nazarov appeared atop a municipal dam in his familiar blue, white and red overalls, before delivering a damning blow-by-blow account of Babikov's mishandling of the case, complete with grainy photographs of Bryce's body at the local morgue and subtitled screenshots of American and British newspaper headlines about Russian criminality. At the end of the video, the camera zoomed in on Nazarov's squat, bear-like figure as he ran, Putin-style, along the top of the dam before getting into a waiting helicopter, hired at great expense from the small Tomsk airfield. 'Grigor Babikov wants to run Kemerovo City,' Nazarov shouted over the screaming engines, 'but he can't even run his own police department. Give your vote to a real man. Vote Nazarov!'

Soon the journalists began asking Olga different kinds of questions – questions about the police's conduct, or misconduct, of the investigation. She imagined the little man with the pointed beard gnashing his teeth at the terrible blow the unsolvable murder represented for Babikov's campaign, and feverishly casting around for some new masterstroke to reclaim lost ground in the polls. (She had decided that a man with such expensive clothes must be more than just an assistant, and was probably more like a strategist or campaign manager.)

Vassily Marushkin, too, had been besieged by reporters in the little police station at Roslazny. It was perhaps for this reason that he was uncharacteristically brusque with Olga when she went to see him after work on Friday, almost a week after the murder of Nathan Bryce.

She had spent an agitated week in her hut. An enlightened employer might have thought Olga was due some time off after the traumatic events by the tracks, but Victor Fandorin, learning of her sprightly involvement in the police investigation on the day of Bryce's murder, had insisted on her returning to work first thing the day after, on the Sunday. She'd spent the days that followed pacing up and down inside the hut, turning over every detail of the case in her mind and wondering what Vassily was doing to solve it. Had he followed up any leads on the train crew or passengers? Did he really think Ivanka Kozar, the friendly *provodnitsa*, worthy of suspicion? If not, why had he tapped his lips that way when she'd left?

By the time Olga set out on her regular Thursday-evening trip to deliver Aunt Zia's groceries, she'd resolved to be patient and await events like everyone else. But on Friday morning she found herself becoming indignant. She might be relieved at the decline in public interest in the case, but that didn't mean she wasn't curious herself. Didn't she deserve some kind of special treatment after all she'd been through – from the police, if not from Viktor Fandorin? Surely Vassily would understand that she was entitled to a little more information than the rest of Roslazny, or Josef Public elsewhere. And they had been to the same village school, after all. Didn't that mean anything? She decided to put these arguments to him in person, and as soon as she finished work at the hut she bustled round to the police station to see what Vassily would say in response.

'Vassily Marushkin,' she called, banging on the door with her gloved fist. 'Vassily! It's Olga Pushkin.' She heard footsteps coming along the corridor and composed her features into what she hoped was a winning smile. She had taken particular care with her appearance that night, putting on her newest fur jacket and hat, and even some lipstick and blusher. It wasn't because she wanted to persuade Vassily by looking attractive – she wasn't that kind of woman – but because she didn't want him to think of her only as a victim, as a lowly trackside worker laid unconscious by a corpse and covered with blood, or even, at best, as a hanger-on who had contributed very little, after all, to an important investigation. She wanted him, in other words, to take her seriously.

In the event all her efforts were in vain. 'Ah, Miss Pushkin,' Vassily said, tugging the door open. She could hear a distant squeaking from within, presumably from his renowned ferret. 'I hope you're fully recovered by now,' he said. 'What can I help you with?'

Olga's smile became fixed. 'What can you help me with?' she repeated. Wasn't it obvious? 'Well,' she went on, 'I wondered if you had any updates on the murder investigation. You know, because I'm a key witness. And because I helped at Tayga station. Or, well, I was going to, anyway, until Babikov came along.'

Vassily nodded. 'Yes – yes, I understand your curiosity. But I'm afraid I can't comment on an ongoing investigation. You're no longer part of it, you see – we've already got your statement, and we managed to get hold of all the platform vendors through other contacts.'

'I see,' she said, her smile slowly fading.

'I really am sorry, Miss Pushkin,' said Vassily, 'but my hands are tied. It's the law, you understand. Look, why don't you come in and have a cup of tea? We can talk about old times together.'

'No, thank you,' said Olga. 'I don't much care for ferrets – I hear you're fond of them. And I was only passing by, in any case.' Vassily looked up the deserted unlit road to the right, then down the deserted unlit road to the left, and opened his mouth to comment, but before he could say anything Olga had turned away and was stalking up the road to nowhere. If Vassily wasn't going to include her in his counsels, she would show him she hadn't really been interested in the first place, and that she didn't have time to idle away on social calls.

Vassily watched her walk off into the darkness and shrugged his shoulders, retreating inside to arrange a meal for Rasputin. The whole of Roslazny might be obsessed with the Trans-Siberian murder, but ferrets still needed feeding, just the same.

On Saturday the local TV station announced that Nathan Bryce's parents had been to Kemerovo to collect his body and take it back to Cleveland, Ohio. They had insisted on coming personally, said the reporter, because they wanted to see where he had died. His friends, two men and a woman from the city where Nathan Bryce had been at law school, had abandoned their holiday to stay in Kemerovo until his parents came. It must have been a comfort for his mother and father, thought Olga, to see how much he was loved. It would have been nice to be invited to meet his parents and friends, she reflected, and to find out more about the dead man – what he was like, what he loved to do, what his dreams and ambitions were, and why he had decided to travel on the Trans-Siberian with his friends. But the police – and in particular police*men* – would never think of that kind of thing. Maybe in America, but not in Russia. Not as long as men like Grigor Babikov were in charge.

Still, Olga was glad that Bryce's parents had come and gone. She was glad not only for their sake, because now they could bury him at home in America, but also because she hoped it would serve as a natural end-point for the villagers' interest in the case. And so, in the event, it proved. No leads had emerged in the investigation, nobody had been charged or arrested, and no convincing evidence had been found to demonstrate police incompetence, and consequently – apart from Babikov's seemingly inexorable slide in the polls – there was nothing new to talk about.

Besides, there was soon something else to occupy people's attention in Roslazny: something equally mysterious, but – as it turned out – rather closer to home. It began with the butcher's wife, Nadya Popov, making a complaint to Vassily on Saturday evening.

'Someone tried to sell me cocaine!' she cried. She had burst into the police station in a state of high dudgeon, red-faced and almost shaking with fury that such a thing should happen in Roslazny. Such goings-on were to be expected in Novosibirsk and Tomsk, and even in Tayga, but Roslazny was different, in Madam Popov's view. 'We can't have that sort of thing happening here,' she said to Vassily, who had come out from behind his desk to calm her. 'It starts with an unpleasant-looking man like that drug-dealer, all greasy hair and leather jacket and shiny shoes, and it ends up with tattoo shops and massage parlours on every corner. What are you going to do about it?'

'I'm in the middle of a murder investigation, Madam Popov,' said Vassily, 'but I'll see what can be done. Why don't I come with you now, and you can show me where the man approached you?'

But the man had long since disappeared. All Vassily could do was look at his footprints, already obscured by fresh snow like those of Olga's letter-writer, and reassure Madam Popov that he and Glazkov would keep an eye on things when they could.

The incident was the first in a rash of unpleasant events brought about, in Odrosov's view, by an influx of newcomers associated with Bogdan Kabalevsky, Anna's entrepreneurial husband. 'They're all the same type,' he said to his daughter Svetlana the next day. 'They're like that man Bogdan had drinks with last week – or was it the week before? Sergei Something-or-other. These men are Sergei's associates, no doubt. Well, we shouldn't worry. We've got Vassily Marushkin here now, and Anatoly Glazkov, of course, when he's sober – and my shotgun below the bar, if things get too hot to handle. On the other hand, I have to admit it's good for business. Yes – as long as they come in here and buy their vodka from me, I've got no complaints.'

Svetlana shook her head. 'Men like that are bad news, Papa,' she said. 'Believe me.'

'And what do you know of men like that?' said Odrosov.

Svetlana could hardly answer him, so she contented herself

with looking aloof and retiring to her bedroom upstairs. Odrosov shrugged and began to count the takings from the lunch service of gherkins and pickled eggs – better than usual, thanks to the group of five businessmen who had dropped in to warm up at Café Astana. He chuckled as he tapped the notes into a neat pile. At this rate, he'd soon be able to afford the piece of cosmonaut memorabilia he'd always coveted: a glove from a spacesuit worn on a mission to Mir, the USSR's space station.

He changed his mind, however, when Bogdan and his new associates overdid the Rocket Fuel one evening and got into an argument with the mechanic Koptev Alexeyev and several of his friends from the garage in Tayga. The resulting brawl damaged a number of Odrosov's precious Soviet space posters, as well as laying waste to three of the tables he had bought from the bathhouse owner when it closed. The row only stopped when Odrosov fired his shotgun over the men's heads, blasting a hole in the café's thin walls and startling Olga, who was walking past on her way to Anna Kabalevsky's. She watched as Odrosov opened the door and threw the men out one by one, shouting colourful abuse after them into the night.

Vassily Marushkin came running around the corner with drawn pistol, roused by the sound of Odrosov's shotgun. He took all the men to the police station, where he interviewed each of them in turn, leaving Sergei and his associates in no doubt as to what would happen if any further disturbances occurred. (He was more understanding with Alexeyev and the mechanics, who, Odrosov said, had been provoked by taunts from Sergei and the others.) Olga thought Vassily looked rather dashing, running around the corner in his police uniform, until she remembered she was still cross with him for cutting her out of the investigation.

After that, and with Vassily and Glazkov undertaking nightly patrols, things quietened down considerably. They quietened down perhaps a little too much, for Olga feared the trouble had merely been driven underground.

Her fears were soon vindicated. Three days after the commotion at Café Astana, she was walking past the old bathhouse on the way back from one of her fortnightly grocery deliveries to Vladimir Solotov. She saw lights glimmering from behind the wooden shutters, where no light had shone for a decade or more, since the *sovkhoz* had closed. She looked around. The road was empty in both directions, and all the houses in the vicinity were dark and abandoned.

She walked closer and put her eye to one of the gaps, then drew back with her hand over her mouth. Weren't there enough such DVDs already, without making more of them? Who were those women? Surely that wasn't Ludmila the waitress doing – doing *that*? And wasn't that Bogdan standing there, half naked, watching and smirking? What could Olga possibly say about such things to Anna? She knew from Anna's frequent complaints that Bogdan had been away from the house more and more frequently, ostensibly on business trips to Tayga and Kemerovo. She knew, too, that he'd been wearing new clothes around the house – leather jackets and expensive shirts, like the ones Sergei wore, instead of his usual indoors outfit of printed T-shirt, shorts, and fake Crocs from the market at Tayga. She knew Bogdan was not to be trusted, but even she hadn't suspected he would stoop to such depths of bad behaviour.

She walked back to the house in the silent snowy night, pondering what she should do. On the one hand, Anna should know the truth about what her husband was getting up to. But on the other, Anna already had more than enough to deal with. And if Bogdan was bringing money in again, perhaps that was worth putting up with certain things for. Anna was becoming quite a drain on Olga's finances, with weekly loans that were never likely to be paid back. It wasn't helping her to save for Tomsk. But then, that was such an unworthy, selfish way to think . . .

She shook her head. She was too tired to dwell on it now, after another long day by the railway – a day with no time for writing, even. She would sleep on it and consider it properly tomorrow.

But events the next day put Bogdan and Anna out of her mind for a while. She woke up earlier than usual because of a nightmare involving a runaway train, and after an hour of fruitless tossing and turning she gave up and angrily got out of bed.

After a hurried shower – the water was never hot that early in the morning – and ten minutes spent getting dressed and brushing her hair, she walked through to the kitchenette to make herself a rare cooked breakfast. Most days, she just had a packet of wafer biscuits and half a cup of stale reheated coffee from the night before, but today would be different, and she needed to fuel up. Already she could tell that today would be different, and it was barely light outside.

On her way to the kitchenette she caught her breath as she saw an envelope addressed to her lying on the doormat. Could it be another poison-pen letter? But then she heaved a sigh of relief. She recognised the handwriting: it was from her brother,

Pasha. He was stationed with his unit in Crimea, where phone calls home were forbidden, and as he rarely had time to write, it had been months since they or Aunt Zia, to whom he sent dutiful letters when he could summon the energy, had heard from him.

She picked it up and saw a muddy footprint on the envelope – it looked like her own. Of course: the letter must have been delivered the day before, and she'd walked over it without seeing it when she came in during the night. Then she noticed the postmark, which bore a stamp from two weeks ago. She knew the infrastructure in Crimea was poor, but this was pushing it. But still, better late than never.

She ripped it open and began to read, her pleased anticipation fading to puzzlement and then shock. Pasha was coming home – but not for leave: he had been *dishonourably discharged*! Olga had never heard of such a thing. He wrote that they were to expect him on 21 January, escorted to Tayga by the army and then to Roslazny by the police. The twenty-first – that was in two days' time! She wasn't to tell her father, her brother wrote, and she was to forgive him for not saying more in his letter: he wanted to explain in person. He should never have tried to pretend, wrote Pasha. He hoped their father would understand.

She sank back on the rickety bench they kept by the front door, wondering what Pasha could have done. It would be wonderful to see him again, of course – but *dishonourably discharged*? Her father would never forgive him.

She sighed. Here was another burden that had to be borne, and she hadn't had breakfast yet. She got up wearily and set off to the kitchenette once more. But then came the thought: couldn't she drop round to the police station before work and ask Vassily if he had any more information? If the police were responsible for escorting Pasha to Roslazny, Vassily might have been given some details about his case.

It was still early, though, and she doubted that the Roslazny police kept the same strict timetable as the railway: Vassily might still be asleep. But, then, his horrible ferret might have woken him already. Yes, she decided, it was reasonable to expect Vassily to be up by now – just as it was reasonable to expect him to divulge confidential police information at the drop of a hat on the sole basis that it concerned her brother. They had been to school together, after all. And he had hardly been forthcoming on her previous visit. He surely owed her one.

She decided to abandon breakfast and set out immediately for the police station. She checked her hair in the mirror that hung by the door, deciding it needed brushing just a little more neatly. This was the second time she'd thought about her appearance before going to see Vassily, she realised. She'd thought she was doing it solely for professional reasons – to convey the impression that she was a serious, businesslike person. But why was she really doing this? she asked herself. Was it for Vassily himself?

He was a good-looking man, she reflected, as she set out into the cold morning air. She thought back to their first meeting since her teenage years, in her bedroom at home, when he'd walked in to question her on the morning of the murder. She had been distracted then, traumatised by the day's events, and haunted by the staring, sightless eyes of Nathan Bryce as he lay on the snow, staining it red with his blood. But since that day her thoughts had often strayed in quiet moments to Vassily Kirillovich Marushkin. In her mind's eye he appeared as she'd first seen him, framed against the doorway of her bedroom: his messy jet-black hair; his tall, stocky physique, like a shot-putter in training; his thoughtful eyes ringed with sorrow. It was a long time since there had been a man like him in Roslazny, or even in Tayga. He would track down whoever had murdered Nathan Bryce, she was sure of it. He would work out who had stuffed his mouth with ten-rouble coins and why. The police were lucky to have Vassily Marushkin as a sergeant, she thought. If every policeman was like Vassily, Russia would be a happy country indeed.

But Vassily was a married man, she reminded herself, as she passed the lime-green house that belonged to Zia Kuznetsoz. Olga had seen the golden ring on his finger. No doubt some beautiful girl called Feodora, or something like that, had snatched him up as soon as she'd seen him. She imagined an elegant creature, almost as tall as Vassily, dressed in expensive clothes and speaking with a refined accent. She would be clever, because Vassily was clever – and clever men wanted clever women around them. She would have gone to university, of course – no Railway Academy for a woman like her! She would have all kinds of certificates and diplomas in picture frames on the walls of the house they shared in Tomsk, or Novosibirsk, or whichever city they had settled upon. Vassily, no doubt, had been posted to Roslazny to get things going again at the dusty, closed-off station, but as soon as he could find a replacement for himself he would be recalled, and would return with relief to his comfortable home in the city with grocery shops, supermarkets and wine bars around the corner, instead of Café Astana and Popov the butcher.

No, the likes of Vassily were not for her. She had to resign herself to being no more than a friend – if that – to the tall sergeant with the brooding eyes. Still, she could always do with another friend. And it didn't hurt if the friend in question happened to be rather handsome.

As she walked up to the door of the police station, she noticed that a police car was parked outside, as well as Vassily's estate. Glazkov sometimes drove around in one, but it seemed early for him to be visiting. Maybe the Tayga police had given Vassily a vehicle. It wouldn't be surprising, given the state of his battered Volvo.

She knocked on the door, hearing voices inside despite the early hour. The voices ceased and footsteps approached. But it was not Vassily who wrenched open the door.

'Anatoly Glazkov!' she cried.

'Ye-es?' he said, eyebrows raised as if she were a travelling saleswoman.

'I – I was looking for Sergeant Marushkin,' she stammered.

'So was Lieutenant Colonel Babikov,' said Glazkov.

Olga caught the tang of alcohol on his breath. 'What? I don't understand.'

'The chief called me yesterday and gave me the order. I had to do it straight away, he said. Finally we could show we were making progress against police corruption.'

'An order to do what?' said Olga.

'I was ordered to arrest Sergeant Marushkin. Vassily's in a cell' – he jerked his thumb behind him – 'as we speak. Well, he's been living in a cell since he was posted here, of course, but now I've locked the door from the outside. We're holding him for a couple of weeks, while we gather more evidence. I've been assigned to watch him, when I'm not out on patrol.'

'*Arrested*,' breathed Olga. 'But how – why – what for?'

'What for?' said Glazkov. 'What for? Can't you guess? For murder, of course.'

9

What Popov Didn't See

Vassily's incarceration at Roslazny police station was unforeseen by most, Olga Pushkin included. But like many things that come to pass, some could have guessed its approach. Popov the butcher, for instance, would have had more to say at Café Astana on the night of Bryce's murder, if he'd had the wit to comprehend what he'd heard at Tayga earlier that day.

Popov had been asked to visit the police station on a matter entirely unrelated to food hygiene, or so he always maintained on these occasions. While waiting for his appointment with the Department of Environmental Health, he'd heard a hubbub arising in the reception area, and bustled back to see Babikov coming in from the railway station, together with the bearded man called Wolansky, Sergeant Vassily Marushkin, and three other policemen escorting a number of Trans-Siberian crew members to the interview rooms for further questioning.

Babikov and his retinue had disappeared behind closed doors, but Popov soon learned the news, or some of it, from the junior sergeant behind the desk – a man who had got to know Popov in the course of his frequent appointments to discuss legal aspects of butchery and animal welfare in the Tayga region. In a couple of impatient sentences between urgent phone calls from Kemerovo and elsewhere, the sergeant had told Popov that a man had been killed on the Trans-Siberian, his throat cut from ear to ear; that his body, falling from the train, had knocked Olga Pushkin unconscious by her railside hut; and that the investigation was already under way – the chief was just back from the platforms, as Popov could see for himself.

After a few moments there was a lull in the phone calls, and the junior sergeant, whose name was Shchetkin, had turned to the butcher. 'Funny thing, though,' he said. 'A phone call came in about the murder from a member of the public – a man. Funny voice. A passenger on the train who saw the body falling out, I suppose.'

'What's funny about that?' said Popov.

'Well, it came in before the radio call from that railway engineer by the tracks. Pretty damn quick, considering she was the one who found the body! And another thing: they hung up before I could get their details. In fact, they hung up before they'd finished their story – before they'd even finished their sentence! They—'

But Sergeant Shchetkin was himself cut off, by another call from Headquarters in Kemerovo. He rolled his eyes at Popov, and got back to work.

The butcher found all this much more interesting than the prospect of being lectured yet again about disease-control regulations and the sale of adulterated meat and poultry. He abandoned his appointment – such things, he knew from experience, were easy to rearrange upon payment of a certain administrative fee – and took up a position at the edge of the reception area, staring with apparent determination at the cracked screen of his smartphone. For a large man Popov could be surprisingly unobtrusive when he wished, and that seemed an ideal spot to await events, while listening to Shchetkin and the others fielding calls from journalists and local politicians.

Vassily Marushkin appeared after a few minutes, emerging from a corridor and walking across the reception area towards a doorway with a printed A4 sheet taped to it, bearing the legend ARKHIV. Swiping his identity badge through the keycard lock, Vassily pushed through the door and turned right towards a series of shelves, dimly visible to Popov through a set of tinted-glass windows. On previous occasions Popov had often wondered what they had on him in the archives, but this time he was more interested in where Vassily had come from. For down the corridor from which Vassily had emerged, the butcher could see a door ajar; and where a door was ajar, words might be overheard.

'What a mug,' said a man's voice, as Popov approached on tiptoe. 'He really believes all that stuff, you know.'

'What stuff?' said another man's voice.

'Oh, you know,' said the first voice, which Popov identified as belonging to Lieutenant Colonel Babikov, the star of countless TV adverts and mini-documentaries. 'Duty and honour. The law and public service. Protecting the vulnerable. All that *der'mo*.'

'He hasn't changed since he was here before, then,' said the second voice. Popov risked a glance through the door, seeing a small man with a pointed beard, the man who called himself Wolansky. At present he was looking down at his hands and fiddling with his jewellery. He seemed to have a silver ring on one hand and a golden ring on the other.

'Not a bit of it,' said Babikov. 'You'd think a couple of years in Novosibirsk would wash that rubbish off a man. But he's still the same. Fussing about rules, laws, human rights, due process and all that. That's why I requested him from Terekhin, of course. A man like that's got no place in the modern police force. That's not how things get done these days. He's no loss, Wolansky, no loss at all.'

'So you're saying you wanted a stickler to stick it to. Ha! Did you hear that, Grigor?'

'I heard it, Wolansky,' said Babikov. 'But this isn't the time for humour.'

'Lighten up,' said the small man. 'You laughed well enough when I told you about the Uzbek grandmother.'

'That was different,' said Babikov.

The small man leaned forward. 'Was it?' he said. 'Was it so different? Didn't someone die then, too? Didn't that have to happen, just like this time? Didn't we have to deal with the Uzbek, just like you dealt with the farmer, the courier, the factory worker, the accountant and the rest? As it was with them, so it'll be with him, too – *and her*. Plus the spare, and the American, of course. Necessary losses. Part of the game. Par for the course. Eggs for the omelette. The price you pay to get what you want.'

Popov watched Babikov as he leaned back in his uncomfortable office chair and rubbed his fingers in his eyes. Then the lieutenant colonel rocked forward again, the chair's metal legs scraping on the concrete floor. 'Wolansky,' he said, in a tone half commanding, half entreating. 'Wolansky, are you sure? Can we really justify—'

'Grigor, Grigor,' said Wolansky, taking one of Babikov's hands in his. 'What is it you want to achieve?'

'Law and order in Kemerovo Province,' said Babikov, after a pause.

'And how do you want to achieve it?'

'By any means possible,' said the chief of police, like a child repeating his catechism.

'By what means?' said Wolansky.

'By. Any. Means. Possible,' said Babikov, in a firmer voice.

'Because otherwise, if Nazarov wins, what would happen to your plans for free school lunches? For armed guards at football matches? For tougher sentencing, and less luxury in prisons?'

'They'd be finished before they were started,' said Babikov, gazing into the distance as he envisaged the fulfilment of his flagship policies, just as Wolansky had trained him to do for television broadcasts. Then he turned his eyes to his head of PR. 'You're right, Wolansky,' he said. 'There can be no going back.'

'No going back,' repeated the small man, shaking his head. 'And now Bryce must occupy centre stage. Him, and his props.'

'Props?'

'The ten-rouble pieces.'

Popov's ears pricked up at the mention of money.

'A young American's mouth, stuffed with Russian roubles,' went on Wolansky. 'So many coins that they spilled all around, like confetti at a wedding, only better – because who can spend confetti? It should be a publicist's dream!'

'Your job is to ensure it doesn't become a nightmare,' said Babikov. 'You need to work more effectively this time. Then we'll discuss the next step.'

'Steps, Grigor, steps,' said the small man, noticing that the door was ajar, and getting up to close it. Popov moved back to avoid being seen. The last thing he heard the man say was: 'We can't rush things. This is the first act. The players are just getting warmed up.'

The door closed, leaving the Roslazny butcher to draw his own conclusions. Unfortunately Popov limited himself, in this endeavour, to the last part of the conversation he'd overheard, like a dog who remembers only the last bone he buried. Nobody in Roslazny judged him harshly, in the weeks that came afterwards, because everyone knew how he was made. Nobody blames a magpie for seizing sparkly, shimmering things, and nobody blames a child for thinking plastic rings are silver. But nonetheless it was unfortunate that it was Popov, and not some shrewder soul, like Odrosov or Fyodor Katin or even Mikhail Pushkin, who had heard Babikov and Wolansky talking.

Olga reflected on this later, when time allowed, and when Popov told them one day what he'd heard at Tayga, rather than just the part he'd found most interesting. But for now, confronted with Anatoly Glazkov at the door of the Roslazny police station on Sunday morning, she could only stare and stammer, slack-jawed with shock, as she learned that Vassily – *Vassily* – was in prison, arrested for murder!

'Murder?' she said. '*Whose* murder? Surely not Nathan Bryce's. How could Vassily have killed Bryce? He was on the ground with you, wasn't he, when you found me and the body?'

'Yes,' said Glazkov. 'But he could've been working with someone on the train, couldn't he? Anyway, he's not in for the Bryce murder. Not yet, anyway.'

Olga had noticed the slight emphasis Glazkov placed on 'Bryce'.

'Wait,' she said. 'Has someone else died?'

Glazkov nodded, then stared at the floor, as if unwilling to look Olga in the eyes. 'Yes,' he said. 'There's another death to account for, another body calling for justice. A *provodnitsa*, this time.'

'A *provodnitsa*?' said Olga, putting her hand on her chest. 'Another railway murder? Which *provodnitsa* was it?'

'Vasiliev,' said Glazkov. 'Her name was Alyona Vasiliev.'

'Oh, I remember her,' said Olga, sadly. 'From that day at Tayga station. She was tired – tired and cross.'

'Not any more,' said Glazkov, looking up at her with red-rimmed eyes.

'What happened?' said Olga.

'She died yesterday, near Talovka,' said Glazkov. 'Look, we're keeping it out of the news for now, so don't tell anyone. They – they hanged her in her own house! It was horrible – horrible.'

'Did you find her, Anatoly? And what's Vassily got to do with it?'

'No, I didn't find her,' said Glazkov. 'But I got there not long after someone else did. A woman called us in. A neighbour. Name of Elizaveta Medtner. She drove past Vasiliev's last night on her way home to Talovka, and saw her front door open, so she stopped to investigate.' Olga nodded – Siberians don't leave doors ajar in January. 'And then – and then—'

Olga stared at Glazkov as his eyes moistened. Was this battle-hardened *ryadovoy politsii*, the veteran of thirty winters on the force, about to *weep*? She was finding it hard to keep up with his shifting moods. But then she remembered his alcohol problem. She was used to this kind of behaviour with her father, who could be spirit-jarringly ecstatic one moment and aggressively fractious, or wearingly emotional, the next.

'And then?' she said, trying to help Glazkov along.

Glazkov shook his head. He didn't speak for fear his voice would betray him. He remembered every word that Elizaveta Medtner had uttered in her testimony, every pause for breath, every choked-off sob and half-finished sentence. He had gone back into the interview room at Tayga station after the others left, and listened to the digital recording of her interview over and over again, as if he could wear out the content by endless repetition, like an old cassette tape. Glazkov was not known for feats of the intellect, but if he chose he could play the whole recording again in his head. It began with Elizaveta Medtner's journey home.

I was driving along the road to Talovka, like every night, said Elizaveta. *It's a rotten road. More potholes than tarmac. Depressions so deep your exhaust pipe shrieks on the rocks.*

It was past six o'clock when I got there. Night was falling fast. There weren't any lights on in her house when I reached it. But that's nothing strange. Alyona's on the railways, as a provodnitsa. You know, a carriage worker. Well, she was . . . So she's often away. But then I saw the door open. Just hanging open. Now Alyona would never do that. Nobody would, with half a brain, in this weather. So I parked up.

You got out of the car? said Lieutenant Colonel Babikov, his voice high-pitched, cautious, precisely modulated.

Yes, went on Elizaveta. *I parked so the car headlights would shine on the house. Then I got out. I wasn't far*

149

*from home, but I felt a bit – a bit lonely, you know? I
wished I had my uncle's gun. I felt like getting back in
and driving off. But Alyona's a neighbour. Well, she was.
Oh, Alyona …*

So you got out of the car, said Babikov again, after
allowing Elizaveta to weep for a moment.

Yes, she said, choking back a sob. *Yes, I got out and
walked forward or, well, sideways, really, at first,
because I couldn't see anything in the headlights – they
were too bright. From the side I could see the house
against the sky.*

*I was afraid then, but I couldn't turn back – I owed it
to Alyona to find out what had happened to her. So I
carried on walking, step by step, into the doorway.
It looked like a dark mouth, or the top of a well in that
horror film. I was frightened, but I kept going, and
pushed the door aside – it creaked and made me jump.
And then – and then—*

Go on, said Babikov, impatiently. But Elizaveta had
dissolved into a flood of tears, and he could get no
more out of her. After a while he sighed and said, *End of
recording.* The audio clicked, and then ran into silence.

But Anatoly Glazkov knew what had come next. Elizaveta
Medtner had told him herself when he'd arrived twenty minutes
after her phone call to the Tayga police station. Weeping with
terror, she'd clung to him, and then, in a lowered voice, as if
the murderer might hear, she'd told him how she had crept into
the house; how she had struggled to make anything out in the
darkened rooms; and how at last, and as if led by some horrible

sixth sense, she had looked up towards the staircase that led on into the house and seen something hanging there, dimly illuminated by the car's headlights. She had screamed, she told Glazkov – she'd screamed again and again until she had shattered the forest's sleep and sent birds flapping through the branches in alarm. Her eyes had rolled up into her head, and she had fallen senseless upon the snowy ground. When she came round, she'd vomited from sheer horror, then ran back to her car, shut and locked the doors, and rang the police at Tayga, begging them to send someone, anyone, as soon as they could.

'Anatoly?' said Olga. Glazkov started: he realised he had become fixated again, tormented by Elizaveta Medtner's version of what had happened.

'Maybe you'd like to sit down,' said Olga.

Glazkov nodded, staggered to the police car, and sank onto its bonnet. 'Thanks,' he said, wiping his forehead. 'It's just been a bit much. All that's happened ... And now poor Vassily locked away, in his own family's station. . . I remember his dad, you know. And the chief's *still* not happy. He wanted a clean sweep this time, he said.'

'A clean sweep?' said Olga, sensing the possibility of some interesting news. She perched next to Glazkov on the car bonnet.

'Private Glazkov,' said a voice from behind him, making him jump, 'I hope you're not about to divulge details of an ongoing investigation to a member of the public.'

'N-no, sir,' he said, getting unsteadily to his feet. 'No, I – I was just—'

'Private Glazkov was telling me that Sergeant Marushkin is currently unavailable,' said Olga to Babikov, who had walked soundlessly down the corridor that led to the station's front door. 'Nothing more.' Glazkov shot her a look of gratitude and opened his mouth to speak. But then he seemed to think better of it and turned, making his way back inside the station with an abject air. Before the door closed behind him, Olga thought she saw another man inside – a bulky, bald man in uniform, with exuberant moustaches.

'Now, Miss Pushkin,' said Babikov. 'It is Miss Pushkin, is it not? I remember your kind offer to help at Tayga station. Be that as it may, I should be sorry to see a respectable member of the railway workforce charged with interfering in police matters.'

'I'm not sure what you're getting at, Lieutenant Colonel,' said Olga. 'And I'm going to talk to Sergeant Marushkin, whether you want me to or not,' she continued, standing up. 'Maybe I can help him. There's two sides to every story.'

'No,' said Babikov, sharply. 'You don't come anywhere near this jail. Private Glazkov will be here to guard the prisoner, when he's not on patrol around the village – I gave him the order myself. And I'll tell him to keep a particular watch on you, if he sees you wandering about. Listen, Miss Pushkin,' he went on, in a gentler voice, 'you can trust me when I say there's good evidence against Sergeant Marushkin – damning evidence, in fact, clear as day. Colonel Terekhin, from Novosibirsk, has inspected it personally. And the last thing we need is a civilian messing around, sticking her nose in police business. Got it?'

Olga was about to take issue with Babikov's condescending tone, but thought better of it.

'Yes, Lieutenant Colonel,' she said instead. 'I understand.' She walked away from the station towards home, hoping she seemed suitably abashed and demure. After a minute she glanced behind her and saw that Babikov was still watching her. She waited until she turned a corner to clench her fists and swear softly. She was so tired of all these men ordering her around: her father Mikhail; his horrible friend, Vladimir Solotov; Viktor Fandorin, the foreman at Tayga . . . Even Odrosov had been rude to her the other day, interrupting her request for fresh vegetables with a peremptory list of the tinned goods he had for sale. They all seemed to think women were a second-class species. But what had these men done to merit such a superior station in life? What had they accomplished that gave them the right to lord it over her? And now here was Babikov, another man with more bravado than brains, bossing her around in her own village. It was her tax roubles that paid for the police, wasn't it? It was her money, after all, and the money of thousands of other Olgas and Ekaterinas and Annas, that paid for the little station in Roslazny, and the salaries of those who worked there.

And so Olga would go to the jail and talk to Vassily Marushkin if she wanted to. Quite apart from her concern for the incarcerated sergeant and a very strong unwillingness to believe him capable of murder, she was inclined to be suspicious of Glazkov, despite his pitiable condition. He had expressed regret at Vassily's imprisonment, and had uttered cryptic hints about some plan for a clean sweep, before Babikov had cut him off. And while Olga knew that old men of an alcoholic persuasion were prone to mood swings, Glazkov's worries seemed more specific than the vodka-induced lows that Mikhail Pushkin presented to the world each morning. There was definitely something going on with Anatoly Glazkov, and – as Olga saw it – she had a duty to find out what it was.

Olga had begun to realise that when things went wrong it might come down to her to fix them. It was no use waiting for someone else to do it, or for the authorities to step in. What if the authorities themselves were the problem?

Yes, she would talk to Vassily, but not now. First she had to go to work, as Russian women did, day in, day out. She had a busy day ahead on the railway, for which she was already late, with sixteen freight trains passing through, plus two passenger trains from Tomsk and a maintenance crew destined for Novosibirsk. And between trains there was the track to inspect, Dmitri the hedgehog to feed, and ideas to jot down for her book, *Find Your Rail Self: 100 Life Lessons from the Trans-Siberian Railway*. So her visit to the jail would have to come later that day, in the evening, once she had fed her father. Glazkov was supposed to be at the station guarding Vassily, Babikov had said, but Olga strongly suspected that he would show up at Odrosov's instead, once night fell, to keep himself topped up with vodka. Once he was safely inside and drinking his fill of Rocket Fuel, Olga could go to the jail. And then she would see what Sergeant Vassily Marushkin, Novosibirsk big shot, one-time Roslazny schoolboy and lead suspect for one (possibly two) murders, had to say for himself. She was tired of men's voices in her ears, but Vassily, at last, might be a man worth hearing.

10

Rasputin by Night

The skies had cleared when Olga finished work that Wednesday, and she walked back to Roslazny in the cold blue glow of starlight. She made her way home as quickly as possible, and cooked a hurried meal for Mikhail from the shoulder of beef Popov had sold her for a few hundred roubles earlier that week. She gave him an extra-large glass of vodka with his dinner, so that he wouldn't pick up on her haste. Soon he was installed in the living room with the television blaring at full volume. He barely noticed when she left.

She glanced at her watch before leaving the house. It was still a little early for respectable people to go out drinking – but, then, Glazkov wasn't very respectable. So she went ahead with her plan and took up a position opposite Café Astana, hiding behind a rusty oil tank outside a derelict house. She looked on as the regulars arrived, heads hunched into their shoulders against the cold. There was Fyodor Katin, with his typewriter under his arm, and Popov the butcher; then Alexeyev the mechanic with his friends, several still in bandages after their battle with Bogdan's associates, and others who came from different parts of the village but with the same aim in mind.

She watched her frosted breath rising in the night. It had always struck her how strange it was to see breath become visible like that. It was such an intimate thing. Only we can occupy the space we are in, she thought, and only we can draw in this parcel of air and expel it again, building up columns of icy vapour that hang above us like a second self. But those second selves are as opaque as the bodies they come from, thought Olga. They, too, surrender no secrets. And there were many secrets to be uncovered if the truth was ever to be known about the murders of Nathan Bryce and Alyona Vasiliev – secrets in Roslazny and Kemerovo, on the railway and in the police force, in the forest and in the city . . .

Everyone has secrets. Glazkov must have a good few, thought Olga. Nobody could be a local policeman for as long as he had without accumulating skeletons in the closet. He must have looked the other way once or twice, or discreetly closed a minor case in exchange for cash in an envelope – quite apart from any larger scheme he might have become involved with more recently. She knew from the papers that policemen often did favours for friends in high places, ranging from covering up fraud and corruption to personal involvement in organised crime and murders. It was quite common for people to be run out of business on some trumped-up technicality, with assets shared between policemen, judges and local politicians. But Glazkov was surely too incompetent to run something big like that. Someone smarter would be in charge, and Glazkov would be a dogsbody, at best. I need to be careful, she thought. There are bigger fish to fry than Anatoly Glazkov.

Thirty minutes after she arrived, Olga decided to give up and go home. She could talk to Vassily another day, after all.

He wasn't going anywhere, whereas she might well be going to hospital if she ignored the intense cold in her fingers and toes for another minute – and nobody wanted to go to hospital in Tayga if they could possibly avoid it. She began to emerge from behind the tank. But then she shuffled back into hiding again, as quickly and quietly as she could, for in the corner of her eye she'd seen a familiar uniformed figure approaching in the distance, walking slowly into the pool of light that surrounded the café and then disappearing into its warmth. Finally she could be sure that Glazkov was safely inside, rather than patrolling the village; finally she could be sure of an extended period alone with Vassily.

Olga waited for a minute or two, just to be certain. Then she extracted herself at last from behind the oil tank and set off to the police station, jogging down the road that led past the old bathhouse to warm her frozen limbs. The dilapidated building reminded her that she still needed to decide whether to tell Anna about Bogdan's all-too-personal involvement in making a particular kind of video. It was dark and empty that evening, but no doubt they would be at it again before long.

She decided she'd think about telling Anna another time, ignoring an inner voice that said decisions to delay decisions were not really decisions. But she had more pressing things to deal with that evening. There was a policeman's reputation, indeed his very freedom, at stake. And she was too cold to think about more than one difficult thing – too cold to do anything very much, except run until some warmth returned to her frozen extremities.

After a few minutes she came to the police station and slowed to a walk. She tried to control her breathing, feeling that the clouds of frosted vapour, her own second self, made her conspicuous in the wan light that streamed from the low windows. She looked around her, but could see nothing except darkness and the faint outlines of abandoned houses that seemed to bow under the weight of snow on their roofs. A host of people might be watching her, and she would never know. She felt a strong temptation to give up on the whole enterprise, and almost turned to go home. But she found herself stepping forward instead.

The door offered some resistance when she tried the handle, but she managed to shoulder it aside. She stepped inside, taking in the ancient décor and faded posters. It was dingy but it wasn't filthy, as she'd half expected. Someone had tried to clean the place – probably Vassily, for she couldn't imagine Glazkov wielding a dustpan and brush.

Beyond the desk that served as the reception there was a door that led to the cells. Glazkov had left it open, and she could see a row of bars, half lit by what looked like a paraffin lamp, and the end of a bench that served as a bed for a prisoner. On the bench rested a pair of feet, clad in thick woollen socks. The feet lifted and swung to the floor.

'Glazkov?' said a voice. 'Drunk Odrosov dry at last, have you?'

Olga walked forward, her heart beating faster as she approached. It was ridiculous, she thought, to be so excited about seeing Vassily again.

'It's me, Olga Pushkin.' She stood in the doorway, and Vassily looked at her in astonishment.

'Miss *Pushkin*,' he said, jumping to his feet. 'What on earth are you doing here?'

'That's no way to greet a lady, Sergeant,' she said, smiling at him. 'Especially a lady who's come to help you.'

'Yes – sorry – I— To help me?' stammered Vassily. 'What do you mean?'

'I mean, the fact that you're behind bars when you should be putting other people behind them,' she said. 'I mean that other policemen should be under investigation, not you.'

'Look, Miss Pushkin,' said Vassily, sitting on the bench again, 'I'm touched at your faith in me. But—'

'But nothing,' she said. 'We went to school together, didn't we? We Roslazny folk have to stick together! And we need good men like you in the police, with the likes of Anatoly Glazkov and Grigor Babikov around. And what about that *provodnitsa*, Ivanka Kozar? The one you suspected – remember? You tapped your lip.'

'I tapped my lip?'

'After you and Glazkov interviewed her at Tayga station, you got up and tapped your lip three times, staring after her, as if you wanted to call her back. I thought maybe it meant something – that you suspected her. She has three golden teeth—'

'So she does,' interrupted Vassily. 'But that wasn't what was on my mind.'

'Well, what *were* you thinking of, then?'

'I had toothache that day,' said Vassily. 'And I probably got up because I'd forgotten to get her contact details. A few of them didn't give us a phone number, or their address. Sloppy, I know, but it was hard keeping on top of the paperwork with an aching jaw and a hung-over Glazkov.'

'Oh,' said Olga, feeling rather deflated. Perhaps being a detective was more difficult than she'd thought. It was always possible to misinterpret things, she reminded herself, and the obvious explanation isn't necessarily the correct one.

She shook her head. 'Well, I'm sure the details, the evidence, the *truth* will prove your innocence, if we can just get to them.'

Vassily was smiling despite himself. Olga's involvement with the investigation had clearly whetted an appetite for detective work. But she didn't understand the complexities. How could she? 'Miss Pushkin, why don't you sit down?' he said, gesturing towards a wooden chair opposite his cell. 'I can't ask you to help me. And the reason is simple. I'm guilty.'

Olga sat down with a bump. 'You're *guilty*?' she said. 'Guilty of *murder*?'

'Yes, I'm guilty of murder – or, at least, I am as far as Babikov's concerned. He just hasn't got the proof yet. But I'm guilty of other crimes, too, in reality.' He grimaced. 'I can't talk about it. Like I said the other day, I'm not allowed to discuss ongoing investigations. If I tell you any details, I'll only incriminate myself further – and you, too, by association. And there's – well, there's other things that you'd be better off not knowing. Babikov would have no problem roping you into his pantomime, believe me.'

She looked at him intensely, as if she could assess his character by doing so. She knew that didn't always work – old Vladimir Solotov looked like a saint in an icon, until he was alone with a woman – but she could have sworn that Vassily had the face of a good man. No, she told herself, as she studied his eyes, his firm jaw, his lined cheeks and forehead. He *was* a good man. Nobody could look like that and not have suffered. And wasn't suffering the key to goodness? Olga had never met anybody who was good who had not suffered.

'Vassily,' she said, 'I can call you that, can't I? And you must call me Olga. Vassily, you must tell me everything. I can help you, I *know* it. I don't care about the risks. You're a good man, and good men deserve a helping hand. And you're a good man who *needs* help. Isn't that obvious? Don't you want to get out of jail? Isn't someone – someone special – waiting for you? The woman who gave you that golden ring on your finger, perhaps.'

Vassily looked away. 'I don't have a wife. And I don't have a child, either,' he said. 'I had a son, Kliment, and Rozalina was my wife. But not any more. I lost them. They were taken from me.' He looked back at her, his eyes boring into hers. 'They were taken from me, long ago. And I've worked ever since to get them back. I've done all kinds of things, Miss Pushkin – Olga, I mean.'

'I'm sure whatever you did was justified, Vassily,' said Olga.

'Listen,' said Vassily, 'I've already told you I'm guilty – not of murder, but of other things just as bad as murder, in some people's eyes. Worse, maybe, under the current regime. I could be *executed* – unofficially, of course. But death by covert arrangement in prison, a plastic knife under the ribs in the lunchtime canteen queue, that's no different from a firing-squad, in the end.'

'What did you do?' she said. 'What are these things, Vassily Marushkin, that you're guilty of?'

Vassily looked at her. He could be putting his life at risk all over again if he confided in the woman before him. He wondered, in turn, if she had the face of a good woman. But why would she have come, if she were not a good woman? How could she possibly benefit from helping him, if it were not from the satisfaction of virtue realised and duty fulfilled?

He decided to trust her. They had been at school together, after all. 'I'd hardly know where to start if I tried to tell you everything,' he said. 'But the last thing I did? Two weeks ago I broke into the military archives in Novosibirsk.'

'You did *what*?' said Olga, horrified on Vassily's behalf. She knew, from her brother Pasha, how far the military would go to preserve its secrets.

'Yes, I broke in,' he said, breathing out slowly, and feeling an immense weight lift from his shoulders. Colonel Terekhin had guessed the reason for Vassily's career path, but even he didn't know the lengths to which Vassily had gone to find his family. Finally he was shedding the burden of concealment and opening his heart to another person after almost two decades of solitude.

'You see,' he went on, 'it was an old soldier, a man called Pavel Prokofy, who kidnapped my wife and son. I've been on Prokofy's trail for fourteen years, and I thought maybe there'd be something on him in those archives. They wouldn't give me access, so I broke in. But there wasn't anything there – it was just another dead end. It was all for nothing. I put my life at risk again for no reason, just like I did in so many other places – Novosibirsk, Ekaterinburg, Perm ... And always with the same result: *nimalo*. Nothing at all. Gone without a trace, like a stone dropped down a well with no bottom.'

They sat in silence for a minute, Olga uncertain what to say, and Vassily staring into the darkness beyond the bars. Confessing his sins to Olga was a great relief, but it did little to assuage the pain of his loss, which had long since taken on the character of a bitter and prolonged bereavement.

'Well,' said Olga, eventually, 'it sounds to me like you've only done what anyone would do, in the circumstances.'

He smiled gratefully at her, and she went on: 'But, Vassily, does Babikov know about any of those things?'

'Oh, no,' said Vassily. 'Not as far as I'm aware. But now I've been arrested, he'll start digging up my past, and who knows what he'll find? At least he'll get nothing out of Terekhin.'

'Terekhin?' said Olga, thinking the name sounded familiar.

'Colonel Terekhin,' said Vassily. 'He was here most of yesterday, and this morning, too. He's my boss in Novosibirsk – I'm only here on a six-month secondment.'

Of course – Babikov had mentioned Terekhin to Olga that morning. And she remembered the stranger she'd seen inside the police station before Glazkov closed the door. 'Is he about sixty? And bald, with a big moustache?'

'Yes, that's him. You saw him at the station? He outranks Babikov – though it doesn't always work like that, in different patches. But, regardless, Terekhin's high enough up the greasy pole to make Babikov play by the rules, and that's all I wanted.'

'What do you mean?' said Olga.

'I got Terekhin over here myself,' said Vassily. 'I managed to text him when I was arrested, before they took my phone away. He came straight to Tayga. Got here just in time. Well, just in time for Ivanka. But he managed to help me, too. He cast enough doubt over the evidence to get me held here at Roslazny over the next few days. It's thanks to him I wasn't thrown in some hell-hole regional jail. Those aren't pretty places for coppers. And he stopped Babikov broadcasting my arrest on TV – said there'd be a lawsuit if I turned out to be innocent. Thank God for Colonel Terekhin.'

Olga blinked, trying to process what Vassily was telling her.

'So – wait,' she said. 'Ivanka was here, too? In prison – in Roslazny?'

'No,' said Vassily. 'At the station in Tayga. But she's gone now – back on the railway, I suppose. They didn't say she couldn't.' Then, seeing the bewilderment on Olga's face, he said, 'Maybe I'd better start again.'

'Please do,' said Olga.

'Well, someone's trying to frame us – me and Ivanka Kozar, I mean – for the murders of Nathan Bryce and Alyona Vasiliev. It must be the murderer, I suppose, trying to shift the blame. Though why he picked us I can't imagine. Anyway, it all kicked off last night. Or a little earlier, depending on how you count it. It was in the afternoon they found the fabric, you see.'

'The *fabric*?' said Olga.

'Yes, they got a tip-off, says Babikov, and found a bit of material from a sergeant's tunic stuck on a thorny bush outside Vasiliev's house. The crime-scene itself was clean as a whistle, but Babikov claims someone walked by, saw the material on the bush, and called it in. And then, acting on another tip-off, Babikov's men did a search of the abandoned buildings around the station here in Roslazny, and just *happened* to find an old tunic of mine in the house across the way, with a missing bit of fabric matching the patch on the bush. I'd noticed the tunic was missing, but it was so old I hadn't bothered to look for it.'

'So someone tipped off the police, twice, about more or less the same thing? Didn't they think that was a bit suspicious?'

'Are you kidding?' said Vassily. 'Babikov's desperate to solve these murders, especially with his precious election coming up. He'll jump on anything he can get, even something circumstantial like a piece of fabric. It's not enough to convict, by itself, but even with Terekhin onside it was enough to keep me in here, pending further investigations. I don't have an alibi, after all, for the night of Vasiliev's murder. I was just here, with Rasputin, minding my own business. Do you know what "alibi" actually means? It means "in another place" – to have been somewhere else. But I was in this place. And things would've looked pretty bleak if the case against Ivanka had held up.'

'The case against Ivanka?'

'The ex-case,' said Vassily. 'It was thrown out, thanks to Colonel Terekhin – but only just.' He sat forward. 'You remember I looked at some people's phones at Tayga – phones belonging to the crew? It's what we do in Novosibirsk, but some little devil must have picked up on it and whispered an idea into the ears of the Kemerovo police. Maybe it was another tip-off from whoever's trying to frame us. If so, it was pretty well directed, coming right after the miraculous discovery of an incriminating tunic in a nearby house. You see, Babikov looked on my phone and found a whole folder of messages I'd never seen in my life, from a certain *Ivanka K*. Once Babikov saw those, they had good reason to arrest Ivanka Kozar – or so it seemed.'

'And those messages were pretty convincing, I'll bet,' said Olga, putting on her detective hat once more. 'Yes, yes – let me guess: they made it look like you and Ivanka were working together. That you'd decided Alyona Vasiliev had to die. That you'd decided to kill her by hanging her in her own house!'

'That was part of it,' said Vassily. 'But there was a lot more stuff, too. Like I said, the killer's trying to frame us for Bryce's murder as well as Vasiliev's. And they tried to use the messages to tie the cases together. They made it look like one murder had led to the other, because Alyona Vasiliev saw us killing Bryce on the train. And then of course she had to go, too. We were just being professional, tying up loose ends. And as soon as Babikov realised the killer was trying to frame us, he pounced. He's trying to finish the job the murderer started, you see. Probably he got his PR man to make up a story to fit the facts and pin us to the wall. And as far as I can make out from Babikov's line of questioning, this is how the story's meant to go: Ivanka Kozar and I were in cahoots because she wanted a tourist killed on the railway. It didn't matter who, or why. The details of her motive could be worked out later.'

'Are you sure that's the story?' interrupted Olga. 'They didn't mention anything like that on TV last week. They were going on about how the murderer had chosen Nathan Bryce because he was American, or because he was rich, or both.'

'Of course they didn't mention it,' said Vassily. 'They never tell you the final story first! They like sending you off in the wrong direction. Then, when they spring the big reveal, it's more exciting. And if it's more exciting, it's more believable. It's like movie directors putting together a thriller. It's all about the twist.'

Olga nodded and bit her lip, thinking hard. This was interesting. She had always known she would have to master the art of plotting a narrative – how else would she write the next Great Russian Novel, while studying literature at Tomsk State University? But she hadn't expected to learn about storytelling in the course of a murder investigation.

'As I was saying,' resumed Vassily, 'Babikov's story was that Ivanka wanted someone killed on the railway. Then she had to get me on the payroll, because she'd need to dispose of the body, once she'd thrown it off the train. And who better than a bent copper – a.k.a. yours truly – to get rid of it, no questions asked? And where better than somewhere quiet and remote like Roslazny, where the bent copper in question can operate in peace? So, of course, I got myself posted over here, by asking Babikov to persuade Terekhin to let me go. No record of me asking Babikov that, but there's no record of it *not* happening, either. Then Ivanka stuffed Bryce's mouth with money and threw his body off the train, for two reasons, says Babikov: first, to pay me off, in dramatic style, and second, to sign the murder.'

'To *sign* it?'

'Yes – killers often do that. Serial killers, anyway. It's a fingers-up to the police. And in this case it's meant to be a very literal signature. She has golden teeth, for God's sake. Anyway, as Babikov seems to see it, I was meant to come along, pick up the body, pocket the cash and hide the weapon – although, as you may remember, we didn't find a knife anywhere near Bryce's body. That was the plan, as Babikov tells it, but then you happened along, and Glazkov soon afterwards, and upset all my plans. There were too many people around for me to get away with hiding the body. I saw the game was up, and started investigating the murder as if I'd had nothing to do with it.'

Olga tried to process what he had said. It was a story told by Vassily about a story made up by Babikov about a story made up by the killer, who was trying, for unfathomable reasons, to frame Vassily and Ivanka for his own crimes . . . Once again she reflected on how difficult, how *complicated*, detective work could be.

After a minute she said: 'But what about the samovar? How's Babikov going to claim that Ivanka killed anyone when she was working on her samovar with that engineer, Zonov, all morning?'

'How did you know about that?' exclaimed Vassily.

Olga was embarrassed. She hadn't meant to let Vassily know she'd been eavesdropping on his interviews at Tayga station after Bryce's murder, but there was no point in pretending now. 'Well,' she said awkwardly, 'I heard you say something to Ivanka at Tayga. I was standing nearby having a coffee. And that other man was there, the engineer, something Zonov.'

'Hmm,' said Vassily. 'I'll have to watch what I say from now on, Olga Pushkin! You don't miss much. But you're right: the samovar *did* make things difficult for Babikov. That's why they arrested us for Alyona's murder instead. I think the big idea is still to pin the Bryce murder on me and Ivanka, later on. Imagine the headlines! An evil golden-toothed *provodnitsa* working with a corrupt policeman, a dead tourist's mouth stuffed with coins, death on the Trans-Siberian Express . . . But Babikov can't pin the crime on anyone yet. And no suspect means no headlines. So I think Babikov wanted to work backwards. First he'd frame Ivanka and me for the Vasiliev murder, and once he'd got us tarred as murderers he'd say we must've done Bryce, too. He'd sketch the picture and fill in the details later. It's already a good story. And, you know, I think he'd have got away with it. People would fix on the ten-rouble coins and accept the rest as background noise. I can't imagine too many judges round here having the guts to overturn that line of argument, especially when put by a chief of police with a chance of becoming Mayor of Kemerovo. Yes, he nearly got away with it.'

Olga nodded, thinking hard as she tried to piece together the various parts of the picture in her mind. She looked quite beautiful, thought Vassily with a twinge of self-reproach, her head tilted sideways as if to see things more clearly, and with strands of hair curving around her cheek. He reached forward and turned down the paraffin lamp, which had begun to sputter as the wick burned to its end. The light diminished yet further, and the cell's harsh features were softened to the point of disappearance. Even the iron bars between them faded into darkness, as if they were just sitting and talking in a room together.

But then her eyes widened in horror. 'What's that?' she cried, jumping up and pointing at something that had begun to move around in the darkness under Vassily's bench. 'Oh, it's a rat!'

Vassily laughed. 'It's only Rasputin. He must've woken up after his evening nap. Come on, boy. Say hello to Olga.' He lifted up a cage to reveal the ferret, which blinked up at them, dazed and disoriented after his long sleep.

Olga gasped. 'Oh, put him back!' she said. 'I thought he'd have been taken away, once you were arrested.'

'To where?' said Vassily, picking up Rasputin. 'I live at the station now, and this cell's my bedroom. Though usually I can open the door when I want . . . Look, he's a cuddly little fellow, really, aren't you, Rasputin?'

He smiled at Olga, but she didn't smile back. 'Well, all right, then, you'd better go into your cage until the lady goes away,' said Vassily to Rasputin. He put the ferret back into his cage and put him into the cell next door, safely out of sight.

'How you can keep such a creature? Didn't you know they eat hedgehogs?'

'They've got to eat something,' said Vassily. 'And what's so special about hedgehogs?'

'I've got a pet hedgehog.'

'Ah,' said Vassily. 'That is a shame. Not everyone can manage a superior animal like a ferret, I suppose. Anyway,' he hurried on, 'you guessed right. About the text messages they found on my phone, I mean. It fits with the story – with me and Ivanka taking care of loose ends. So Vasiliev had to die.'

'I suppose so,' said Olga. 'But why was Ivanka released, while you're still here?'

'She was released because the framers got it wrong,' said Vassily. 'By chance Ivanka had changed her phone contract a few days before Vasiliev's body was found, and had a new number. Colonel Terekhin told me himself – he was at her interview in Tayga. And since Terekhin was there, Babikov had to follow up with Rostelecom, the service provider. Turns out she was right. The old number hadn't been used since she got a new one – except for the fake messages in my phone. They searched her house, too, but found nothing. Place was like a showroom, Glazkov said. Clinical, almost. So they had to let her go. She's back at work, on the Trans-Siberian. Probably halfway to Vladivostok by now.

'Yes, the killer got it wrong, when he tried to frame Ivanka Kozar,' he continued. 'Babikov was spitting fire yesterday when he realised he had to let her go – no golden-toothed Trans-Siberian killer for Wolansky to spin – and he was even angrier when Terekhin imposed a news blackout on Vasiliev's death, and stopped him running to his tame reporters to get my arrest on the evening news.'

'Who's Wolansky?' said Olga.

'Babikov's PR man,' said Vassily. 'Not sure what his first name is – I don't think I've ever heard it. Everyone just calls him

Wolansky. Short, pointy beard, shaggy hair, wears boots – like an eccentric professor, or an Irish leprechaun. He's even got a tinge of red in his hair. And he's quirky – the type who wears odd socks on purpose. You've probably seen him on TV, standing next to Babikov – Grigor, he calls him – at some press conference or other.'

So Wolansky was the small man Olga had seen at Tayga station, marshalling the reporters and doing important business on his smartphone. She'd been right, then, that he was more than a PA. Another feather in her detective's cap!

'So much for Babikov's story,' said Vassily. 'But it's just a story. Someone else knows what *really* happened – maybe more than one person. Somebody sent those messages to my phone, and somebody had to steal my tunic, tear off the fabric, stick it on that bush outside Vasiliev's house, then hide the rest in the house across the way before tipping off the police. And, of course, somebody had to kill Bryce and Vasiliev in the first place. But we don't know who that somebody is, and Babikov doesn't care, as long as he gets a couple of names to trumpet in his damn press conferences. It's just me saying I'm not guilty, and nothing to prove it.'

'Haven't you thought about who'd want to frame you, Vassily?' said Olga. 'You must have a lot of enemies from past cases – people you've put in prison.'

Vassily shook his head. 'I've been thinking about that,' he said. 'I've run through all the cases I can remember, but I can't think of anyone who'd go to all this trouble instead of just putting a bullet in my head one night on a quiet street in Roslazny or Tayga. It doesn't make sense to get revenge this way. It's too complicated, and too doubtful. I mean, look what's happened – Terekhin was able to stop Babikov making a song and dance about me on TV, because the evidence isn't strong enough. What kind of payback is that?'

'Well, what about Ivanka Kozar?' said Olga. 'She's the other half of your criminal double act. Maybe she's got some enemies.'

'True,' he admitted, 'but I can't imagine a *provodnitsa* making enemies on a scale like this. Seems unlikely to me.'

'But not impossible,' said Olga. 'You say you've been through your past, thinking about who it could be. Maybe we need to do the same for her. Maybe she was the target all along, and you got mixed up in it by mistake, or as a means to an end.'

She stood and walked up and down beside the three tiny cells. 'Somebody, somewhere, knows something, and it's our job to find out what it is, that's all. The murders both involved Ivanka Kozar, in one way or another. If someone did want to frame her, there must be a reason why they picked her, and not some other *provodnitsa*. They work in twos, don't they? So why her and not her partner—'

'Yelena something,' put in Vassily. 'Yes – Yelena Koriakin. We talked to her as well. But she was spotless.'

'Why Ivanka Kozar and not her partner,' continued Olga, 'even if it's only that Ivanka's golden teeth would help them to frame her? That would still tell us something about them, wouldn't it?'

'I suppose so,' admitted Vassily. 'I suppose she could be worth looking into a little more. And Ivanka's a woman, too.'

'What difference does that make?' asked Olga.

'Oh, just something Terekhin said,' replied Vassily, quickly. 'Some rumours he'd heard about a female serial killer operating in the sticks.'

'Because, of course, Roslazny and Tayga are "the sticks" to important sergeants from Novosibirsk.'

Vassily laughed. 'I just mean it'd make sense to frame a woman working in more – more *rustic* areas, because of all the rumours.'

'Well, luckily for you, I know a lot of people in *rustic* areas,' said Olga. 'And on the railways, too. I'm sure I can find something to fill in Ivanka's background while she's away. And then we can interview her when she gets back from Vladivostok.'

But Vassily shook his head. It was difficult for him to trust in hope, after all the fruitless years he'd spent searching for his family. 'I think you're letting your imagination run away with you, Olga,' he said. 'I know people like to believe that the truth will out, or that justice will be done, or whatever cliché you want, but it doesn't happen that way. I'm sorry, but I've been a policeman for a lot of years now, and it just doesn't. Not in Russia, anyway.'

'Perhaps it hasn't so far,' said Olga. 'That doesn't mean it can't in the future. Look, we *know* you're innocent. So the truth is still waiting for us to find it. Out there,' she added, gesturing at the window in the cell wall, barred and glazed, through which only the snowy outline of an abandoned house was visible, and above it a single glimmering star.

'I don't think there's much chance of you finding it,' said Vassily. 'I mean, well, I can't help you, stuck in here. And you're not a copper, so you can't access the usual resources – records, databases, networks . . .'

'Maybe not,' said Olga. 'But sometimes you have to take a different approach. You have to think creatively, like a wr– like someone with imagination.'

Olga didn't want to tell Vassily that she was a writer until she had more to show for it. A published book, perhaps, or a place at Tomsk State University. She had too much pride to let him think of her as some kind of tragic dreamer. That was Fyodor Katin's fate, not hers.

'I suppose that's true,' said Vassily. 'They didn't put it quite like that at the Police Academy. But just try to keep it in check. Policework's more about elimination than imagination.'

She smiled and put her hand between the bars. 'Partners, then?' she said.

Vassily shook his head in bewilderment. An hour ago he'd been lying on the bench in mute despair, awaiting his fate – trial, or prison, or worse. And now he was looking at Olga, her eyes shining in the lamplight, her face full of energy and determination. She was just a civilian – a railway worker. What could she do against a serial killer and the entire police force of Kemerovo Province? But, then, what other choice did he have?

He shrugged, smiled, and shook her outstretched hand. If the choices were trusting Olga or giving in to despair, he'd try trusting Olga.

'Partners,' he said.

11

Olga Investigates

The following day, a Thursday, was one of Olga's rare days off. Viktor Fandorin, the foreman at Tayga station, was responsible for drawing up the rotas for the trackside engineers, and always made sure that third-class ones, like Olga, received the minimum amount of leave mandated by law. His reasoning was simple: the more engineers on duty, the less likely things were to go wrong; and if everything ran smoothly, it was less likely that he would be discovered absent from the office on one of his frequent trips to Misha's nightclub on Privokzalnaya Ulitsa. Misha had recently got some new girls in, girls with Arctic skin and high cheekbones from the far eastern reaches of the country – Kamchatka, or somewhere exotic like that – and Viktor couldn't resist appreciating their charms during long luncheons, or elevenses, or afternoon teas, or all three combined. But even Viktor couldn't deprive his engineers of all leave. He was obliged, by law, to write 'H' for holiday beside one day for every five weeks on each engineer's rota. And this Thursday it was Olga's turn.

Usually she spent her days off reading in bed at home or, on the rare occasions when she allowed herself to spend the money, on trips to Tomsk. On those days she would walk alone into Tayga and buy the cheapest ticket for the train, just as she and her mother used to do, long ago. In the city, she would go to a café near the university, where she would order the cheapest item on the menu and linger over it, dreaming of life as a budding writer. After an hour or two she would walk around the campus to admire the buildings, before visiting the admissions office for updates on course fees and starting dates. If she could, she would sneak into the back of a lecture hall in the languages department and sit for a while, imagining herself a student like all the others, wearing strange clothes and reading interesting books with incomprehensible titles. She would dream of a different life for a few hours, until it was time to walk to the station and get the train back to Tayga, then walk to Roslazny and the house she shared with her father.

But today would be very different from her usual holiday routine. Today she was trying to pick up the trail of a ruthless killer, a man – she presumed it was a man, despite the rumours Vassily had heard, because most of the horrible things in the world were done by men – a man who would stop at nothing, it seemed, until some other person or persons had paid in full for his crimes. With Vassily imprisoned, it was her job to make sure that didn't happen – and not just for Vassily's sake, but because it was the right thing to do. She didn't want people from other countries thinking Russia was a terrible place, full of thieves and murderers, and criminals who made others pay for their wrongdoing. Whatever Vladimir Solotov and the others might say, Olga knew that Putin had made Russia unpopular enough in the world, without a railway murderer in Kemerovo Province making things worse. But if Olga spent the day finding out about Ivanka Kozar, the golden-toothed *provodnitsa* with jittery manners and a helpful smile, perhaps she could do something to redress the balance. If she could find out why the murderer had decided to frame Ivanka as well as Vassily, she could help show people from those other countries – the Germans and the Americans and even, grudgingly, the Dutch – that the Russians could keep their house in order, that Russia wasn't just a Wild West run by the Kremlin and the army.

The army, she thought, with a sinking feeling. *Pasha.*

When she woke up that morning, she realised she'd completely forgotten to ask Vassily about Pasha's dishonourable discharge. The excitement of conspiring with Vassily to fight for justice had driven her brother out of her mind. That, and, if she was honest with herself, the way Vassily's eyes had glowed in the pale lamplight, and the way he had spoken to her in the tumbledown police station on the abandoned road that led to nowhere in particular.

It was true that being accused of murder was more serious than being discharged from the army, but still it seemed unforgivable to cast aside a much-loved brother in favour of a man she barely knew. But, then, Vassily was a good man who'd been deprived of his family by an old soldier, this Pavel Prokofy character. Surely Pasha would understand that the honour of the army was at stake. Pasha might even know Pavel Prokofy, she reflected. Stranger things had happened. She resolved to ask him when he returned from Crimea. But other things had to come first.

She felt an unaccustomed thrill running through her as she got dressed that morning and ate a hurried breakfast. Was it horrible to be exhilarated at the prospect of chasing down a murderer? No, she told herself, as she pulled on her boots. It would be horrible to be excited by doing the murdering. And anyway, hadn't Olga spent enough time on the same old things, the same job, errands, chores and duties? Didn't life owe her a little excitement?

Popov the butcher was one of the few people in Roslazny who owned a car, and by paying him an exorbitant sum the night before, Olga had arranged its use for her expedition. She left the house straight after breakfast and made her way to the Popov residence, where an Opel Corsa with a 2002 registration awaited her. She found the keys under the rock near the butcher's front door, just where Popov had said they would be. She started the engine, trying to ignore the strong smell of rotting meat that filled the dingy interior. Then she got out again, to scrape the ice off the windscreen. Finally she got back in and put the car jerkily into gear, trying to remember what order the gears were in and how to work the clutch.

The skies had stayed clear from the night before, and the low winter sun was in her eyes as she set out on the three-mile drive to Tayga. But she didn't mind. On days like this, when the pale sunlight turned the snowy fields into dazzling golden carpets set beneath a sky of purest chalk-blue, Olga could dream she was a little girl again, laughing and running with her mother Tatiana hand in hand through untouched snow-blankets in carefree winters long ago. Then, later, they would collapse exhausted in front of a crackling fire, and her mother would tell her tales of the Lodge at Astrazov, of the old housekeeper Lubov and the woodsmen, of Count Lichnovsky and the dowager countess, and fairy tales of old Russia, with tsarinas and swans and magical creatures that could not be trusted. She smiled as Popov's car bumped along the narrow road, her eyes distant from the muddy, rutted surface and the leafless trees beside the pathway.

Her smile faded as she remembered her mother's sickness and, before that, how her happiness had dwindled away with the passing of the years. Olga had not understood at the time, but now, looking back with an adult's eyes, she saw how unhappy Mikhail had made her with his absences, his drinking, his abusive language and behaviour. Perhaps he had *made* her sick, she thought for the first time. Not literally – not even Mikhail was capable of poisoning his wife – but he had made her sick, maybe, in the way one can make a plant die by putting it in a dark cupboard. The princess had married the woodsman, but she hadn't known that the woodsman was already married. He was married to vodka and indolence, money and sin.

'*Suka, blyad!*' she swore, as she had done when she received the hateful letter. There was nobody to hear her in the car, driving alone along the muddy track with the frozen fields beyond. So she cursed with wild abandon, freeing all the resentment and anger that had piled up within her against her father, day after day, month after month, year after year. All these old men in her life, and Mikhail the worst of them all. He had destroyed her mother, sent his son away to the army, and imprisoned his daughter in a cage, a prison of a life in Roslazny, so she could attend to his every need. Well, no more, she said to herself. When this business with the murders was over, and Vassily Marushkin was free, she and her father would have words. Maybe Anna would have words with Bogdan, once she found out what was going on. And Olga would get Vassily to help with tracking down her letter-writer. Then she would have words with them, too. Things were going to change in Roslazny, and for the better.

That was what she'd said to Vassily the night before, after she and Vassily had declared themselves partners. But she felt less confident now, as she made her way cautiously through the outskirts of Tayga and down the streets that led to the centre of the town. What had seemed exciting the night before, sitting in the lamplit police station with Vassily, seemed daunting on her own in the cold morning light.

It took all her courage to make herself carry on driving through Tayga towards the town centre, to cross the square and park in front of the station, and finally to walk through the high doors out onto the platform in search of her friend Ekaterina.

'Ekaterina Chezhekov,' called Olga, as she spotted her. Her voice betrayed her relief: she was nervous about her proposed activities for the day, and felt in need of a familiar face.

'There you are, Olga Pushkin,' said Ekaterina, with a smile. She was a short, round woman of indeterminate age, with a face that could have weathered forty winters or sixty. She had a scarf wrapped around her hair and a fur collar pulled up over her ears against the cold. She was smoking, as usual – Olga thought she must smoke more cigarettes than she ever sold – and was standing in the lee of a small cabin that sold hot food, talking to Burian Menandrov, one of the porters who carried tourists' bags across the bridges for a handful of roubles.

Olga beckoned her over. She made her excuses to Burian and came bustling across. 'How are you, my friend?' she said. 'Did you sleep, after we talked last night?'

'Not much,' said Olga. 'But I'll be fine when you tell me Viktor Fandorin's not here.'

Ekaterina made an expressive noise. 'Ha! Of course he's not. I told him about that new girl from Vladivostok at Misha's, like you said, and he was off like a shot.'

This was excellent news, for Olga had a plan that would be immeasurably facilitated by Fandorin's absence. But it was also terrifying, for now, after fifteen years' conscientious work at Roslazny, Olga was about to break railway regulations for the first time.

To Ekaterina's astonishment, Olga reached over and plucked a cigarette from an open packet. She put it to her lips and lit it, inhaling deeply and closing her eyes.

'Hey, you don't smoke!' said Ekaterina. 'Or – do you?'

'I used to,' replied Olga. 'And I'm smoking again today. I need to steady my nerves. Give me ten packets from your box. No, not for me! I've got a signalman to bribe.'

Thirty minutes later the Trans-Siberian came into view, the bright red engine visible from afar. The platforms shuddered underfoot as the vast weight drew near, the carriage brakes squealing as the six-thousand-ton juggernaut swayed over the junctions, wheels clattering in shrill metallic voices as they navigated the thin steel tracks and their interweavings, the couplings straining and banging as the endless train came finally to rest beside the low concrete platform. The usual hubbub ensued, with hundreds of people getting off just as hundreds of different people tried to get on. Crew and passengers thronged the narrow aisles, the alighting passengers loaded down with their luggage and blocking the way for the impatient guards and *provodnitsi*, and tourists who wanted to get off for a quick photo and some hot food from the carts. On the platform, the loud voices of the cigarette and food vendors vied with the porters advertising their services and the booming sound of a station announcement, at once deafening and incomprehensible. Meanwhile, the station dogs ran up and down the platform, hoping for scraps of food from kind-hearted tourists.

The train was scheduled to stop for twenty minutes. By the end of this period most of the excitement had died down, and the station announcer had fallen silent. The *provodnitsi* stood by their carriages, chivvying lingerers back on board with cold-eyed stares, and smoking sly cigarettes with their hands hidden by their sides. Soon they got back on board, pulling up the ladders behind them and closing the doors with loud bangs. But still the train did not depart.

Time passed, and people began to get restless. Tourists leaned out of whatever windows they could open, while the crew got on their radios and tried to find out what the hold-up was. But nobody seemed to know what was going on. Eventually the station manager and his staff came out of their offices on the platform, conferring with each other as to what was causing the delay, and making cross-sounding calls to signalling engineers. Finally, after another ten minutes or so, the train got the signal to depart, and rumbled into motion once more. As it began to move, a person – a woman in a fur-lined coat, with one hand inside her jacket – came out of an office towards the northern end of the station building and bustled towards the main exit. A freight train was coming in, but the woman didn't look up: she kept her head down and moved quickly on, almost running now, and disappeared through a door that led to the station café. The freight train thundered by, pulling fifty wagons of iron ore bound for Novosibirsk. When the Trans-Siberian service finally cleared the station, the woman was nowhere to be seen.

Olga closed the Corsa's door. 'One down, two to go,' she said, patting a dog-eared folder that lay on the passenger seat, displaying several semicircles from coffee mugs, and packed with variously sized pieces of paper – all the records Olga could find on Ivanka Kozar in the poky personnel office. She had parked a little way from the station, but she still felt nervous with the stolen materials on the seat beside her. Common sense dictated that she should start Popov's car and drive off. But common sense was nothing compared to curiosity.

She opened the folder and leafed through the records. 'Just a quick look,' she said to herself. 'Work rota and train schedules – that might be useful later. A promotion application – refused. Mandatory time-management course, after chronic lateness over several months . . . Another promotion application – also refused. Several leaves of absence, all stress-related . . . Passenger complaints – rudeness, missing blankets, poor service.'

She closed the folder and sat back. Ivanka Kozar, it seemed, was struggling. Olga had thought her a model employee, energetic, courteous and ever-smiling, but judging by these records she was on the brink of being fired. What had Ivanka said to Vassily, at Tayga station? Her mind was full of holes? Maybe she wasn't the type who could hold down a job. You never know, she said to herself. You just never know.

She turned the key in the ignition and drove jerkily away in a cloud of grey smoke. If he were to consult the archives, he would soon find an Ivanka Kozar-sized hole in them. But there seemed little chance of him looking at Ivanka's records, unless—

Fandorin himself might be involved, she realised. After all, it was Fandorin who'd sent Olga up the line on the morning Nathan Bryce had died, to investigate the jammed point mechanism. He must have expected that job to take longer than it had done – it would have taken many times as long, if it hadn't been for her father's trick of using lighter-fluid to warm the cylinder, and then Olga would have been nowhere near her hut when the body landed. And he'd expected her to confirm when she was coming back, but she hadn't been able to, because of the poor radio reception.

Come to think of it, how had that point jammed, anyway? Maybe Fandorin had jammed it himself, earlier that day, just to get her away from the hut. Her father Mikhail had said the points could jam if it was very cold, and if someone worked the switch too often. Had Fandorin been that someone? She brought his appearance to mind: a short man, not slender but not fat either, with a shaved head covered at all times with a peaked railway cap, red star pinned on the side, and close-set, dark and beady eyes above a fleshy nose and a straggling pepper-and-salt moustache, stained yellow around the mouth from endless cigarettes. Yes – he had the face of a man who would profess Communism till his dying day, and yet do anything for money. But on the other hand, that in itself was hardly proof of anything.

A blaring horn made her jump, and Olga realised she had fallen into a reverie, and nearly a ditch into the bargain. She slammed on the brakes, waved a hurried apology to the car behind her, and lurched back onto the road. She looked anxiously into the rear-view mirror, resolving to focus on driving and reserve thinking for other times. But that only brought her book to mind again, and specifically another life lesson she could add to the list. Life Lesson No.73: *Life goes best when we do one thing at a time. If we try to save time by doing two things at once, we might drive into a ditch – or come to the wrong conclusion.*

Olga liked this life lesson. Not only did it remind her to focus on driving while she was behind the wheel, but it aligned with her plan for the day, which she'd neatly written out that morning on the back of an old Russian Railways calendar:

1. *Obtain Ivanka's official personnel files, including recent work schedule*
2. *Speak to people who knew Ivanka when she was growing up*
3. *Speak to Ivanka's ex-boyfriend*

She'd already achieved the first objective, which seemed good going for ten in the morning. Vassily would be pleased: it was he who'd suggested the railway's personnel records might be useful. But she sensed the other two objectives might prove trickier.

It was inconvenient not being able to talk to the golden-toothed *provodnitsa* herself. It would be so much quicker, Olga thought, if she could sit down and communicate with her, woman to woman. She was sure that she would soon find out whatever had drawn the murderer to her, if she could just share a plate of gherkins and a few vodkas with her. Having to investigate Ivanka in her absence was frustrating. But what else could Olga do? Ivanka was far away in her little compartment, on a Trans-Siberian *spalny vagon* trundling to the Far East. That was life on the railways. All of them were ruled by time-tables and schedules that had been written by others.

From one point of view she was pleased that this necessity had arisen, since it echoed all the soap operas and police dramas she'd ever seen. It was a rule of daytime TV that basic detective leg-work was the starting point for every criminal investigation. And that always seemed to involve finding out about people's childhoods and talking to their partners. Items two and three on her list had practically written themselves.

Olga had been surprised to learn from Ekaterina the night before that Ivanka lived locally, probably within ten miles of Tayga. She thought she knew most of the crew who lived in the region, and she'd never met Ivanka at any social events with other staff. But Ekaterina had told her that Ivanka kept herself to herself, when she wasn't working, and that nobody knew exactly where she lived. The police knew, of course, but if their search of Ivanka's house had turned up nothing of interest, as Vassily had said, it was hardly worth Olga trying to access the property herself.

The only thing anyone knew about her, said Ekaterina, was that she'd been brought up in foster care in Yashkino, another railway town about ten miles from Tayga. Ivanka had let that slip one night years ago, when her train got stuck in a snow-drift and the heaters broke down. A friend of Ekaterina's, Julya Brentanov, had been on board, too, for romantic purposes – specifically, an assignation with the engine driver, Karol – and had told Ekaterina about it afterwards. The crew had tried to stay warm by sharing a bottle of Karol's home-made gin, which Julya said made Odrosov's Rocket Fuel taste like mineral water. After several glasses Ivanka had let her guard down, telling the others how her parents had died when she was eleven, the victims of a criminal gang who'd taken offence when her father refused a bribe at work. Ivanka had seemed a little strange when she'd told them about her parents' death, Julya said. She was wide-eyed and staring, gazing past them as if she could still see the terrible scene she'd discovered outside her front door when she came home from the village school one night. She had seemed oddly agitated, too, stimulated almost, as if she was telling them something that had happened that day rather than twenty years ago.

Ivanka had gone on to tell the crew of her adoption by an elderly local couple, said Julya Brentanov, and after that a series of foster families. But then she seemed to think she'd said too much, and fell into a silence she had rarely broken since. She never joined the other *provodnitsi* on their nights out in the Tayga bars, or attended any weddings, christenings or birthday celebrations that crew members organised locally. She kept her smiles for when it suited her, said Julya, and otherwise vanished from the station as soon as she could.

Olga found this surprising. Hadn't she seen Ivanka chatting to the other crew members at Tayga station, making jokes and jollying them along as they waited for Vassily to interview them? Maybe she had changed over time, thought Olga, or perhaps she had found it was advisable to be cheery rather than taciturn at work, given that her job was hanging in the balance. Yes, a successful career required a certain degree of acting, she mused.

Olga had thanked Ekaterina for the information and hung up, thinking it didn't give her very much to go on. But overnight, while she lay awake turning the case over in her mind, she'd had a flash of inspiration: she could go to the social services office in Yashkino, where Ivanka had been brought up, and make enquiries there. They might be reluctant to tell her anything at first, but Olga knew that civil servants who worked in places like that were poorly paid, and might not be averse to an exchange of cash for information. Consequently, when she set off to Popov's house to pick up his car on Thursday morning, she did so with a reasonably sized wad of 100-rouble notes in her handbag, taken from the emergency stash she kept under her mattress.

But she had shaken her head as she'd counted out the notes earlier that morning, asking herself what on earth she thought she was doing. Did she understand that she was planning to bribe state officials with her hard-earned savings, solely on the off-chance that she might – *might* – learn something useful about Ivanka Kozar?

And how, she'd also asked herself, will you decide what is useful and what is not? The information will hardly come pre-sorted into categories relevant to the investigation. You might get yourself into a good deal of trouble – *serious* trouble – in exchange for a carload of useless trivia about one of a thousand Russian Railways *provodnitsi*! That hardly seemed prudent. And hadn't her father Mikhail said that prudence is the Russian virtue?

But Olga was sick of thinking about what Mikhail said about this virtue or that duty. It was like hearing Putin extol the merits of democracy, or the value of a free press. Hypocrisy was a waste of time for all but the hypocrite himself. Anyway, a change in her situation was long overdue. From now on, she, not her father, would decide what was prudent or not. She, not Mikhail Pushkin, would decide whether prudence itself was even prudent, in certain circumstances.

And so, rather to her surprise, it was with a degree of excite ment that Olga Pushkin approached the social services offices in Yashkino, following a half-hour drive from Tayga. As she pushed through the swing doors she reached into her handbag and fingered the crisp wads of banknotes, feeling not trepidation but an unaccustomed sense of power. She had suffered the effects of corruption in Russia – they all had, for many years: the queues and fees and endless rounds of paperwork that never seemed to get to the right people at the right time. It was only fair, she told herself, that she was now going to use corruption for good purposes. Bribing a public official wasn't really bribery if one did it for public-spirited ends.

In the event, however, no bribery was necessary. The public official in question, who went by the name of Leonid Almosya, was quite willing to share private information free of charge, as long as it meant doing something different from his normal routine. He simply nodded at Olga and disappeared into a back room beyond the reception desk of the adoption bureau. 'Come on, then,' he shouted, after a minute or two, and Olga, lifting up the wooden folding desk and ducking under it, found Almosya at an ancient desktop computer, which all but shook from side to side as it booted up.

'Kozar, was it?' he said, typing on the rackety keyboard. 'Ivanka Kozar, you say? That rings a bell. Ah, yes – adopted in 1995, when she was eleven. Her biological family was killed.

Some sob story about a local gang, it says here. And you want to speak to the adoptive family? Here's the record we need. Well, they're dead too, I'm afraid. Died in 1999, both of them – on the same day, too. That's odd. But they were pretty old when they took her on, it says here.'

Olga counted up in her head. 'So Ivanka was fourteen or fifteen when they died. Was she adopted again after that? How does that work?'

'Not adoption,' said Almosya. 'Foster families. She was booted into the system when the old couple kicked the bucket. Assigned to a family near Tayga, the Nikitins, and then another, I think – can't say for sure. The records haven't been digitised yet. But it looks like that might've happened, if I'm reading this right. Sad story,' he added, in a flat tone.

'Isn't it unusual,' said Olga, 'to go from family to family like that?'

'Not really,' said Almosya. 'Especially if there's some trauma early on. Messes them up, see? They can't stay put.'

'I do see,' said Olga. 'Well, are there more details about the first foster family – the family near Tayga?'

Almosya sighed and turned to the computer monitor, typing again on the keyboard and staring myopically at the ancient screen. 'Hmm,' he said. 'Looks like they kicked her out. They had a couple of kids of their own, too – seems they didn't get on with Kozar. So Ivanka got put back into the system and, as I said, it looks like she went to another family.'

He frowned. 'That's odd,' he said. 'There's some kind of a block on the system. The police do that sometimes, if someone's involved in an investigation. But only for something big – homicide, or fraud on a large scale, things like that. Can't imagine the Nikitins being involved in that kind of thing. Maybe someone dobbed them in as suspects to get the cops off their trail. Dodgy neighbours, or the like. It happens. Well, anyway, that's all I've got, so don't ask for any more.' He switched off the computer, which sighed and shuddered as it returned to its slumber.

Olga realised that Almosya was bored again, and wanted to be rid of her. She looked curiously at him, thinking how difficult her life would be if she got bored as quickly as that. Still, she wasn't complaining: she'd been miraculously lucky to get so much information out of him, and without having to sacrifice any of her Tomsk money. But she no longer felt exhilarated, as she got back into the creaking front seat of Popov's Opel. She felt desperately sad instead.

Poor Ivanka, she said to herself. First her parents get themselves killed, then the kindly old couple who adopted her pass away unexpectedly, and *then* the foster family who took her on send her back into the system . . . All that in her past, and now a failing career to contend with, too. There weren't many options on the railways, once you got fired as a *provodnitsa*. An attendant in the dining-car, maybe, though it would be hard to keep that job once the crew found out about her employment history. And people always seemed to find out about things like that.

Maybe that's why she became a target, thought Olga, as well as her golden teeth. The killers think she's weak and traumatised – that she would confess to anything when put under pressure. Well, Ivanka had proved them wrong, hadn't she? said Olga to herself, with a touch of pride in her gender. Ivanka hadn't buckled when they'd arrested her for the Alyona murder. She hadn't made up a false confession or begged for mercy. Russian women were tough – tougher than their men, in many ways. And it was high time they grasped that.

Olga breathed in deeply and exhaled again, gathering her thoughts. All these discoveries were fascinating, but she couldn't sit cogitating in Popov's car all day long. Now that she'd ticked two items off on her list, it was time for her to tackle the third task of the day: Ivanka's former boyfriend. Ekaterina, once again, had come through with the goods when Olga had asked her if Ivanka had ever had a partner of any kind. Ekaterina knew a man who knew a man, and that man, a policeman called Igor Troponovich, was friends with Ivanka's (apparently one and only) ex-boyfriend in the little town of Pikhtach, a few miles north of Roslazny.

'He's an odd sort, Igor says,' Ekaterina had told her. 'Bit of a loner. A hunting obsessive, you know the type – guns and knives and so on, always wears old army gear. Anyway, I've given you his address, so you can look him up yourself. His name's Taras Sviatoslav.'

Twenty minutes after leaving the adoption bureau at Yashkino, Olga pulled up outside Taras Sviatoslav's Soviet-era apartment block in the small town of Pikhtach. She got out of the car with relief, glad to escape the meaty aroma that had built up over the course of the morning. She walked past a derelict car on blocks and a dinghy on a trailer, and rang the front doorbell. She rang it again, then again and again, until eventually there came a noise of movement within. The door opened a crack and a sleepy eye pushed up against it.

'What?' said a voice.

'I'm – I'm a railway engineer,' said Olga, a little nervously.

'But I'm working with the police on an investigation. I just want to talk. Can I come in?'

'What?' said the voice again.

Olga sighed. She could see this was going to take some time. 'Look,' she said, in a louder, slower voice, 'I want to talk to you about a police investigation I'm helping with. You know Ivanka Kozar, don't you? You were her boyfriend once, I understand.'

At the mention of Ivanka's name the door slammed shut, making Olga jump. Then she heard the rattle of a brass chain, and the door swung open, revealing an overweight man with an unkempt beard wearing combat trousers and a camouflage top.

'You'd better come in,' said the man. 'I'm Taras – but you know that already. Who told you about me and Ivanka?'

'Igor Troponovich,' said Olga, walking cautiously into the house and wrinkling her nose at the damp, mouldy air, mixed with what smelt like anchovies and strong cheese. Detective work, it seemed, involved a lot of unpleasant smells. 'He said you wouldn't mind talking to me about Ivanka.'

'Igor, eh?' said Taras, clearing space on a couple of chairs by dumping fresh piles of rubbish on the floor. He sat with a grunt, indicating with a wave that Olga should do the same. 'He's a good man. Owes me six hundred roubles, though. So, you're working with the police. What's Ivanka done now?'

'Well,' said Olga, sitting warily on the grubby chair and wondering how to begin, 'it's not so much what she's done as what's been done to her. Look, I have a few questions for you, if you don't mind. Can we start with how you met Ivanka?'

Taras shrugged his shoulders. 'She showed up at one of Troponovich's parties a year or so ago. She was all dolled up, and she stuck to me for the whole night. It was nice. I enjoyed it. I got her number and saw her again, quite a few times. She even stayed over now and then. Funny thing was, she didn't mind the mess. In fact,' he said, leaning forward, slightly too close to Olga, 'I think she might've actually made it worse. On purpose, like. Rooting through things. Now, what do you make of that? Is that something to do with your investigation – robbery? Identity theft?'

'Well,' said Olga, shifting in her seat and trying to avoid answering his question, 'it does sound a little odd, I agree.'

'Oh, that was nothing,' said Taras, sitting back again. 'There was heaps of other weird stuff. Let me see . . . Well, she used to make really crazy food, with whale-meat, or something, that she got special from some Chinaman in Tayga. She'd get really worked up watching TV sometimes. Like, if there were stories about celebrities getting away with breaking the law. Wealthy people and that. It seemed to make her angry, as if she wanted to be something different from what she was. I told her there's nothing wrong with working the railways. We can't all be rich, can we? Or celebrities? Another thing, too – she kept going on about the police. Who I knew in the force, what friends I had at the Tayga station, all that. I told her I didn't know anyone in the police, but she never believed me. It was like someone had told her I was pals with loads of coppers, and she thought I was lying when I said I wasn't.'

Olga nodded, thinking that Ivanka's jealousy of wealthy celebrities was easy enough to explain, given her terrible childhood and her professional difficulties. She wasn't sure what to make of Ivanka's interest in the police, but then she smiled. Of course! Ivanka must be thinking of switching careers. There wasn't much hope of progress for a demoted *provodnitsa* in Russian Railways, so it made sense to look for alternatives – to search for contacts who could give her a helping hand.

'Something funny?' said Taras.

'Not at all,' said Olga, resolving to control her expression more in future, and wondering what to ask next. She hadn't thought before how much policework boiled down to knowing which questions one should ask. What would Vassily do? Surely he would insist on covering all the bases – on questions that would confirm without any doubt that Ivanka was innocent. Olga knew she was, of course, because someone was trying to frame her as well as Vassily – but knowing something and having proof of it were two different things. Olga would be doing Ivanka an important service if she could establish her innocence once and for all, particularly with regard to the murder of Nathan Bryce. When Alyona Vasiliev died, there'd been no doubt of Ivanka's innocence because of the phone records. But there was no such definitive proof when it came to the unfortunate American tourist. There was only the broken samovar and Andrian Zonov. It had been enough to spare her from investigation first time around, but Zonov was hardly the most convincing witness she had ever seen. The problem was, though, that she didn't know *how* to prove Ivanka's innocence. All she knew was that she shouldn't approach the topic too directly. Detectives always wove their way in, she had noticed on TV, like a yacht tacking into the wind. Perhaps she should just set sail and see what happened along the way.

'Umm,' she began, 'did you ever . . . When Ivanka was staying here, did she mention anything about tourists? On the train, I mean. Perhaps she disliked them, like she did celebrities?'

'No, I don't think so,' said Taras, scratching his head. 'She didn't talk about work that much. Like I said, I reckon she wanted to be something else.'

Olga nodded, thinking hard. 'And did you ever see her with ten-rouble coins? Did she ever take money out of the bank that way – in bags of coins?'

'You mean like the murder on the train? I read about that. Wait – don't tell me she was involved?'

'We're not sure, really,' said Olga. 'Can you just answer my question about the coins?'

'I never saw her with coins,' said Taras. 'Why carry coins when you can carry notes, or a card? Even Ivanka's not that stupid.'

'You think she's stupid?' said Olga, quickly.

'I didn't say that,' said Taras. 'But you've met her, right? You've got to admit, she's no intellectual. She's no Viktoriya Panovsky.' Olga looked blank. 'You know, the Channel Two presenter? The model? Oh, you should hear her talk about football! Beauty *and* brains.'

'Right,' said Olga. 'Right. Well, er, what about . . .'

But she could think of no more questions to ask. Perhaps Taras didn't know anything that could help Ivanka, after all – and even if he did, perhaps Olga wasn't skilful enough to wheedle it out of him. She decided discretion was the better part of valour. 'Actually, I think that's all the questions I have, Mr Sviatoslav,' she said, trying to sound professional.

'Oh, just Taras, please,' he said eagerly.

'Thanks again for your time,' she said, getting up to go.

'You don't want tea, or some pickles?' said Taras.

'No, I've got to go, thanks,' she said, edging towards the door.

'Wait,' he said, getting to his feet. 'Maybe there's something else. I've just remembered it. What you said about the tourists jogged my memory. If you'd like to stay for a cup of tea? I don't get a lot of visitors.'

'Oh,' said Olga, who had been looking forward to escaping the smell. 'Well, if you've remembered something . . . Yes, that would be – nice.'

Taras bustled around his kitchenette preparing the drinks, finally bringing through a tray laden with snacks and tea-making implements.

'What is it you do for a living, Mr – I mean, Taras?' she said, belatedly remembering another question she should have asked.

'I work with animals,' he said, sitting down and putting the tray on a little table by their chairs. 'Abattoirs, mostly.'

'Abattoirs?' she said, trying to hide a shiver of distaste. 'Well, that must be – interesting.'

'Yes,' he said. 'I suppose it is. Never really thought about it. Ivanka liked it, though.'

'She *liked* it?'

'Seemed to,' said Taras. 'Like I said, she was into eating weird animals, and stuff like that. Probably found it interesting to learn where meat comes from. More people should. It doesn't grow in packets, y'know.'

Olga shook her head as if to express disapproval at people's lack of knowledge about meat production. 'So,' she said, trying to think of something to say, 'she was interested in your work with animals. And you liked talking about your work with her. That sounds like a good relationship. So what happened to end it? Did you get tired of her questions?'

'It wasn't me who ended it,' said Taras. 'I should've done, though. Didn't get round to it, somehow. She just stopped calling a couple of months ago, stopped coming round. I guess she found someone else. I saw her once after that, in Tayga, but she pretended she didn't see me and walked off the other way. I haven't had a girlfriend since.'

I can't imagine why, thought Olga, looking around at the apartment.

'But you know,' Taras continued, 'maybe it was for the best.'

'Why's that?' said Olga.

'Well,' said Taras, sitting forward until she could smell the pickles on his breath, 'there's something else I could tell you about her. I overheard her on the phone, not long before we broke up. She thought I was on the toilet, see. I have these problems, and sometimes it takes me a long time to— Well, you don't need to know about that. Anyway, I couldn't go – I think it was those pickled bear paws again – so I came back through to the kitchen. I don't think she heard me coming. I heard her talking, and it was a bit, well, *creepy* . . . Not like the times she used to burst into laughter for no reason, though that was weird. But at least she sounded happy then. But this time . . . You should've seen her face, when she realised I'd heard her talking – it scared me a bit. So when we broke up, I thought maybe it wasn't such a bad thing. Maybe she was a bit too weird for me, after all.'

Olga nodded, looking at Taras's camouflage gear, the wall-mounted crossbows, the stuffed hares and rabbits dotted around the room. 'Yes, I – I can totally understand that,' she said. 'But what was it that she was saying on the phone – can you remember?'

'Pretty much,' he said. 'It stuck in my mind, y'know? Not the kind of things you want to hear your girlfriend saying, really. Anyway, it sounded like she was talking to someone about some work she wanted done. "It'll be around New Year," she said. "It can't be earlier, because of the work rota. It has to be then. Don't let me down – remember, you need the money to keep on looking. And keep your mouth shut. You know what happens to blabbermouths round these parts." That's what she said.

'But it was the next bit that really creeped me out,' Taras went on. 'She started off talking normally, but then she went into this intense voice. Like something off a horror film.'

'But what did she say?' said Olga.

'It wasn't a lot – it was more how she said it. Maybe it'll mean something to you. She said: "The name? Oh, it's easy to remember. Even you can get it first time. It's just this. *Anyone*."

'Are you listening?' he said after a minute, making Olga jump.

She had fallen into another reverie, but this time it was a dream of mounting terror.

Olga returned Popov's car in Roslazny some time before Glazkov could be expected to arrive for his usual evening drinking session, and therefore some time before she could share her news with Vassily. She found this intensely frustrating, for it was news of immense importance. Finally it was clear why Ivanka had featured in both murder cases, something that had puzzled them from the start. She featured because she herself was the killer.

Everything Olga had learned that day had pointed towards Ivanka's innocence, but then, in a chance remark, like a twist in the murder mysteries Vassily had spoken of, Olga had learned of a phone call that seemed to portend a motiveless murder. *Anyone* . . . Hadn't they all wondered why Nathan Bryce had died? Hadn't everyone struggled to produce a clear reason for his death, as opposed to the death of any other tourist on the Trans-Siberian? Well, now they knew. Ivanka hadn't cared who died. It hadn't mattered, as long as someone died – *anyone*, anyone at all!

But perhaps the stranger Ivanka had chosen was not wholly random, after all. He was an American tourist – a wealthy man, by most Russians' standards, though only a trainee lawyer; a man with expensive clothes and straight white teeth. Ivanka hated celebrities, Taras had said, and people who got away with breaking the law. Well, who broke more laws, internationally speaking, than the Americans? And who supplied the world with its celebrities – ridiculous actors and rappers and comedians? So maybe Ivanka had decided to find an American tourist, cut his or her throat, stuff their mouth with money to symbolise America's destructive wealth, and dump them out of the train – having first arranged an alibi with the engineer, Andrian Zonov. Not that Olga really suspected Zonov: like Glazkov, he was too stupid to be anything but a liability as an accomplice. But as an *unwitting* accomplice he had served his purpose. No doubt Ivanka had offered to fetch him some vodka to help with his hangover, or something like that – the hair of the dog, her father Mikhail called it – and he'd been happy to accept it, and her brief absence, and not think of mentioning it to anyone afterwards. A brief absence, but long enough for murder. No wonder Ivanka laughed to herself in sudden glory from time to time: her scheme was a stroke of genius.

And Alyona Vasiliev – maybe she'd seen Ivanka do something the day Nathan Bryce had died, and so needed dispatching to keep her quiet. Hadn't she been nervous and irritable that day in Tayga? Hadn't she looked exhausted, as if she bore a heavy burden? Or perhaps it was Alyona whom Ivanka had called from Taras's flat long before Nathan Bryce died, telling her of her plans to kill a random stranger on the railway, and threatening her with some dire fate if she didn't go along with Ivanka's scheme – a fate that had eventually befallen her, nonetheless.

Vassily, of course, had been involved only by accident, Glazkov too, and herself. Ivanka hadn't cared where she'd dumped the body, or who found it – or whom it struck on its way to earth. She had alibis for both murders, so it didn't matter what happened to anyone else. But there was still the puzzling matter of the text messages found on Vassily's phone. Could Ivanka herself have tried to frame Vassily, changing her phone number at the same time to avoid suspicion falling on her? But how would Ivanka, a simple *provodnitsa*, achieve such a feat? Did she have an accomplice, as yet unknown, with technical know-how? She pondered on this for a while without reaching any resolution. That was too complex for her to settle by herself. Digital technology was not her area of expertise. But maybe Vassily could help, later on.

Detective work was really quite interesting, thought Olga, if one put aside the murders and suffering. Vassily was right: it was just like all the police dramas she'd watched on TV, with a series of clues leading to the wrong suspect – or, as in this case, making a guilty person look innocent until the very end. Ivanka had almost got away with it. Ivanka *would* have got away with it, if it hadn't been for Olga calling on Taras! She shivered as she thought of that smiling golden mouth, grinning and laughing and smirking, and at other times talking evil words to a wicked accomplice.

Olga was itching to tell Vassily all about it, but by seven o'clock that evening there was still no sign of Glazkov at Café Astana, and she was reluctant to walk to the station in case she ran into him en route. So she told herself that patience was a virtue and went into the café instead, buying a drink at the bar and chatting to Fyodor Katin to distract herself. Fyodor had forgotten his attempt to establish a new monarchical constitution in Russia and was now obsessed with the history of serfdom.

'If we introduced serfdom again, we could have all the benefits of Communism without any of the wretched Party machinery,' he said to Olga, over his typewriter. 'Just think – we could spend the mornings working for our needs, farming and mechanics and what-have-you, and the afternoons and evenings would be ours for the taking!'

'And who would make all the decisions?' said Olga. 'The aristocrats who used to own us all? Fyodor, this is just your new monarchy in a different form.'

'No, you don't understand,' he said. 'This would be quite different. You see, it would involve a collective expression of the natural virtues of the Russian peasant – all the things we've lost, but that lie buried deep inside us, in our very blood!'

While Fyodor talked, Olga treated herself to a second drink and a plate of Odrosov's pickled herring. Finally, when she could nurse her empty glass no longer, she had to accept that Glazkov wasn't going to come that night. It was maddening: she was desperate to speak to Vassily about her long day's work. But it was too risky just to set off and take her chances: if she ran into Glazkov en route, or (even worse) at the station, Babikov would soon hear about it – and then maybe he'd move Vassily somewhere else, or even arrest Olga herself. No – it would have to wait until the following day.

She made her goodbyes to Fyodor, got up from the bar and turned towards the door. Then she stopped dead, her face white with shock. A man was standing there, a man she had not seen for almost two years.

'Pasha!' she said.

12

Musical Chairs

Olga's older brother Pasha had the same flaxen hair as she did, but he was taller than her and of a slimmer build, more like their mother Tatiana than their father Mikhail. The girls in Roslazny, in the days when there were still girls in Roslazny, had expressed great admiration for how Pasha looked in his uniform when he joined the army in 1999. Army uniforms, said the girls, tended to make a man look like a sack of potatoes, all baggy and wrinkled and shapeless. Odrosov, who had been in the military police and still wore his old fatigues when he cleaned the toilets at Café Astana every second month or so, was a case in point. But Pasha somehow looked gallant and dashing in the dull grey camouflage of a private's uniform. The heart of Anna Kabalevsky – at the time her name was still Anna Sorokin – was not the only one he left aching behind him when he strode out of Roslazny one summer morning, his kitbag over his shoulder, marching off to Tayga station and the army train that would take him to his barracks at Novosibirsk. Anna had met Bogdan Kabalevsky the week after that.

Now Pasha was back once more at Café Astana, standing in the doorway with the westering sun behind him. His flaxen hair was a little thinner, perhaps, and a little paler, but he was still as tall and slender as ever. He had returned over the intervening years as often as his postings allowed, always arriving proudly wearing his uniform. This time, however, he was clad in jeans, jumper and fur-lined jacket, like any other man in Kemerovo Province. He wore them self-consciously, as if they were a new and uncomfortable kind of tunic that his superiors had just issued.

'Young Pushkin, as I live and breathe – and in civvies, too!' called Odrosov, from behind the bar. 'Kicked you out at last, have they?'

Olga gave him a withering stare. 'Mind your own business, Odrosov. Come on, Pasha,' she said, putting her hand on his arm to guide him out of the café.

'Said the wrong thing, have I?' said Odrosov to Fyodor Katin, as Olga slammed the door behind them.

But Fyodor shook his head. 'I rather think the opposite is true, my friend,' he said. 'You may, by chance, have said all too much the right thing.'

Outside the café, Olga hugged Pasha fervently. 'Thank God you're here, and a day early, too,' she said. 'So much has happened here . . . I need you now more than ever.'

'Then I'm glad to be back,' said Pasha.

'But I'm being so selfish,' she said. 'You have your own problems, of course, and here am I wittering on about mine. The army, the police escort home . . . You must tell me all about it.'

Pasha smiled briefly in the way he'd always done, a flicker of emotion passing across his face but leaving his sad eyes untouched. 'No,' he said. 'At least, not here. I want to tell you and Father at the same time.'

'Oh, Pasha,' said Olga, her hand over her mouth. 'What is it? What's happened to you?'

'Olga, Olgakin,' he said, 'every word you say betrays your goodness. Some would say, "What have you done?" But you say, "What's happened to you?"'

'Well, I know my brother could never do anything wrong,' she said.

'I hope you still think so in ten minutes' time,' he said. 'Come on! Let's go home. I've had a long journey and I want to get this over with.'

'But, Pasha,' said Olga, scurrying to catch up with her brother's long strides as he set off towards the house, 'you haven't been back for ages – Father's got worse, you know. He barely laughs, these days, except when his horrible friends are round. Old Solotov and that lot. I don't know how he'll be about your discharge.'

'We'll find out,' said Pasha. 'I've made up my mind, Olga. This is how I want things to be. I've endured enough, suffered enough, over the past twenty years. I can't take it any more! It's time to have it out.'

'Don't speak like that, Pasha,' she said. 'I can't bear to think of you suffering. Why didn't you say something? Why didn't you tell us you've been unhappy?'

'You'll see,' he said. And she couldn't get him to say anything else until they were inside the house, kicking the snow and mud from their boots. It was dark by now, and since Mikhail rarely left the living room after lunch, the rest of the house was still unlit. Olga looked at her brother as he closed the door behind him, his face lost in the darkness. What could he possibly reveal that could be so disastrous? What could have caused him twenty years of suffering? She wished he would tell her first, so that she could find a way of framing it for her father's ears. Pasha didn't know Mikhail the way she did. And she had a feeling of dread inside her, a conviction that somehow this was going to end badly for Pasha. But he rejected her last whispered entreaty, squeezed her arm affectionately, and walked through to the living room.

'That went well,' said Pasha, standing outside the house ten minutes later.

'Oh, *Pasha*,' said Olga. 'What are we going to do now?'

As Olga had expected, Mikhail had reacted negatively to the news that Pasha had been dishonourably discharged from his regiment in Novosibirsk. But he had reacted even more negatively to the reason.

'You're *what*?' he'd roared, jumping to his feet, and seeming to forget the crutch that never left his side.

'I'm gay, Father,' said Pasha, holding his ground, standing opposite Mikhail in the dingy living room. 'Homosexual,' he added by way of clarification.

'I know what bloody gay means,' shouted Mikhail. 'Dishonourably discharged, that's what it means. So this is why you turn up here after almost two years away – almost two years, with hardly a letter or a phone call – but that was fine, I understood. I accepted that, because I was proud of my son being in the army. Damn sight better than any of those other idiots managed round here. And now this! Did they find you with another man, in the barracks? Or did you ask the colonel out for dinner? No, don't tell me. I'm disgusted. I'm *ashamed*.'

Olga saw that Mikhail had tears in his eyes – something she hadn't seen since Russia had lost to Japan in the 2002 World Cup. 'But, Father,' she said, 'he's still our Pasha, isn't he? Still your little boy, your firstborn? Think of what Mama would say if she heard you talking to him like that!'

'Aha!' he said, turning on her. 'You're going to stand up for your brother, are you? You're both useless. One of you's a pansy, and the other dresses like a man with a ponytail. I'll never have grandchildren. I've resigned myself to that. I might just as well be alone and save myself the trouble.'

He had begun to walk around the living room, navigating between the piles of old magazines and delicately balanced ashtrays, gesturing and waving his arms.

'Father, you'll give yourself a coronary,' said Pasha.

'And what's that to you?' shouted Mikhail. 'I'd be better off dead than listening to this rubbish. And if I do have a stroke, it'll be you who's given it to me!'

He really did look like he might have a heart attack, thought Olga. His face had turned deep puce and his eyes were bulging from their sockets, while his fists were clenched so tightly that his knuckles stuck out like white mushrooms. 'Look,' she said, 'I think we'd better leave, Pasha. Let's go to the café and have a drink. We'll come back later, Father, when you've calmed down.'

'You can go to the café,' he said, 'but no damned *pansy* will ever set foot in this house. Be off with you! And you can go with him, Olga. I've had enough of you as well.' He seized a heavy poker from the hearth. 'Go on! I bloody mean it. I'm better off alone.'

Olga stared at him for a minute, finally allowing herself to realise how much she hated him. She hated him because of how he had treated her mother, because of how he had betrayed Tatiana's hopes of happiness and taken her to a cold, damp house that had sealed her fate, and because of how he'd left her to care for the children while he drank away what little money they had. She hated him, too, for the callous way he had always treated her, Olga, belittling her achievements, her character and even her appearance.

Still, leaving the house she had shared with her father for so long was a big step. Not because she would miss her father, but because she would miss her mother. This was the house to which, all those years ago, Mikhail had brought Tatiana, and which Tatiana had filled with treasures from the Lodge at Astrazov, until Mikhail had sold them. It was the house where Tatiana had had her children, the midwife coming from Tayga to deliver Olga and Pasha, putting them into their mother's arms in the same bedroom that Mikhail had now filled with stacks of DVDs and old food wrappers and empty cigarette packets. Olga had stayed so long not because it helped her to save up for her course at Tomsk, but because it had been a part of her mother's life. And now she would have to leave it behind, because her father didn't like who his son had turned out to be. All those years of patience, politeness and prim decorum that Olga had endured to keep her father happy, and it still wasn't enough.

She looked at Mikhail, red-faced and staring as if they'd confessed to murdering the entire populace of Roslazny. At last, and quite suddenly, her patience ran out. 'Fine,' she snapped. 'Come on, Pasha. You can help me pack.'

'With pleasure,' said Pasha, staring coldly at Mikhail until he looked away. 'I might be a *pansy*, but I can still make myself useful.'

Olga threw some things into an old suitcase of their mother's that she kept under her bed. It didn't take long. It was pathetic to see how little she possessed: a small pile of clothes and shoes, a few accessories for the cold weather, a couple of handbags, some cosmetics and toiletries, and the patchwork quilt from Astrazov, as well as the red-and-gold table she had salvaged from the skip in Tayga. She couldn't take the new sofa with her, of course. It was too big, and in any case, as she finally allowed herself to admit, it was perhaps rather smelly and discoloured. She decided to leave it for her father. Let him rot on it, she told herself. It's all he's good for. Anyway, her most prized possessions were her mother's books, and those were safe in the little hut by the railway tracks.

'Come on, then,' she said to Pasha. She stood at the door to the bedroom where she had lived for so many years, and to which she had returned after so many days working on the railway. But it wasn't the later years she was thinking of, as she stood in the doorway. It was the times before, when her mother had sat on the side of her bed, reading to her or playing with her or just watching her fall asleep. Can furniture or walls or beds remember us? she wondered. Do they keep some trace of us upon them, some scent or shape or sound from us, when we leave them and go away? If so, she thought, let this place remember me as well as her. That way we will always be together. She stifled a sob and turned away.

'Good riddance,' Mikhail called after them, as they put on their snow-boots and opened the door to leave. Olga shook her head. That was what Mikhail had said about the dead American.

Then she took Pasha's arm and walked out into the night.

After they'd left the house Olga no longer shared with her father Mikhail, she led them quickly towards the centre of Roslazny, but with no particular destination in mind. They couldn't stay at Anna Kabalevsky's – the hostel rooms were full of paying guests, for once, and anyway Pasha had always disliked Bogdan. There were rooms at Café Astana, above the bar, but Svetlana, Odrosov's daughter, had shown Olga what they were like a year or two ago, and they fell firmly into the last-resort category. Short of getting themselves arrested and sharing the cells with Vassily and Rasputin, Olga could think of no other option but Aunt Zia's.

'Zia?' said Pasha, as they trudged through the darkened streets, Olga struggling with her suitcase and Pasha carrying the red-and-gold table on his shoulder. 'But she'll take Father's side! She'll throw us out as soon as he tells her.'

'No, she won't,' said Olga. 'Father will never tell anyone about this.'

'Right,' said Pasha, quietly. 'Because I'm so disgusting.'

'It doesn't matter what he thinks, Pasha,' said Olga. 'It doesn't matter what anyone thinks.'

She put her suitcase down in the snow, and threw her arms around him again. 'You'll always be my big brother,' she said, 'and anybody who has a problem with you can take it up with me!'

'You've changed, Olgakin,' he said, looking down at her. 'There's a fierceness about you, like – like a Siberian tiger. What's happened to you?'

'A lot's happened since you went away,' she said. 'I'll tell you about it later, and it takes some telling, believe me. But not now. I want to hear about you.'

'That takes some telling, too,' said Pasha. 'And I suppose it begins with Ruslan.'

'Ruslan Yozhin? Your friend from Tayga?'

'Yes, Ruslan Yozhin,' said Pasha. 'It began with him.' And he told her how he had first discovered his feelings for Ruslan when he'd said goodbye to him, the day before he left for the army. 'Aren't partings always like that?' said Pasha, as they navigated through the frozen carcasses that littered the ground outside Popov's shop. 'You don't realise what you have until you lose it. There've been others since, but Ruslan was the first, the forerunner.'

'I remember him,' said Olga, picturing a thin boy of average height, but with stark, high cheekbones and a shock of dark hair, like Vassily Marushkin's. 'So that was why you always used to write to each other. I remember you bringing a sheaf of letters back from the barracks on your first visit.'

Pasha smiled, but again in that fleeting way he had, like sunlight cutting through a break in the clouds only to be covered up again. 'Yes, that was why. But his mother found the letters, and that was that. They took him away from me, west to Perm, where his father's family lived. I never saw him again.'

'Oh, Pasha,' said Olga, reading the old pain living still in his eyes. 'But you said there were others. Was that how they found out in the army?'

'No, no,' said Pasha, as they passed Café Astana. 'They found out the same way Ruslan's mother did: by reading my letters. I always kept Ruslan's letters – couldn't bear to throw them out, though they were a ticking time-bomb in my locker. I suppose I always knew it was a matter of time before someone got suspicious and went through my stuff. It happens all the time. And I'm relieved, in a way, that it's over now – the waiting, I mean. But I'm sad, too. Father forced me to join the army, but the strange thing was, I loved it, Olga! The marches, the weapons training, the secret deployments overseas . . . I'm no fan of Putin, and he'd be no fan of mine, either, if he knew me. I know what he thinks of people like me. But, still, I loved the army he made. Is that crazy? And now I'm out of a job, and all I can do is wear a uniform and shoot a rifle. What can I possibly do for work in Roslazny?'

They arrived outside Aunt Zia's house, the faded lime-green paint transformed into sickly yellow by the faint light of the streetlamp. Olga knocked on the front door, and turned to Pasha. 'I wouldn't worry about that just yet,' she said. 'I can think of something to keep you busy for a couple of days.'

Aunt Zia offered them two rooms at the back of the house, away from the road. Olga had to explain why she and Pasha had left Mikhail's house, but Pasha wasn't ready for anyone else to know the real reason. So Olga just said that Pasha had quit the army after a row with an officer ended in blows – and that Mikhail had flown into a rage when Pasha told him, throwing Olga out for good measure when she tried to defend her brother. That much was true, anyway.

'But you can't tell Father we're here,' said Olga. 'That would make him angry with you, too, Auntie. And he's angry enough for now.'

'Well, my dear,' said Zia Kuznetsov, 'looking after house-guests doesn't come cheaply, these days. You can have the back two rooms, so nobody sees you. And you'll have to stay out of sight during the day, too, so you won't be under my feet indoors when I want a bit of peace. I don't know – it's a lot to ask, even for family.'

Olga sighed. 'We could pay, of course, Auntie, if that would help.'

'Pay?' said Zia. 'Oh, no, I'd never let family *pay*. Not rent, anyway. No contracts or bills for family! Maybe a few roubles, here and there, to keep things going, eh? To buy some food and drink. Oh, I know how much you young people eat! Why don't you give me two thousand now, to get some shopping in tomorrow, and then three thousand a week? For the both of you. That's fair. And I'll heat up something for your dinner now, free of charge.'

'That will be fine, Auntie,' Olga said with a sigh, taking the money from her handbag and putting it on the sideboard. But here was another expenditure she could barely afford, especially as she would have to pay it all herself. She knew Pasha hadn't a kopek to his name after his discharge, for which the army had, somewhat ironically, charged him handsomely. Olga would have to dip once more into the savings she'd put aside for the course at Tomsk University, at least until Pasha could find work again. Hopefully that would happen soon, and then she could continue saving – less quickly than before, because she no longer had free accommodation at Mikhail's house, but she should be able to save a thousand or so a week. There might be some other small savings, too, now that Mikhail would have to find someone else to run his errands for him. And at least dinner tonight was free.

'Come on, then,' she said to Pasha. 'Let's get settled in. I don't know about you, but I'm ready for bed as soon as we've eaten.'

'All right,' said Pasha, as they walked up the stairs to their bedrooms, 'but not before you tell me what's been going on in Roslazny.'

'No – after dinner,' said Olga. 'I can't tell you with Aunt Zia around. We'll find somewhere quiet and you'll learn all my secrets!'

But the evening didn't go quite as planned. They had finished what passed for pudding at Aunt Zia's – half a can of condensed milk each, in a bowl, with some stale hot chocolate powder sprinkled on top – when Olga's mobile rang.

'It's Anna,' she said to Pasha, after her brief and hurried conversation. 'Well, it's Bogdan. He's at the house, drunk. Anna said he threatened to hurt the children. We'd better go around.'

'*Hurt the children?*' said Pasha. 'What kind of man threatens to do that? Let's go, then. I just wish I still had my bayonet.'

They got their coats, put on their snow-boots and dashed out, ignoring Zia's protests about irregular hours, and her request that they use the back entrance at all times and give a thought to what the neighbours might say.

'What neighbours?' said Pasha, as they walked along the muddy street. 'This place is even emptier than it used to be.'

'And yet still full of *pridurki*,' said Olga, thinking of her father, of Solotov, and of Bogdan.

'Everywhere is,' muttered Pasha. 'If it isn't, you just haven't met them yet.'

'Not Tomsk,' said Olga. 'Tomsk will be full of people like . . . well, people like Mamochka, I hope.'

Pasha looked at her fondly. 'I hope so, Olgakin,' he said.

In a matter of minutes they arrived at Anna's house. Pasha remembered the place from visits there as a teenager with Olga, when Anna was young, and hopeful of attracting Pasha's attention. But even if he hadn't remembered, he would have known which house it was because of the shouting.

'You're *disgusting*,' screamed Anna. 'How could you do those things? And *on film*, too? Don't you realise our children could see them in the future? Can you even *imagine* how *mortifying* it was to be told about the DVDs by a sleazy man at the hospital at Tayga, who'd seen you there with me and the kids, and recognised you from your – your *performances*?'

'Don't you want me to – to – to earn a living?' said Bogdan, slurring his words. Olga could imagine his face, looking stupider than ever, if that were possible, and crimson with the effects of Odrosov's vodka.

'Not like that, you idiot!' shouted Anna. Then came the sound of something smashing, then another and another.

Olga thought of the china plates that stood in a row on the dresser, a wedding present from Anna's mother. 'We'd better go in,' she said to Pasha.

'Yes, before she kills him,' he replied.

'Oh, look who it is,' said Bogdan, as they entered. 'So you called your – your friends to help, did you? Olga Pushkin, and – is that Pasha? Hello, Pasha!'

'It's no time for pleasantries, Bogdan,' said Pasha. 'Look where you're standing!'

Bogdan had taken refuge behind a door, half closing it on himself to protect him from the dinner set. Anna stood across the room from him, scarlet with fury, a plate in each hand. Upstairs the children were crying. There was no sign of the hostel guests: presumably they had beaten a hasty retreat.

'Put the plates down, Anna,' said Olga. 'And come out from there, Bogdan. You can't carry on like this.'

'You're dead right,' said Bogdan, emerging from behind the door. 'In fact, I've – I've had enough of all this – this *nagging*. If you can't accept what I do to earn a living for this family, then to hell with you! This is my house. It's my name on the whatsit. The paperwork at the bank. You can get out, all of you! The children too. I've had enough of their whining.'

Olga looked at him in horror, with a strong sense of déjà vu. Had she accidentally caused a second eviction in one day? 'Come on, now, Bogdan,' she said, trying to calm him down. 'You can't just—'

'Oh, but I can, Miss Olga Pushkin, Miss Olga-too-good-for-the-likes-of-us-but-only-works-on-the-railways-bloody-Pushkin! Just watch me. I'll throw them out myself, or get whatshisname – the policeman, Glazkov, to do it for me. That's the law. It's my house.'

Now Olga lost her temper, too. 'You wrote that horrible letter, didn't you, you – you – *pridurok*? You didn't have the courage to say it to my face until now – until you're so drunk you can hardly stand!'

Bogdan looked puzzled. 'What letter?'

'Oh, don't pretend,' said Olga. 'It's no use pretending now I've found out.'

'Olga, he can hardly write one word in front of another,' said Anna, who was calmer now the crisis had come at last. 'He can hardly *think* with one word in front of another. So whatever letter you're talking about, someone else must have written it. Anyway, he's right. It *is* high time for us to leave. All of us. Olga, will you help me get the children ready? And, Pasha, it's nice to see you again. Will you watch my husband to make sure he doesn't hurt the children as we leave?'

Bogdan, deciding it was unwise to continue standing, slumped onto the sofa and promptly fell asleep, or pretended to. 'Are you sure you want to leave, Anna?' said Olga. 'Maybe he'll feel better tomorrow. And where will you go? I'd take you in myself, but I can't, just now. I'll explain later.'

'He won't feel better tomorrow,' said Anna. 'He'll spend about half of it being sick into the toilet, and I've heard him do that far too many times. No. We'll go to Café Astana and stay in Odrosov's lodgings until we can get a nicer home for the children. Better to live in squalor there than share a house with – with *that*,' she said, pointing at Bogdan as he snored on the sofa. 'The lodgers have gone, too. They couldn't stand the shouting. Can't say I blame them.'

Olga gave in, helping to pack the children's belongings and assuring them that Daddy was fine, that they were going to stay at the café for a while, for a holiday!

Anna looked at her friend and thought what a treasure she was.

She thought the same at Café Astana when Olga insisted on paying a week's rent for Anna and the children. It was quite a significant sum, for they needed both rooms for the children and all their belongings, but Olga said she was happy to pay

– that it was no more than any friend would do for another, and that she was glad to see Anna free of Bogdan at last.

'We should have been here years ago,' said Anna. 'I'll pay you back as soon as I can, Olga – I'll wash dishes for Odrosov, if I have to. Now we can start a new chapter, God willing, and in peace, without *him* to drag us down.' She put a hand on Olga's arm, and turned to go upstairs to the children.

Pasha came down from the rooms upstairs, where he'd been unpacking the children's belongings and reading to them before bedtime. He sat on a stool beside Olga, and ordered a large vodka for both of them. '*Nazdarovya*,' he said, clinking his glass on hers.

'I need this,' said Olga, drinking deeply. 'It's been a long day. A long month, really.'

'Are you going to tell me what's been going on?' said Pasha. 'We hear nothing in Crimea – they stop us reading the papers, you know. The whole of Siberia could be in flames, and I wouldn't know. You said something to Bogdan about a letter – what's that all about?'

Olga put down her glass. 'There was a letter,' she said, 'a poison-pen letter, from someone in the village, I think. It was horrible, at the time. I should have kept it, to show the police, but I burned it. Anyway, more pressing things have come up in the meantime.'

'More pressing than a poison-pen letter to my sister, my Olgakin?' said Pasha, angrily.

'Yes, a little,' said Olga. 'Where to begin? Well, I want you to think of a samovar on a Trans-Siberian carriage, sabotaged to provide an alibi, of an American tourist, his throat cut and his mouth stuffed with ten-rouble coins, thrown dead from a carriage door, and a poor *provodnitsa* hanged to keep her silent. And another *provodnitsa*, a terrible one, golden-toothed and smiling, always smiling, but with murder in mind . . .'

13

The Turn of the Screw

Wolansky stood at the edge of the studio and watched the make-up artists dab blusher on Grigor Babikov's cheeks, nose and temples. Normally the lieutenant colonel relished the attentions of the (invariably young and attractive) beauticians, but today he seemed distracted, barely mustering a smile when Natasha fell onto his lap as if by accident. Sensing his disinterest, she pouted and stalked away on her stilettos, leaving Samara to finish by herself. Wolansky felt sorry for them, having to fuss over unattractive men and hiring themselves out as escorts at night to make ends meet. Babikov had little pity for people like them, saying they were all part of the same pretence, and that they were adequately paid for their trouble, which was more than one could say of the police. But Wolansky wasn't so sure. He thought good acting was always undervalued.

Wolansky watched Natasha clacking away and wondered how long the charade could be maintained. Babikov had persuaded Colonel Terekhin to allow a press conference about the murder of Alyona Vasiliev, but at the last minute Terekhin had rung the TV station from Novosibirsk to insist that Vassily's name be kept out of all broadcasts unless any new evidence had emerged. The press conference had already been announced and Babikov had no choice other than to proceed, but he'd been white-lipped with anger. 'Damn Terekhin!' he shouted at Wolansky. 'He waited till now on purpose, to humiliate me. What the hell's the point of a press conference without a bloody suspect?'

'I'll manage it, Grigor,' Wolansky had replied. But in truth there was little Wolansky could do in the time available. He wrote a press release hinting that police corruption lay at the centre of the case, and called in a few favours to get the papers to send journalists he knew were supportive of Babikov rather than Arkady Nazarov, his rival in the mayoral race. Wolansky thought he might be able to do more later on, under the table. But while he'd worked miracles before, there was no getting around the embargo on Vassily's name. And Vassily's name was what Babikov wanted to mention above all else, since Ivanka Kozar was out of the picture for now. She was the one Babikov had wanted most, a woman with a metallic grin and a mysterious past – but then, on the other hand, bent coppers like Vassily always played well in local papers. And in the end, all Babikov really needed was a clearly identified scapegoat to take the fall, while his clearance rate shot ever higher. But as long as Terekhin's ban stayed in force, their options were few and unattractive.

'Not this time, Grigor,' muttered Wolansky, as the lieutenant colonel, now fully made-up, nervously downed a glass of water. 'Not while Terekhin lives and breathes.'

He wondered if things were getting out of hand at last. Anyone else would have thought so months ago, he reflected. And it was hard enough keeping Babikov going, without having to persuade himself, too. He had the same concerns as Babikov did, after all, but transposed to another register. Could one really *act* oneself into a position of influence, into a municipal office in Kemerovo and then a federal office in Moscow? Perhaps, but a time might come when enough was enough – when justice had been done and it was time for the curtain to fall. The challenge was how to know when the moment had arrived.

It hadn't come yet, anyway: Wolansky knew that much. So he made his way to the desk where Babikov was sitting with his head in his hands. It was time for a pep-talk.

'Grigor, remember what we discussed – the brutal murder of a poor working woman. Linked to the Bryce case, for sure. Lots of leads, many promising lines of enquiry. Activity, assertiveness, energy! And don't forget to mention police corruption. Every second policeman a danger! Because of things before your time, though – we don't want you taking the fall. Because of Ryanov, and Moussakin, and the rest of your predecessors – crooks one and all, with cronies everywhere. You could hint we've got someone in custody, the lawyers tell me, but no more. Don't mention Marushkin or Roslazny, let alone Kozar!'

Babikov shook his head. All these rules and limitations – it was a far cry from the press conferences he was used to holding, the gleeful centre of a media circus focused nightly and benignly on him, the golden boy of the force in Kemerovo and beyond. That was in the days before the Bryce case. He wished he'd never heard of the damn Trans-Siberian.

'All right, Wolansky,' he said. 'I've got it. God knows what people will think of this. A broadcast without a criminal – it's like a funeral without a bloody coffin.'

Later that day Igor Odrosov expressed the same thought at Café Astana, albeit in rather cruder terms relating to massage parlours in Moscow's red-light district. 'I mean, what's the point?' he went on. 'Look at him!' He gestured at the TV above the bar, which showed Babikov shifting uncomfortably in his seat as the journalists fought among themselves to be the first to ask him a question. 'He's in over his head. Two murders and no clear suspects! Maybe Nazarov's the man for me, after all.'

He was addressing Popov, who had stopped by to sell Odrosov some sausages of indeterminate origin. Popov shrugged. 'Ah, what does it matter?' he said. 'It makes no difference, once they're in.' The butcher tapped his nose. 'Let me tell you a secret, Igor: campaigning's different from governing. They'll promise you the world and give you the back-end of Tayga!'

'Ha!' said Odrosov. 'Hear who's talking. You promise sirloin steak and deliver goat's arse!' Popov sniffed and made as if to leave, but Odrosov reached out a hand. 'All right, I'll take 'em,' he said. 'Twenty roubles a sausage?'

'Done,' said Popov, with suspicious eagerness.

By good fortune Olga and Pasha had already eaten a hasty dinner at Aunt Zia's before Olga went to Café Astana that evening. She therefore avoided the unpleasant consequences that several customers experienced overnight as a result of dining upon Popov's uncertain sausages. One of these unlucky diners was Sasha Tsaritsyn, the journalist whom Olga had encountered at Tayga station on the day of Nathan Bryce's murder.

'Olga Pushkin!' he called, as she walked into the café. 'Come and have a vodka and a sandwich.'

'Just a vodka, thanks, Sasha,' said Olga, sitting on the stool next to him. 'Good to see you again. What brings you to Roslazny?'

'Same thing that brought me to Tayga that time,' said Sasha, through a mouthful of Odrosov's sausage special. 'Murder.'

'Not Nathan *Brrryce* again,' said Odrosov, who was standing behind the bar stacking glasses. 'That's old news.'

'Not Bryce,' said Sasha. 'The *provodnitsa* who was hanged – you know, Alyona Vasiliev.' He nodded at the TV above the bar. 'Didn't you see Babikov on there earlier?'

'Yes, but Vasiliev wasn't killed in Roslazny,' said Odrosov. 'Babikov said she was murdered in Talovka.'

'Ah, but you don't know Babikov's head of PR,' said Sasha, winking at him.

'What did Wolansky tell you?' said Olga, before she could help herself. This sounded ominous for Vassily.

'You know Wolansky?' said Sasha. 'Then you know he's dangerous to know. So I can't tell you what he said to me. But I'm here because of it, that I can tell you.'

So Wolansky *was* tipping off journalists, thought Olga, just as Vassily had suspected. No doubt Wolansky had hinted to Sasha that one of the Roslazny policemen was in jail for Vasiliev's murder. She and Pasha would have to be careful later that night.

There was something else, too, on Olga's mind. She thought back to the time she'd spent at Tayga station watching Vassily and Glazkov at work. 'Did he send you to Tayga that day?' she asked Sasha. 'The day of Nathan Bryce's murder? You all got there very quickly.'

Sasha looked at her but didn't speak, merely letting an

amused smile play around his lips. He picked up his shot glass of Odrosov's Rocket Fuel, inclined it towards Olga, and downed it in a single gulp. He reached into his leather jacket and pulled out a few notes, which he threw onto the bar next to the remains of his sandwich. 'Thanks, Igor,' he said. 'Keep the change. Evening, all!' Without another word, he walked out of the café.

Was that a yes or a no? wondered Olga. If it was a yes, didn't that mean Wolansky – and therefore Babikov – had known about Ivanka's murderous activities in advance? Or did it just mean Wolansky was well-informed – that he had spies on all the trains, perhaps, telling him everything that was going on? It would depend on the timings . . . She'd have to talk to Vassily about it. But then Odrosov cut across her thoughts.

'Bloody cheek,' he said, counting the money. 'Keep the change, he says! A six-rouble tip. What use is that to anyone? You drove him off, Olga, with your questions. Next time keep your feminist remarks to yourself!'

Then he, too, left Olga sitting at the bar, leaving her wondering if Odrosov had the faintest idea of what feminism meant. Perhaps he took feminism to mean anything women did that he found inconvenient. Maybe it was as good a definition as any. She was happy to create inconvenience for men like Odrosov, who had had too many years of people – and women in particular – running after him and attending to his needs. One might have thought that the departure of his wife, Henrika, who'd taken up six years ago with a carpet salesman from Sochi, would have sobered him up. But then his daughter Svetlana had slithered back from Novosibirsk or Tomsk or wherever she'd gone after school, and stepped straight into Henrika's shoes, looking after her father and tending the bar when he'd had too much to drink. Sometimes we're our own worst enemies, thought Olga. It was no use calling yourself a feminist and doing things like that.

An uncomfortable idea crossed her mind. Did *Ivanka* consider herself a feminist? Did she think of herself as a female trailblazer because most serial killers were men? She pondered this as she drank her vodka, said her goodbyes to the café regulars, and took up her position outside once more, watching and waiting until Glazkov turned up for his evening tipple.

No, decided Olga, Ivanka couldn't be called a feminist – not even if she limited herself to killing men. Being a feminist, to Olga's mind, was about freedom. Well, there wasn't much freedom in taking other people's lives away, was there? That didn't make people happy – or, at least, it shouldn't, even if the person whose life had ended early was an unpleasant superior or a wealthy relative.

She watched Glazkov stagger up to the café door at last, apparently drunk already. Some might say he wouldn't be much of a loss to the world, she reflected. If Glazkov were to die, his salary could go to a younger, more professional man (or woman), someone less corrupt and more capable of getting through the day without a quart of neat vodka every six hours. But that was no way to think, she said to herself, as she set off towards the police station. That was how the Kremlin thought, seeing people as dots of ink on a page, or grains of sand on a beach, and just as dispensable. She'd heard someone say that Glazkov had kept working long after he should have retired because he was supporting his elderly mother in a care home in Suranovo. The person had meant it as a criticism of his unprofessionalism, but it was a point in his favour, to Olga's mind.

'Who's there?' she cried, startled by a figure that emerged from a shadowed doorway and made its way towards her. But it was only Sasha Tsaritsyn again. 'Oh, Sasha, you gave me a fright! What on earth are you doing, loitering around that old house?'

'Sorry, Olga,' said Sasha, looking pale and sweaty. 'I was just out for a walk. But those damn sausages – I thought they smelt off. I've got to get back to the café.' He pushed past her in a decidedly odd gait, one gloved hand clutching his midriff and the other clamped against his bottom.

Pressing her hand to her heart in the way people do after they've had a fright, Olga hurried on to the old crossroads where she had arranged to meet Pasha. She had tried to persuade him to come to the café first for a glass of vodka to keep him warm, but he'd insisted on a more private rendezvous near the police station, saying he didn't feel like answering hundreds of questions from all and sundry. 'That's fine with me,' said Olga. 'I wouldn't want to answer them, either. But Glazkov doesn't run to a timetable, remember. Don't blame me if you're half frozen by the time I get there!'

In the event, Pasha was only two-fifths frozen when Olga reached the meeting-point. She told him about Sasha Tsaritsyn. 'Ha! Serves him right,' said Pasha. 'I'm sure it was Sasha who put those laxatives in my borscht at school lunch on Revolution Day in 1989 – you remember? Anyway, did you get the smokes?'

Olga had mentioned Vassily's habit to Pasha, and her plan to bring him some cigarettes so he wouldn't run out. Pasha had made much of this, teasing Olga about her concern for Vassily's welfare until she felt rather uncomfortable. If she was honest with herself, she hadn't just been thinking of his welfare but also of his sad eyes, and his stocky, well-built physique, and the way his black hair fought its way out from whatever kind of hat he had on . . . When she found herself drifting into thoughts of this kind, she would sternly tell herself that she'd gladly bring comfort to any poor soul stuck in prison on trumped-up charges. What did it matter if she wasn't wholly convinced?

As it happened, however, she needn't have troubled herself about the cigarettes.

'Glazkov gave me a whole carton yesterday,' said Vassily, when they got to the station. 'Good of him, though I hope I'm not in here long enough to finish it.'

'Sounds like he's got a guilty conscience,' said Pasha. 'Anyway, it's good to see you, Vassily, though I wish it were in happier circumstances. It must be twenty years since we met.'

'At least,' said Vassily, shaking his hand through the bars. 'I was sorry to hear about what happened. You know, with the army. I would've liked to be the one to bring you home, instead of some duty private from Tayga. But I was otherwise detained.'

'I know,' said Pasha, smiling. Then the smile left his face. 'I'm sorry, too. I loved the army. But I think my sister might've found me something to do instead.'

'So she's roped you into her little project,' said Vassily. 'Look, sit down on that bench. I'm glad to see you, Pushkins, and not just for the company. I've got some news!'

'News, Vassily Marushkin?' said Olga. 'How on earth can you have news, stuck in here?'

'Misfortune can lead to good fortune, it seems,' said Vassily, smiling at her. 'To be more precise, imprisonment might be inconvenient for a number of reasons, but it does furnish something busy sergeants are usually short of. *Time to think.*'

'And what does a busy sergeant think about, when he finds himself falsely imprisoned?' said Olga.

'Oh, this and that,' said Vassily. 'The birth of stars, our place in the universe . . . and the identity of murderers who slit tourists' throats and stuff their mouths with roubles.'

Olga shook her head. 'Well, joking aside, I've also been busy,' she said. 'I think I actually know who the killer is.'

'You do?' said Vassily. 'You mean, you've worked out it's—'

'Ivanka!' said Olga, in triumph.

'Babikov!' said Vassily, at the same time.

Silence fell over the tiny police station, a silence broken only by Rasputin's chitterings from his cage under Vassily's bench.

'*Ivanka?*' said Vassily.

'Babikov?' cried Olga. 'No. It's Ivanka Kozar! The *provodnitsa*. I heard it from Taras himself.'

'Taras?' said Vassily. Then Olga remembered that he didn't know who Taras was, because she hadn't had a chance to tell him about her detective work the day before. With more than a hint of pride in her investigative brilliance, Olga told Vassily every detail of her explorations in Tayga, Yashkino and Pikhtach, where Taras Sviatoslav lived. Vassily nodded and smiled and exclaimed as he was meant to, but before she finished her tale Olga sensed disagreement behind his eyes.

'You see, Vassily,' she concluded, 'it was Ivanka all along. She wanted to kill *just anyone* . . . I think she was on the phone to Alyona, that time at Taras's. And—'

But Vassily cut across her. 'Olga – Olga, hold on a minute! Listen, you've done excellent work, worthy of the best detectives in Novosibirsk, and you've found out many important things. But it's not the whole story. You have to realise that you can be right and wrong at once in policework – and that people can be guilty in different ways.'

'What are you talking about, Vassily Kirillovich?' said Pasha. 'How can a person be right and wrong at once, or guilty in different ways?'

'Look,' said Vassily, 'everything you've said fits perfectly. But it fits with a different story. It means *Babikov*'s guilty – Babikov, and Wolansky, and Glazkov, and God knows how many others too – but not Ivanka. She's the victim here – well, her and me together, painted into a neat little picture to hang inside a cell, or two. That's how Babikov operates. I've worked it all out, sitting here all day with nothing else to do. We thought he was acting on tip-offs, making up a story based on someone else's clumsy attempt to frame me and Ivanka. But no!' he cried, making Olga and her brother jump. 'Babikov himself is behind it all! He sets people up – frames them for crimes they haven't committed. That way he gets to look good on TV and in the papers, without the trouble of having to solve any real crimes at all.'

'He *frames* people?' said Olga sceptically. 'What people?'

'First you have to understand that every police force relies on local knowledge,' explained Vassily. 'Scraps of information about what deals are going down and where. Supplied by crooks, mostly, in exchange for reduced sentences. But Babikov's taken it to another level – he's known for it, across the region. As far away as Novosibirsk, even. He's got a network of inform-ants, collaborators, agents provocateurs – you know, people who set other people up, offer them something tempting and see if they take the bait. Not all his little drones are crooks, either. Sometimes they're busybodies, or local people with an axe to grind or something to prove. I saw a few of those joining up when I was at Kemerovo. Babikov would swear them to secrecy on a copy of the Constitution and give them a speech about duty and honour, that kind of thing, though I doubt he believes any of it himself. I remember their faces – the crooks and gullible fools that Babikov recruited. And their faces turned out to be very important.'

'What about their faces?' said Olga, slightly crossly. She wanted to arrive at the truth, of course, but it did seem a shame that Vassily was getting there by debunking the results of her inspired detective work.

'I saw them in a report on murders in the Province,' said Vassily.

'So what?' said Olga. 'Why wouldn't they appear in a report, if they're helping the police?'

'No, you don't understand,' said Vassily. 'They didn't appear in some appendix or sidebar, thanking locals for their support. No. They appeared as *convicts*. The people I remember were all convicted of murder, and other things, too. *All* of them. I mean, three or four might be expected to have got up to no good – a lot of them were crooks in the first place, don't forget. But *every single informant* I can remember being framed for murder? That's more than thirty people we're talking about. It's too much to be a coincidence – far too much – but it's genius, too. Because nobody would bother to question their guilt. If someone's already a crook, why wouldn't they carry on being a crook? And if they weren't crooks already – if they were just busybodies or cranks – it would look like they really had been crooks all along, and that they'd got involved with the police to find out what was going on, or how to cover their tracks. Like I say, it's genius.'

Vassily leaned forward. 'But that's not all,' he breathed, lowering his voice as if someone might hear. 'Because there has to be something to frame people for, doesn't there? If there's a person to convict of murder, there has to be a body to prove the murder took place. But that doesn't present a problem for our ingenious chief of police – oh, no, not him! Grigor Babikov doesn't let anything as inconvenient as human life get in his way.'

'You don't mean . . .' Olga was staring at Vassily.

'I do mean,' said Vassily. 'I think he carries out the murders himself, or gets his cronies to do it. Cronies like Anatoly Glazkov, I suppose, and the others he has hanging around – Stasevich, Yaroslav, and the rest. And Wolansky's a big part of it all, I'm sure, like a little troll perching on his shoulder, whispering evil thoughts into his ear and driving him on.

'Oh, Olga, the whole thing's been a piece of theatre all along! The dead tourist with money in his mouth, the fake text messages, the tip-offs, the tunic and the missing scrap of fabric, as if a killer was trying to frame me and Ivanka . . . It's all been *The Babikov Show*, every bit of it, right from the start.'

'Let me get this straight,' said Olga. 'You think Babikov tried to frame you and Ivanka by murdering Nathan Bryce and pushing him out of a carriage at Roslazny, with his mouth full of gold, as if Ivanka had signed the body. And there you were, waiting for the corpse, ready to incriminate yourself in front of Glazkov and the rest, as if you were in on Ivanka's plans. And—'

Pasha cut across her. 'Hang on,' he said to Vassily. 'How could Babikov know you'd be there to get the body?'

'Probably he got someone to call the murder in – or would've done, if Olga hadn't happened to do it first,' said Vassily. 'The

Roslazny station's closest to that bit of the track, so if someone called the Tayga police, they'd have to radio and send me first.'

'But doesn't your theory mean that Babikov knew Ivanka already?' said Olga. 'He had to know about her teeth, at least, if he had coins to stuff in Bryce's mouth.'

'That's what I'm saying,' said Vassily, patiently. 'I said Babikov frames his informants. And I think she was one of them. Didn't you say Ivanka's parents died when she was young – the victims of some gang or other? Well, there you go. There's her motivation to join up, to help the police in their work, and get one over on the criminals who did for her parents. She probably volunteered her services during a routine follow-up – or else Babikov got her to. Now I come to think of it, she all but said as much to us, when we interviewed her at Tayga. Nothing pleases her more than helping the police, or something like that.'

'The timing of the murder's interesting, too,' said Pasha, 'with the election coming up.'

'Exactly!' said Vassily. 'Babikov knew he was lagging in the polls – that he needed something big to push him over the top. And what could be bigger than solving a murder on the Trans-Siberian, with the eyes of the world upon him? So maybe he sat down to think, asking himself who he knew on the railways. The answer was Ivanka, of course – she's made for publicity, with her golden teeth, odd manners, tragic childhood, the lot. Then he asked himself if he knew any cops he could get posted to Roslazny to take the fall. And Babikov must have thought of me. I wasn't exactly his favourite employee when I worked with him before – he'd shed no tears at my taking the blame for his publicity exercise.

'But then you made your unexpected entrance in Act One,' said Vassily to Olga, 'and upset all his plans. So he needed to write another bit of the play – an Act Two, in which he could pin the murder of Alyona Vasiliev on me and Ivanka. Like I said when you visited me before, Olga, he could work backwards from Vasiliev to Bryce easily enough, the way things are in the media, these days.'

'But, Vassily,' said Olga, 'what about the phone call Ivanka made from Taras's? You can't just pretend she didn't say those things!'

'You're putting a lot of weight on the word of a man who, from what you say, sounds fairly disreputable. But supposing he's telling the truth, do you really think your Ivanka Kozar, hardened murderer and master of evil cunning, would have let herself be overheard on the phone to Alyona Vasiliev, or whoever, by a man like Taras? *By mistake?* No chance!'

'But then – why?' said Olga, mystified. 'Why would she make a call like that, only to be overheard?'

'Why do actors speak their lines on stage?' said Vassily. 'To be heard, not overheard! Think about what she said. It has to be after New Year, she said. And you need the money, she said, to keep looking. Well, who does that fit? *It fits me*, Olga,' he went on, seeing the blank look in her eyes. 'I didn't get here till after New Year, did I? And I'm looking for my wife and son, aren't I? Well, obviously I need money for bribes, then. That much is true, actually – I've spent pretty much every kopek I've got, greasing wheels all across the region. So I think Babikov instructed Ivanka to let Taras hear her, so that later on, when the police finally got round to investigating Ivanka, that phone call would turn up in evidence – and hey presto! Another damning link between Ivanka Kozar and Vassily Marushkin. Only, you got to Taras before the police, because Ivanka, by sheer good fortune, happened to have alibis. So, to sum up, I think her phone call was another bit of play-acting; and who was the illustrious producer, you might ask, of this celebrated performance? None other than our very own Lieutenant Colonel Babikov, with Wolansky directing from the wings. No doubt Wolansky wrote the script for her phone call himself.

'Babikov must've worked his charm on Ivanka,' he went on, 'getting under her skin and persuading her to cultivate Taras, get close to him, ask about his work at the slaughterhouse. He probably told Ivanka that Taras was a suspect for murder himself, that she should try to coax secrets out of him – say terrible things in his presence, and see if Taras took the bait. But Taras wasn't up to anything in particular – nothing very bad, anyway. So she abandoned him, again on Babikov's suggestion, I expect. But she'd already laid a trail of guilt that would come back to haunt her, sooner or later. If that samovar hadn't gone wrong on the Trans-Siberian, and if she hadn't happened to change her phone contract, Babikov would already have laid her bare on TV and banged her up for life.'

Silence fell over the police station as Olga and Pasha digested Vassily's arguments.

'I suppose it could make sense,' Pasha said, with a wary glance at Olga – he knew how proud she had been of her detective work the day before. But somewhat to his surprise she nodded distractedly, as if her thoughts were elsewhere. Vassily's words had brought memories to the surface, half-remembered fragments of overheard conversations.

'He said she won't see it coming,' she said. And then, in

response to Vassily's look of enquiry, she went on: 'Wolansky, I mean. He was talking to Babikov, when they met at Tayga. I might've overheard something that time, as well. Don't look at me like that, Vassily! It's a good job some of us keep our ears open. Anyway, Wolansky was talking about them still having the leading lady – that she was the key. And then he mentioned a chance for a man to redeem himself, though I'm not sure who, or why. At the time I thought they were talking about Babikov's mayoral campaign. But it's clear who the leading lady was, if you're right, Vassily. It was Ivanka. She was going to be the star of a public-relations exercise, only she didn't know anything about it. I'm sorry, Vassily – I should've mentioned it before, but I didn't think it mattered.'

Pasha whistled and made to speak, but Olga carried on, her heartbeat quickening as she thrilled with the pleasure of weaving disparate threads together: 'There's another thing, too, about how Babikov came into the station building at Tayga. He walked in quickly, and pulled on his overcoat. Who comes into a warm railway station and pulls *on* a coat? Only a man who's just changed out of a disguise! He must've been on the train, of course, like you said, Vassily, and had just cut Nathan Bryce's throat, maybe disguised as a guard, or as a tourist. Oh, we should've known he was the murderer, there and then, but we were stupid. We let him go on. We let him kill Alyona.

'Yes, yes,' she went on, her eyes glowing as they did when inspiration seized her in her little hut, 'there was a phrase Glazkov said, too, when I came to the police station after you'd been arrested. He was muttering about Babikov, saying he wanted a clean sweep this time. I think he meant that Babikov wanted Ivanka in a cell next to you. But she'd got away for a second time, because she happened to change her phone number.'

'Well, well,' said Vassily. 'So old Glazkov is in on it . . . That fits, now I come to think of it. It would be easiest for him, of all people, to frame me for the Vasiliev murder. All he had to do was steal one of my old tunics from the station. And as for the Bryce murder, it explains how he got there so fast, doesn't it, when Bryce was killed? He turned up early, like all those journos – sent by Wolansky, I suppose. It must've been Glazkov you saw disappearing behind your hut.'

'I wish I could be sure,' said Olga, shaking her head. 'But I just can't remember seeing him for certain, Vassily. It's all a bit of a blur.'

'Don't worry – it might come back to you later. I've seen that happen before. Anyway, I think Glazkov took a camera with him, so he could snap an incriminating photo of me standing by the body, waiting to collect my pay-off and do my duty by my partner in crime. And it made sense to pick Roslazny. The trains slow down going past your hut, because of the bumpy ground. And the path near the forest – they knew I'd be able to get there when the train was still going past, if I drove fast from the police station. Makes a better photo, doesn't it, if the train's still moving when they take the photo of me and the body? Gets the Trans-Siberian in. That's what Babikov wanted, for publicity.'

'Yes,' said Olga, excitedly. 'But Glazkov failed, didn't he? He forgot the camera and the picture when he saw me on the ground. He was too kind, too good a man, after all, to let me lie there unattended. So – so if he failed by the tracks, maybe he's the man who needed to redeem himself, like Wolansky said.

But how could he redeem himself at Tayga station? He could hardly go back in time and take another picture of you.'

'No, but he could do something else,' said Vassily. 'Did you hear them talking before or after we interviewed the crew, Olga?'

'It was before,' she said.

'So Glazkov had a chance to make someone hang for the murder,' murmured Pasha. 'He could try to frame Ivanka in the interviews, even if you were out of the picture. But they didn't know then that Ivanka had been working on the samovar with Zonov.'

'Remember how cross Babikov was – how *pale*, and then how lost he looked – when Glazkov told him there was nothing doing?' said Olga.

Vassily recalled the lieutenant colonel's puzzlement. 'Yes,' he said, 'he must've pinned all his hopes on getting Ivanka for Bryce's death, at least, even if I was out of the picture. And he'd just realised he couldn't even have her.'

Olga turned to him, her eyes glimmering in the dark. 'You must be right, Vassily. It *was* Babikov, all along.'

'It's the only thing that makes sense,' he agreed.

Pasha stirred. 'And Fandorin – the broken points. Olga thinks that—'

'I thought of Viktor Fandorin, too,' cut in Vassily, as he lit another of Glazkov's cigarettes. 'But I expect he's pretty small beer. Probably Babikov got Glazkov or Wolansky to call him up with a disguised voice, and offer him a few thousand roubles to break the point. That way they could get you out of the hut.'

'He asked me to confirm when I'd finished the repair,' said Olga, thinking back, 'but he couldn't, because the radio reception was so bad – so I got back to my hut sooner than anyone expected. I remember him laughing through the static, and saying rude things about me, because he thought I couldn't hear him.'

'He might've been laughing then, when he hadn't realised he'd got tied up in murder,' said Vassily. 'I bet he's scared stiff now. Well, we'll just have to scoop him up, at the same time.'

'At the same time?' said Olga.

Vassily exhaled until his face was wreathed in smoke. 'We're going to get them all, Olga. Babikov, Glazkov, Fandorin, Wolansky, the lot. But first we've got to make a couple of phone calls. We'll start with Colonel Terekhin, who can help us with some logistical necessities, and then we'll call your friend – what was her name? The woman with all the contacts?'

'Ekaterina Chezekhov?' said Olga.

'That's the one,' said Vassily. 'Tell her we need to speak to a *provodnitsa*, currently far away on the Trans-Siberian, as soon as possible. Lives might depend on it! Not to mention the fate of a certain poor sergeant, locked into a cell in the Roslazny jail, with only a ferret for company.'

Pasha poured each of them a healthy slug of vodka from his hip-flask, and Olga got busy on her mobile. Less than twenty minutes later the phone calls had been made, Ekaterina's networks had been mobilised, and Ivanka had been tracked down and contacted. She was in Vladivostok, she said, thousands of miles away at the end of the line. Everything she said confirmed Vassily's theories to the last detail, even down to the very words she'd uttered in front of Taras Sviatoslav, which had been written out for her sentence by sentence, she said, by Babikov's head of PR, the man called Wolansky.

'I can't believe this is happening,' said Ivanka Kozar, her voice tinny and distorted on Olga's speakerphone. 'After everything I've done for the police – for the lieutenant colonel . . . He said I could have a new job – that it didn't matter I wasn't wanted on the railways any more. And now he turns out to be a *murderer* – a serial killer! I'm sorry,' she went on, breaking down in tears and sobbing. 'It's just – all this *death* . . . My parents, my adopted parents, and all the others, too – and now those poor souls on the railway . . . Oh, I can't bear it,' she went on. 'Just tell me – no, *promise* me – you'll catch them all, and put them away. That's all I want.'

'Don't worry, Ivanka,' Olga said. 'That's all *we* want, too. And we've got a plan.'

'Have we?' mouthed Vassily.

Olga nodded, smiled, and inclined her mug towards the sergeant, just like Sasha Tsaritsyn. 'We have now,' she whispered. And then, as the silent streets of Roslazny dreamed under the frozen, star-scattered sky, she began to speak, telling Ivanka Kozar, the golden-mouthed *provodnitsa*, what she had in store for Lieutenant Colonel Babikov and his accomplices.

When Olga had finished Ivanka laughed, a harsh, crackling sound on the tinny speakerphone. 'That'll do it,' she said. 'That'll cook the little geese, yes, and leave plenty for all to eat. Plenty for all.'

14

The Return of Baba Yaga

Just before nine o'clock on Saturday morning, a figure could be seen trudging down the forest pathway towards the little railside hut where Olga worked. Dressed in Olga's roomy fur-lined parka, and with sunglasses and a fur hat pulled down about the ears, the figure looked prepared for any weather – too prepared, perhaps, given the relatively balmy temperature of minus five. The figure behaved strangely, too, when it got to the hut, struggling to unlock the door as if they were unfamiliar with the lock.

All these riddles were solved when the figure ducked inside, put down the satchel, and took off the fur hat with a sigh of relief – for it was Pasha, rather than Olga, who would man the hut that day. Olga had lived up to her promise of finding him a job to keep him busy, and had pressed him into service as a workable Olga replica. 'We're in luck,' she'd said earlier that morning, over a scanty breakfast at Aunt Zia's. 'It'll be a quiet day. A few freight trains to wave through, and the standard track inspections, plus the weekly checks once the passenger service's gone through in the evening. Easy enough, for an army man like you! And if you wear my sunglasses and hat outside, and keep your distance, nobody will be able to tell. If you've got to use the radio, just pretend you've got a cold. But you shouldn't have to, today.'

'But what if there's something wrong with the track?'

'Oh, don't worry about that,' she'd replied airily. 'That hardly ever happens.'

'But – but it does happen sometimes?' Pasha had replied, beginning to sweat as he imagined a six-thousand-ton train derailing at forty miles an hour.

'It's more important to remember why we're doing this,' Olga had said briskly, bossing her big brother around as if she were still ten years old. 'This is the only way to free me up without Fandorin knowing I'm off work. He's tied up in this somehow, remember. And don't forget there's an innocent man in prison, and murderous policemen on the loose.'

'A rather attractive innocent man?' said Pasha. But she'd only hit him on the arm and begun to squeeze him into her parka. He thought again how much Olga had changed since he had last seen her. The strange thing was, he felt it was an older version of her he was seeing, not a newer one. Pasha remembered how his little sister had changed after their mother's death, shrinking into herself and prioritising obedience to their father Mikhail above all else, as if she could ensure, through sheer virtue, that this second parent would not also perish. Since then, she had most often been subdued and submissive, a lesser version of the woman she would have been, perhaps, had Tatiana Pushkin lived. But now at last she seemed to be coming back to herself.

But Pasha's realisation had made him still more anxious about Olga's plan for that Saturday . So much was at stake – not just the freedom of Vassily Marushkin, but also justice for Babikov's victims, including Nathan Bryce and Alyona Vasiliev alongside the informants and collaborators whose faces he'd brazenly printed in his report, not to mention the poor souls he'd murdered to frame his victims in the first place . . . And now Olga herself would be at risk, too. But Pasha had forced himself not to show his fear. She didn't need to carry that burden, too, after all she had been through.

'You'll be fine,' Pasha had said, before he set off to the hut that morning. 'I know you will. There's no policeman on earth, lieutenant colonel or otherwise, who can get the better of Olga Pushkin.'

'I hope you're right,' Olga had replied, looking up at him, suddenly tearful. 'Thanks, Pasha. I just wanted to say—'

'I know,' he'd said. 'Me, too. Now, I'd better go! I'll see you at Café Astana this evening, unless you come and get me from the hut first. I promised Anna I'd play with the boys.'

Olga had nodded, choking back a sob as she watched Pasha leave Aunt Zia's house and walk down the road towards the hut. It had been a long time since she'd realised how much she cared for those around her: Pasha, of course, but also Anna and her boys, Popov the butcher and Fyodor Katin the Dreamer, even Odrosov and his daughter Svetlana . . . They were a community, after all. They didn't have much in common, perhaps, but they all lived in Roslazny and had a right to dwell there in peace and safety. Her eyes had filled with tears not because she was worried for her own safety, but because she couldn't bear the thought of anything happening to Pasha or the others at Babikov's hands, or the hands of any other murderer who might be lurking in their midst.

And then there was Vassily Marushkin, whose face was rarely far from Olga's thoughts. She had relished working with him on the case, and not just because of his haunting eyes. She'd found herself coming alive during their partnership, forgetting the dull routines of everyday life and concentrating all her energy on the goal of freeing him from the Roslazny jailhouse. And they'd already accomplished a great deal together. But one task still remained.

After Pasha left, Olga had tried to distract herself by sitting in bed and reading her way through Aunt Zia's enormous collection of *Sovetskaya zhenshchina* magazines from the 1980s. But it was hard to concentrate on a day like that, and despite the dangers hanging over her she found it a relief to slip out of the house that afternoon and be on her way to the rendezvous at last. She marched along the path that led away from the centre of Roslazny, her jaw set in a firm line, her hands and feet swinging purposefully. 'You'd better watch out, Lieutenant Colonel Grigor Babikov,' she said. 'I might only be a third class engineer, but we have our own ways of getting things done. And we don't like dead bodies littering the tracks!'

Private Anatoly Glazkov left the police station at his usual time that evening, muttering a goodbye to Vassily and pulling on his fur-lined gloves as he stepped out into the cold. He set off on his normal route to Café Astana, past the abandoned bathhouse and through the graveyard that straggled outward from the ruined Church of St Aleksandr. His repeated journeys had scored a pathway into the snow, beating it down into muddy ice that was more treacherous than the virgin surface. But Glazkov stuck to his path nonetheless: the worn-down track was the quickest way to the café and Odrosov's Rocket Fuel.

Each night he'd walked there a little more quickly, more and more desperate for a bottle that would grant him blessed relief from the despair that filled his waking hours. If only he could talk to someone, unburden himself, confess his terrible deeds like a repentant sinner, hold up his hands and experience the ecstasy of honesty at last . . . But talking about what he'd done would seal his fate. Others wouldn't understand. Others wouldn't excuse him, even if they knew why he'd gone along with Babikov's plans – why he'd done anything he could to protect his elderly mother and pay her care-home bills, which mounted month by month . . .

No, he couldn't talk. Only the bottom of a glass could help, the delicious oblivion that swept over him as the crude alcohol sank down his throat. But the more he drank to forget, the worse he would feel the morning after, which only heightened the despair.

And all the time he had his police duties to carry out – running the Roslazny station in Vassily's place, conducting daily patrols to ensure that Bogdan's associates were behaving themselves, and avoiding awkward questions from journalists and others about the murders of Nathan Bryce and Alyona Vasiliev. Wolansky had quite a few hacks in his pay, Glazkov knew, but lately they'd seemed more aggressive in their enquiries – more aggressive than one would expect, for pen-pushers in the little man's pocket. Maybe it was part of some grand plan above Glazkov's pay grade. But in any case, Glazkov had never fully trusted Wolansky. He wasn't one of them. He hadn't proved his worth over decades of policework, fighting a constant battle against chaos and trying to balance the law's stern diktats with the simple human need to get by and make ends meet. Involving people like Wolansky was risky – who knew where his loyalties lay? And at any time there could be a reckoning that would spell disaster for all of them. But for the moment Glazkov had to keep going as he was. He had no choice. He had never had a choice – not as long as his mother was alive.

'Bloody snow,' he said, as the skies clouded over once more and heavy flakes began to fall. He hunched his head low and hurried as fast as he dared, keeping an eye out for three low gravestones near the path, each of which had been his downfall on previous occasions. Then he stopped, uttering another curse, for his mobile was ringing in his pocket. Who could be calling at this time of day?

He looked at the screen. 'Number withheld,' it read. He decided he'd better answer it.

'Yes?' he said. 'Who's this?'

'It's me – Babikov,' said a muffled voice at the other end. 'I'm in Roslazny. We need to meet. Now.'

'Right now?' said Glazkov. 'Can't it wait, sir?' In his mind he was already halfway through the door at Café Astana, drinking a triple vodka with a bowl of pickled gherkins, and talking about the usual things with Igor Odrosov and Fyodor Katin and Odrosov's daughter Svetlana, whenever she emerged from the kitchen, cigarette in mouth, to dish out hot food to whoever was brave enough to order it.

'No, it has to be now,' said the voice. 'Things have changed, and I need to discuss them with you. It's urgent.'

Glazkov sighed. 'All right, sir. Tell me where you are, and I'll be on my way.'

'I'm at the edge of the village, by the old road to Tayga. There's an old warehouse here, with machinery inside.'

'I know it,' said Glazkov. The run-down warehouse had housed a processing plant in the days of the *sovkhoz*, when the farmers used to package their produce before sending it on to Tayga. In those days there had been another road to Tayga, running south-east at first rather than west, but the municipality had ripped up the tarmac and sold it off for aggregate after the *sovkhoz* closed, and the road was now overgrown. The building had stood empty for more than a decade, apart from the occasional group of teenagers who wanted a private place to smoke or drink.

'I'm still in the middle of the village, though,' Glazkov continued, 'and the paths are thick with snow. It'll take me a few minutes to get there.'

'I'll be waiting.' The phone went dead.

Reluctantly Glazkov turned, and trudged back the way he had come until he reached the winding path that led towards the old road to Tayga. If he had looked behind him after passing the old bathhouse, down the road towards the police station, he might have seen a man emerging from a nearby doorway and entering the station, then coming out again, accompanied by another man; and then he would have seen both of them following him at a safe distance. But Glazkov didn't look back. He tramped on in the snow, now falling so thickly that it all but obscured the faint light of the Roslazny lampposts, which were few and far between at this end of the village. Glazkov could hardly see his feet beneath him.

'Damn him,' he muttered to himself. 'Bloody Babikov! Can't a man have a drink in peace?'

Finally the old Tayga road came into sight, and then the abandoned warehouse next to its overgrown threshold. Glazkov went on towards the warehouse, stumbling on the potholes hidden under the blanket of fresh snow. He tripped again as he made his way inside, falling heavily against the flimsy door and knocking it off its hinges at last.

'You make quite an entrance, Anatoly Glazkov,' said a figure inside. He looked up, gasping from the pain in his shins and struggling to see clearly in the gloom of the warehouse. As his eyes adapted, he could make out a woman's figure leaning against one of the workbenches in skirt, boots and puffy jacket.

'What are you doing here?' he said.

'The lieutenant colonel invited me,' said the woman. 'Didn't you know I've been working with him?'

'Of course I did,' said Glazkov. 'But I thought you were off to the east, on the railway.'

'I'm back now – regular as clockwork, Anatoly,' said the woman. 'You could set your watch by me. Speaking of which, here's the lieutenant colonel, right on time.'

Glazkov turned to see Babikov standing in the doorway, framed against the snow-drifts outside. Behind him was a smaller man with a pointed beard, who hung back, looking up at the building as if reluctant to enter. Babikov spoke quietly in Wolansky's ear, too quietly for the others to hear. 'How will we know if she's okay – if she's cracked? Or been turned? It's odd that she asked to meet me here.'

'I'll know, Grigor,' said Wolansky. 'I know acting when I see it.'

Finally Babikov nodded and stepped gingerly over the edge of the fallen door, taking up a position a few feet from the entrance. Wolansky stayed nearer the door.

'Private,' said Babikov, nodding at Glazkov. And then, to the woman: 'I should tell you that I'm not used to being summoned from restaurants to abandoned warehouses at short notice, Miss Kozar. Nor am I accustomed to being threatened by a person whose formal relationship with the force is tenuous, at best.'

'I'm not threatening you,' said the woman. 'I want a few points cleared up, that's all.'

Babikov didn't answer straight away. Then he spoke with a quizzical tone: 'You sound different,' he said. 'Have you caught a cold?'

'I'm the same, Lieutenant Colonel,' she said. 'It's you who's changed.'

'What do you mean?'

'It's just that I'm beginning to wonder . . . Look, when I signed up, you said a lot of things about duty, service and justice.'

'I probably did, yes,' said Babikov. 'What of it?'

'Well, then you made me get together with that man – with Taras Sviatoslav,' she went on. 'That didn't seem very – very *ethical* . . . And I couldn't understand why you said I had to ask him about the abattoir, and laugh to myself at times, and – and eat strange food in front of him. And then you made me drop him, out of nowhere – you said he'd served his purpose well enough.'

'I don't remember saying that,' said Babikov. He and Glazkov were staring at the woman, and neither of them noticed

Wolansky moving slowly towards the entrance, pulling a phone from his pocket.

He paused before he left the warehouse and looked once more at Babikov. The time had come at last, thought Wolansky. He'd told Babikov that he knew acting when he saw it – and so he did. He didn't know exactly what had changed, but something surely had, and that was enough. The curtain was about to fall, and it was no part of his plan to be caught under it. He smiled briefly, almost sadly, in Babikov's direction, then stepped silently into the falling night, merging into the snowflakes and disappearing into the dark grey beyond.

'You made me ask him about the police, too, for no reason I could follow,' continued the woman, 'and you made me say those things on the phone in front of him, without really being on the phone at all!'

Babikov smirked. 'That I do remember,' he said, turning to where Wolansky had been. 'Where did he go?' he said to Glazkov, who shrugged.

'He'll be back,' said Babikov. 'Now, Miss Kozar, I'm sorry to hear of your concerns. But as long as you keep them to yourself and continue your important work with the force, there needn't be any trouble. If, on the other hand, you decided to talk about your concerns to anyone else – to the media, let us say – well, that would be a different story altogether.'

The woman paused. 'But you haven't heard all the things I'm worried about. Like how it was that my name kept coming up in connection with murders. How text messages with my name on them were sent to some crooked copper, from a phone number I don't use any more. And how another poor *provodnitsa* from that train – the train that tourist died on – ended up dangling from a rope, and not by her own hand. People are dying all over the place, and it seems like I'm in the firing line for deaths I'm beginning to think were your fault. Oh, no, I'm not going to keep quiet – you can rely on that! I'm going to the papers. Let's see how you get on with your mayoral campaign after they print what I've got to say.'

The woman stopped speaking, as if breathless after her outburst. There was silence for a moment. Then Babikov laughed. 'My mayoral campaign will be just fine, Miss Kozar. In fact, it will be better than ever in about half an hour, when I've had time to prepare the scene. Death by hanging again, maybe. Or perhaps we might try something a little more inventive, like we managed for the American on the train. Yes, I rather like that idea! Maybe something involving this old machinery . . . Do you agree? Might make rather a splash in the papers. Wait till Wolansky gets hold of it!'

But the woman didn't reply. She looked sideways instead, raising her head as if seeking permission to do something. Then she nodded and stepped behind the workbench. In an instant, a series of floodlights crashed on, bathing Babikov and Glazkov in a sea of scorching blue light. At the same time, two men stepped forward with raised pistols, shouting at them to get on their knees and put their hands behind their heads.

Dazedly they complied, blinking as they tried to understand what was happening. Had Ivanka Kozar brought back-up of some kind? Had she thought they'd try to kill her, and hired a gang of hitmen to take them out instead? But then Babikov saw the reflective bands on the men's arms and the familiar peaked caps of the Russian police, and finally he understood what had happened. Ivanka had worked out what was going on, and the authorities had caught up with him at last. He groaned and slumped forward.

'Sensible not to resist,' said a stentorian voice. Babikov looked up, shielding his eyes, and saw Colonel Terekhin stepping forward, with Vassily Marushkin at his side.

'Vassily!' gasped Glazkov, who had left him locked in his cell only twenty minutes earlier. 'How did you get here?'

'I was happy to release Sergeant Marushkin myself,' said Terekhin. 'Someone called me on his behalf yesterday, and presented me with enough evidence to convince me that I needed to get involved again – and more effectively this time. We followed you here in time to hear what you were saying. The game's up. But don't think this gives me any pleasure, Babikov,' Terekhin went on, as Vassily helped the two policemen, rank-and-file privates from Tayga, to cuff Babikov and Glazkov's hands behind their backs. 'No copper should ever have to arrest another.'

'It doesn't give me much pleasure either, *sir*,' spat Babikov, as Vassily got him to his feet. 'Brought down by a bloody *provodnitsa*!'

'I *told* you Kozar was trouble,' muttered Glazkov, out of the side of his mouth.

'Oh, that's not Ivanka Kozar,' said Terekhin, waving towards the woman. 'Kozar's on a train somewhere east of Irkutsk. Sloppy work, Grigor. You should've checked the railway schedule before you came.'

'Not Ivanka?' said Glazkov. 'Then who . . .?'

Glazkov and Babikov watched in astonishment as Olga came forward out of the gloom, taking out the padding from her fur-lined jacket, and giving them a little curtsy. Glazkov managed a smile. 'Well, Miss Pushkin,' he said, 'you make a good Ivanka.'

But she didn't smile in response. 'I'm not sure how flattered I should be, Anatoly,' she said. 'I don't set much store by the praise of murderers.'

'*Murderers?*' said Babikov. 'Who said anything about murder?'

Vassily and Olga looked at each other. 'You did, about five minutes ago,' said Olga.

'Unfortunately for you,' added Vassily, picking up a small device hidden behind a rusty vice, 'we took the liberty of recording your discussion with Miss Pushkin just now, to aid your future prosecution.'

'You've already confessed to the murders of Nathan Bryce and Alyona Vasiliev,' said Terekhin. 'And as Sergeant Marushkin was clever enough to work out your MO while imprisoned in a cell—'

'Sergeant Marushkin *and* Miss Pushkin,' Vassily cut in.

'As Sergeant Marushkin *and* Miss Pushkin were clever enough,' said Terekhin drily, nodding at Olga, 'we now have a long list of old murder cases we're reopening, starting with those you put in your own report, Grigor, for God's sake! Did you really think you could get away with it for ever? Going on a killing spree and framing your own snitches for the deaths? Killing women and teenagers in Kemerovo, and foster families in Yashkino?'

'It wasn't me,' said Babikov. 'It was Wolansky's idea. My head of PR. He's got things over me. Where is he? He was here a few minutes ago! If you check outside you'll find him. Quick!'

Terekhin jerked his head at one of the privates from Tayga,

who spoke urgently into his chest-mounted radio, drew his pistol again, and left the building in search of Wolansky. But he soon returned, shrugging his shoulders. Wolansky had vanished, his footprints merging with others, already obscured by the falling snow.

Terekhin turned to Babikov, but Glazkov spoke first, in tones of puzzlement. 'Foster families in Yashkino? We didn't do those, did we, sir? Unless I'm forgetting, or you did them alone, like the Bryce murder and Vasiliev. God, there were so many.'

'Foster families?' said Olga. 'In Yashkino?' Why did that information set alarm bells ringing?

In her mind, slowly at first but then with mounting speed, she seemed to see the old steam engine at Tayga station pulling an enormous train through the Siberian night, lit by unearthly light and filled with evil creatures: goblins, imps, sprites, boggarts, ghosts and demons of every kind. But worst of all was the engine driver. Olga found herself swept closer to the locomotive's cab, lit from within by scorching flames from the firebox, and inhabited by something vile. She could see skirts flapping in the rushing air as the engine accelerated to breakneck speed, the tortured steel of bearings and couplings and wheels shrieking in the night as the spectral driver drove the train faster, faster, ever faster . . .

A bony hand grasped her arm and dragged her into the cab, and then Olga saw her, facing away, hunched over in the corner beyond the glowing firebox. As if compelled by another power Olga stepped forward. Her own hand crept out, defying her will. She felt as if she were bound to the floor in a gigantic iron frame, and that she had no more control over its movements than a puppet over its master. Then came the thing she dreaded most of all: her hand touched the crouching figure. It sprang up and turned to face her, taller than it had looked in its huddle, revealed now as a darkling witch with golden teeth and whirling clothes of a deeper black than the night alone. The teeth shivered in laughter, then swooped to engulf her in a murderous embrace—

Olga blinked: she was remembering a nightmare she'd had that morning, when she'd lain half asleep in the pre-dawn quiet, dreading the day ahead. It was silent in the abandoned warehouse, too, for a few seconds, except for the soft hiss of snowflakes falling on the roof, louder than might have been expected.

And then came a different sound: a gentle thumping, distant and subtle, but definite, like the ends of a rocking-chair banging against a wall. The policemen heard it also – Olga could see Babikov's head turning, then Vassily's and Glazkov's and Terekhin's, too, as they sought its source. The empty warehouse confused their ears, sending echoes everywhere. But then came a particularly loud bang, and she gasped: the noise seemed to be coming from *behind* her, from the side of the warehouse furthest from the road. Had the police checked for hidden entrances? Olga thought back to the briefing Colonel Terekhin had given them when they'd gathered at the warehouse earlier that afternoon, perched on old gas cylinders, some rusted through and some still bearing their bright warning colours, to make their plans for the capture of Babikov, Wolansky and Glazkov. But she couldn't remember Terekhin mentioning an entrance at the back. And Olga was nearer that side than any of the others.

Another bang came to her ears, louder this time, and now she was filled with fear. She was thinking of Baba Yaga again, the old woman who dwelled in the woods, and who drove herself around in a mortar, banging the pestle upon the ground as she chased down Vassilia the Beautiful. Suddenly the glaring blue floodlights went out, casting them into darkness. The policemen called out in surprise, and drew their weapons; Olga screamed and shrank to the ground, clinging to the dusty workbench and dreading further sounds that might herald the coming of the witch, or a bony hand upon her shoulder in the dark and the foetid stench of evil breath in her face . . .

The banging stopped. Silence reigned once more in the abandoned warehouse for a few minutes, long enough for Olga to wonder if she'd imagined the banging. Or perhaps it had just been an old shutter blowing in the breeze and knocking on the side of the building. There was a slight breeze, she realised, that flowed across the warehouse from a loose plank to her right. She breathed slowly, deeply, drawing in the fresh, chilled air and trying to calm down. One of the policemen muttered something to the others, and they laughed. The privates from Tayga took out their torches and flicked them on with familiar ease. The power supply, after all, was notoriously unreliable in Roslazny.

But then came a voice in the darkness beyond Olga's workbench.

'Glazkov,' it said, in sing-song tones. 'Oh, Glazkov . . . Babikov! Oh, Babikov . . .'

It was a harsh, cracked voice, like the fractured ice at the edge of a lake – a woman's voice, an evil witch's voice, full of ancient cruelty and hate. And the hideous imitation of a child at play filled Olga with terror, not least because the speaker was behind her. She *had* come in by a secret way, then, creeping through the darkened warehouse with infinite care, avoiding all the machinery and clutter that lay about, while tormenting them with faint percussion, the threat of blows to come.

'Glazkov, Babikov, are you there, my children, my naughty little boys?' said the voice. Olga dared a glance over the workbench and saw a figure standing in the gloom, neither tall nor short, and stocky in the *provodnitsa* winter uniform of boots and skirt and fur-lined jacket. The woman held a heavy wooden staff in one hand – it looked as if she'd taken it from an old barrel in the warehouse. Then she turned her head, and Olga's heart quailed – for the woman was smiling, and she saw a glint of metal in that horrid mouth. But there was no golden colour on her teeth, in that bleached and dusky light. Ivanka Kozar the golden-toothed had become Baba Yaga the iron-mouthed.

'I'm here,' said Glazkov, making Olga jump. He stood forward, silhouetted against the faint twilight, and Olga could see that he was afraid, that he knew what had happened – that he'd realised, like her, who had really been responsible for the deaths of the foster families. Glazkov was suddenly aware, like Olga, of an evil deeper than the mere Machiavellian ruthlessness of Grigor Babikov.

While the others stood still, Anatoly Glazkov walked slowly towards Ivanka, like a condemned man on the way to his place of execution, defenceless, his hands cuffed behind his back, and Olga thought it was the bravest thing she had ever seen.

'And what does Anatoly Glazkov want from Ivanka?' said the *provodnitsa*, moving forward, still speaking in mockery of a child's voice.

'I'm s-sorry, Ivanka,' said Glazkov. 'I – I see we underestimated you. We shouldn't have treated you like—'

'Like an idiot?' said Ivanka, raising her heavy wooden staff to his throat, like a sword, and at the same time throwing a heavy scarf around her face, hiding her mouth and nose.

'Y-yes,' stammered Glazkov, looking at the staff beneath his chin. 'Like an idiot. I'm sorry,' he said again. 'It was – it was wrong.'

Ivanka laughed. Even muffled by the scarf, it came to Olga's ears as a terrible scraping sound, like an avalanche of frozen snow. 'I'm glad you see that now, Anatoly.'

'I do, I do,' said Glazkov, eagerly. 'I just hope you can forgive us.'

Babikov found his voice. 'Glazkov's right,' he said, pulling free of Terekhin's grasp with surprising ease. 'We can find a solution that suits everybody. Well, *almost* everybody.' He turned and nodded at the others. 'We don't need them. Or Wolansky, wherever the hell he's got to. Glazkov and I are *experienced*, just the same way you are. We could work together – collaborate. We underestimated you,' he went on, with an obvious effort. 'We – we should never – we should never have—'

He tailed off into silence and began retching. He bent over as if in pain, then tried to stand up straight again. But again he bent double, and then, with his hands pressed against his stomach, collapsed onto the ground and lay still. Olga registered, in some part of her mind, the oddity of his patch of white hair against the black, like some kind of animal with swirls of fur, some dark and some silver. She struggled to bring its name to mind. A badger! Of course. A badger. But a badger lying still on the ground, instead of rooting in the earth; a badger that had been shot, or tranquillised.

Tranquillised, she thought. Tranquillised, or drugged in some other way . . . Ivanka had drugged Babikov – she had drugged them all. Or *gassed* them: she remembered now the brightly coloured gas cylinders by the doorway, too new and unrusted to be a survival from the *sovkhoz*. They'd hidden in plain sight, too obvious to be a source of suspicion. Colonel Terekhin had sat upon one! And the hissing noise she'd heard, when the warehouse was silent – it had been too loud, she now realised, to have been snowflakes alone. But she must already have fallen under the insidious substance's influence by then, or she would have grasped that straight away. Yes, she'd fallen under its influence – but not, perhaps, as much as the others. She hadn't fallen to earth like Babikov. Why?

'So Babikov's the first,' laughed Ivanka, her voice thick with menace through the scarf.

Scarf? No, it must be a gas mask, thought Olga, dully, her mind moving slowly, as if she were wading thigh-high through the last and wettest snow of the season.

'Shame,' said Ivanka Kozar. 'I wanted Babikov to know. After all these months and years of bossing me around, treating me like an idiot – like one of his pathetic army of devoted citizens, or the small-time robbers and extortionists that prance around the province for him . . . I wanted him to know that it was *me* pulling the strings all along. I knew all about the ridiculous scheme he dreamed up with that long-haired fool Wolansky, and how he planned to ensnare me and the good Sergeant Marushkin. You got somewhere, Marushkin, I'll give you that,' she added, turning to face Vassily. 'You and your little railway engineer deduced more than I expected, chewing over the titbits of information I left lying around, just for the fun of it.

'And when you called me yesterday, I knew I'd have to come back, and in a hurry, too. But, still, I knew you'd never guess it was me who sabotaged the samovar, and got Zonov to help in exchange for a couple of bottles of vodka – or that I deliberately gave Glazkov my old phone number after we talked at Tayga, in case Wolansky's IT minions tried sending fake messages from it. It was so easy I began to get bored. But this – *this* is exciting again! So, well done, Colonel Terekhin – I see you at the back there – and Marushkin, and Pushkin, and the rest, for organising it. Still, I can't linger too long. It's exciting because it's risky. But I want to carry on for a few years yet.

'So, who's next?' went on Ivanka. 'Let's go down the chain of command. We've done away with a lieutenant colonel, so why not a *ryadovoy politsii*? Why not Private Glazkov?'

'No!' said Glazkov. 'I'm innocent – I only did those things because *he* made me.' He jerked his head at Babikov, lying on the ground, but the movement unbalanced him, and he fell to his knees. 'Oh please, Ivanka,' he went on, his words slurring into each other, 'think of my mother. She's the only reason I got involved. I had to do all those things, all those murders, for *years* – and then setting up Vassily with the American's body, and Alyona Vasiliev. But that was all Babikov's idea. Please – just give us another chance to help you.'

The American's body, thought Olga, as if in a trance. So it *had* been Glazkov behind the hut that time. They had reasoned it out already, but now they had proof from the horse's mouth.

Glazkov's voice tailed off and, like Babikov, he retched and stumbled. He recovered briefly and, with a final desperate effort, begged her to spare him, to let him work with her, as Babikov had suggested, to think of his poor mother stuck in a care home and relying on him, to give him a second chance to prove his worth to her.

'Another chance?' said Ivanka, laughing behind her scarf. 'Nobody ever gave me a second chance. They said I was odd, strange, uncanny – *unearthly*. A queer little girl, they said – and that was my own parents, behind my back! No loss, when they went. And then the two geriatrics who adopted me said the same things, only this time to my face. And when I told them the things I'd been doing for fun, they dispatched *themselves* that very day, and spared me the trouble. Best day's work they ever did. But by then I'd learned the pleasure in lingering over a tasty morsel. And so the fosterers, the Nikitins and the Rybakovs and the Zhuravlevs, had to wait a while for their reunions with me – they had to wait until December, to be precise. I thought it would be a nice Christmas present for their families – their precious flesh-and-blood children, who were just *far too good* for me to mix with!

'But between times I kept my hand in. I had to – I don't like to see a job done poorly. And it was fun, besides, to hunt them down – the hangers-on, I mean. The folk who run around after the rich to make their easy lives even easier – accountants and lawyers and nannies and life coaches and all the useless *pridurki* who ride through life in the handbags of oligarchs' wives like lapdogs. Do you know what it means to be rich and famous? It means to be *accepted*. Even if you break the law! You don't have to convince or persuade or force people to do anything, or to like you. And now that I've killed enough of the hangers-on,

I'll graduate to the rich themselves, the oligarchs and the media barons and the politicians and the TV presenters and the rest. The lieutenant colonel here might've got it wrong, when he tried to frame me, but at least he was thinking along the right lines when he killed that rich tourist. Those *idiots*, parading up and down my carriage in their pyjamas, in their *underwear*, telling me to do this, do that – to bring them bedlinen and tea and all the other things! And if you get the slightest thing wrong, it's off to the conductor with them, and you're up on a report with one chance left . . .

'No, Anatoly Glazkov,' she went on. 'I never had any second chances. Why should you?' Without warning she lifted her staff and swung it viciously at his head. Glazkov saw the blow coming and tried to duck, but his responses were too slow, too dulled by poisonous gas on top of decades of too much vodka. Ivanka connected with a sickening crunch, followed by a heavy thud as Glazkov fell to ground, blood spurting from his temples.

Vassily and the others watched in silence. Their eyes were distant and glazed, and Olga, too, felt her mind drifting away.

'Oh, forget about Glazkov, dear policemen, dear poodles,' said Ivanka, cutting through Olga's stupor and bringing her dazed thoughts back to the present. 'He never mattered, and neither did Grigor Babikov, or his pet Wolansky – or was it the other way round? Don't you see? As soon as I gave Babikov that babushka doll, nothing he did – nothing Babikov even *thought* – was hidden from me.'

Babushka doll? thought Olga. What did a babushka doll have to do with anything? How could a doll spy on a policeman?

'No, none of these stupid policemen matter,' went on Ivanka. 'Look at those two,' she added, pointing to the Tayga policemen

Terekhin had brought to support the operation, who were now collapsing onto the floor, like Babikov. 'A waste of space – a waste of *air*. If you can't be cunning, if you can't be *original*, don't take oxygen from those who are.'

'You witch,' stammered Terekhin. He lurched forward, but stopped abruptly, reeling on his feet. Then he, too, vomited uncontrollably and sank to his knees. Vassily stepped forward and tried to help him up, but then they both fell, dragging each other down and slumping upon the floor. Olga's eyelids were closing, but with a momentous effort she forced them open, and instinctively lurched towards the loose plank on the side of the warehouse, putting her face close to the lifegiving stream of cold, inflowing air. It bought her a moment of clarity, and with a tingling sense of unfriendly eyes upon her back she turned and saw Ivanka Kozar staring directly at her. Ivanka smiled under her scarf – Olga saw her eyes tighten sideways – and began striding quickly towards her.

But Olga had expected that, and began to move towards the far end of the warehouse, with the aim of getting outside and circling round the building. Then she could surprise Ivanka from behind, just as they had been surprised themselves. Perhaps she could get her hands on one of the policemen's pistols. Then she could deal with the golden-mouthed killer, once and for all.

Her thoughts raced as she went. So Ivanka Kozar *was* guilty, just as Olga had thought at first. The devilish *provodnitsa* with the chilling grin was, after all, the Baba Yaga of whom Fyodor Katin had spoken, the merciless killer whose reputation had reached even as far as Novosibirsk.

As Olga stepped quickly but carefully between the tangled

wires, wooden boxes and broken machinery strewn across the floor, she became aware of her returning strength and certainty. Of course: she was moving away from the gas canister at the entrance, and its poisonous, enfeebling contents. With this realisation she gained new courage. But she still had to find the hidden doorway that the *provodnitsa* had used earlier. And she could hear Ivanka coming up behind her, turning over bits of junk with her staff and calling to her in that terrible, broken-ice voice, taunting her and telling her the things she would do to her when she caught her.

At last Olga found a handle in the darkness. She pulled on it until her hands ached and her knuckles cracked, but to no avail. She tried pushing it instead, and the door suddenly gave way. She fell with a crash, landing on her hands and knees in the snow outside.

'I know where you are now, little goose,' called Ivanka, walking more quickly towards her. 'Didn't I say your plan would cook the geese for eating? Only you didn't know you were one of them. Don't move, little one. I'll soon be there.'

She was talking like the characters in Lubov's stories, Olga thought – the myths and legends her mother had learned at the Lodge in Astrazov, long ago. She talked as if they were in a fairy-tale filled with the hidden dark magic of Russia, as if she really *was* a forest-dwelling witch come once more to haunt children's dreams.

Olga shook her head, forcing herself to remember that Ivanka was just a woman, just flesh and blood like the rest of them. She was no sorceress with supernatural powers. She was a woman who needed a gas-mask to avoid being drugged herself.

Olga got to her feet and peered around her, breathing in the outside air, a fresh and cleansing draught thick with tingling snowflakes. To the right, and straight ahead, she saw high walls and thick, bushy undergrowth. But to the left a narrow alleyway seemed to offer a clear path down the side of the warehouse. Dimly she noticed there was already a set of fresh footprints leading that way. But there was no time to waste on pondering such things: she could hear Ivanka's footsteps echoing in the cavernous warehouse, quickening as they drew near to the exit.

But as Olga set off to follow the footsteps she paused, staring to her right, and trying to understand what her eyes were telling her. She saw a swelling in the snow, several feet across, like a monstrous toadstool dressed in white, covered with smooth snow but for a marked indentation near the top. Vaguely, Olga had understood what it meant. Anyone from Roslazny would know what it meant. But Ivanka had not grown up there, had she? Olga tried to remember what she'd learned about Ivanka in the course of her detective work, but her mind was still sluggish and unresponsive, her memories sticky and beyond her reach. She would simply have to stake everything on Ivanka *not* knowing.

As quickly as she could, she shuffled behind the bell-like shape, taking care not to tread on it, and pushing the snow clumsily back into place, as if attempting to conceal where she'd stepped. She ducked behind the snow-covered swelling, but took care that Ivanka would still be able to see her.

She heard the *provodnitsa* squeezing through the narrow doorway. Then she heard her laugh again, but this time a simpering, high-pitched twitter that made her shiver with fear.

'There you are, little goose, little one,' said Ivanka, swinging her wooden staff from side to side. 'I see you. Now I will conjure you a dream,' she went on. 'A dream that never ends.'

She stepped forward. Olga ducked more deeply, as if she were cowering from Ivanka.

'Come, little goose,' Ivanka kept saying, as she stepped nearer and nearer. She wasn't looking closely at the ground, but gazing steadily at Olga, the prey she would soon consume.

But it was not to be.

Ivanka stepped too close to the swelling, just an inch too close, but it was enough: for Olga had remembered it was a disused well with a wooden cover, a mass-produced fitting bearing the hammer and sickle, and distributed long ago to *sovkhoz* properties across the Kemerovo region. The ancient well-cover creaked as Ivanka stepped onto its edge. For a moment the ice that had wrapped itself around the wood held it together – for a moment: but then it cracked, the rotting fibres ripped apart, and the cover collapsed, just as Olga had hoped. Ivanka Kozar screamed as her foot plunged into the abyss that yawned beneath. The wooden staff fell from her hands and she scrabbled desperately at the snow, but now her other foot, too, slipped into the well, coming to rest on the thin lip of a protruding brick.

She flung out a hand and seized Olga's jacket. Olga gasped as she felt herself toppling towards the well, but she managed to stick out a foot in time to arrest her fall. Ivanka's weight was intolerable, a deadening pull on her arm that felt like it would tear the joint from its socket. The *provodnitsa* looked up at Olga, her face twisted into a demonic parody of entreaty, pleading for help, just as Glazkov had pleaded for his life. 'Oh, please, Miss Pushkin, *please* help me – I'll admit to anything, incriminate anybody you like! I'll kill all your enemies – get rid of Victor Fandorin! Or – or I'll say a prayer, offer a Divine Liturgy, for each and every soul I killed – a whole month of services! Just pull me up, help me, please, *dear* Miss Pushkin!'

Olga knew that her strength was failing – that soon she would topple forward and be cast down into the dark herself. Her head was pounding and the sweat ran freely down her back as she strained against her quivering legs and the scorching pain in her arm. It was her or Ivanka: her own self or a remorseless killer.

Slowly she reached down and began to prise Ivanka's fingers free of her arm. Ivanka screamed, and the hairs rose on Olga's neck as her face transformed, the pleading smile becoming a fierce grimace as she shouted obscene and terrible curses. She became a loathsome, bloated creature, a thing to be squashed and erased from the Earth. Olga grappled with the last finger, a pincer stuck deep into her, and then, with a scream of desperation and the end of her strength, she flung it from her arm. Ivanka Kozar fell with a great clattering and shrieking, the echoes reaching Olga's fading consciousness until there was a heavy crash, and the sounds of life abruptly ceased.

She sank back onto the snow. 'Vassily,' she tried to say, but the breath would not come. 'Vassily . . .'

Her eyes rolled up into her head, and she fell unconscious onto the ground.

15

Journey to Astrazov

'I think he's getting tired of me,' said Olga.

'Nonsense,' said Pasha. 'It's his job! Though he did say something about a loyalty card . . .'

It was Sunday, the day after Ivanka's death, and Pasha was sitting in a small armchair by Olga's bed at Aunt Zia's house. Dr Zinovev had been to check on her again, cautiously predicting a full recovery. The gas Ivanka had used on them had turned out to be an anaesthetic mixture in use at Taras Sviatoslav's abattoir, with powerful but mostly temporary effects. Olga shuddered as she wondered what Ivanka had planned once they'd all been knocked out – hadn't she said something about eating the goose, once it had been cooked?

Those who are foolish enough to fall unconscious in the Siberian winter can expect frostbite, hypothermia and, in due course, death. Luckily for Olga, however, Sasha Tsaritsyn had arrived soon after Ivanka fell down the well, and had immediately called the Tayga police station for assistance – upon which Pasha, hearing the commotion on the emergency frequency of Olga's radio, instantly abandoned his post at the railside hut to rush to the warehouse himself. While Sasha helped the paramedics administer first-aid to the stricken policemen, Pasha searched for his sister among the rusting machinery and rotting benches. Finally he came across the exit at the rear of the warehouse, and saw Olga lying motionless beside the disused well. Thrusting himself through the narrow door, he threw himself down beside her, and called her name again and again until, to his immense relief, she stirred and half opened her eyes. He picked her up and struggled around the side of the warehouse to the paramedics' ambulance, and within an hour Olga was safely in bed at Aunt Zia's with a mug of hot, sweet tea and a warm blanket around her shoulders.

Vassily had also spent the night at Aunt Zia's, in Pasha's bed next door; Pasha had volunteered to stay on the sofa for a few nights, since Vassily could hardly convalesce at the police station. Colonel Terekhin had signed his pardon with a knowing air, and now Vassily was free once more to sleep wherever he wanted.

Babikov, however, was at the Tayga community hospital under armed guard; he had been the worst affected by the gas, and was urgently awaited by the courts if he should recover. Colonel Terekhin, by contrast, was relaxing in the best hotel Kemerovo could provide, while the other two policemen had been taken back to their families in Tayga. But for Anatoly Glazkov there would be no return home. Ivanka, too, had perished, though in her case of a presumed broken neck.

Presumed, because her body had not been recovered, and never would be. The well was too deep, and when a fireman from Tayga tried to descend on a harness the following morning the well-mouth began to collapse, necessitating his swift escape. They finished the job by tumbling stones down on top of her.

'It's for the best,' said Pasha, when he heard the news. 'Nobody wants to give her a decent burial, anyway. Let her stay there and freeze for ever. It's a good kind of Hell, for a killer like that.'

'I don't know who was worse,' said Olga, after a pause. 'Ivanka or Babikov.'

'Babikov killed a lot more people,' said Pasha. 'He'd been at it for years, Vassily said.'

'But at least Babikov was doing it to advance his political career. I mean, it's terrible, but you can understand why he did it. But what was Ivanka's motive?'

Olga tried to sum up her confused impressions of the dead *provodnitsa*. 'People didn't like her, so she hated them. Her parents feared her, and so did her other guardians – so she made them even more afraid of her. And she said she'd killed others, too – servants of the rich and famous, people who were accepted and liked whatever they did, just the opposite of herself . . . And she didn't just want to kill people. She wanted to fool the police, the railways, the media, the whole *world* at the same time.'

'But doesn't that make Babikov worse?' said Pasha. 'He did what he did for political gain, but who can say why Ivanka did those things?'

'Not I,' said Olga. 'But remember what Ekaterina Chezhekov told me about Ivanka, when she talked of her parents' death. She seemed agitated, said Ekaterina, worked up, somehow. I think she was *excited*, not traumatised, by her parents' death. Maybe it triggered something lying deep within, a longing for suffering and death . . . Vassily's sure she killed her foster parents – all of them. But perhaps she began with her parents. Maybe that was what she told that old couple, before they killed themselves – that she'd already killed her own mother and father.'

'But they haven't found the bodies,' said Pasha. 'The bodies of the foster parents, I mean.'

'Not yet,' said Olga. 'But Vassily says they're working on a lead – a lead that I supplied, if you can believe it.'

Pasha thought for a minute. 'Taras's abattoir?'

'Taras's abattoir,' she said, with a brief smile. It had been a stroke of genius, she thought, to conjure that idea from her brief interview with Taras Sviatoslav. Olga had been struck by Ivanka Kozar's interest in his work at the abattoir, and by her private laughter – things that she'd guessed weren't part of Babikov's instructions for his tame *provodnitsa*. Didn't that suggest something horrible, some evil secret? And mightn't abattoirs have huge freezers on the premises, in which meat could be preserved when necessary – meat, or human corpses?

And so, in the event, it proved. Vassily came into Olga's room later that day with a satisfied look on his face. 'You were right, Olga,' he said. 'They found the bodies – the foster families. All three sets – the Nikitins, the Rybakovs and the Zhuralevs. The first two couples we knew about from the records in Yashkino, but Ivanka was sent to the Zhuralevs, too – they got missed off her notes somehow. Probably the Zhuralevs had something to hide, and bribed someone to keep it that way. Anyway, like you guessed, Ivanka hid their bodies deep in the abattoir freezers, laying a paper trail that pointed to Taras. Babikov thought he was setting *her* up by getting them together, but she was doing the same thing to Taras! It's brilliant. Evil, of course,' he added, 'but brilliant, from a purely professional point of view. Think of how she fooled us on the phone that time – making us think she was stuck on the train at Vladivostok, when she was already at the bloody airport!'

Acting on Terekhin's instructions, the Russian transport police had discovered footage of Ivanka boarding a flight from Vladivostok to Novosibirsk the night before last, less than two hours after she had spoken to Vassily and the Pushkins on the phone. She had abandoned her post on the Trans-Siberian, having paid her colleague Yelena Koriakin a small fortune to keep quiet and pull both shifts on the return leg west. Then she had paid a man to drive her to Roslazny, where she'd hidden near the warehouse until Babikov and the others arrived. After a few minutes she'd cut the power line to the floodlights, walked along the outside of the warehouse (banging on it as she went), and entered the building at the rear. Olga had seen her footprints, before Ivanka fell down the well.

'And she had Babikov dancing to her tune all along,' Vassily continued. 'Imagine, a chief of police controlled by a *provodnitsa*!'

'They thought she was a stool pigeon,' said Olga, pleased with a writerly turn of phrase that had just occurred to her. 'But she was the cat among the pigeons.'

Once Babikov had recovered, he confirmed all this himself, in a series of interviews conducted by Novosibirsk detectives under the supervision of Colonel Terekhin. (All the Kemerovo senior policemen were themselves under investigation, following the revelation of Babikov's murderous activities.) Babikov and his men later proved responsible for more than half of all the homicides in Kemerovo Province over the past four years, earning Babikov, as the man behind the scheme, the dubious honour of the most prolific Russian murderer since Stalin.

'I'll tell you everything,' Babikov said to his interviewers, his fussy, punctilious speech replaced by a desperate chattiness. He was eager to secure house arrest, rather than be incarcerated alongside the hardened criminals he'd put away over the years.

'Kozar?' he said. 'Oh, she was in charge. I thought I was running her as an informant – a scapegoat. That's why we spread all those rumours about a Baba Yaga, an evil witch in the forest. But it was the other way round all along. Kozar was running me! She got me to recruit her as an informant, playing her role as a tragic loser, swearing never to reveal her involvement with the police force . . . And all the time she was laughing at me behind her sleeve, with those golden teeth of hers – taunting me, pretending to be a submissive pawn of the force, while coming up with clever alibis to stop me doing what I wanted.'

Grigor Babikov could still remember every detail of his first meeting with Ivanka Kozar three years previously. She had come into Kemerovo for a routine update on the murder inquiry into her parents' death, and had asked to speak with the chief of police personally. She'd asked Babikov if normal people ever worked with the police, as informants, perhaps, or in other roles; and she spoke of her desperate yearning to help the Kemerovo detectives in their enquiries, so that other families weren't left in the dark for years and years, as she had been. She'd smiled her golden-toothed smile as she ranted about the rich and well-connected, who could do whatever they liked and get away with it. And she'd complained about the dullness of life on the lines, and her struggle to be recognised by the idiotic bureaucrats who managed her. Yes, it was duty and honour she longed for, she'd told Babikov – but it was excitement, too.

'She certainly jumped at the chance to get close to that idiot from the slaughterhouse,' Babikov went on. 'Kozar was meant to take the fall for the dead tourist, you see. Yes – yes, I killed Bryce. What of it? What's one less tourist in Russia? It didn't take much planning. Just a pay-off to that *provodnitsa*, Vasiliev, so I could dump the body out of her carriage, and a disguise from a charity shop, so I could get on the train at Yurga incognito, and off again at Tayga. Bryce took a knife in the neck – easy. It's in the River Tom, if you're looking for it. And the money in his mouth – that was my idea. Golden teeth, as if Kozar was putting her signature on the body.

'Sergeant Marushkin was supposed to collect the body. That was the story – and that idiot Glazkov was supposed to snap him standing by the corpse. And Fandorin was meant to get the engineer, Pushkin, away from her hut. Wolansky and I went to Roslazny on recon a while back and worked out that was the best spot, because it was the closest place to the Roslazny police station. But Kozar was on to me, and worked up that samovar thing with Zonov, so we couldn't get her for that, either. And Fandorin cocked up, too – no surprise there. He didn't bother to confirm that Pushkin was still up the line, didn't bother letting me know she might be on her way back. Glazkov had to message us from the tracks to let us know. He messed up, too, like I said – panicked, and didn't take the photo. He started giving first aid to Pushkin instead, the fool. And then Marushkin radioed in, reporting that Glazkov was there. There's only so much even I can cover up. And all those journos were already en route, primed for my announcement. We had to hide that podium pretty quick! And then bloody Terekhin stopped me pinning it on Marushkin. If I'd been able to do that press conference my way instead of his, things would've been different, let me tell you.

'Anyway, when that didn't pan out, I decided Kozar and Marushkin had to swing for the Vasiliev murder. Vasiliev had to die, of course – you don't leave loose ends lying around, in my line of work. Kozar still seemed onside as an informant, and Marushkin didn't know what time of day it was – he didn't even notice when Glazkov stole his tunic. And I almost got them, too. But Kozar dodged that one as well. You know how she did it? A babushka doll! Yes, a bloody babushka doll with an electronic bug in it. She was listening to us all along. We never found her audio equipment. But then I suppose she knew where we might search for it. And we laughed at the doll, when she gave it to me. We *laughed* at it . . . Little did we know she'd end up trying to murder us all, so she could carry on her own killing spree.

'Who's we? Me and Wolansky, of course. You haven't found him yet? Well, he'll turn up. He was behind it all. Him and Ivanka, in different ways, I suppose. The murders, framing people, getting my clearance rate up so I could run for mayor . . . Well, no, it's true he only joined me two years ago. So I suppose some things were already going on. But he speeded everything up. And the Trans-Siberian scheme, that was his idea – high-profile, with lots of media attention, to get my ratings up. It was Wolansky who dropped me off at Yurga the night before so I could get on the train the next morning in disguise. He was the one who called Tayga station to get Vassily at the tracks when I chucked Bryce's body out. It was Wolansky's idea, too, to get the ten-rouble coins from the lab at Kemerovo. No fingerprints, you see. And it was Wolansky who kept all the journos hooked, like fat sturgeons on a fishing-line. He got his computer nerds to plant the messages on Marushkin's phone, too. Find him and you'll have the mastermind behind everything. I was just the frontman. Find him, I'm telling you!'

But nobody could find Wolansky. The small man with the pointed beard had backed out of the abandoned warehouse and vanished from the face of the Earth. His final act in the world of the living, it seemed, had been to message Sasha Tsaritsyn, telling him that Babikov was ready to fall. Sasha confirmed, too, that Wolansky had tipped him off personally about Vassily's arrest, although Popov's sausages had prevented him from writing his exclusive in time. Wolansky had a large network of journalists at his beck and call, said Sasha, many of whom he'd rallied to Tayga station on the day of Nathan Bryce's murder.

'I *knew* they got there too quickly,' said Olga, when Vassily told her. 'He was such a strange little man. Who on earth was he, after all?'

That mystery was never solved. There was a rumour, some months later, of a young actor, Mikhail Azazelov, who had been a star of the avant-garde theatre scene in St Petersburg years ago – a brilliant young man with crooked teeth and radical political views, who'd suddenly vanished one day. An old, indistinct photo of Azazelov appeared in the *Kemerovo Herald* alongside a speculative piece by Sasha Tsaritsyn, which suggested that Azazelov and Wolansky might have been one and the same. The *Herald* also published a recent CCTV image of a long-haired, neatly dressed pedestrian on a street in Westminster, London, which purported to prove that the man called Wolansky was now plying his trade, whatever it was, in foreign climes.

Sasha had to be careful what he wrote – every journalist had to be careful what they wrote in Kemerovo Province – but he managed to drop enough hints to make his own views fairly obvious: Wolansky was an agent provocateur, acting on behalf of some other agency to provoke crooks like Babikov into ever more serious misdemeanours – encouraging their embryonic malfeasance to gestate into full-blown criminality, and giving them enough rope to hang themselves.

This raised a host of ethical questions. Was it excusable, for example, to assist a murderer to prevent even more deaths taking place? But it also raised a more pragmatic issue: the identity of the person, persons, or agency for whom Wolansky had been working. Sasha thought it probable that Wolansky's true employer was Arkady Nazarov, who had now become Mayor of Kemerovo in a landslide poll following Babikov's arrest and subsequent life imprisonment in one of his dreaded federal penitentiaries – but this was unprintable in Kemerovo, or any neighbouring *oblast*. In any case, there were plenty of other possibilities, including various vigilante groups active in Russia and, most appealingly of all from a newspaper-sales perspective, the Central Intelligence Agency of the United States of America. And, of course, there was always the chance that he was simply unbalanced, or one of a thousand varieties of anarchist or conspiracy enthusiast. It was not unknown for unbalanced people to become involved in politics.

Olga saw the article, but was unconvinced by Sasha's theories about the obscure Azazelov, the fallen star of St Petersburg's avant-garde scene. It was true, she admitted, that a theatrical background could have helped Wolansky to realise she'd been acting, when she'd impersonated Ivanka Kozar in the warehouse. But then again, Wolansky's teeth had been perfectly straight . . .

Olga put down the newspaper and looked out of her window, on the first floor of Aunt Zia's house, into the cold distance that lay beyond. There was something about Wolansky's name, something about his appearance . . . What was it? Was it a faint recollection from one of the books she'd tried to read – one of her mother's books from that visit to Tomsk long ago, whose words spidered over page after yellowing page in bewildering, dazzling, otherworldly brilliance? And the man himself, when she'd seen him in Tayga, and on Babikov's broadcasts . . . There'd been something not quite right about him. She couldn't put her finger on it, but the note of uncertainty, of difference, was certainly there. Was it because he, too, was acting – putting on a persona?

But didn't everyone do that? Didn't she do it herself, when she pretended that she was only an engineer and not a great writer in waiting? Or was it something worse, she thought, or at least something stranger, deeper, *darker*? If Wolansky had really driven Babikov on, as Babikov had claimed, was it for his own purposes, for some kind of poetic justice beyond the half-baked claims of vigilante groups and the crazy anarchism of cults and secret societies?

The hairs rose on the back of her neck as she remembered the book she'd been thinking of, and the character, or rather characters, of whom Wolansky had reminded her. But then she laughed, a little uncertainly, and shook her head. She was not Anna Kabalevsky, to believe in such things. There are enough demons in the world around us, she thought, without imagining yet more into existence. No: he was just someone playing a part, probably modelled on the very book she had in mind. The man who called himself Wolansky was just a former actor who'd got in too deep, and who'd fled when he had the chance – and just in time, too.

The net had, however, closed tightly around others. Igor Troponovich, for instance, the policeman who had told Ekaterina Chezhekov about Ivanka's ex-boyfriend Taras. He was arrested as an accessory to murder, for it had been from him that Babikov had learned of Taras's existence and occupation. Viktor Fandorin, the foreman at the Tayga railway depot, had also been arrested. Using phone records, it had been easy to prove his connections with Babikov and his cronies, and specifically the phone call in which Glazkov, using a payphone in Tayga, had asked Fandorin to jam the points the following morning. Following Fandorin's arrest, he was replaced by his second-in-command, Boris Andreyev, raising Olga's hopes for a less repressive working environment, and perhaps a long-overdue promotion. And Yelena Koriakin, Ivanka's erstwhile *provodnitsa* colleague, was arrested for corruption, and questioned at length about Ivanka's activities and movements.

As the police continued their investigations, further revelations came to light about Ivanka herself. It seemed unlikely that a post-mortem would reveal any new information about the deaths of her parents, but they dug up the bodies anyway, using huge gas heaters to thaw the frozen ground and free the corpses from their graves near the cottage on the edge of Yashkino. As the icy mud yielded its wicked secrets, the forensic team, veterans of many crime scenes, staggered back in horror. At least thirty other bodies were buried there besides Ivanka's parents – men and women, young and old. Many had hideous mutilations, and some had been cut into so many separate parts that identification proved impossible. But those who were identified confirmed Ivanka's boast to have killed the servants of the rich: they identified exclusive hairdressers' assistants and junior stylists, trainee accountants and legal clerks, PAs for luxury car dealerships and secretaries for escort agencies. And Ivanka had been clever: each person had been lowly enough in their line of work to avoid a hue and cry when they disappeared. She had lured them somehow into the dark forests of the *taiga* – the early stages of the investigation found some paperwork relating to get-rich-quick schemes – and then struck, as Fyodor Katin had said, when their backs were turned. Then Ivanka had returned to her childhood home to bury each new corpse at the scene of her first crime, as if to show her dead parents what she was capable of. The police thought there might be other places, too, where she had buried her victims, since so many murders in the region were still unaccounted for. As one of the forensic doctors said to Vassily, he and Olga had ended the career of a real-life Baba Yaga, a woman quite as murderous as the witch of the old folk tale.

But Olga was not much inclined to celebrate. As Vassily had said, enforced idleness aids the memory, and as she lay recovering on the narrow bed, dozing or staring out of the window at the steadily falling snow, she encountered new strands of remembrance emerging from the depths. She recalled, for example, Babikov's pale-lipped anger when he saw her for the first time, the person who had derailed their plans by returning to her hut ahead of schedule. And Glazkov, she realised, was permanently drunk not because he was a hopeless alcoholic but because he was trying to drown his guilt in

Odrosov's Rocket Fuel. He might not have murdered Bryce or Vasiliev himself, but he'd surely guessed that Babikov had. It was to Glazkov's credit, she supposed, that he had felt it so deeply.

There was something else, too – something about Ivanka. Something so frightening that even now, with Ivanka buried under twenty tons of Siberian rock and ice, Olga shivered with fear. For she'd known all along what Ivanka had said to Vassily, when he interviewed her in Tayga station.

'Oh, Pasha,' she said later. 'Do you know what she said? She said she was no good – no good at all. She said her mind was like Swiss cheese. That it was *full of holes*. And I thought she meant she was forgetful at work . . .' Olga shuddered as she remembered how Ivanka had grinned at Vassily at the end of her interview, taunting him, perhaps, by admitting her evil character to his face. But was evil the right way to describe a woman like Ivanka? Was there another word – one a writer might use – for someone whose soul was a window into wicked, forgotten pasts, a pathway to lost iniquities and the frozen darkness beyond, in which death was the least of terrors, a blessed relief from torment and pain?

She shook her head and gave up. There were no words for such people. Not even a writer could find them.

On Monday morning, two days after Ivanka's death, Vassily got out of bed and walked to Olga's room. He was still feeling rather weak and shaky, and as such he was glad to sleep in a proper bed rather than on his bench in the Roslazny police station. He had to admit, though, that his initial welcome had been less than warm. Aunt Zia had been unenthusiastic about Vassily's installation as a temporary lodger – 'Family's one thing,' she'd said snootily, 'but a policeman, a public *servant*, is quite another' – and she'd been yet more unwelcoming when one of the Tayga policemen had arrived with a bag of dead mice in one hand and a cage containing Rasputin in the other. Seeing the ferret's whiskered face sticking out between the bars, Zia had shrieked, gathered her skirts together, and run upstairs to her room, calling to Pasha that he was now in charge of the household until Sergeant Marushkin was well enough to leave. Since Pasha was a more skilled (and more generous) cook than Aunt Zia, this was to everyone's liking, and thenceforth the invalids were excellently looked after during their recovery.

Vassily knocked on the door. 'Olga?' he called. 'Can I come in?'

'Please do,' she said. 'I'm bored half to death here.'

He saw Olga surrounded by a pile of books and magazines that she had borrowed from Aunt Zia, mostly from the *Sovetskaya zhenshchina* back catalogue. 'You need some new reading material,' he said.

'No,' she said. 'I need some writing materials.'

'Writing materials?' he said, sitting on the chair by her bed. And then at last Olga Pushkin told Vassily Marushkin about her mother Tatiana and the books she had left her, the most prized of all Olga's possessions. She overcame her fear of his scorn, and told him of her ambitions to be a writer, and about saving up for the literature course at Tomsk State University. She even told him about her work in progress, *Find Your Rail Self: 100 Life Lessons from the Trans-Siberian Railway*, and some of the new ideas she'd had for the book while she was involved with Babikov and Ivanka.

'Well,' said Vassily, shaking his head, 'an engineer who's also a criminal investigator, who's also a writer . . . You have hidden depths, Olga Pushkin.'

'I don't know about that,' said Olga, smiling. She was happy to have him sitting by her side while she rested and recovered, feeling safe and peaceful in the old-fashioned room with a warm stove in the corner. Vassily looked different out of uniform, less stern and more approachable. But his eyes still conveyed a soul in torment. His imprisonment had been torture, she knew, not only because he had been falsely accused but because every day in jail meant a day wasted in the hunt for his wife and son.

Olga's smile died away. 'I think we all have hidden depths, Vassily,' she said.

He nodded but didn't say anything, so they sat in silence, listening to the clock ticking and Aunt Zia's samovar bubbling on top of the stove, Olga thinking how sad Vassily's face looked in the pale afternoon sunlight, and Vassily thinking of Rozalina and his son, Kliment.

Olga frowned as an idea came back to her – an idea she'd had a few days earlier, involving Pasha, his friends in the army and a soldier-turned-businessman called Prokofy, who'd stolen Vassily's wife and son from him. She smiled a little, imagining how happy Vassily would be if she could reunite him with his family. She'd already freed him from jail, so putting his family back together was the obvious next item for her updated 'To Do' list. But first she and Vassily had to convalesce. And after that, as Vassily suggested, she planned to get in touch with the families of Babikov's and Ivanka's victims.

And so, a week later, Olga visited a house near the town of Beryozovsky to the south of Tayga, where Alyona Vasiliev's mother lived. She hugged Olga when she arrived as if Olga could replace her lost daughter, and fed her honeyed cakes until Olga could eat no more. Alyona had spent some of the money Babikov had given her on her own house, in the days after Bryce's murder. Olga should have seen the fresh paint and new woodwork, said Alyona's mother. The house looked so pretty! Alyona had been too unhappy to enjoy it – too guilty, as her mother frankly acknowledged. But she'd kept some of the money, too, to give to her mother. 'She was a good girl,' said Mrs Vasiliev. 'Only she liked to have nice things. And she wanted me to have everything I needed.'

She reminded Olga of Glazkov's mother, whom she had visited in her care home with Vassily the day before. Mrs Glazkov hadn't fully understood that her son Anatoly was dead, but she was very aware of his good points, which she recited to them at considerable length. 'He's been a good son,' she said again and again. 'He's been a good son to me.' They didn't have the heart to disagree. Glazkov had been paying a fortune to the care home for years, and had provided for her in his will, by the sale of his house.

'He wasn't all bad,' said Olga to Vassily afterwards.

'No, he wasn't,' said Vassily. 'When Bryce's body hit you, he could've left you lying bleeding in the snow, and got his picture, as Babikov ordered. But he went to you first, to see if you needed help. It's because of Glazkov that things worked out as they did.'

'He was brave, too, when Ivanka was there, in the warehouse,' said Olga. 'It makes me sad. We had to wait for the end to see his virtues.'

'But we did see them,' said Vassily. 'That's something.'

Finally, after her visit to Glazkov's mother, Olga called at the Tayga police station, where an interpreter helped her to make a telephone call to the Bryce family in Cleveland, Ohio. When she came out of the room later, her eyes were filled with tears, but she was smiling. 'At last they know everything that happened to their boy,' she said. 'Now they can grieve in peace.'

Aunt Zia asked Vassily to leave as soon as he was well enough to walk without discomfort, upon which he returned to the Roslazny police station and relieved the temporary commander, Nestor Ivanov. Ivanov left with alacrity. 'I don't know how you stick it, Marushkin,' he said, gathering his belongings and throwing them hastily into his rucksack. 'The freezing cold, the damp . . . And there are rats here at night. You can hear them scraping on the walls, trying to get in.'

'Oh, it's not so bad,' said Vassily, looking around at the walls he'd known since childhood. 'And rats don't bother you if you've got a ferret!' He held up Rasputin's cage for Ivanov to see.

'Well, each to his own, I suppose,' said Ivanov, shouldering his rucksack. 'I'll be off, then. Glad you got everything sorted out, Marushkin. Watch you don't lock yourself in at night, out of habit!'

Once the door had closed behind Ivanov, Vassily put Rasputin's cage down and opened the door, smiling as the ferret scampered around the jail, patrolling his old haunts in search of rodent prey. I'll have to get Olga to bring a bag of mice, he thought. But then he remembered, with a surprising pang, that he was a free man again, and could fetch his own dead mice. He shook his head. Olga Pushkin was an attractive woman, he admitted to himself, and he'd enjoyed the excitement of her clandestine visits – but he wasn't in the business of looking for attractive women. He was in the business of looking for his wife, Rozalina. That was what he should be doing, not thinking wistful thoughts about track engineers who worked in little huts by the railside.

As it happened, the track engineer in question would soon be ejected from Aunt Zia's house as well, and less politely than Vassily had been. It turned out to be an absolute necessity – for Olga. But first she had to deal with her father Mikhail. She'd had little to do with him since he'd thrown her and Pasha onto the street. She'd seen him now and again, limping along the narrow paths that criss-crossed Roslazny like the threads of a string bag. With Olga living elsewhere, Mikhail had to get his own shopping, and he didn't look very happy about it. He didn't even have the courtesy to acknowledge her presence when he came across her, unless an unfriendly grunt could be interpreted as a social nicety. In itself, that didn't bother Olga: she was still furious with Mikhail for his hateful reaction to Pasha's news. But she needed to speak to him to make the arrangements for her plan.

'Just corner him in Café Astana some time,' said Pasha one night, as they sat in Olga's room and schemed by candlelight. 'He'll have to talk to you if there are other people around. You know what he's like. He's as proud as Lucifer.'

'And as unpleasant,' said Olga. But Pasha had made a good point. Mikhail wouldn't want the village to know there was a rift between them, and above all he wouldn't want people knowing why he'd thrown Pasha out in the first place. Earlier that very day, Odrosov had related some nonsense Mikhail had told him about Olga being forced to live nearer Tayga station for work purposes, adding that Pasha had gone with her of his own free will. Odrosov knew it was nonsense, of course, and so did Fyodor Katin, the Dreamer, who was sitting next to Olga at the bar at the time.

'And why would Olga and her brother Pasha want to live nearer Tayga, when life in Roslazny is closer to the real life, the *authentic* life, of the peasants?' said Fyodor, enthusiastically. 'I can't think of anything better, for a true Russian, than to live in the heart of a small village. There are sights here one could never see in St Petersburg or Ekaterinburg or Nizhny Novgorod. Just the other week I saw an old woman walk out one morning, dressed in a red coat, her jagged nose sticking out from under a fur-lined hat, carrying a besom brush in one hand and something white – perhaps an envelope – in the other. How romantic, I thought – how very tsarist Russia! An elderly serf, perhaps, delivering a letter of love to an ancient sweetheart, and a brush to conceal her steps afterwards . . . What is it, Olga?' He'd noticed she was staring at him.

'Is it that you agree with me?' he went on. 'Oh, you do!' he said, clasping her hand. 'I always knew you and I were alike. Odrosov, two more vodkas! And make them large ones. I've found a kindred spirit at last.'

Olga drank the vodka mechanically, smiling at Fyodor as if in agreement. But in truth she hadn't heard a word. Her heart was thudding and her breathing was tightly constricted. Fyodor didn't know it, but he had just told her that Aunt Zia had been her mystery poison-pen letter-writer all along. A hand-written envelope, a red coat, a crooked nose, and above all a besom, like Baba Yaga, to conceal her steps afterwards...

But why would Aunt Zia have written that to her? Olga thought back to that week. Wasn't that the week she had failed to deliver Zia's shopping? Yes – she remembered now. She'd had to go to help Anna Kabalevsky, because Anna needed to go to the hospital and couldn't look after all the children at once. So Olga had telephoned Zia to apologise. But clearly that had not been enough to pacify her. Zia had taken pen and paper, scribbled the vicious note and set out the following morning to put it through the letterbox before Mikhail and Olga were awake.

'So she slept on it, and *still* put it through your letterbox?' said Pasha, when Olga told him later that evening. 'And all because you didn't bring her shopping round one evening!'

'I still can't fathom how she found out I want to be a writer,' said Olga. 'I'm certain she knows. She wouldn't have written that line about "never being anything else", otherwise. What is it, Pasha?'

Her brother had blushed crimson, just as Olga did at times. 'Well – er – I think I might have told her,' said Pasha.

'*You* told her?' said Olga, astonished. 'Why?'

'It was by accident, Olga. I used to write to her from Crimea sometimes. It was so hard to think of what to say, so I used to write about you. Oh, I'm so sorry, Olga! I should never have—'

'Pasha, Pasha!' said Olga. 'There's nothing to be sorry about. How were you to know she'd write such terrible things? But how could she do that and then take us in?'

'To make some money,' said Pasha, simply.

Olga laughed a brief, bitter laugh. 'Of course,' she said. 'Why else would anyone do anything?'

'Listen, Olga, you have to tell her you know it was her. She deserves to be confronted. She can't get away with it, just because you're family. That makes it even worse.'

Olga nodded. 'She won't get away with it. And neither will Father. He's got away with too much for too long.'

'Tomorrow, then?' said Pasha. 'You'll speak to him tomorrow?'

'Tomorrow,' said Olga, 'or as soon as I see him in the café. And after that, the three of us will pay a visit to the Lodge at Astrazov. And we won't be going alone.'

Olga had only been to the Lodge at Astrazov a few times, during holidays from the school in Roslazny, when the caretaker would let them stay for a few days in exchange for potatoes or vodka or both. The Lodge had been sold to meet some debts, Tatiana had said. She didn't know to whom, or why they had chosen to leave the Lodge empty. And she had loved it so much that Olga hadn't had the heart to go back when she was gone. It would be like visiting a grave, she thought.

So Olga had few memories to draw upon when it came to ensnaring Mikhail. But she remembered enough to entice him. She cornered him in Café Astana the day after she'd talked to Pasha. She made a great pretence of being uncomfortable in his presence, and of being tormented by some secret that she felt duty-bound to share – she made some obscure remarks about money and treasure and hidden things, and she mentioned Astrazov, too, by means of the Pushkin poem 'To K—' that Mikhail had quoted to Tatiana at the Lodge before they were married.

Her mother had told her about it many times. She had persuaded Lubov, the housekeeper, to allow Mikhail to come for dinner on the understanding that they should dine on game that Mikhail would provide from the forest. And the birds and animals of the woods around Astrazov saw a strange sight that day: a huntsman, clad in a chequered jacket and forager's cap, rifle at the ready, muttering delicate literary words to himself as he padded through the rows of leafless trees. Mikhail had resolved to learn his namesake's most famous poem, 'To K—', and, with a momentous effort, he had managed to memorise it in time for a recital after dinner. He stood by the fire, a crackling blaze of scented apple-wood from the Astrazov orchard, and spoke the most famous lines in Russian literature.

> *I recall the wondrous chance:*
> *There before me I saw you.*
> *Like a ghost, like a fleeting apparition,*
> *Like genius of the purest grace.*

With the first words Tatiana's heart was firmly, disastrously his.

Now, many years later, Olga said the same words from Pushkin's poem to her father. 'Do you remember the wood-chimes at Astrazov, Father?' she went on. 'I can't stop hearing them in my mind. They remind me of what Mother said before she died. Something about a treasure and the whispering wood . . .' Then she turned and left, as if overcome by emotion. But she turned back unseen after she'd left the café, and looked through the window by the door. As she'd hoped, Mikhail's face was a picture of greed.

'Hook, line and sinker,' she said to Pasha later that night. 'He thinks Mamochka hid something valuable in those old chimes by the summerhouse. As if she'd leave anything worthwhile hanging in the open air! Whatever she had in mind for the treasure, if there is any, it wasn't that. Now we just have to reel him in. He'll go tomorrow, I'm sure of it – it's too dark for him to go now. Is your man ready?'

'He's ready,' said Pasha. 'He jumped at the chance. I think he gets a commission for every fraud he uncovers. But are you sure you want to do this, Olga? He'll never forgive us.'

'You've got it the wrong way around, Pasha. It's us who will never forgive him.'

The next morning, Olga and Pasha borrowed Popov's car once more, this time in exchange for a promise of help in shifting a consignment of horse-meat. Soon they were bumping along the road out of Roslazny and towards the Lodge at Astrazov.

'Do you remember them?' Olga said to Pasha.

'What?'

'The chimes.'

'Of course,' said Pasha. 'I dream of them sometimes. I dream of Mamochka standing by them, or dancing around them, laughing with me at the sounds they made in the wind.'

'Those are good memories, Pasha,' she said. 'I'm sorry, then, to have used them like this – to punish Father.'

'No, you were right,' he said, his jaw set firmly, just as Olga's had been when she'd made her way to the abandoned warehouse. 'He needs to be punished. And it won't kill him. It'll probably do him a favour, in the long term.'

Olga nodded. 'I think it's down here,' she said, squinting at the faded sign that stood lopsidedly at the entrance to a narrow single-track road.

'Yes, that's it,' he said, his eyes distant as he recalled hot summer days from long-ago holidays.

'Where will your man be?'

'I'm not sure exactly. He just said he'd be here at dawn, in a position where he could watch Father getting out of his car.'

'Assuming, of course, that Father can get his hands on one,' said Olga. 'But I think he'll borrow Solotov's old Lada. He got it for me once, when I collected my table from Tayga last year. Solotov rarely goes out, these days, so it should be available – if it starts.'

'Then we'll just have to wait and see,' said Pasha. They fell silent – the road was a little too bumpy for talking – and didn't speak again until they pulled up in the place Pasha had indicated, beyond the Lodge and out of sight from the track. Olga switched off the engine and they sat for a minute or two, as if bracing themselves to see the Lodge again.

'You know,' said Olga, 'I haven't been here for more than twenty years. I don't even know if the chimes are still there.'

'Let's find out together,' he said.

Five minutes later they had completed a circuit around the Lodge, each new angle revealing some forgotten memory, some new chink of light that brought the past vividly to life, recalling their mother's smile or the smell of roasted chestnuts in autumn or the helter-skelter laughter of some childhood game. The Lodge was still empty, as it had been in their childhood. Olga stood close to the windows and peered through the dirty glass, seeing white sheets over a few pieces of furniture, and rolled-up carpets piled in a corner. She wondered who owned it, and why it stood so empty and forlorn. Wouldn't it be wonderful to own it again? She smiled to herself. She could no more afford to buy a Lodge than she could imagine having children of her own. Such things were for others, not for her.

They walked past the Lodge's east wing and saw the summerhouse across the snow-covered lawn, with its wrought-iron gates and gossamer frames frosted like a fairy palace. Most of the glass in the panes was broken and the painted wood was covered with green mildew under the ice, but the chimes still hung where they always had, under a little canopy that jutted out from the side of the summerhouse. They heard them moving in the gentle breeze long before they saw them, giving forth soft, resonant echoes that drifted across the icy garden.

'We'd better not walk on the lawn,' said Olga. 'Father will see the footprints. Your man must've been very careful, getting into position. I wonder where he is,' she added, looking around curiously.

'No idea,' said Pasha again. 'But he must be close by. He said to pretend he wasn't here and—' But then Pasha turned his head towards the direction of the single-track road they had driven up earlier. 'Ssh – someone's coming now.'

'Let's take cover,' said Olga. 'Quick – behind the Lodge.' They ran back the way they'd come and ducked behind a wall, bringing back a fleeting memory of hide-and-seek. But this time it was their father they were out to uncover.

Soon Vladmir Solotov's rusty orange Lada came up the track towards the Lodge, moving slowly and cautiously between the potholes and frozen depressions in the road. Olga peered at the windscreen but couldn't see the driver for the reflections on the smooth glass. But he soon revealed himself.

The Lada drew up to the Lodge's main entrance and stopped. The door opened, and Mikhail Pushkin got out, looking left and right, as if to check he was alone. Then he closed the car door decisively, and set off on foot across the lawn towards the summerhouse. He walked quickly and freely, with no sign of a crutch or walking-stick. Olga looked at Pasha. 'That should do it,' she said.

As she spoke, a man holding a small video camera emerged from the undergrowth beside the summerhouse and shouted across the lawn: 'Mikhail Pushkin, I am an officer of the Fraud Unit, Kemerovo Province. You have been caught committing benefit fraud. Specifically, defrauding the Municipal Government of Tayga, Kemerovo *Oblast*, and Russian Railways by feigning injury since 1988. You should now consider yourself under arrest.'

Mikhail stood still in the middle of the snowy lawn, looking from the man to the summerhouse and back again, as if he were trying to work out what had happened. Then he clenched his fists. 'Damn Olga!' he cried. 'Damn that bitch of a child!'

Pasha took Olga away from the Lodge after Mikhail's arrest: he didn't want her to hear any more of Mikhail's shouted abuse, and he could tell she'd been affected by what they'd seen and heard. Mikhail was her father, after all, and she had lived with him all her life. But that didn't stop him, Pasha said, from being a lazy and ill-natured man, who had defrauded honest taxpayers like themselves for decades.

'Are you sure he won't go to prison, Pasha?' said Olga, anxiously. 'I wouldn't want him to go to prison, not at his age.'

'We've discussed this before,' said Pasha. 'Like I told you, Paninoff said he'd probably just get a slap on the wrist and a fine, or something like that.' Paninoff was the name of the fraud officer who had arrested Mikhail. 'And he'll have to go back to work for a couple of years, until he gets to retirement age.'

'That's not too bad, I suppose,' said Olga. 'He can't argue with that.'

'Of course he can't,' said Pasha. 'You're a good person, Olga, to worry about him after all he's done to you. To us.'

Olga nodded, but didn't reply. When they reached the turn-off to Roslazny she kept on driving. 'Do you mind if we go on for a bit?' she said.

'I don't mind,' said Pasha. 'It's not my petrol.' She drove on past frozen streams and bare-branched trees and snow-mantled fields, past tumbledown shacks and rusting farm equipment lying in muddy yards, past little hamlets and billboard advertisements and queues of Ladas at the level-crossings, until the flat grey horizon had soothed her and quietened her jangling nerves.

'I worked it out, you know,' she said, breaking the silence at last.

'Oh, yes?' said Pasha. 'What's that?'

'What Mother meant, when she said that thing about the whispering wood. You know, about the treasure, just before she died.'

'Tell me, then,' said Pasha.

'It's Pushkin, of course. *The* Pushkin. Another poem. One with a simple name, just "The Poet". I read it the other day. It's in one of those books Mamochka left me. It's about what happens when a poet is summoned to work.'

'Do poets work?' said Pasha, smiling.

'Hush,' she said, but smiling too. 'Anyway, I can't remember the exact lines, but it's something like this. This is before the poet's called to work – *His holy lyre silent is, and cold sleep his soul locks in.* But later he gets the call, the summons from his muse. *The world's pastimes him now weary, and mortals' gossip now he shuns.* And then the poem ends: *Wild and stern, rushes he, To the shores* – I think it's shores – *To the shores of desert waves, Into the widely whispering wood.*'

'The widely whispering wood,' repeated Pasha, staring at Olga. 'So the great treasure Mother hid – you think it was just poetry?'

'It's not *just* poetry,' said Olga, her eyes shining. 'It's *poetry* – everything that's wild and strange and beautiful in the world. Art, and music, and literature too . . . Mother left me those books because she knew I'd find that line, sooner or later, and work out what she meant. Don't you see, Pasha? She wanted us to be poets, like she was – to shun the world's pastimes and find true treasure! I really think she would've wanted me to be a writer.'

'I'm sure of it,' said Pasha. Then he stirred in his seat, and turned to face his sister. 'Look, it's time, Olga,' he went on. 'It's time for you to apply to university – today, when we get back. You've got enough money for the first year or two, haven't you? I'm sure you'll be offered a place – you could start this autumn, and work part time in a café there, or a library, or something. I'll help out if you need more cash – I'll get a job working security, or in a garage in Tayga, whatever it takes. It's time to think of yourself now. You have to do this.'

'You're right, Pasha,' she said, smiling at him as she drove. 'Of course you are. God knows I've waited long enough. But, first, we have to talk to Zia. All the Pushkins are being called to account today.'

In later days, what happened after that always seemed rather opaque to Olga, like a half-remembered dream. Perhaps it was because there was no great confrontation, no screaming or throwing of china plates. Ever since she received the letter, Olga had been imagining the moment when she discovered the identity of her hateful correspondent, conjuring scenes in which she floored her hidden enemy with a right hook, or tripped them so they fell into the barrel of offal that Popov kept outside the butchery, or showered them with dirty, half-full glasses from Odrosov's untidy bar in Café Astana. The details of the punishment she administered varied from daydream to daydream, but the gist, the essential take-home message for her semi-literate assailant, was clear and unvaried.

The confrontation with Aunt Zia, though, had been nothing like any of those scenarios. For one thing, Olga had known it was Zia for at least a day before she confronted her, which had the effect of dulling the initial shock and dampening the fierce rage she felt. By the time the moment came, Olga almost felt sorry for her aunt, standing in front of her in her ridiculous red coat – too vibrant a colour for such a frumpy, miserable old creature, thought Olga, then instantly regretted it.

She'd gone into the house with Pasha as soon as they got back from their extended drive – none too soon for Pasha, who was less familiar than Olga with the strong odour of decaying flesh that pervaded Popov's car. They'd packed their belongings into their suitcases, and only then had Olga gone downstairs into Aunt Zia's drawing room to tell her what Fyodor Katin had said.

'She didn't even bother to deny it,' Olga said to Pasha afterwards, in the car. 'She shrugged and pointed to the door. When I asked her why she did it, she wouldn't answer, just stared at me. Then she said . . .'

'Yes?' said Pasha. But Olga didn't tell him. She didn't feel she could. Pasha had enough on his plate without hearing that Mikhail had told Zia about Pasha being gay, and what Aunt Zia thought about gay people, and how disgusted she was with him, and how she thought Olga was a nasty, lazy girl and a bad daughter, and how women shouldn't work on the railways, and how she had only taken them in because the roof needed repairing.

Olga shook her head, angrily wiped away a tear or two, and started the car.

'I just want to forget it,' she said, putting the car into gear with a jerk. But then, as she drove off down the uneven, potholed track, she found herself smiling, even laughing. She felt quite different somehow, as though she'd been wading through deep mud that had suddenly dissolved into clear, sparkling waters. Even though the confrontation with her correspondent had been less cathartic than she'd hoped, she felt infinitely better for knowing who it was. And she felt better for having made a clean break with her father's family at last. The Pushkins were poison.

Pasha looked at her, smiling in response to her infectious laughter. 'Where to, then?' he said.

'Well, let's go to Popov's first and drop off the car. And then to Café Astana. I think their guest accommodation is about to get a little crowded . . .'

16

Endings and Beginnings

'Oh, Pasha, I'm exhausted,' said Olga, finally giving up on sleep and sitting up in bed.

Pasha shushed her. 'Gyorgy's asleep,' he whispered, pointing at Anna Kabalevsky's seven-year-old son, who was lying on a ragged mattress next to him on the floor.

'*Now* he sleeps,' said Olga, quietly, 'after keeping us up all night . . . Just when I feel it would be death to lie here another minute, he drops off.'

'Anna said to let him sleep until seven, if we could,' said Pasha. 'And don't moan too much – you've got the bed, don't forget!'

'Some bed,' muttered Olga, pressing down the lumps in the mattress and trying to find a position that didn't make her back ache. 'I can't take another night of this, Pasha. We've got to find somewhere else.'

This was the third night of their stay in the guestrooms above the bar at Café Astana. Anna hadn't hesitated when Olga and Pasha arrived: she'd thrown open the doors of the little box-rooms she was renting from Odrosov, and soon had Olga and Pasha installed in the larger room with Gyorgy, while she took baby Ilya and Boris into her room. It was a relief to have a roof over their heads, but the cramped and noisy quarters took some getting used to.

'Yes,' murmured Pasha. 'I think today's the day to get Anna's house back. And not just for us. This is no place to bring up children.'

'Do you really think you can?' whispered Olga.

'I can try,' said Pasha. 'If what you heard Bogdan's friends say last night is true, they're about to start their operations again. Better to get started now than wait for them to get established.'

The night before, Olga had been walking back to Café Astana from her railside hut when she'd heard low voices and stifled laughter coming from a ramshackle building that had once been the Roslazny church hall. In the 1990s, when the *sovkhoz* was still going, Olga had been there many times, sometimes for awkward discos, but more often for jumble sales and bazaars to raise money for the crumbling Church of St Aleksandr. They had closed the hall in 2001, and the church the year after. The church roof had fallen in during the Great Storm of 2003, but the hall had somehow survived, and Olga, trudging past its low eaves, had seen a dim light trickling through cracks in the shutters over the windows. Moving closer and taking care not to dislodge the icicles that hung from the low eaves, she'd put her ear to one of the cracks. She'd been unsurprised, somehow, to hear the voice of Bogdan Kabalevsky, who was holding forth on the need to seize the initiative again, now that things had quietened down after the Babikov case.

'We owe it to ourselves,' Olga heard him say, 'and to the art of filmmaking. And to the beautiful girls of Kemerovo Province, who might otherwise find themselves unemployed!'

She'd pursed her lips as Bogdan's friends laughed and cheered. Then she'd spotted a wider crack to her right, and slowly moved sideways until she could peer around the edge of the shutter, watching Bogdan pour vodka for a group of men who sat around a table lit by a battery-powered lamp. In the background she could see piles of broken chairs and prayer-books, and a heap of rotting fabric that looked like old curtains. Clearly the men had made an effort at tidying the place, though they'd obviously stopped for vodka before finishing the job.

Olga had spent a few more frozen minutes eavesdropping, before making her way back towards the café and its grateful warmth. Over a plate of Odrosov's goat stew, she told Pasha what she'd seen and heard at the old church hall. 'It'd be the perfect place for their *activities*,' she said. 'It's off the main path, so it'd be quiet – I only saw them because I took a short-cut back from my hut. We can't let Bogdan carry on like this, Pasha! It's too horrible to think of him prancing about with his women and sleeping in luxury in that empty house, while Anna kills herself looking after three children in Café Astana, with no money to speak of.'

Pasha looked thoughtful. 'You know, there might be a way to get rid of Bogdan and his friends,' he said. 'I remember a sergeant major who made our lives miserable. But we set things up so the colonel thought the sergeant major was undermining him. It's amazing what a few faked memos will do! And the colonel was a veteran of Afghanistan in the eighties – he wasn't someone you'd want to cross. Once the sergeant major knew the colonel had turned against him, he put in for a transfer, and that was that.'

Olga looked at him blankly. 'What are you suggesting? We fake some memos from Bogdan? I don't think they use memos in that kind of operation, Pasha.'

'Not exactly memos,' said Pasha, smiling. 'I was thinking more of posters. And maybe some empty DVD boxes. Don't worry, Olga – I'll take care of everything.'

The next day brought a strange harvest. By late afternoon, a slew of brightly coloured posters advertising certain films, and stalls selling the advertised films in lurid DVD boxes, sprang up across Roslazny and Tayga. In addition to portraying scenes from the films – scenes in which the face of Bogdan Kabalevsky was comically prevalent – the posters relayed a link to a website, promising a thirty per cent discount on bulk orders of titles including *Whore and Peace*, *Behinds and Punishment* and *Doctor Big-Hard-Go*.

Most of the villagers in Roslazny found the posters amusing, and a few even bought copies of the films, dropping a few roubles into the honesty box on each stall. This might have been expected to make Bogdan happy, as presumably he would benefit from the sales and publicity. Oddly, though, he seemed to take the opposite view, and by the time night fell he'd made his way around the whole of Roslazny, sweeping the DVDs into a large bin-bag and tearing down all the posters. When Alexeyev the mechanic said he'd seen more in Tayga, Bogdan set off at a run to his car, and raced down the road to do the same thing there, on a larger scale.

Even this did not seem to set his mind at rest, as Popov revealed later that night in Café Astana.

'I was coming back from Tayga,' said the butcher. 'I was there on municipal business. Meeting the mayor, actually – and no, Igor Odrosov, it had nothing to do with food hygiene inspections.' Odrosov nodded seriously at Popov, and winked at Fyodor Katin.

'Anyway, Bogdan Kabalevsky was driving home in front of me. He hadn't closed the boot of his car properly, though, and things kept falling out – things that that looked a lot like those DVDs he was hawking in town earlier. And when we got to his house, he screeched to a halt and ran inside. I hung back a bit in the car, to inspect part of the road—'

'You mean, you killed the lights and reversed into the darkness to spy on him?' said Fyodor, laughing.

'And then I saw him coming out again,' said Popov, ignoring Fyodor. 'He had a suitcase bulging with clothes, and a couple of smaller bags, too. He slung them into the back seat, revved the engine, turned the car and drove off, nearly taking my wing-mirror with him.'

'No wonder, if your lights were off,' muttered Fyodor.

'And that's that,' finished Popov. 'He didn't come back – I waited for ten minutes. I think he's gone for good.'

'Then we must tell Anna she can go home,' said Fyodor, earning himself a glare from Odrosov, who'd been delighted to find someone willing to pay for the use of his dingy guestrooms. But Anna was coming down the stairs at that moment, holding baby Ilya and leading Gyorgy by the hand, and she heard her name above the hubbub.

'You must tell me – what?' she said.

'Good news, Anna,' said Fyodor. 'Your house is yours once more. Bogdan has left the village.'

Anna turned to Pasha, who was coming down the stairs behind her. 'Was this your doing, Pasha?' she said to him. 'I thought I heard you saying something about Bogdan last night.'

Getting Bogdan to leave of his own free will had been Pasha's aim all along. First he'd borrowed a roll of hundred-rouble notes from Olga, assuring her it was for Anna, and that he'd pay her back as soon as he could. Then he'd borrowed Popov's car again, driving to Tayga to buy a few copies of Bogdan's films from the adult store by the railway. After that, he'd gone to the printers to get posters and DVD covers made, and to the computer shop to buy blank DVDs and empty DVD cases, which he'd filled with copies of the films. The assistant had helped him set up a rudimentary website, with enough functionality to look convincing. Finally, Pasha had gone to a second-hand furniture shop to hire a few folding tables for the stalls, and after that it was just a matter of driving round to set everything up.

The plan was simple. Pasha knew that Bogdan's associates would think he was trying to undercut them and set up on his own. And he'd guessed that Bogdan's associates, like the colonel in the barracks, were not people you crossed if you could help it. Bogdan would have the strongest possible reason for getting out of town: to save his skin – or, rather, his fingertips. And the beauty of it was that nobody had been hurt in the process.

But now Pasha looked at Anna and wondered if he'd done the right thing. Bogdan was her husband, after all, and the father of her children. But then she rushed up the stairs and hugged him.

'Thank you, Pasha! Oh, thank you. This is the best news I've had for many years.' She carried on up the stairs with Ilya in her arms, calling to Boris to start packing their things, for they were going home. 'You and Olga, too, Pasha,' she called down the stairs. 'You must take the lodgers' room. We will all be happy together.'

In the event, however, their happiness was short-lived. Bogdan had left the place in an unholy mess, for one thing, so they had to spend hours cleaning before they could go to bed. And then, first thing next morning, there came a heavy knock on the door.

'Open up,' came a gruff voice. 'Bailiffs.'

'Bailiffs?' said Anna to Olga. 'Oh, no – surely Bogdan didn't . . .'

But Bogdan had. He had secretly remortgaged the house the year before to keep his business enterprises afloat, and had then failed to meet the repayment schedule. 'We're here for the house and everything in it, up to the value of a million roubles,' said the bailiff, looking at the information on his clipboard. 'I'm sorry,' he added, seeing the look of shock on Anna's face, 'but there's nothing I can do. I'm just doing my job.'

Olga and Pasha tried to comfort the children as they watched the bailiff's men pack their toys and clothes into large plastic crates and load them onto the truck outside. But it was Anna who sobbed the most, holding baby Ilya to her as if he was the last thing she possessed in the world. Olga watched her friend standing by the open door, eking out the last few moments before the bailiffs threw them out and they had to trek back to the café and Odrosov's dingy rooms. And suddenly Olga knew what she had to do. She knew as if she'd been planning this all along, as if she'd always known that this was what the money was for, as if her mother Tatiana had set her on this path and that nothing could shake her from it.

'Anna,' she said, placing her hand on her friend's arm, and startling her from her sadness.

'Yes, Olga?' said Anna. 'What is it? Do you want something?'

Olga looked at her. 'Do *I* want something?' she said gently. 'Yes, I do. I want to borrow Popov's car again, drive with you into Tayga, and go to the estate agent's – you know, the place they have next to the boxing school, with pictures of houses in the window. And then I'm going to the bank to speak to the manager. I'm going to set up a mortgage to buy us a house in Roslazny. I should have more than enough for the deposit, with my savings.'

'Olga, you can't!' said Anna. 'You've saved that money for Tomsk! You've worked so hard, for so long. You can't throw it away on us! We can live at the café. It's perfectly comfortable.'

'It's nothing of the sort,' said Olga. 'And I won't change my mind. It'll take a bit longer for me get to Tomsk, but the university will still be there in a few years' time. And in the meantime we'll all live in the house together, and there'll be no more evictions, or rent to pay, or noise from men drinking at the bar in the café, or anything horrible. You see, I'm really being selfish. You are the friend I love most in the world, and I want you all to myself. You, and Pasha, and the children.'

'Oh, Olga, no,' said Anna.

'Anna, yes,' said Olga, squeezing her arm.

Anna looked at her for a long moment, until her eyes spilled over with tears. 'Oh, Olga, Olga,' she said at last, 'thank you, thank you, thank you and bless you. With such things we make Heaven on Earth. Bless you, bless you, a thousand times bless you.'

Sergeant Vassily Marushkin looked up from his desk, hearing boots crunching on the thick blanket of snow that had fallen overnight and then frozen hard that morning. The sound stopped as the postman halted outside the police station and rummaged in his shoulder-bag. With a clattering sound he rammed the mail through the letter-box before setting off for the next address on his round, his footsteps gradually dying away into silence. Vassily walked to the door, chirruping at Rasputin in his little cage on the floor. But Rasputin was cross at having been locked away so early in the day, and ignored Vassily quite pointedly.

'Hmm,' said Vassily, as he leafed through the envelopes. 'Nothing of interest, it seems, Rasputin ... But what have we here?'

Vassily had seen a postmark from Ekaterinburg. Could it be from Major Davlovsky? Davlovsky specialised in veteran criminology, occupying a dedicated post in the renowned Ekaterinburg force. If anybody knew who Pavel Prokofy was, and why the soldier-turned-businessman had abducted Vassily's wife and child, it was Major Davlovsky. Or so Colonel Terekhin had said, anyway. And now Vassily had a response! Eagerly he ripped open the envelope and scanned the hand-written letter. But his face fell as he read. Davlovsky had never heard of a Prokofy, and neither had his associates in other cities. Vassily had come to another dead end.

'Oh, well,' he said to Rasputin, sitting down at his desk again, 'there's always another day. We'll never give up, will we, Rasputin? Not till we find our dearest Rozalina, and my round-head sweetheart, my little Kliment. Not till we find them and bring them home. What do you say, Ra-Ra-Rasputin? Would you like a snack?'

Vassily took the bag of dead rodents he kept under the desk and popped a small rat through the door on the top of Rasputin's cage. 'That'll keep you happy for a while,' he said to the ferret, which pounced on the furry corpse with relish. 'I wish I was so easily pleased. What else have we got here, then?'

He flicked through the rest of the mail, most of which related to everyday police business. But there was also a letter from Police Headquarters at Novosibirsk. It was from Colonel Terekhin, and as usual he didn't mince his words:

> Marushkin,
>
> I got your request for the transfer to Roslazny. Have you lost your mind? First you nearly get yourself killed, and me into the bargain – and now you want to bury yourself in the sleepiest village in Siberia? You'll go mad with boredom now you've captured, or killed off, all the murderers in the region! But each to his own. Maybe the rest'll do you good. But if you'll take my advice, try to forget the past. Dwelling on what's gone does nobody any good.
>
> Terekhin

'Easier said than done, sir,' he said, his voice echoing in the empty police station. 'Easier said than done.'

After a moment, Vassily tucked Terekhin's letter into a folder on top of the filing cabinet, then swept out the cells and the office, and took a bag of rubbish outside. He checked in by radio with the Tayga control desk: all was quiet. He nearly sat down at his desk again, to deal with some paperwork, but instead he picked up his coat and hat, left the station, and took a walk down to the railway to see Olga Pushkin at her little hut. Walking for pleasure was almost unheard of in Roslazny, and Olga's response when she saw him was to ask what was wrong, with a worried look.

'Nothing,' he said, smiling at her. 'I've come to say hello.'

'Oh,' said Olga, somewhat nonplussed. 'Well, come in, then. Sit down and have a cup of tea. The samovar's nice and hot.'

They talked for a while, Olga ignoring the radio whenever a cross voice called for her attention. 'I'll just say the battery was dying,' she said. 'It happens all the time.'

'You're quite a rebel, aren't you, Olga Pushkin?' he said.

'I suppose I am, these days,' she said, returning his smile. His face was less worn and tired than it had been during his imprisonment, she noticed, but his eyes were as sad as ever.

'And what's this I hear about your new property empire?' said Vassily. 'I thought you wanted to go to Tomsk – to become a writer?'

'I do want to be a writer,' said Olga. 'I *am* a writer. And I'm still planning to go to Tomsk – I've had to delay it, that's all, while I save up some more cash. A couple of hundred thousand roubles should do it. Anyway, I've already written sixty thousand words of a book. A book about the railway.'

'Sixty *thousand* words?' said Vassily, astonished. The longest thing he'd ever written was his transfer request to Terekhin the week before, in which he'd tried to explain why he wanted to stay in the little village – and that had taken him all day. He'd found the letter difficult to write, partly because he wasn't exactly sure why he wanted to stay. One reason was that he'd given up hope of stumbling across Prokofy's trail in inner-city crime. Recent events had convinced him there were just as many criminals, and therefore leads to follow, in the countryside. But there was also a part of him that had fallen in love with the little village that held so many memories for him. And there was Olga, too, but he didn't let himself think about her.

'Most books are eighty or ninety thousand words,' continued Olga, who had looked it up on the internet at Tayga public library, 'so there's some way to go for mine. But I'm happy to finish the book here, in my little hut. I've got plenty of time to write, when the trains are quiet. And even when I'm busy, the trains inspire me. Do you know the Pushkin poem "To K—"? It was a favourite of my mother's. Look – here it is,' she went on, picking up one of the volumes that Tatiana had left her, and flicking to a well-thumbed page. 'I think Pushkin could almost have been talking about the railway, about a speeding engine flying past him in the night – and who could ask for a better example than Pushkin? Listen: *I recall the wondrous chance: There before me I saw you. Like a ghost, like a fleeting apparition, Like genius of the purest grace.* Pushkin was writing about a woman, I know, but to me he could've been writing about the trains. Those are the things *I* love, just as Aleksandr Sergeyevich Pushkin loved Anna Petrovna Kern.'

'I'm staying in Roslazny, you know,' said Vassily, after a moment's silence. 'I got a transfer.'

'I'm glad,' she said, smiling at the non-sequitur that perhaps was not entirely a non-sequitur. Then she said, 'Tell me, what was the name of that man who took your wife and son? Something Prokofy.'

'Pavel,' said Vassily, quietly. 'Pavel Prokofy was his name.'

312

'Let me talk to Pasha,' she said. 'He still knows many men in the army. And the army is a closed book to outsiders. Maybe you need Pasha to help you open it.'

Vassily shook his head. Olga was trying to help, but what could her brother possibly do – a brother, moreover, who'd just been discharged from his unit? Nevertheless he forced himself to smile at her. She had such a kind face, he thought. It was no surprise that she'd given up half her university savings for her friend, just as it was no surprise that she wanted to help him find his family.

'All right,' he said. 'I'm grateful. To both of you.'

'Then we will see what we will see,' she said.

A week later, on a Saturday morning when Vassily was off duty, Olga dressed Pasha in her jacket and hat once more, and packed him off to the hut with a bag containing his lunch and some meal-worms for Dmitri. Anna's children laughed to see him in that outfit, not least because Olga had been to the fancy-dress shop in Tayga, so that Pasha now sported a short blonde pony-tail that stuck out over his collar.

'Laugh now, but you'll both be wearing it later,' said Pasha to Boris and Gyorgy, in a menacing growl. 'Good luck, Olgakin,' he added to his sister. 'It's a good thing you're doing. But what am I saying? Do you ever do anything else?'

'No, she doesn't,' said Anna Kabalevsky, coming through from the living room of their new house with a paint pot in one hand and a brush in the other. 'She's a saint in living form, aren't you, Olga?'

'Oh, stop it, you two,' said Olga. 'I'm nothing of the sort, as you both well know. Now I'd better go, or I'll keep Sergeant Marushkin waiting. Here he is now.'

Olga had heard the booming exhaust of Vassily's ancient Volvo 240, which came to a juddering halt on the icy road as she trotted down the steps from the house.

'Nice place,' said Vassily. 'I'll have to invite myself to dinner sometime.'

'Why not tonight?' said Olga, smiling nervously at him.

'Can't see why not,' said Vassily. 'It's either that or a tin of microwaved beans at the station. Now, where are we going? What was so important that you took the day off work again?'

'You'll see,' said Olga, taking a deep breath and trying to suppress the feeling in her chest, part excitement and part anxiety. 'I've marked it on the map. It's not too far from here. About twenty miles or so. You have enough petrol? Then let's go!'

'You're the boss,' said Vassily, putting the car into gear and moving off. They didn't talk much on the way. Perhaps Vassily had picked up on Olga's mood, and wasn't sure how to react. She noticed that he turned to her several times and opened his mouth, then closed it, as if he'd decided against speaking.

Soon they pulled up outside the place Olga had marked on the map. A large sign in front of a low wooden barn read 'Smirnov Agriculture'. Beyond the barn they could see men and women at work, using pitchforks to move piles of hay from a large wagon to troughs dotted around the snow-covered fields, where cattle awaited their food.

'Is this the place?' said Vassily. Olga nodded, looking past him to where a worker was standing a few hundred yards away.

At the sight of the Volvo, he jammed his pitchfork into the ground and began to walk towards them.

'Vassily,' she said, her heart thumping in her chest. 'Vassily – look, Pasha found a man who'd known Pavel Prokofy in the army, only that wasn't the name he used, and— Well, it doesn't matter now. I'll tell you everything later. The important thing is that Pasha tracked Prokofy down. And he said Rozalina's *gone*, Vassily. I'm so, so sorry . . . They moved her on from a farm in Itatka years ago, and Prokofy swears he doesn't know where. He said he didn't even know if she was dead or alive.'

Vassily nodded slowly, staring ahead through the windscreen, so sad that Olga couldn't bear to look at him. She tore her gaze from his face and gazed past him, towards the worker who had jammed his pitchfork into the ground, and who was now drawing near to the car.

Vassily saw the direction of her gaze and turned his head. 'Who's that?' he said, in a strangled voice, as if he couldn't quite get the words out. 'Olga, who's that coming towards us?'

'Oh, Vassily, Pasha's friend couldn't find Rozalina, but – but he did find Kliment, Vassily. *He found Kliment!*'

Olga nearly went on to tell Vassily about the brilliant work she had done earlier that week. She'd been longing to tell him about her visit to the Smirnov farm in Popov's much-travelled car – about how she'd cajoled and threatened the man on the front gate until the manager appeared, and how she'd offered the manager steadily increasing sums from her savings until finally, after the appearance of crisp banknotes worth fifty thousand roubles, he'd admitted that a certain Karol Matslavsky, a fifteen-year-old employee of the farm, was in truth Kliment Marushkin, Vassily's son. Olga had sighed with relief: from what Vassily and Pasha had said, Prokofy sounded an extremely dubious character, and she'd hardly dared to hope that he'd given Pasha the correct pseudonym.

She longed to tell Vassily, too, how she'd laid down a further seventy-five thousand roubles to buy Kliment out of his contract and secure his freedom, with just three days' notice to work off. Above all, she wanted to tell him how, after much wrangling from the manager and the requirement of a further fifteen thousand roubles, she had at last met Kliment in person.

Olga had asked the manager to introduce her to Kliment as the representative of a charity and nothing more, sensing that Vassily would want to tell his son everything himself. After the payment of yet another fee the manager agreed, and brought him to her, a tall, gently spoken presence with Vassily's eyes and hair, who told her, in a slow country burr, of life on the Smirnov farm and, before that, a series of other places whose names had faded from his memory. He didn't mind the work, he said, he'd never known anything else, and the other boys were all right, though they all envied the workers with families of their own. He told her of the apprenticeship contracts the manager had hurriedly arranged with him and the other under-age workers after the farm had got wind of an impending federal investigation. When Olga asked after Rozalina, he told her he hadn't seen his mother since he was five or six. He was told she'd died in a farming accident, but once he learned that all the other boys had been told similar stories, he'd begun to wonder if she might still be alive, after all.

'And your father?' said Olga. 'Do you remember him?'

'No,' said Kliment. 'Can't remember him. Always dreamed of meeting him, though. Don't suppose I ever will.'

'Oh, well,' said Olga, trying to hide her emotion. 'You never know.'

'Why – have you met him?' said Kliment.

Olga was unsure what to say next. She had a strong feeling that she was straying onto private ground. In the end she said she'd known Kliment's father when he was younger, but that she didn't know where he was at that moment. (This was true, she told herself, if one took the words literally.) She knew his name was Vassily, she said, and she'd heard that he was a good man – that he was a policeman by profession, and a credit to the force. She'd heard, too, that he drove an old Volvo 240 estate, and that perhaps, in future, she might be able to find him and bring him to see Kliment at the farm. She decided not to tell him that Vassily was in nearby Roslazny, or that Kliment would soon be free, or even that Karol Matslavsky was not his real name. These, she thought, were gifts that only Vassily should give. She'd left Kliment, instead, with vague promises of enrolment in some charitable scheme for disadvantaged teenagers, hoping he would forgive the deception later. The last thing she did was to instruct the manager, in exchange for a final wad of roubles, to put Kliment to work near the road on the coming Saturday.

Olga was proud of her detective work on Vassily's behalf, even though it had cost her yet more of her precious savings, and she had been looking forward to telling Vassily all about it when they got to the Smirnov farm on Saturday. But as she opened her lips to speak she saw that Vassily was crying, and in an instant her eyes, too, were brimming with tears, and she found she had no more words to utter. Then Vassily wrestled off his seatbelt and jumped out of the car, as if he would run to the boy and claim him as his own.

But he paused before he reached him, and looked back towards Olga as if in doubt. 'Is it really him?' he called. 'Are you *sure*?'

'Look at him, Vassily, and tell me,' she shouted through the open door, leaning across the driver's seat.

Vassily turned to the boy, and stepped forward, taking his head in his hands and staring at his face. 'Is it you?' he said. 'Can it really be you, after all these years? Are these – are these *my* eyes? They are – my God, they are. They are! And my hair, and – and' – his voice broke – 'and your mother's lips.'

Then, at last, he flung his arms around his son and embraced him as if the world was ending. 'Oh, Kliment, Kliment,' Olga heard him say. 'Oh, Round-head, Mousekin, you've come back to me. You've come back to me at last.'

Olga got out of the car then, quietly, and walked down the road, wiping her eyes on her scarf and feeling so full of sadness and joy that she could hardly bear to be alive.

'Oh, Mamochka,' she said, to the cold Siberian air, 'what was it Lubov used to say to you, at the Lodge in Astrazov? Russian stories end in sorrow, yes – but oh, my mother! There is so much happiness, too.'

Vassily Marushkin took his son Kliment from the Smirnov farm and gave him the other cell in the Roslazny jail, thinking to find him more suitable accommodation in due course, but Kliment persuaded Vassily to let him stay in the police station.

'I don't need anything more than this, Papa,' he said to Vassily. 'If it's good enough for you, it's good enough for me.' So father and son lived together and played with Rasputin and watched the changing seasons through the barred windows that looked out over the abandoned buildings that lay beyond.

A few hours after they'd found Kliment together, Olga told Vassily how Pasha had tracked down Pavel Prokofy. Vassily was understandably keen to learn how a disgraced soldier had seemingly clicked his fingers and made Prokofy appear like a rabbit out of a hat, while Vassily, a professional detective, had scoured Kemerovo Province and elsewhere for years with no success.

'You remember I said the army was a closed book to outsiders?' said Olga, 'Well, Pasha managed to open it. He got in touch with his friends and asked if they knew a man called Pavel Prokofy. And it was pure chance, Vassily,' she went on, sensing his wounded professional pride. 'Nobody else could have done it. You could've searched for ever and not come across him.

'You see, Pasha has a friend called Artyem, who shared a cell with Prokofy in the military prison at Novosibirsk. It was back in the eighties, before Prokofy met your wife – he was serving a two-year sentence, in those days, for embezzling army funds. Pasha's friend Artyem was in for false accounting, though Pasha said he only did it to help out a comrade who had fallen on hard times. Pasha says Artyem's a good man, really, only he finds it hard to stay on the right side of the law. I think he's got a soft spot for him. Anyway, Artyem discovered that Prokofy was using a false name – Denis Petrov. He actually managed to enlist in the army with a false name! It was quite a feat, Pasha said.

'Well, Artyem only found out about the false name because Prokofy was beaten up by some of the other prisoners. Prokofy had been dealing in cigarettes on the inside, and had foolishly ripped off one of the gangs. After that, Prokofy was carted off to the infirmary, and then they cleared his things out of his cell. But they left something behind – some kind of identity card with Prokofy's real name, which he'd hidden under his mattress. Artyem found it while moving the mattress down onto his bunk for a bit of extra comfort, and then he had that information hanging over Prokofy, you see, in case he ever wanted something from him in the future. That seems to be how things work, in prison. I'm learning such a lot about the criminal world!

'Anyway,' she went on, 'it's no wonder your enquiries never made progress, because everyone in the army thought Prokofy's name was Denis Petrov. And once Pasha found that out, he persuaded Artyem to get back in touch with Prokofy, and blackmail him about enlisting with a false identity – that'd be twenty years in federal prison, Pasha said – so he would tell us about your family. And it did the trick. Prokofy made a few calls, and that was how we got Kliment's location, and his pseudonym, too.

'But Prokofy said that was just good luck, and that he couldn't find Rozalina no matter how much Artyem threatened him. He said his involvement had ended the moment he delivered Rozalina and Kliment, drugged and bound, to the people-traffickers sitting in a truck parked on the outskirts of Tomsk. He took the roll of cash they gave him and walked off into the night, Artyem said. But Prokofy did say it's the usual policy to keep mothers and children together until the children are five or six, so the mothers can look after them, then split them up when the kids are old enough to start doing something useful on their own. Artyem said that was all he could get out of him.'

'Just tell me where Prokofy is,' said Vassily, grimly. 'I'll get more out of him, believe me.'

'No, Vassily,' said Olga. 'Artyem only spoke to Pasha on condition that nothing would go any further. He wouldn't tell Pasha where *he* was, never mind where Prokofy might be. I think Artyem's on the run again, or hiding out somewhere. And Prokofy only spoke to him on condition that Artyem didn't say where he, Prokofy, was hiding.'

'Honour among thieves, is it?' said Vassily, bitterly. 'Typical. Twenty years in the police, and I finally come across it when my family's at stake. Look, can't Pasha speak to Artyem again – try to persuade him, maybe? I'll pay any amount of money.'

'Again, no,' said Olga, sadly. 'Pasha says Artyem got rid of his phone after they talked about Prokofy, so he can't call him again. And Pasha doesn't know how to find him. He could be anywhere in Russia – he could even be out of the country, Pasha says. He's gone. And so is Prokofy.'

Vassily nodded. It was some time before he could bring himself to speak. 'Artyem's gone, and Prokofy's gone,' he said at last. 'So you say. But I'll find them, Olga. I'll find them, and then I'll find Rozalina, too.'

She nodded. 'I know you will. You're a good man, Sergeant Marushkin, and a good father, now, as well. And I hope you can be a good husband again, too.'

In the weeks that followed, Olga settled into the house she shared in Roslazny with her brother Pasha and her friend Anna Kabalevsky and her children. She walked home more quickly from her little hut than she used to, in the days when she shared a house with her father. Mikhail Pushkin had to go to work these days, after his arrest at the Lodge in Astrazov, and though he was perfectly fit, and well able to do his job at a processing plant in Tayga, he still cursed her every time they ran into each other in the streets of Roslazny. Soon he sold the house in which Olga had lived since she was a little girl, and moved in with Aunt Zia, whom he paid to look after him. 'They suit each other,' said Pasha, when he heard the news. 'Let them stew together, like rotten apples. We won't think of them. We'll think of the future and forget about the past.'

'You're right, brother,' she said that night. 'And I've been thinking of the future. I've got some news for you: I finished my book!'

'You wrote the hundredth life lesson!' said Pasha excitedly. 'Oh, well done, Olgakin! A hundred lessons, from life on the railway! I could never have imagined such a thing. You make me proud. You should've made Father proud, too. But I know Mamochka would be proud of you, and I can think of no higher praise than that.'

Olga smiled, for Vassily had said something similar earlier that day, when she ran into him on the outskirts of Roslazny. He had never met Tatiana Pushkin, but Olga talked about her so much that he almost felt as if he had. She and Vassily talked often, in those days, sometimes in chance meetings, or in Café Astana over a glass of Odrosov's vodka, if they happened to be there at the same time.

As the weather improved, and the snow gave way to grass and flowers and young pink cones on the budding larches, they started going for walks together in the fields or by the River Tom, taking a picnic basket or filling their pockets with apples to eat as they wandered, Olga talking about her plans for her book and the publishers she would send it to, and Vassily smoking and listening. His eyes, she noticed, had lost something of their haunted look. His whole being seemed lighter somehow, like a man who'd put down a long-carried burden. She knew, of course, that Vassily's wife Rozalina had still to be found, and that he would soon begin searching for her once more. But in the meantime it made Olga happy to see him with his son Kliment – a calm, patient soul who, against all logic, had fallen deeply in love with the country fields during his indentured servitude on the Smirnov farm, and other estates. He soon became firm friends with Fyodor Katin, the Dreamer, who preached to him about his latest enthusiasm from Russian history, the time of Catherine the Great. And Olga saw these things and thought how joy could come by surprise on the heels of sorrow, just as a well, deepened in time of drought, might see its level rise to yield a rill of sweet, clear water in place of dust.

One day Vassily came to Olga's hut by the tracks, bringing with him a letter that the postman had given him at the police station, knowing it would reach her more quickly by Vassily's hands. He knocked on the side of the hut and stuck his head through the low doorway. 'Post's here,' he said.

Olga looked up from the desk and saw the envelope in his hand. 'Surely it can't be the publishers already,' she said. She had finally sent off the manuscript of her book the month before, after weeks of tormenting herself with endless revisions of *Find Your Rail Self: 100 Life Lessons from the Trans-Siberian Railway*. But Vassily shook his head.

'I don't think so,' he said. 'It's got a Russian Railways stamp.'

'It could be about my promotion,' said Olga. 'Oh, I can't look at it! Can you open it?'

'Of course,' said Vassily, 'but I don't know why you're so nervous. They're bound to give you a rise, at least, after all the help you gave us with Ivanka, Glazkov and Babikov, not to mention Viktor Fandorin.'

'You don't know Russian Railways the way I do,' said Olga.

'Well, it says – oh, it's good news, Olga,' said Vassily, smiling as he read the letter. 'You've been promoted to Track Engineer, *Second Class*, if you don't mind! And you've been – hang on . . .'

He turned the page to read the reverse, and his face fell.

'What is it, Vassily?' said Olga. 'Give it to me, if you won't read it,' she said, and standing up she took the letter in her hand.

'I've been posted away,' she said slowly. 'To Ulaanbaatar. To – to *Mongolia*.' She looked at him in despair. 'Oh, Vassily,' she said. 'What am I going to do now?'

He stared at her in astonishment. 'Mongolia? But – but how can Russian Railways post you to Mongolia – to another *country*?'

She sat down. 'I don't know,' she said, shaking her head. 'But I think there used to be an exchange programme for railway staff, in the old days, when it was run by the Communists. I remember my father talking about the Railway Academy at Ulaanbaatar. But they must be really angry with me, to have resurrected some ancient Soviet scheme from the ashes.'

Vassily perched on the desk and looked at the letter again. 'Could you refuse to go – decline the posting?' he said.

'Yes, if I want to be fired,' she said. 'But I can't do that. I need to start saving again, if I'm ever to get to Tomsk. And

I've got a mortgage now. I can't risk Anna being kicked out on the street again.'

'I could help,' he said, gently touching her shoulder.

She looked up at him, laid her hand on his, and smiled a brief smile. 'Didn't I say you were a good man, Vassily Marushkin? But you can't carry my burdens as well as yours. You have a son to provide for now. And you still have a wife to find.'

She got up and walked to the window, gazing at the trees along the railway line, steepling pines and lissom birches whose leaves seemed to float in the shimmering midday heat. Beneath their boughs, running between the pea-shrubs and willow bushes that crowded the forest eaves, and resting on an endless bed of gravel, she saw the track itself, gleaming in the sun like rivulets of molten steel, and vanishing into the unseen distance on either side. All her life she had lived by the track, cared for it, maintained and repaired it. And now it would bear her to a faraway place – a place so distant that even the gauge was different – and who knew when she would return, or what might have changed when she did?

She breathed out and closed her eyes, placing her hand on the windowsill. Then she opened her eyes and clamped her lips together with firm resolution. She would carry on. She would travel down the line and deal with whatever awaited her there. That was what Russian women did. They carried on, day in, day out, regardless of the challenges that arose along the way. The tracks lay always before them, the horizon forever receding. Maybe one day they would reach it. Maybe one day.

Acknowledgements

Writing a book incurs many debts, some self-evident and others harder to trace, some of recent vintage and others from the dawn of memory. Because of my father, my sister and I were surrounded from our earliest days by railway paraphernalia, and as a child I stood by him on the footplate as he fired steam locomotives on the Poppy Line. From his *Life on the Lines* (Moorland, 1984) I learned not just of English railwaymen and engines of the past, but also what it is to write a book. My father, too, introduced me to Russian storytelling – and Baba Yaga – by reading us Arthur Ransome's *Old Peter's Russian Tales* each night.

In more recent years, my wife Claire suggested an expedition from Moscow to Bangkok, travelling by Trans-Siberian, Trans-Mongolian, Chinese, and Vietnamese railways as well as the occasional bus, and tarrying at some of the places in between, from Ekaterinburg and Listvyanka to Ulaanbaatar and Hội An. To Claire, I owe my first-hand knowledge of *provodnitsi*, samovars, and the endless rolling depths of the Russian *taiga*. More recently still, I spent a stormy night walking my daughter Acacia to sleep in the darkness, during which the figure of Olga

Pushkin, and her snowy vigil beside the tracks, came unbidden to mind. Claire read each new chapter as it emerged from my pen, and remains the most perceptive (as well as the first) of all my readers.

I must thank my wonderful agent, Bill Goodall, for his dedication, enthusiasm, and deep insight throughout the journey from first paragraph to published novel, and my editor Krystyna Green for her passionate and good-humoured engagement with Olga and her Roslaznyan entourage. I am also most grateful to Martin Fletcher and Hazel Orme, who provided invaluable comments on the manuscript, and to Amanda Keats and all at Constable and Little, Brown for their assistance and support.